I Can Handle Him

By

Debbie K. Lum

Dedicated to the person in my life
whose number one goal is to be unremarkable

[ONE]

If only it hadn't rained.

Quinn Corbin steps wide to avoid a puddle on the downtown sidewalk and dodges water dripping from the building eaves. The twenty-four-year-old catches her reflection in a storefront window, backlit by a tangerine sunset across the southern Texas sky. She stops and latches on to the arm of her best friend, Tory Taylor.

"Seriously," Quinn says, shaking her head at the sight of her frizzed-out hair. "My hair just doubled in size. I haven't seen some of these people in two years and they're going to think I roll like this every day." She attempts to smooth down her long, wavy buttermilk blonde hair.

Tory squeezes Quinn's arm, facing their reflection. "I couldn't get my hair wavy if I paid to try. You're lucky."

Quinn tilts her head, staring at the image of the two of them. Her boho-inspired, free-flowing style is so opposite of Tory, the denim with anything black, straight-haired brunette, rock of her life. They stand arm-in-arm, like they've done for years. Like they'll do forever.

A soft light from the Indigo Exchange sign bathes the sidewalk in a blue glow. Quinn casts an uncertain look toward Indigo's double glass doors. "What a bunch of mixed-up memories in there."

Tory nods agreeably.

Indigo is San Antonio's largest independent coffeehouse and bookstore, covering a downtown city block. In a few steps they'll be inside, seeing former coworkers from two summers ago now gathering for Al Thomas's retirement party. And likely inside will be two guys who are the biggest jerks on the planet. But with any luck, another guy will be here who they are both anxious to see: Nick Allen.

A wave of anxiety sweeps through Quinn at the thought of Nick. He's the most warmhearted guy she's ever known. Damn sure the cutest. *It's not fair what he's gone through. Totally not fair.* She turns to Tory. "I'm a little nervous."

Tory's chin rises and she flashes her trademark confident smile. "For Al's sake, don't be."

The sight of Tory's smile gives Quinn a sense of calm. Heck, Tory's smile could give her enough confidence to run a marathon and she hates running. She squeezes Tory's arm as they step toward Indigo's entrance. "Do you think Nick's here? I mean, would he come? So soon?"

Tory gives a cautious shrug. "I hope he's here, but it's only been a month since the accident. I don't know how upset he still is."

Quinn looks down at her tan suede sandals and the swinging hem of her floral dress. *How long does it take to get over watching your girlfriend die in an accident that everyone thinks you caused?* "I can't imagine what he's gone through."

"Me either."

Tory flashes another sure smile, tugs hard on the door and they step inside. It's not unusual for Indigo to be busy on a Thursday night and tonight, it's shoulder-to-shoulder with a crowd of young professionals and hipster students. Quinn and Tory stand for a moment, listening to the whir of a frothing machine and breathing in the aroma of freshly brewed coffee.

"Smells like work, huh?" Tory whispers.

"Smells like…a cinnamon macchiato." Quinn eases into a smile. "Mmm…with almond milk."

Tory raises an eyebrow. "Why did you always ask *me* to make that damn drink for you?"

"Payback. Because *you* always made *me* make the hot chocolates."

Indigo's fancy espresso machine required eight steps to produce one hot chocolate. And when Quinn was barista, Tory would drive up hot chocolate orders by convincing customers to order two: one for here and one to go. Even in the hot Texas summer.

Tory points over Quinn's shoulder. "There's the sign. Al's retirement party, upstairs." They head for the stairs leading up to Indigo's second floor, where there is a large gathering room, a rare book collections room and staff offices. With each stair they climb, the bustling sounds from the coffeehouse below fade and they begin to hear music playing from a room in full party mode.

Quinn tightens with nerves. Crowds have never been her thing. She'd rather be alone with the curled pages of a romance novel, lost in an imaginary adventure. But the chance to see Nick was worth the trip. Even though the thought of him is making her hands feel sweaty.

"Two of my favorites!" a man's voice booms out. Al Thomas stands at the gathering room door with his arms open wide and Quinn and Tory rush into him for a hug. He squeezes them confidently, exactly how he lives his life. A slender man of average height with silver hair, he's strikingly attractive. Everything has always seemed to go this man's way. He married his college sweetheart, turned this neglected building into a money-making, coffee-brewing gold mine and raised Blaine, his twenty-four-year-old son. His pain-in-the-ass, cocky-to-the-hilt, avoid-at-all-costs son. Well, maybe not everything has gone Al's way…

"Al!" Quinn says, pulling back from their triple hug.

"Congratulations on your retirement," Tory says.

Al beams with pride. "Having everyone come tonight is the best retirement present I could ask for. And seeing you—both of you! Quinn, you've graduated now, right?"

"Just finished my master's," Quinn says.

"And she's already landed a teaching job at Miller Elementary," Tory adds.

"Good! Tory, how's law school?" Al asks.

"Hard as hell but I love Texas Law," Tory says.

"And she only has one year to go," Quinn adds.

Al shakes his head. "You two; still finishing each other's sentences. So, what are your summer plans now that you're back in town?"

"New teacher orientation and lesson planning," Quinn says.

"She can't wait for fall," Tory says.

"But first we need to find Tory an internship," Quinn says, nodding Tory's way with a troubled expression.

Tory's smile fades. "I was supposed to begin an internship

with the Federal Public Defender's office in Austin next week, but the attorney I was assigned to had a heart attack. Her deputy is out on maternity leave and their office is swamped. No one has time to train new people, so yesterday they cancelled all summer interns."

A line of concentration creases Al's forehead. "I can make some calls around town to find you something."

Tory squeezes his arm. "You're the sweetest, thank you. I might need that. My dad is also trying to see what he can find."

"I forgot your father is a lawyer," Al says.

"But don't forget, Tory makes the best cinnamon macchiato. You know, in case she has to come back here." Quinn gives her a teasing nudge.

Al's eyes tighten. "Actually, we should talk. I could use some help with a few business issues here, working with our legal firm on some matters I want to wrap up before I go. Let's talk later."

Tory nods.

"On to more important matters," Al says, wearing mischief on his face. "Do both of you have boyfriends?"

"For real?" Tory asks.

"She does." Quinn points to Tory.

"She doesn't." Tory points to Quinn.

"Don't you start again, Al," Quinn says with a smile. "Don't try to set me up with Blaine."

He shrugs. "I'm a proud father. I always look out for my boy."

"And I bet your boy is here," Quinn says, looking over Al's shoulder to find the guy she's desperate to avoid. "Who else is here that worked with us?"

"So many," Al says, turning to glance over the crowd. "I was surprised to see Nick Allen tonight. I didn't think he would be out and about so soon."

"Nick's here? He came?" Quinn says, rising up on her toes to see if she can spot him.

Al's eyes darken with concern. "He did. But I don't think he should be here. I mean, it's wonderful to see former employees, but his new coffeehouse is my competition now. And not everyone here is excited to see him."

"Why wouldn't people want to see him?" Quinn asks in a disbelieving voice.

"Dear Quinn, always so optimistic. It's no secret: Nick is trouble. He was trouble when he worked here, he's trouble to my business now and his negligence has killed a beautiful soul. The best thing for Nick would be to leave town."

"Really?" Quinn asks.

Tory draws her hands to her hips.

"Hey, Al!" a young couple holler as they enter the room. Al turns to greet them as Quinn and Tory wave him goodbye.

"When did Al become such a Nick hater?" Quinn asks as they walk away.

"Nick's negligence? That's a heavy accusation. Even nice people can screw up but claiming negligence takes it to a new level. And he wasn't charged for that accident. I wonder what really happened," Tory says.

"Nick isn't trouble," Quinn says, head shaking and eyes cast to the floor. "He'd never do anything to hurt anybody. At least not the Nick I knew. I mean, we all pulled pranks on each other but he always was a gentleman. He covered shifts and stayed late; he gave people rides to and from work. Remember how he stood up for us when that old lady in the bookstore accused us of stealing? He saved our jobs that summer! Even though he never asked me out, you know, if he would have I would have totally said yes and—"

Tory squeezes Quinn's arm. Quinn stops talking and looks up into Tory's eyes, set with a stone-cold glare.

Tory leans closer. "Trouble is walking this way."

[TWO]

"Nick?" Quinn asks, her face feeling instantly flush.

Tory rolls her eyes. "You just babbled on and on about how Nick isn't trouble, so why would I say he's the trouble that's coming?"

"Ah, yeah. Okay, I won't look. Rank who's coming."

A devious smile creases Tory's mouth. "Qutor scale?"

Quinn excitedly nods. The Qutor scale is their favorite party game. The "Qu" of Quinn plus "Tor" of Tory spells the name of their secret scale for ranking guys. A Qutor rank of one is husband material. A ten means run for your life.

"Nine."

Quinn groans. It must be Blaine. It wouldn't be Reed, his best friend. Because if Reed was coming, Tory wouldn't be playing this game. She'd be halfway to the exit. "It's Blaine."

Tory nods and the two high-five each other just as Blaine Thomas walks up.

"Quinn and Tory, always inseparable," he says.

"And Blaine," Quinn says, "always…here!"

He smiles as if he received a compliment. He's a reflection of his father, attractive in a youthful way, trendy with slim-fitting pants and a tight-fitting blue button-down shirt. His brown hair is parted in the middle with a fade on the sides. He lingers at every mirror and reflective surface he meets. He leans in for an air kiss and Quinn politely dips toward him. He turns to Tory to do the same, but she stands still, her wide eyes watching Blaine's head come closer to her and then pull away.

"How's it going?" Tory asks.

"Business is good. Did you see the crowd downstairs?" he boasts.

"We did! So nice to see everything going well," Quinn says. "Are you still running as tight of a ship as when we worked here?"

He fans the air. "Oh please. We all had fun. You can't blame me for wanting to be sure the family business was running well."

"Nah…" Tory says. "Even though you'd yell at us for not hanging up brooms. Who knew bristles touching the floor makes brooms wear out faster?"

He points at her. "That's legit. Brooms do wear out faster if you don't hang them up."

Quinn's not sure if she wants to laugh or bump up his Qutor rank to a ten. "So, if we helped those brooms last longer, are they still here?"

Tory snort-laughs.

He shrugs. "Saving pennies has paid off for my family. Look around! We are successful, even with—how can I say it—the recent competition. I guess you could say Indigo is the proven classic and not just a *faze*." He slaps his thigh, smiling at his joke.

"I see what you did there," Tory says, not amused. "That's a dig against Nick and his Faze coffeehouse."

"Well, why not? Nick learned all about the business here and then stabs my father's heart by opening a shiny new store not far away. I know that's why he's here tonight. He's spying."

Tory squints, looking at both sides of Blaine's head.

"What?" he says, gently running a hand over his picture-perfect hair.

"Just looking…" she says, "…for a visible screw loose."

Quinn struggles to bury a laugh. "Blaine, not everyone is out to get you. Remember when you made us open dozens of coffee bags to be sure the beans were the same color because you thought the vendor was selling you different beans? And they were all the same color? Your imagination just lives in overdrive. It could be, wild as it may be, that Nick wants to wish your dad well."

Blaine tenses. "Welcome back to town, Quinn. You've missed a lot. Nick's not here to wish anyone well. He's here to spy and to try to mend fences with Reed, you know, since Nick killed Reed's sister in that accident. I'm sure he thinks a little social mingling will make us forget that Sienna is dead."

Tory's eyes ignite. "You cold hearted—"

"Hey!" Quinn interrupts. "Look who's here!"

Two women and a man join their group, with jolly hellos and hugs. While they air kiss with Blaine, Quinn leans in to Tory. "Be patient with Blaine. You need Al's help. He knows so many people in town and can help you find an internship."

"God, Blaine's a jerk," Tory whispers back. "And when he mentioned Reed I wanted to scream. Fair warning, if Reed shows up, I'm out of here."

Quinn nods. *Oh, Lord, why did she and Tory bother coming here tonight?* She should be back in her new apartment, decorating it. She's supposed to be home anyway waiting for a delivery, an old sofa that her parents are giving her. She and Tory could be ordering pizza and splitting the bottle of chardonnay she got as a graduation gift instead of dealing with this drama.

They stand among a circle of people, filled with meaningless conversation and then Blaine eases back to let someone else join them. *Oh, hell no!* Reed Brown joins their group. So fashionable with hipster black-framed glasses, Reed has more money than everyone in this room combined, plus add on the value of this room, the entire building and the land it sits on. His family owns six of San Antonio's largest car dealerships, all named after Reed, of course.

Quinn frantically looks to Tory. *Maybe she hasn't seen...*

Tory raises two hands in the air to show her ten fingers and mouths, "Ten. I'm out." She shakes her head and walks away.

"Hey, Quinn," Reed says, a simple smile on his face. He looks over her shoulder. "Where's Tory going? I haven't said hi to her tonight."

Quinn glances behind her, watching Tory disappear into the crowd. "Oh, well, probably the ladies' room."

Reed gives her a quick hug. As they draw apart, Quinn keeps one hand on his shoulder. "I was very sorry to hear about the accident and Sienna's death. I didn't know her but I always heard lovely things about her."

Reed's face softens. "Thank you. I appreciate it. It's been a rough month for my family." His shoulders droop and Quinn can't help it: she hugs him again. They straighten and he shows the barest hint of a smile. "You remind me a little of my sister. Your hair and your smile and how nice you are. It's really good to see you."

Quinn nods with dismay. What a strange, sweet conversation with a terminal jerk. He was never nice to her when they worked together. Her family wasn't rich enough, he told her once, which was funny coming from someone who worked at the same coffeehouse as her, probably making the same hourly wage. Evidently his parents made him work at Indigo that summer, before giving him the keys to their Lexus dealership. From what she's heard, he now runs that place, plus their Subaru and Volvo dealerships too. It's only a matter of time before his father retires and the Reed's Motor Car empire all belongs to Reed. Back when they worked together, he only seemed to have eyes for Tory. Her family is wealthy and he respects that. And he wants that. But for some reason, Reed irritates Tory and Quinn has never found out why.

She tries to see if she can spot Tory in the crowd.

"It's really very tragic," Blaine says to Reed, drawing Quinn's attention back into the group conversation. "A car accident is what took your sister. Of course, had Nick maintained his car, Sienna would be with us tonight, at this party."

"And instead, only Nick is here," Reed says. "I'll never get over what he's done. Never. And someone needs to make him pay."

Reed and Blaine lock eyes, glaring at each other with building anger. It's as if Nick were between them and they were tearing him apart with their eyes. The space around them feels hotter and no one around them speaks. Quinn's skin bristles. *Get out of here.*

"Hey, I'll catch you guys in a minute," she says and slips away.

What. Was. That. It felt like she was watching Blaine and

Reed doing their own imaginary rating scale like she and Tory have, only they were rating their enemy by the scorching glare of their eyes. From what she saw, and felt, Nick must be an eleven.

Quinn smiles politely as she passes unfamiliar faces. Some are older than her, who probably worked here years ago. Others are younger, and may work here now. It's true what they say: you can never go back. You can't go back to where you worked before and feel the same. Walls will be painted a new color or furniture will be moved. The way you did things before will be different. People you used to know will have changed, for the better or for the worse. It's never going to feel the same. And tonight, here at Indigo, doesn't feel good.

Her phone vibrates with a text.

Movers left a few minutes ago, so you better be home.

Mom never was one to mince words. Now Quinn needs to find Tory and leave.

She notices a bar across the room and gradually moves that way. Tory will be there, for sure. She'll have a rum and Coke in hand, and since it's probably an open bar and the drinks are free, she may already be sipping drink number two. She needs to get Tory, say her goodbye to Al and try to forget about this odd night.

Someone across the room waves hello. She recognizes them and waves back, still edging around people in happy conversations, trying to make her way to the bar. She doesn't have the time, nor the interest, in talking with anyone right now.

"Quinn?" Someone gently squeezes her arm.

She turns and comes face-to-face with Nick Allen.

[THREE]

A soft gasp escapes from Quinn's mouth. "Nick!" Happiness shines in his eyes and spreads to his smile. "I've been looking for a friendly face. Looks like I hit the jackpot."

She opens her arms and hugs him; he warmly returns her squeeze. They pull back and she can barely contain her flutters. *Oh, he's delicious.* Chestnut hair, parted to the side and perfectly messed up. His tan face sports a barely there mustache and beard. A white, button-down shirt is generously unbuttoned, lying flat under his crisp, linen blazer. His shoulders are wide but his waist seems small and she stops herself before she looks lower. If she stares at everything below his belt, he might think she's being rude. Plus, she might go dizzy and faint.

She does it anyway.

Slim, dark jeans. Tan, classic suede bucks. *Oh my God, he's perfection.*

She looks up into his interested eyes. "I've been looking for you! It seems everywhere I go tonight everyone has something to say about…"

He timidly nods as if he knows what she's about to say next.

"A lot has happened since I saw you last. There's a lot to say."

"Are you all right? I heard about the accident but I haven't seen you post anything since then."

"Social media is not a good place for me to be right now."

"That explains why you haven't messaged me back. I've been worried about you."

He runs a hand across his forehead, gently sweeping back a stray lock of his hair. His hand is discolored with light spots. She looks down to his other hand, also blotchy with spots. *From the accident maybe?*

She leans closer. "I mean, not that I expected you to respond to my messages. I don't want you to feel badly or anything. I just wanted you to know I was thinking about you."

"I would have noticed your message for sure. But I stopped reading all of them because most were not supportive."

Her heart aches and she wants to hug him again. "I just… can't imagine. I feel helpless. And awkward."

"It's a long story," he mumbles.

She doesn't have time! Forget it: make time. "You have my full attention if you want to talk about it."

His eyes look as hurt as his heart must be. "I don't know what you heard, but it was an accident. We were leaving Greene; we had just eaten dinner at the Blue Talon on the river. Sienna had been working in Greene all day, so I met her there. She asked if she could drive my car."

"I remember your car," Quinn says. "The convertible?"

He nods. "Yeah, the '66 Mustang I bought a few years ago from Reed's. Sienna remembered it from the showroom. When she was in high school, she used to sit behind the wheel and pretend it was hers. Of all the cars at all the Reed dealerships, she said that Mustang was her favorite because of the blue color."

"So that's why she was driving?" Quinn asks.

"She wanted to drive it on the back roads. I mean, this was only our second date but I let her drive it because it was so familiar and special to her."

Quinn's shoulder gets bumped from someone walking past her, reminding her that they're in the middle of a crowded and obnoxiously loud room. Somehow, listening to Nick and his story has made everyone around her disappear. She only has ears for him. And his eyes are only on her.

"So, she drove my car and I drove hers, following her. We took the back way, down the 46, because she wanted to drive with the top down. There was a big curve and the car suddenly… all I saw was flames." He swallows hard and looks away.

God, this is worse than she had heard. And the burn spots on his hands? He must have tried to save her. She gently rests her hand on his shoulder and leans closer to be heard above the conversations around them. "Nick, I am so sorry."

"I didn't want to come tonight, especially because of Reed. But I don't know when I'd ever see Al again and I wanted to wish him well, even though I know he's not happy with me either."

Quinn leans closer with a smile. "So, maybe there are people here who aren't your friends, but you have at least two who are."

"You?"

"You bet."

"And where's your other half?" he says, looking around.

"Ah, well, I lost Tory a few minutes ago when Reed walked up. See? You aren't the only person in this room trying to avoid him."

"I was hoping you both would be here. You two were my brightest memories of this place."

"Then let's focus on those memories and not the present. Like, remember that costume party?"

He grins. "How we Googled 'two girls and one guy costume ideas' and ended up as the cast of *Three's Company*?"

"That was the best! Remember hanging out at my parents' house while we binge-watched *Three's Company* because we had never seen the show?"

His eyes crinkle with amusement. "You were perfect as Chrissy, Tory was an amazing Janet and I was an outstanding Jack Tripper."

"Daniel was so mad he didn't get to be Jack until he realized Jack's character really wasn't gay."

"Daniel! I forgot about him. Is he still Tory's other BFF?"

"Lord, yes. Sometimes I have to fight him to get any time with Tory. Between her splitting her time with me, Daniel and her new boyfriend, I'm lucky to ever see her."

"Tory…she has a boyfriend?"

"I know, right? She hadn't dated anyone serious since we all worked together and then this guy comes along."

"Wow. How about you?"

Quinn breaks eye contact for a quick second and shrugs. "Not seeing anyone. Although if Al had his way, he'd have Blaine and I married by now."

"Al's been trying to set you up with Blaine for ages."

"I love Al, but not enough to date his son."

Nick's eyes glass over.

Oh boy; slow down. Probably shouldn't talk about people dating and boyfriend/girlfriend stuff so soon after his loss.

"Hey, I was heading over to the bar to find Tory. Want to join me?"

His glassy look disappears. "Absolutely."

She turns and begins winding her way through the crowd again, Nick a breath behind her. People notice Nick, launching lingering stares and questioning glances. Quinn reaches behind her and grabs Nick's hand to lead him through the crowd.

The bar is set against the back of the room with a few bar stools in front. All of the stools are taken. Perched on one in the middle is Tory.

Quinn stops, leaning toward Nick's ear. "She's been there long enough to have finished a drink and you know, only one drink can cause her to surprise-slur."

"Her surprise-slurs are epic! Remember that time at the club when a cop came up behind her and she yelled, "I'm gonna be an astronaut like you!"

Quinn playfully slaps his shoulder. "That *was* epic." She wraps her arm around his; so close; so comfy; so perfect. They plow forward together and approach Tory from behind. One empty highball glass sits in front of her and there's another half-empty one in her hand.

"Hey, look who I found!" Quinn says, elbowing Tory's shoulder. "An astronaut!"

Tory turns so fast she almost falls off of the stool. "Holy shit, you are flippin' hotter than I remember! Nick!"

He leans over to give her a hug but as he's hugging her, her face screws up. "You're an astronaut now?"

Suddenly what sounds like a spoon clinking against a glass quiets the crowd.

Nick wraps his arms around Tory in a hug. "I'm just me and

I have missed you, Tory." He looks at Quinn. "I've missed you both." Quinn slips her arm around his waist and he drapes his arm over her shoulders, his other arm over Tory's.

"Okay, everyone," Blaine says, standing on a side of the room where people have cleared an open space. Al stands next to him, beside a cake that looks as big as half of a car. "Glasses up to toast to a legend, someone we all have learned from, someone we all want to be. I love you Dad, and I'm happy to pick up where you left off while you enjoy the next adventure in your life. To your retirement! Hear, hear!" He raises his glass.

Glasses of all shapes and sizes rise up in the air and the crowd echoes Blaine, "Hear, hear!"

Quinn and Nick have no glass in hand so they smile and squeeze each other. "Hear, hear," Quinn says.

Tory lowers her glass to take a sip but Nick leans toward her ear. "If you're driving, you should try the coffee." Quinn nods.

Tory shrugs. "Actually, a hot chocolate sounds pretty damn good but only if Quinn makes it. Plus one to go."

Hilarious. "Speaking of "to go", my mom texted. The sofa's on the way. We've gotta go." Quinn pats Tory's shoulder, then faces Nick.

"You guys are leaving already?" he asks.

"I've got a new, old sofa on the way," Quinn says. "I wish I could stay and talk with you longer."

"Hey, in case you didn't know, I opened a new coffee bar and bookstore a few blocks away."

"Oh, I heard."

"Why don't you guys come by on Saturday night. We've got a book signing by Wally B., the soul poet. His poetry book is a best seller and he's going to do one of his famous spoken word poetry performances."

"I'd love to," Quinn says.

Nick leans down to Tory. "Bring your boyfriend too."

Tory winces. "Won't happen unless he's got a coupon."

"A coupon?"

Quinn squeezes his arm. "Yeah. There's a super long story there."

Nick nods. "Can I walk you guys to your car?"

Tory stands. "Seriously, you are sweet, but I'll have my drink shaken off by the time I fall down the stairs. Good to see you, Nick." She hugs him, steps back and points a finger in his face. "By the way, Blaine and Reed are shitheads and we don't listen to what they say."

"Good," he says, pleased.

She lowers her finger and looks to Quinn. "I really have a super bad case of the munchies so I'm gonna grab me a slab of cake and I'll meet you by the door." She walks away in a perfectly straight line.

Nick watches her leave, his expression worried. "Will she be okay?"

"Please. She can handle more than one drink. It's her loose lips and cursing that I worry more about in times like this. Thanks for asking though."

They stand, toe to toe, under the antique chandeliers glittering in the soft light. A waiter pauses beside them, offering a tray of dainty party food that neither of them looks down to. The waiter moves on, leaving them surrounded by the gentle hum of conversations and the booming rhythm of the DJ's pop music.

"I'm glad I could get you to smile," Quinn says.

A new smile stretches across Nick's face. "It felt good to smile again."

TORY

Tory falls into line with a few people who are hovering around the cake table. *Screw healthy eating.* She burned off enough calories in her morning TRX class to earn this slice. Besides, with Reed in this room breathing the same air as her, getting a forkful of comfort from some buttercream icing sounds real good. With any luck, she'll have her slice of cake polished off well before Quinn finishes up with Nick. And with super good luck, this cake will be chocolate.

Tory nods a few polite hellos to others in line before the waiter hands her a serving. *Girl, play the lottery tonight because you are winning: it's chocolate!* She's got a bite of cake heading for her mouth as she turns to look back at Quinn.

Quinn. Seeing her face-to-face with Nick brings a smile to Tory's face. And Quinn's doing her cute, nervous-energy, rocking back-and-forth on her toes thing. *So adorable.* She always does that when she's with a good-looking guy and Nick surely fits that bill. Quinn's nervous energy started the minute they received the invitation to come tonight because she knew Nick might be here. Quinn is genuinely worried about him, and Tory is too. Then again, Quinn's been known to obsessively worry, even over complete strangers. Back when they were undergrads at UT Austin, they saw one of the campus tour guides trip on an uneven sidewalk. Quinn worried about that girl for weeks. Tory was concerned too, but was more curious to know if the girl's fall was a tort.

Tory takes another bite of cake, still watching Quinn and Nick. Even from across the room, she can see his relaxed smile. *Good.* She can't imagine what he's been through. And she's mad at herself for not reaching out to him sooner. But she's back in town now. And her legal mind-in-training is spinning with questions.

Why on earth would Al say that Nick caused Sienna's accident? How could Nick make a car explode? Why would he even want to kill Sienna? It's ridiculous to think he would have done anything intentionally malicious. That's not the Nick who Tory knows. At least, not the Nick she used to know.

And she used to know him…very well.

[FOUR]

QUINN

Pure joy fills Quinn's heart and her smile feels like it can't be contained.

She pushes a shopping cart through a brightly lit aisle at Lakeshore Learning Center, where colorful classroom decorations surround her. One display has twisted brown vines and tropical leaves for a jungle theme and next to that, there's fish netting with inflatable sea creatures for an ocean theme. She stops at the circus theme display and picks up a red-and-white crepe-paper package to read the instructions for how to make a big top. Since she was a little girl, she's dreamed of this day. What began as silly, imaginary classroom play with her stuffed animals and dolls led to six years of college to earn the degree she needed to teach elementary education. Finally, she's shopping for supplies for her own, real classroom. Even though it's only May and she doesn't report to work until the end of July.

A pink feather boa flies through the air and lands in her cart.

"You must have one," says Daniel Clay. Tory's good friend strikes a pose with a sassy smirk and then he spins to find treasures down another aisle.

"Um, no," Quinn says, picking up the wad of feathers.

Tory rushes past her down the center aisle, then turns, wearing sunglasses on her head and a grin. "They have sensory sand over here!"

"Why did I bring you two?" Quinn mutters.

Tory disappears down another aisle and Daniel reappears. "Next aisle! Hurry!"

Quinn shakes her head and pushes her cart after him. Tory's already there, rifling through the dramatic play display.

"Second graders need dress-up stuff, right?" Daniel asks. "Look, they have costumes for everything!"

Tory holds up one. "A doctor!"

Daniel pulls out another. "A chef!"

Tory grabs another. "A fireman!"

Daniel plants his hands on his hips. "Girl, that reminds me of the last three guys I dated."

Tory smirks. "Reminds me of the last romance novel I read."

Quinn reaches into her basket and removes the feather boa, returning it to the shelf. "Alphabet strips, you guys. We're looking for alphabet strips and number lines."

"But…over in the science section the anatomical torso with removable body parts is twenty percent off!" Daniel says.

"No."

He pouts. "I'm concerned with what kind of teacher you are going to be."

Tory holds up a policeman costume. "Hey, this reminds me of last night."

"Oh baby, what did you do?" Daniel asks. "Were you arrested or did you take a policeman home? Were handcuffs involved and how'd you like them?"

Tory suppresses a sigh. "I'm certain there will be a day when you need a lawyer and maybe I'll remember you when you call." She looks to Quinn. "This reminds me of the cops and what I heard about why Nick wasn't charged for the accident."

"From who?" Quinn asks.

"A girl I was standing next to at the cake table. I totally don't remember how we started the convo, I think we were talking about hot guys so Nick came up, but she told me it was a faulty fuel line that exploded. It was a complete accident."

"So how could Al claim that Nick was negligent?"

"It seems like there's a big batch of misinformation out there."

"It's worse than that," Quinn says. "Reed said he wanted to make Nick pay."

"Reed is a prick. He's stupid to try to get revenge for an accident caused by a bad fuel line from a car bought at his own dealership. There were no charges. It wasn't Nick's fault. Reed needs to let it go."

"Charges or not, I wouldn't get near Nick," Daniel says, setting down the box of play food he was holding. "There's some shady shit around him."

Quinn shakes her head. "Years ago, maybe. He was arrested for drug possession when he was eighteen. That's not cool but he told us back when we worked with him that he hasn't used drugs since."

"Look, what's said in the chair stays in the chair but I have to tell you this," Daniel says. "The woman who lived next door to the Allens was a client of mine. Cut and root touch-ups, once a month. Anyway, she used to tell me she'd hear yelling from the Allens' house all the time. And remember, Mr. and Mrs. Allen died in a car accident too. It's too sketchy for me."

"So," Tory says, "you don't like Nick because his family was loud and then his parents were tragically killed the same way his girlfriend died and he used to snort some lines?"

"Uh-huh. Oh, and don't forget that pesky little hit-and-run," Daniel says.

"We know about that," Quinn says. "We were working at Indigo then. He had no idea he'd hit a dog in my neighborhood until the police came to Indigo to question him. He was really upset."

"See? Basically every year of his adult life there has been some shady drama," Daniel says. "Those are the facts."

"I see someone different," Quinn says. "He's not intentionally shady; he's been dealt a bad hand. But look at him now. Running his own business and getting back on his feet."

"You know he hired one of the managers from Indigo, right?" Daniel adds. "One day that guy was working at Indigo and the next he's at Faze. Not cool. I mean, stealing backup dancers caused the whole Katy Perry and Taylor Swift feud. You can't take people like that. I wouldn't touch Nick."

"Right," Tory says. "You wouldn't touch Nick even if he sat in your chair begging for a haircut?"

Daniel's expression brightens. "Totally different. That's business. And I've dreamt about touching Nick's amazing hair for years now."

Quinn laughs. "So, I guess you don't want to go with us to Faze tomorrow night?"

"Nick's hair will be there," Tory says.

Daniel holds out a stiff arm. "Oh hell no. You two can get mixed up in Nick's drama. Besides, it's taco night at Mama Margie's."

"Of course it is," Tory says.

"Honey, you know I moved to San Antonio for the street tacos and brown men. And I can't meet my men at some coffee shop."

Tory's phone buzzes with an incoming text and she looks down. "It's my man. And he wants to go out tomorrow night."

"Oh, I can't wait to hear: where does Jake have a coupon for?" Quinn asks.

Tory squints at her phone and shakes her head. "Whataburger has a two-for-one."

"Jake's going to drive an hour from Austin to take you to Whataburger?" Quinn asks.

Tory's head is still shaking and she lowers her phone. "No. He wants me to meet him halfway there."

"For Whataburger?"

Daniel shakes his head. "How long have you been dating again?"

"Like, a month," Tory says.

Daniel nods. "Exactly. He's putting in less than half the effort, as usual. You've got to lose this guy."

"He's still never taken you anywhere without a coupon?" Quinn asks.

Tory bites her knuckle. "I've got to lose this guy."

"I'm all about saving coin but Jake's obsessive about this," Daniel says.

Tory tucks her phone into her purse. "I've offered to pay

and suggested places to go! Couponing is all he talks about."

Quinn leans closer. "You've got to lose this guy."

"Tomorrow," Tory says, looking at Quinn. "I'll break it off when I see him tomorrow. You'll have to go to Faze without me."

Not ideal. Now the pressure is on. Without Tory, this feels more like a date she's driving herself to. She's nervous just thinking about Nick and now the thought of going to Faze alone? Tory gives her cover; Tory gives her confidence!

Quinn twists her hands.

She's buried her crush for Nick for years, and now isn't the time to let her feelings be known. When she first saw him at Indigo, she, Tory and Nick had just graduated from UT Austin. They didn't know Nick from college but hit it off with him during that summer job. He was the resident pro operating the La Marzocco espresso machine. Everyone else was afraid of that damn thing, but Nick was an effortless master. She watched in awe how he gripped the coffee cups and squeezed the stainless-steel handles. His blue eyes were compelling and there were touches of humor around his mouth. His smile made her melt and she desperately wanted to reach out and dab away a drop of moisture that clung to his forehead. Her crush-at-first-sight was ruined when another girl came up behind Nick, slipping her hands around his waist. His attention turned to her, his girlfriend at the time. She knew then she didn't have a chance.

The thought of dating any guy gives her a primal need to run and hide. If she could get her nerves in check, she could be bolder—like Tory. And now, the guy she's always wanted isn't available because he's reeling from disaster. This isn't the time to make a move for Nick; she's got to hold back her feelings.

Quinn tunes in to Tory's waving hands. "Whoa, where'd you zone off to?" Tory asks. "You'll be okay going to Faze without me, right?"

"Oh, sorry, yes. It'll be fine. I mean, once I figure out what to wear and I should Google 'Wally B.' so I know a little about that poet who's coming and I need to be sure I arrive at the perfect time and—"

Tory interrupts. "You like him."

Quinn's mouth tightens.

Tory tosses her a reassuring smile. "Nick's a great guy, Quinn. I like him too. Breathe and live in the moment. Follow your heart and don't listen to all of these haters. Nick is hurting and he needs friends. Don't feel bad if you secretly want to be more than that."

Her tension suddenly releases like a needle piercing an over-inflated balloon. *Thank God Tory gets it.* Tears well up behind her eyes. "One day, I'm going to be as cool as you."

Tory smiles warmly.

Daniel moves closer, gently placing a hand on each of their shoulders. "And one day, you both can be as awesome as me."

[FIVE]

Gut check time.

Quinn gives the fabric belt of her pale red, floral maxi-dress a final tug. Four chains drape around her neck, starting with a black choker and layering down to a long pendant resting so low it tickles the skin between her breasts. The V-neck front of her dress shows just enough cleavage to be interesting but not too much to make her blush.

She clutches a straw handbag, walking up to the entrance of Faze. An evening breeze sweeps through Town Centre, a circle of two-story buildings that surround a tiered, limestone water fountain. The breeze feels good on her hair, bouncing with amazing fullness thanks to the professionally blown-out waves that Daniel styled. It was a good trade on her part: a free blow-out in exchange for her finally buying him the anatomical torso from the science section at Lakewood Learning. *God only knows what he's been doing with that thing.*

Up ahead, the sign for Faze makes the sidewalk around it glow just like the sign at Indigo Exchange. But at Faze, the bright, fresh turquoise color seems to make the entire area happy. With each step forward, a delicious smell grows stronger.

She's heard about this. It's coming from the signature item at Faze: cinnamon rolls.

She follows a group of people through the front door. Cool, crisp colors of turquoise, white and pewter gray surround her. A calm gray sea of glossy stained concrete covers the floor; glass globe lights dangle like stars overhead. Steel stools surround high, round tables not far from the coffee bar with beer on tap and liquor bottles stacked on clear, lighted shelves.

So fresh; so urban; so trendy. This feels so Nick.

The familiar hum of an espresso machine fills the air, along with happy conversation among everyone here. Well, almost everyone. At tables where there are fist-sized cinnamon rolls drizzled with turquoise-colored icing, those people aren't talking. They're eating.

Quinn slowly makes her way through the crowd, looking for Nick. Her mellow mood reflects the vibe of this place. Her mellow mood is also from the glass of chardonnay she enjoyed an hour before coming. Without that drink, she'd probably be nervously chewing her fingernails by now.

She spots Nick across the room and the sight of him makes her stomach tingle. He's talking to an African-American man. Nick's got his linen blazer on again, and this time he's added a brown pocket scarf. It looks like he's wearing a pale blue button-down shirt underneath and from here she can look at what's below his belt without being caught: another pair of dark, fitted jeans. His smile is curved perfection. Also perfection is his five-o'clock shadow. His conversational hand gestures are confident. He's in his element, his place, and she feels damn lucky to have been invited by him to be here.

Every second standing alone feels wasted. She came for

him, *so get moving.* She walks closer and closer, afraid that any moment some jaw-droppingly beautiful woman will get to Nick first, sliding her fingers around his waist and claiming him like on the day she met him. Fear rages through her gut, excitement pulses through her heart but logic rules her brain. He wouldn't be dating anyone right now. *Relax: just be his friend.*

She's a good twenty feet away when he notices her. "Quinn!" His excited smile makes her move faster. He welcomes her with a soft, strong hug.

What a greeting.

"I love your place," she says, sweeping her hand in the air and looking around. "I see why it's so popular."

He hasn't stopped smiling. "Thank you. That means a lot." He turns to introduce the man he was speaking with, but Quinn recognizes him first.

"You're Wally B., right?" she says.

He extends a sturdy hand and a broad, white smile. "Nice to meet you, Quinn. Nick was just telling me about you."

She shrugs with disbelief, turning to Nick. "Really? What were you telling him?"

Nick smiles at Wally B. and then at her. "That reacquainting with old friends is the best feeling ever."

She tilts her head and smiles.

"I'm going to check in with my musician," Wally B. says, then turns to Quinn. "You're staying for my performance, right?"

"Wouldn't miss it. I want to pick up your book too," she says.

"All right you two," Wally B. says, pointing his index fingers at both of them and turning and walking away.

"He's nice," she says. "I was looking online at some of his stuff. Very motivational. Inspirational. Especially for teenagers."

"He has a huge following among young people. His *Heard 'Em Say Teen Poetry* radio show has really taken off. Good messages. We were lucky to get him."

Quinn glances around. Over in the corner she sees a silver sign that says Book Nook. "Is that your bookstore section?"

Nick looks over. "It is. Not as large as Indigo's though. I carry mainstream bestsellers in half of the nook and the other half is for indie authors only. I give priority to local authors."

"Who knows? One of those indie authors might be discovered here! I love how you're giving people a break."

He turns and looks into her eyes. "I know what it feels like to just want a break."

She softens. All over.

He gives a *let's move on* look. "Anyone else with you? Where's Tory?"

"She had something to do with her boyfriend and was sorry she couldn't be here." Quinn glances at her watch. By now, Tory's with Jake and one of three things could have happened. One: she's already broken up with him. Two: she's waiting until she finishes her free Whataburger and then she'll crush his heart. Or three: she's figuring out how to grab his phone to delete all of his damn coupon apps and then eat her free burger and then crush his heart. Whichever of the three: that boy will be ditched tonight.

Nick looks off to the distance. "Oh. I was hoping to catch up with her too." His face softens as he looks back to Quinn. "I'm happy that you could come. I'd love to show you around."

"I'd love it!"

Nick leads her toward the main coffee bar. The crowd has already grown since she arrived. Many people have moved closer to the Book Nook area, waiting for Wally B. The line at the coffee bar is at least fifteen customers deep. Nick looks over his shoulder back at her. "Want to try a cinnamon roll?"

"Oh my God, yes."

"Cinnamon macchiato?" he asks.

"You remember? Yes, perfect."

He leans over the bar and whispers to a barista. She stops what she was doing to prepare his order. In seconds, he turns to hand Quinn her coffee mug and takes his own mug and a plate with a massive cinnamon roll. Getting anything instantly is a nice perk of hanging with the owner.

"I have a happy problem: there's nowhere to sit," Nick says. He nods to the side. "Let's go up to my office."

She follows him down a back hallway and then up a set of open stairs. His office sits at the end of a brightly lit hallway and following him here feels sneaky, like she's in a place she's not supposed to be. Almost as off-limits as if she was following him into his bedroom.

"I feel like I'm in a secret back area I'm not supposed to be in," she says.

He walks into his office and turns. "Please, you're always welcome here." He gestures to a meeting table and she places her cup down. Everything around her feels manly and warm. Abstract art that looks like a melted tic-tac-toe board hangs behind his dark wood desk. Two guest chairs are in front of his desk, upholstered in a brown, black and white geometric pattern. He pulls out one of the meeting table chairs and sits down. "It's quieter up here too."

"So, this office is where all of the ideas come from?"

"Sure! Here or up here." He points to his temple and then slides the cinnamon roll closer to her.

"This looks sinful. And what an awesome touch to use colored frosting to match your logo. You're a branding genius."

He cuts the roll into smaller, bite-size pieces and helps himself to one. "It's also giving customers what they want. When I worked at Indigo, I always wondered why they couldn't offer something better than day-old muffins and pastries. Adding a small kitchen for cinnamon rolls, sandwiches and salads wasn't a huge expense either." He pops a bite into his mouth.

She follows with a bite of her own. *Still warm.* "These make you want more coffee too."

"Exactly." He clinks his coffee cup against hers in a toast. "Surprisingly though, our most popular drink with cinnamon rolls is Faze Out, a bacon-infused whiskey with cold brew coffee and bitters."

"I'd faze out and need a nap after drinking that." She gazes around his office and his floor-to-ceiling windows that face the plaza fountain. "How did you ever pull off opening a place like this? The financing, the decorating, the staff?"

"I was lucky, in a bad way, that I had money. I used most of the inheritance from when my parents died."

"I cannot believe what you just went through was so similar to the accident with your parents."

His eyes lower to his coffee cup. "Both times, it should've been me. I should've been in the car. I don't get it."

Her heart feels heavy. "I didn't know Sienna. Tell me about her."

His eyes remain on his cup but a small smile stretches

across his lips. "She was beautiful and kind. There wasn't a bug on the planet she'd ever harm." He looks up. "We were friends for so long but only went out on a few dates. God, if I could only have that minute back. That split-second moment when I agreed to let her drive my car. I'll never get that back. She'll never be back."

Tears burn behind her eyes. "How did you move forward after the accident?"

He shakes his head. "I don't know. I don't know what I did those days after the accident. I don't know what I'm doing now. I just get up every day and do the things everyone else is doing. I still don't feel. I can't feel anything."

"Do you feel anything when you smile? Because I do see you smile."

His eyes briefly close. When he opens them he looks at her. "I do. Actually, I take that back. I do feel something. I smile when I'm here. I smiled when I saw you and Tory the other night. It does feel good to smile."

He smiles then, as if to show her he's okay, but it doesn't reach his eyes. Maybe she should lighten the subject.

"We're not missing Wally B., right?"

He looks at his watch. "We've got a few more minutes. So, tell me about your new job." He takes another bite of cinnamon roll.

"I'll be teaching second grade at Miller Elementary. I was lucky to get my assignment so quickly. Their enrollment numbers are up so they knew how many teachers they needed. I'm blessed."

"Perfect for you."

"And, breaking news: my room will have a camping theme." She smiles, taking another bite of cinnamon roll.

"Can you imagine being in second grade again? In a cute classroom with a camping theme? Think of all of the decisions ahead of you. All of the life you have left to live." His voice cracks and she knows his thoughts have drifted back to Sienna. She searches around for a new topic of conversation but he beats her to it. "So," he says, "how are your parents?"

"Great! Still living in Canyon Lake. They're obsessively planning their 'final Fiesta' bash like they always do at the end of Fiesta. This year, they arranged to borrow the giant cowboy boot balloon that's always used in the downtown parade. It's insane."

"I remember them from the parties and things at your house. Especially your mom and how she wasn't happy with me that time I accidently broke a glass."

Quinn shakes her head. *Her mom.*

"Still, you're lucky to have family," he says.

"What about you? Do you keep up with your stepbrother or are things still—"

"We still don't talk. He's busy with his job and life. You know, he's so much older than me and we've never been close. We probably never will be."

"I'm sorry about that. And of all times, this is when you need family."

He nods and sips from his cup. "I spend time with my new family now."

Her eyes widen. *He has...kids? Oh my God, major information fail. No one ever mentioned he has kids!*

"Your...new family?"

"Yeah. Here. Faze is my family. And," he looks at his watch, "it's time for us to head downstairs."

The lump in her stomach dissipates. For a second, an adorable toddler named Nick Jr. flashed before her eyes, his mother some gorgeous woman not named Quinn.

They stand and take their plate and cups with them, walking down the stairs, dropping off their dishes before walking back into the coffeehouse.

"Whoa," Quinn says. In the fifteen minutes they were upstairs, the crowd has doubled.

"We thought this might happen," Nick says. "I've got a manager at the door in case we have to close due to capacity."

"Wow. This never happened at Indigo."

Nick takes the compliment. "Indigo doesn't have me."

Damn straight.

Her arm brushes his as they walk together, closer to the Book Nook so he can introduce Wally B. The sound of smooth, chill alternative music floats through the room and the atmosphere seems magical, the crowd eagerly waiting for the show. Walking next to Nick, it doesn't seem like her feet touch the floor. She feels like the first lady of Faze, the emotional supporter of the man-in-charge. Who else here was just invited to spend time alone with him in his office? She sees wall-to-wall happy faces. She knows Nick sees the dollar signs of paying customers.

Suddenly, Blaine steps in front of them.

"There's the thief," Blaine says, arms crossed. Reed and his angry eyes are inches behind him.

"Blaine," Nick says, stopping. "What a surprise."

"Is it? You didn't think I'd come to see the author you stole right out from under Indigo?"

Quinn inches closer to Nick.

Nick rolls his eyes. "You didn't execute Wally B.'s contract and you can't blame me for that. He wanted a signed contract and I was ready to deliver. You should have moved faster."

"Faster, like a speeding car?" Reed says, disdain in his eyes.

"What does that have to do with anything?" Nick asks.

"My sister died because of you."

"Reed, I'm sad about Sienna's death too but you can't keep blaming me for an accident."

"You caused it, Nick. And I know a little bit about cars. Hell yeah I can blame you until the day you die, which won't be soon enough for me."

"Are you threatening me?"

"Someone needs to make you pay."

"It. Was. An. Accident!" Nick says, narrowing his eyes.

Blaine uncrosses his arms. "You stole my night manager too." He stands on tiptoes, looking around. "Where's that little traitor?"

"You mistreated him, so he quit and came to me. I hired him. End of story."

Blaine raises a finger. "Your day is coming. All of this trouble will catch up to you."

Quinn shakes her head. These two are ridiculous. If Tory were here, she would have already smacked them down with a well-timed insult. Time to channel her inner Tory. "Have you guys tried the cinnamon rolls?" she blurts.

Blaine and Reed look at her like she's lost her mind. Nick faces her.

What the hell was that? Save yourself! "The famous Faze cinnamon rolls that you can't accuse Nick of stealing?"

Nick smiles.

"We're working on our own new signature item," Blaine

says, chin in the air. "It's on, Nick. As soon as my dad retires and I'm in charge, it's war. Indigo versus Faze. Me against you."

Nick purses his lips. "Oh goody."

Blaine grips Quinn's arm. "Be careful, Quinn. Watch which team you're on. I'm keeping a list of who's supporting him."

She shakes off his hand. "A list? Well, use permanent ink and put my name at the top."

Nick nods curtly, gently takes her hand and they walk away.

Her pulse races. "That felt good. Though that was difficult to watch."

Nick leads her toward the Book Nook. He lets go of her hand and turns. "Blaine comes in here all the time to spy. I had a hunch he'd show up tonight. All of our employees know who he is and they watch for him. Although one time he confused us. We swear he was here dressed up like a woman."

They both laugh but Quinn notices the hurt in his eyes. He's wounded. It's deep and it's painful. Even a confident person would be rattled with an ambush and threats like that, especially from two former friends. A warm flush covers her; an instinct to help him but she knows she can't fix everything tonight. The crowd is shoulder-to-shoulder, anticipating Wally B.'s performance. Nick needs to start the show and once he does there's no guarantee he'll come back to her.

"Hey," she says. "I know it's about to get crazy in here and I'm not sure where you'll be after the show and if I'll have a chance to say goodbye but I just wanted to know if you had any plans next weekend." A wave of nausea rolls through her. *Did she just blurt that?*

Nick's eyes widen. "Next weekend?"

She nods, shocked with herself. *Of all the times to be bold, that was it.* "Yeah. You know, I thought you might want to come to my parents' final Fiesta party and it would be nice to, you know, have someone to go with me. You know, as a friend."

He looks around and she's not sure why. Is he looking for an excuse to say no? His focus goes back to her.

"Well, sure. That sounds nice."

Oh my God, she's never asked a guy out. *But this wasn't really an ask out, right? It was a "go somewhere you've been before and just hang with me as a friend," right? Did he really... say yes?* She feels like she's going pale. *Why can't she talk?*

She clears her throat. "Okay, great. Good. I know you have to do the introduction thing and I didn't want to miss asking you that."

He looks stunned, but he's smiling. "Yeah, it's good." He points to the small stage, where Wally B. stands, waiting to be introduced. "I've got to do this...introduction thing."

She nods. *This is getting awkward.* "Of course. Good luck! Oh, and thank you for the coffee earlier."

He's already taken a few steps toward the stage but he's still looking at her. "Anytime," he says with a smile so hot it burns into her memory.

He jumps on stage, microphone in hand. "Good evening, everyone!"

Everything else she hears is a blur. She's already backing away, a mix of euphoria and pathetic pity racing through her brain. For a split second, she felt so bold. *Was that a mistake?* She's got to leave, *now.* That was the perfect ask and at the perfect time, even if her ask was a little awkward. It might spoil everything if she runs into him later. She looks at her watch. *When can she call Tory!?*

Applause erupts as Wally B. takes the stage. Quinn nears a table where his autographed books are stacked in a neat display. She picks one up and buys it.

Before she reaches the doors, she stops to listen. A smooth, soulful rhythm gives Wally B. a musical backdrop while people nod along to the beat and his words. She crosses her arms, the bag with his book crunching against her chest.

The life is simple; the struggle is not
The friends that you keep; the things that you bought
Why are you here? What do you do?
The only one who answers for your life
…is you.

She breathes in the fresh cinnamon roll smell and then she leaves.

[SIX]

Six days later

TORY

Tory clutches her purse, keys in hand, and slowly heads up the stairs to her and Quinn's apartment.

The sweltering afternoon heat has zapped her energy, as has the reality of what she's done today.

She felt the same emotional exhaustion last Saturday when she broke up with Jake. Part of her exhaustion came after listening to Jake yell every known expletive at her. The other part was from her second-guessing the snarky way she ended it. She had no idea that today would also end with the same kind of weighted, guilty feeling.

Today had begun with such excitement too. She wore her favorite royal blue and black suit and met Al for lunch, hoping he'd have a job lead for her. Then she was blown away when he offered her a generously paid position as his liaison with their legal firm on some issues he wants wrapped up before he retires. Even the food at lunch was amazing: warm, grilled garlic shrimp served on an ice-cold Caesar salad so delicious, she ate every bite. She was already thinking of how great this job will look on her resume and felt on top of the world, until the drive home when reality sank in.

She'll be working for Indigo. As in, the rival to Faze. This feels so disloyal to Nick it's like giving him dozens of stabs in the back, and at a time when he's trying to get on his feet after the accident. *How could she?*

Tory exhales a sigh as she reaches the top of the stairs and turns the corner, walking down the hallway leading to the apartment door.

Nick.

He'd always been more than kind to her. Back when they worked together, she was in awe of his drive and determination. Hell, Nick seemed more like the manager at Indigo than Blaine was. Nick was boldly handsome and the number of girls interested in him was as long as the line of girls that always seemed to hilariously form whenever he worked the front counter register. But it was her that he'd turn to when he wanted advice or was bursting with a new joke or eager to discuss the day's news. And she found herself seeking him out every day for the same. She'd catch his eyes following her, whenever she'd be wiping down tables or rearranging the merchandise display. The jealous eyes of his girlfriend at the time followed her too; even when Tory and Nick would take out the trash together she'd give him a hard time. He was trying to break it off with that girl. What Nick was going through then reminds her a little bit of what she just went through with Jake.

Tory stops outside the apartment door and takes a resetting breath. She owes Nick. He was helpful, more than helpful, keeping that godforsaken creep Reed away from her. And she and Nick did have a special friendship, a closeness she's never felt with any guy before. So now, years later, how's she going to repay him? By taking a job with his competitor.

Some friend she is anyway. When she left Indigo, she didn't return his calls and texts. Back then, she had her reason. Since she's been back, she still hasn't had a decent conversation with him. But tomorrow at Quinn's parents' house, he'll be there. She needs to tell him about her Indigo job. It's the right thing to do.

She unlocks the door to her and Quinn's apartment which, actually, is Quinn's place. When Tory's internship in Austin fell through, Quinn invited her to crash at her new apartment this summer. They'd been roommates before in college and their living styles mesh pretty well. Tory likes to eat out and live simply, decorating her room with white, black and gray. Quinn likes to eat out and live cozily, preferring softer shades of white, gold and rose gold. Since it's Quinn's furniture in the apartment anyway, her style and colors rule. The only thing they disagree on is how Tory never makes her bed. Quinn always says that Tory's twisted sheets look like she wrestled with a gorilla all night.

Tory steps inside and into the calm scent of a lavender candle burning on the kitchen counter and the sound of Quinn's busy humming from the bedroom.

"Honey, I'm home," Tory says, tossing her purse and keys on the counter.

"Well get in here and help me!" she hears Quinn's muffled voice call.

Two steps into Quinn's bedroom and Tory knows: Quinn's

mother would disown her if she saw this. Summer skirts and lacey shirts lay unwanted on the floor. Mismatched shoes are tossed everywhere.

"What are you doing?" Tory asks.

"Starting to panic," Quinn says, sticking her head out of the closet. "I'm trying to figure out what to wear to my parents' party tomorrow."

"Your date that's not a date with Nick."

"Exactly. Usually, I wouldn't have given five minutes' thought to what I would wear but this time, it's impossible." She leans back in her closet and pulls out a pair of shorts and a tank top. "I would have probably worn this, but because I'm arriving with Nick, my mom would say my shorts are too short." She disappears again and reappears with a pink floral maxi-dress. "And this is perfect but it looks too fancy and I don't want Nick to think I tried too hard since, remember—"

"This isn't a date," Tory says, finishing Quinn's sentence and sitting down on her tightly made, wrinkle-free bed.

Quinn lowers the dress she was holding up. "I know my mom would think my outfit was perfect if I wore whatever you were wearing. But I'd like something colorful and you always wear denim or black."

"Life is easy that way. And my outfit will be colorful. Your mom always has those flower crowns at the party, so I'll grab one of those for my decoration and boom, my outfit will be done."

Quinn moves out of the closet and sits down on the foot of the bed. "My outfit isn't what's making this so complicated. When I told my mom I invited Nick, she wasn't happy."

"Why the hell not?"

"She's bought into all of the sketchy hype, like what Daniel was selling. And she probably heard it from Daniel because he just did her hair. She thinks Nick caused the accident and is dangerous to be around."

"What's with people? Who started this rumor and where's the proof? Do they think that Nick made his car explode and now every car he drives will do the same?"

"I got the feeling she was more worried about Nick being in her house rather than it being dangerous for me to ride in a car with him."

Ugh, poor Quinn. "You're bringing a guy, any guy, into her house. And in her world, no guy will measure up to your first boyfriend. Your mom loved Brian and thought he was the one for you. I think she was more upset than you when he broke it off."

"You mean, when he cheated on me."

"You haven't brought a guy to your parents' since Brian, so bringing Nick is a big deal. For her."

"But she knows Nick! We're friends! This shouldn't be a big deal."

"Has there been anything in the last—oh, I don't know—ten years or so that you and your mom agreed on?"

Quinn slowly shakes her head. "I want to see Nick but I know it's way too early for him to date again yet, so what else would we do?"

"Could you just hang out at Faze together? Not as a date?"

"Well, sure. But going to my parents' is an easy hangout thing that's not a date. And he's been to my parents' before."

"Our *Three's Company* binge-watching party."

"And that pool party we had when Daniel quit."

Tory scrunches her nose. "Yeah, that wasn't supposed to be a pool party, remember? We just all ended up in the pool."

"So, see? This party should be a no-stress hangout for Nick."

Dread sinks Tory's shoulders. "Until…"

"Until what?"

"Until I tell him something. I mean, I should probably tell him something."

Quinn tilts her head. "What?"

"Well, I just got back from a meeting with Al. He's had some trouble with Indigo's law firm and needs someone to work with them to get some issues resolved before he retires."

"Oh no you aren't…"

"Working with Al would give me some experience until I can find a replacement internship. My dad has some leads for something in Austin, but even if I got a spot he said I'd probably not start until July. I need to get as much law experience as I can this summer."

Quinn tosses her hands up. "Indigo is Nick's competition!"

"I know. I feel awful. But Al really does need the help."

Quinn fusses with a corner of her comforter, running her fingers down the seam to lay it flat. "How can you work anywhere with Blaine again?"

"I won't be near him. I'll only work with Al. And when Blaine takes over, I'll be gone."

"Be careful. Blaine really laid into Nick the other night with an 'it's on,' 'it's war,' 'Indigo versus Faze' thing."

"I don't think Al sees it as that cutthroat. That's just Blaine being immature."

"I was hoping Al could connect you with something in town but I never thought it'd be at Indigo. You'll have inside information that's meant to compete with Nick."

"I'm not going to learn all of the family business secrets in less than a month."

Quinn crosses her arms. "This makes no sense. You *want* to be in a place where Reed goes all the time?"

Hearing Reed's name makes Tory feel like she's having five instant brain freezes. "The chance of running into him is the biggest risk of this whole thing, honestly."

"He's probably at Indigo every day! He and Blaine are inseparable. And he keeps talking about getting revenge on Nick. I've heard him say it twice!"

"If Reed gets in my face, I'll deal with it. And if he tries to get Nick back for the accident, well, I'm not a lawyer yet but I'd throw everything I know toward Nick's defense."

Quinn plops onto the bed. "This summer is way too much stress. I'm on an enemy list because I'm friends with the guy who'll probably be mad at you by this time tomorrow, which will be the day my mom fumes at me because she doesn't like the color of my dress or something. How did this summer get so complicated?"

Tory's phone buzzes with a text. She looks down to see the four letters she was hoping to never see again: Jake. *Shit.* "It's Jake. Again."

"Oh no. He's not handling this breakup very well, is he?"

Tory shakes her head, looking at her phone. His nasty texts have been persistent since she broke up with him Saturday. "This is the worst one yet." She reads from her phone. "I'm glad I never spent a dime more than I needed on you. I'd say go to hell but I think you're already there. Stay there."

"Oh my God," Quinn says. "This is getting scary."

Tory screenshots the text. One thing she's learned from law school is the importance of collecting evidence. "He's messing with the wrong bitch."

"And people think Nick is dangerous?"

"It will pass. Jake will find another girl who's down for a discount and they will live happily—with coupons—ever after."

Act tough; push it deep. That's her motto for handling bad shit. Her method will work just fine with Jake. Her method worked fine years ago, with Reed.

"Are you going to be okay, with this thing with Jake?" Quinn asks.

"I can handle him," Tory says, putting her phone down. "You're the one about to go into the lion's den with your mother and bring home a guy she thinks is dangerous. There're a lot of people who are teaming up against him. Are you going to be okay with Nick?"

Quinn breathes deep and then nods.

"I can handle him."

[SEVEN]

QUINN

Winding roads that Quinn has known since she was a little girl now seem blurry and unrecognizable on the drive to her parents' home. She's lost in a fuzzy, nervous haze riding in the passenger seat of Nick's car.

"It's a left turn here, right?" Nick asks.

She hasn't been able to take a full breath since he picked her up at her apartment. "You have a good memory. Yeah, right. I should say, correct. Take a left." She exhales. Being in his presence has her unstitched at the emotional hem. When she opened her apartment door, she almost fell over with a wave of sudden heat, and it wasn't just from the rising temperature of this mid-May afternoon. She was hit with Nick's grin, his outfit, his smell...the fact that he was standing at her door made her freak. Plus, not knowing what kind of greeting she'll get from her parents when she shows up with him isn't helping her nervousness.

She twists the fringe along the bottom of her sleeveless

woven top, the honey-yellow color a perfect match with her hair. That's one reason why she picked it. The other reason was she had been running out of time and it was the last shirt she had been holding.

Nick looks Fiesta ready in cobalt blue shorts with a white canvas belt and a white polo shirt. But his grin has been tentative, his movements slow. He has been stealing glances at her, though. She's caught her reflection in his Ray Ban sunglasses a few times. It feels crazy strange to see herself on his face.

The homes are becoming larger in this section of Canyon Lake. Nick slows as they near the Corbins' two-story home with a limestone brick front and terra-cotta barrel roof tiles. At the same time, they both see the massive red-and-white cowboy boot balloon anchored in the front yard.

"Oh my God," Quinn says. "They put that thing in the front?"

Nick's jaw drops. "That's awesome!"

Whew. Glad he doesn't think a twenty-foot parade balloon on the front lawn is tacky.

"Park on the street?" he asks.

"Yeah. Right there, pull up behind Tory's car." She points to Tory's white BMW.

Nick reaches into the backseat to grab a tall, colorful gift bag. "What's that?"

"A hostess gift for your parents. A bottle of Tito's, of course."

"What a nice thought. They'll love it," Quinn says. "They've probably used up most of their vodka soaking watermelon cubes."

"Spiked watermelon cubes? I should make a drink with those at Faze!"

"Well, when you invent that drink, call it the Corbin."

His grin broadens. They step out of the car and immediately hear Tory yelling.

"Good God, Daniel! Stop humping the boot!"

Quinn and Nick look at each other, trying to read each other's reaction. Since they parked on the street, they can't see the side of the balloon facing the house, where Tory apparently is. But they can see that the balloon is bouncing.

"Take another!" they hear Daniel say.

Nick and Quinn walk around the corner to find Daniel posing like a fool in front of the balloon with Tory, his paparazzi enabler.

Tory notices them. "Hey, you guys! Take one of us!" She hands Daniel's phone to Quinn then runs toward Daniel, who has already smooshed himself into the side of the giant boot. Tory does the same.

"Say, Fiesta!" Quinn says, taking pictures, trying to crop out the cars on the street and neighbors' front lawns while Daniel and Tory strike cheesy poses.

"Get in there too," Nick says, smiling. Quinn hands him Daniel's phone and runs to the side of the balloon. All three of them wildly wave their arms. "One, two…Fiesta!" Nick says, taking a few pictures before a silly look covers his face. He runs toward them too, smooshing himself into the balloon, holding the gift bag in one hand and Daniel's phone in the other. They all squeeze together. "Fiesta!" he says, snapping what seems like dozens of selfies.

Tears of laughter fill Quinn's eyes. Then a voice calls out from the front door.

"Have you guys been drinking already?" Quinn's father says. Chet Corbin stands in the open door, a smirk on his face.

Quinn stands up, straightening the fringe on her shirt. "Dad!" She glances at Nick, who pulls himself together and gives Daniel his phone back.

"You were surprisingly fun," Daniel mumbles to Nick. He glances over Nick's hair and flicks a stray strand back into place for him. And then another. And another…

"Hey, C.C.!" Tory says, already on her way to hug him. "Happy Fiesta!"

Chet opens his arms to hug her. A tall man with a full head of graying hair, he's as good looking now as he was in his twenties. At least that's what Quinn thinks from seeing the old photos of him hanging in his office.

Daniel has stopped organizing Nick's hair and approaches. "What's good, C.C.?" They both hug.

Her dad takes another look at Daniel. "Where'd you get that shirt?"

Daniel strikes a pose to show off his white t-shirt with an image of the state of Texas in a colorful serape print. "Taco Cabana! Only five dollars when you buy a combo. Want me to get you one?"

Chet smiles. "I couldn't pull it off like you."

Daniel beams.

"Hi, Dad," Quinn says, moving closer.

Chet has saved his warmest hug for his daughter. "Hello, buttercup."

She squeezes him and then lets go to introduce Nick, but Nick's already extending a hand.

"Mr. Corbin," Nick says.

"Nick, it's been a few years," Chet says, shaking his hand and keeping his expression cautious.

Pleasant enough.

"What were you all doing to that balloon?" Pam Corbin steps into the foyer. Slender with a stylish pixie blonde haircut, she draws her hands to her hips.

"I was loving up on that balloon like I love you, P.C.," Tory says, pulling Quinn's mom into a hug, bringing a rare smile to Pam's face.

"Mama Corbin," Daniel says. "Are you gonna make me a mojito?"

She hugs Daniel. "You're quite old enough to make one yourself."

"Hi, Mom," Quinn says. They share a brief hug. Nick stands behind Quinn's shoulder.

"Nick," Pam says, not extending a hand to shake or her arms for a hug.

Nick nods and offers her the gift bag. "Thanks for having me."

Pam takes it and glances inside. "How thoughtful." She looks up. "So, why don't you all go back outside and make sure those ropes are still anchored into the ground. I'll be in trouble with the Fiesta Committee if that balloon gets damaged."

Tory whispers to Quinn. "Daniel and I got it." She winks, grabs Daniel by the elbow and heads out the front door, leaving Quinn and Nick alone in the foyer with Quinn's parents.

Man, that girl is clutch.

Quinn seizes the moment. "Do you remember the last time you were here?" she says to Nick.

He looks around the foyer. "I think it was your birthday party, years ago."

Pam's eyes slowly roll toward Chet.

"Yes," Chet says, the lines around his mouth tightening. "A lot has happened since you were here last. Listen, Nick. We're a little worried—"

"Pam!" a woman yells as she barrels through the front door. She greets Pam with a robust hug and three or four other people follow, loudly saying their hellos.

Nick stares at Chet with narrowed eyes. Quinn reaches for Nick's arm. "Let's go out by the pool," she says, leading him away.

He slides his hands into his pockets, his eyes canvassing the family room as they walk through to the pool. Outside, a small band is setting up on a concrete patio. Colorful beach balls float in the pool and paper picado banners swing overhead with the hot breeze. A bar has been set up to the side and they walk toward it.

Quinn's eyes are on the ground. "I'm sorry for that chilly reception there."

He straightens his collar, stops and faces her. "I get it everywhere I go. I didn't expect it here."

Really? What's she doing? Why did she ask him here? She's putting him in an awkward social spot, thanks to her stupid parents.

Nick approaches the bar, nodding to the bartender. "Hello there. What's your signature drink?"

The short, Mexican man smiles. "Sol de Flare, sir."

"I'll take one and I'd love to see how you make it."

Nick leans over the bar to watch, seemingly more interested in bartending than continuing a conversation with her. He's back at work, studying for new ideas. He's retreated to a place that's comfortable for him.

"Blood orange juice," Nick says, watching. "Ah, agave."

"Yes, sir, but this is the secret." The bartender reaches under the bar and pulls out a small bottle of pepper-infused tequila. He pours a splash into the drink, gives it a stir and hands it to Nick.

Nick sips and smiles.

"Fiery. Is this your personal creation or can I use this recipe?"

"I wish I invented it, sir. I found it on the internet." The bartender's mustache stretches with his smile.

Nick turns to Quinn. "Have a sip."

He holds the glass as she sips, his eyes curious for her reaction. She swallows. "It's good." And then she starts coughing.

The bartender laughs. "It's the pepper."

Nick laughs. "Told you it's fiery."

The bartender slides a glass of water her way. She takes a few sips and finally stops hacking. Nick's smile is totally worth the embarrassment. At least they can talk about something else besides her rude parents. *Saved by the Sol de Flare.*

Nick waves his thanks to the bartender and they move away.

"Everywhere you go, you like to study and learn new things?" Quinn asks.

"I do," he says. "My goal with the business is to keep things fresh, interesting. I like for employees to suggest new things too. That's one reason I'm thinking about renaming our employees and calling them partners."

"You've always been the type of person to support people and give them a chance. I'll never forget how you went to bat for me and Tory when that cranky bookstore manager at Indigo accused us of stealing."

"I knew you were innocent and I was happy to help. I like to give people a voice, even in my business. When people feel heard, they become more loyal. And loyalty is very important to me. Especially right now."

Quinn sips her water and it feels like a rock just went down her throat. Loyalty is about to be thrown into his face when Tory tells him her news. "Let's go down to the garden."

They walk together through the backyard, down a few steps leading to a small garden filled with yucca and heather bushes. The band has begun to play and more guests have arrived to the pool and bar area. Quinn sits on a bench. Nick leans against a four-foot-high rock wall. Sprawling branches from oak trees help cover them with needed shade.

"I'm glad you came with me today. I wish people would get over this weirdness with your accident."

"It's unbelievable how some people blame me. I know Reed is saying things around town." He looks to his feet. "I can't imagine losing a sister. I feel for him, but this campaign of hate he's launched against me is starting to get old."

"What he said the other night, wishing you were dead. Do you think he's mad enough to get revenge?"

"He'd be stupid to do that. But he has the motivation to try."

"What do you do? How do you move forward?"

"I do what you just saw: learn and make my business better."

There he goes again: back to business. *Has this man even grieved?*

A loud splash draws their attention to the pool.

"I bet that was Daniel," Quinn says, smiling.

Nick looks toward the house. "Where'd Tory go?"

"Let's see," Quinn looks at her watch, "it's about a half hour into this party so she's probably been nibbling the vodka watermelon cubes and is now in the kitchen stalking the caterer and begging them to bring the queso out."

Nick grins with amusement. "Is her boyfriend coming?"

"They, well she, broke up with him."

His eyebrows tighten. "Really? Is she okay?"

"She will be when he stops stalking her."

Nick's arms drop to his sides and he straightens. "What? What's he doing?"

"You know, Tory and I have a policy. After the headline, if it's my news, I tell it. If it's her news, she tells it. So, for more details, you'll need to ask her."

"Good policy. That's probably why you've stayed friends since you were little girls."

Up by the bar, Quinn notices Tory getting a drink. Tory sees them too and heads their way.

Halfway to them, Tory shouts, "Do you need a drink?"

"We're good!" Quinn shouts.

"Do you want one of these?" She points to her head and the paper flower crown she's wearing.

"No, I'm good," she says.

Nick shrugs, smiling.

Quinn yells back at Tory, "Nick really wants one but he's good too."

A few seconds later, Tory has reached them, swinging her long, brown hair to show off the colorful ribbons hanging from the back of the crown. "I love that your mom has these things every year. I always feel like a Fiesta princess."

"I can't wear them." Quinn looks at Nick. "One time, one

of the red paper flowers got wet and red stain rubbed all over my hair."

Tory swings her hair again. "Hashtag: blonde problems. See, brunettes don't have that issue. Seriously, the man of my dreams can give me one of these instead of a ring and I'm good." She sips the drink she's holding. "The bartender is pushing this drink. Have you ever tried a Sol de Flare?"

"I drank the first one he made," Nick says.

"It's so yummy and spicy." She looks at Nick. "I didn't properly greet you out front." She hugs him in an embrace so long, his eyes close. He lets go of her, leaving Quinn hoping the moment of warmth between them will last after Tory tells him her news.

"We haven't properly talked at all since you rolled back into town," he says.

She raises her index finger. "True. And that's my fault. I'm really sorry about what you've been going through. It's ridiculous for people to blame you for the accident. If there's anything I can do to help, please tell me."

"I appreciate your support. Hey, Quinn was just saying you broke up with your boyfriend and it hasn't gone well."

Quinn puts up her hands. "But I only told him the headline, not everything."

Tory looks back to Nick. "His salty texting apparently makes him feel better."

"His texting is starting to scare me, for her," Quinn says.

Nick's cheeks begin to throb. "Let me know if you need me to take care of anything. No guy should make you feel scared in any way."

Tory gives him a stiff nod. "Thanks."

Quinn's eyes dart back and forth between them. *Good to have Nick around.*

Norteno Mexican music now blares from the band, the polka sound inspiring a couple of guests to start dancing. So many people are outside, Quinn can't see the floating beach balls in the pool anymore.

"The food must be out by now," Quinn says. "Want to head back up?"

"I'm perfectly fine here with this present company," Nick says, smiling at both of them.

Tory takes a sip of her drink and then another. "While we're down here, there's something I wanted to tell you, actually."

Nick looks to her with interest.

Quinn braces herself.

"Quinn!" her mother yells, standing at the edge of the pool, motioning for her to come to where she is.

Seriously? Not now!

"Quinn!" she calls again.

"I have no idea what she needs," Quinn says. "I'll be right back, okay?"

Tory nods.

"Sure," Nick says.

Quinn quickly moves away, cutting through the grass to get to her mom as fast as she can.

"You need to say hello to Mike Bentley," her mom says, pointing to the living room.

Oh Lord. One of her parents' neighbors? She would have said hello to him, eventually. *Why right now?*

Quinn glances back to Tory and Nick, who are standing face-to-face, talking. *Okay, good.* Quinn quickly steps into the living room, where her mother leads her in a parade of hugs with people she hasn't seen in years. A few minutes pass until the conversations stop and Quinn heads back outside.

No! Oh no! Tory's shaking her head and Nick's arms are outstretched and animated. Quinn rushes down to them.

"It's not a big deal," Tory says. "It's stuff like city permits and legal approvals to sell alcohol and expand with a kitchen."

Nick's head jerks back. "A kitchen! And selling alcohol? They're coming after me by copying me! That's what Blaine meant when he said they're working on their own signature item. You'll be working on projects that are meant to take me down!"

"No, no. I don't think that's what—"

"Oh yes, it is!" Nick begins pacing. "And Blaine's screwing with me by taking one of the few friends I had. He's doing this on purpose."

"No, Blaine doesn't have anything to do with this. I'll be working with Al. Just for a month."

"Tory…" His eyes burn with hurt. "I didn't know you needed a job. You could have asked me for help. I could have asked people I know if they needed your help for a month. Why Indigo?"

Quinn stands an arm's reach between them and she really wants to reach out and hug them both right now.

"It's not to hurt you. It's to help Al," Tory says.

"Helping Al hurts me!" He runs a hand through his hair and takes a few deep, calming breaths. "You know what? I'm happy for you. I'm glad you'll be working where you want to be."

"Thank you."

Quinn exhales relief. *Thank you, Lord.*

"But loyalty means something to me, Tory. It means everything to me right now. It seems like this whole town is up my ass saying I'm nothing but trouble and I'm looking for friendly faces."

"I'm still a friendly face! I totally support you!"

He shakes his head in anger. "If you're working for Indigo, you can't be a friendly face to me."

Tory shrinks. "That's a little harsh, don't you think?"

"I don't know what to think," he says. "I'm heading to the bar." He brushes Tory's shoulder as he passes.

"Nick!" Quinn calls out. She faces Tory. "Are you okay?"

Tory looks past her, watching Nick walk away, her eyes filling with tears. "Please, go after him and make sure he's okay."

Quinn holds Tory's hands. If Tory's hurt, she's not going anywhere.

"Seriously, Quinn," Tory says with a slight sniffle. "Be sure he's okay."

Quinn nods. "I'll be right back." She takes a few running steps to catch up to Nick. The festive music has some people dancing in the grass but to her, the screeching accordion has become the most irritating sound ever. She reaches his side, just as he notices the long line at the bar. He glances over to the food table, where a group of teenagers hover, filling up their plates. He looks back down to the oak trees where Tory still stands, her back now to the crowd. The long ribbons dangling from the back of her flower crown gently blow in the breeze. Every few seconds, her hand touches her face. Lines of hurt crease the sides of his eyes as he stares at Tory, shaking his head.

Quinn taps his shoulder. "Let's go inside."

His posture is rigid as they walk through the family room, Quinn leading Nick somewhere where he can cool off, where they can talk. She takes him into her dad's study.

Formidable floor to ceiling bookshelves in a dark mahogany stain line the walls. A sturdy, masculine desk is centered in a room that has always felt intimidating to Quinn but now it's the safest place she can think of. And the fastest for her to reach.

"Nick," she whispers, turning to him just as his angry eyes focus on her.

"How long have you known she was going to do legal work for my rival?"

"Yesterday. I found out yesterday."

He pinches his lips. "And you didn't warn me? A little... heads up?"

"It's her news to tell you."

"I might have mentioned a new idea we're working on at Faze, or a new event. If she heard my ideas, she might tell Al."

"I don't think she would."

"I've told *you* about ideas and you might mention those to her!"

"I'd never..."

"And Blaine? She wants to work with him? And...Reed?" he starts pacing. "Reed is probably there every day. What's she thinking?"

"It's not as bad as..."

A man's voice interrupts. "What's going on in here?" Chet says, walking into the study.

No, no, no! Not now!

"Dad, can we have a minute?"

"Actually, I'd like to speak to Nick."

Nick faces Chet with a cold smile. "Of course, Mr. Corbin."

"Look, Nick. I know you were involved in a terrible accident and I'm very sorry for what has happened to you."

Nick stands taller.

"There're a lot of people who think the accident was your fault."

"Chet?" Pam calls, walking into the study.

No! Not Mom too!

Pam sees Nick and Quinn and hits her hips. "Oh." She turns and closes the study doors, leaving the four of them alone.

Quinn explodes. "What the hell are you two doing? Why are you cornering Nick?"

"Buttercup," Chet says, "it's not a good idea for Nick to be here."

"Nick," Pam says, stepping closer to him. "Mrs. Finn is one of my guests here and she was very upset when she saw you."

"Mrs. Finn?" Nick asks, baffled.

"She's the owner of the dog you killed in that hit-and-run."

Nick covers his mouth with his hands.

Pam crosses her arms. "I've been sitting with her in my bedroom for the last half an hour, calming her down."

"It was an accident. Years ago," Nick says, his voice rising. "I apologized!"

"Oh no, she says you never did. She says you never said you were sorry."

"I wrote her family a letter! I put five hundred dollars in cash in there to pay for any expenses they had!"

"I'm afraid you didn't. She never got it."

"You're kidding me," Nick says.

"Come on, Mom, this isn't fair," Quinn says.

"Nick," Chet says. "Son, I think it's best for everyone if you leave."

"What?!" Quinn yells.

Nick straightens his shoulders and the room quiets. The only sounds are from muffled laughter and party music pressing at the door.

Quinn fists her hands. "You're both being ridiculous!"

"Nick…" Pam says.

"Hold on, Mom," Quinn says. "You're asking Nick to leave because one of your guests is upset? What about me? Nick is *my* guest. Making him leave makes *me* upset and I'm your flipping daughter!"

Pam glares at Quinn. "You should have never asked him to—"

"It doesn't matter," Chet says. "This is our home and we are asking him to leave now."

A few seconds that feel like forever pass before Nick finally moves. He stands tall, eye-to-eye with Chet. "Of course, Mr. Corbin."

"Oh no, no," Quinn cries.

Nick sends Pam a cold glare and steps toward the door. Quinn's on his heels. He looks over his shoulder and turns to face her.

"Will you be able to get a ride home?" he asks her flatly.

"Yes, you. I'm leaving with you."

He shakes his head. "No, stay. Enjoy the party." He looks over to Pam and Chet and then back to Quinn. "Enjoy the party with your family."

She trembles with disbelief.

His eyes are wet. "And enjoy this time with your loyal best friend, too."

Her knees buckle. It feels like everyone here has turned on Nick!

"Nick…" she whispers.

He shakes his head again, his eyes in a wet, glassy stare. And in one swift move, Nick opens the study door and disappears.

[EIGHT]

A pot of noodles boils on the stove, the bubbles raging larger and larger. Suddenly, the pot overflows, the hot water meeting the stove's burner in a violent hissing fit.

Quinn stands next to the stove, wearing her faded and well-worn pajamas, and looks down at the rising steam. *Guess she should turn that off.* She turns off the burner and slides the pot over.

Dinner's ready.

She stands motionless, looking at the pot of cooked elbow noodles. *Nifty. She made something.*

She slumps and walks back to the sofa, crawling under her furry white blanket. This has been her safe place since Saturday's disastrous Fiesta party, two days ago.

The door handle rattles and she cracks one eye to look at the door. Tory walks in and sniffs. "Are you burning something?"

"I cooked dinner."

Tory glances at the mess on the stove and then the mess on the sofa. She exhales so loudly it sounds like air being released from a beach ball. She walks farther in and then sits down by

Quinn's feet, tossing her purse and keys in exasperated fashion on the coffee table.

"How was your first day at work?" Quinn mumbles.

Tory presses herself into the couch cushions, kicks off her black patent leather pumps and rests her feet on the coffee table. "I thought about Nick all day."

"Yep. Know the feeling."

"Yeah, but I'm toast. Nick's going to be mad and stay mad at me until this Indigo project is over. Then maybe we can be friends again. But you? You need to go talk to him."

Quinn rubs her face in her blanket. "I've been thinking about texting him."

"A text? Your parents kicked him out of their house. That's brutal. And that's not an apology you do with a text."

Quinn sinks deeper into the sofa. She suffered a stomach-retching wave of anxiety the night of Al's retirement party just thinking that Nick could be there. Then, two days ago, she couldn't even see straight when she was with him, driving in his car. And they were on good terms then! How's she supposed to see him face to face now without crumbling in a pathetic freak-out? "I've got to fix this. I just don't know how."

Tory types on her phone. "You, my friend, need a crutch. There. Sent. Check your email."

Quinn stares at the coffee table, where her phone is lying. It lights up but she doesn't move.

"You. Are. Pathetic." Tory sits up, grabs Quinn's phone and hands it to her.

She glances at the screen and then sits straight up. "Oh my God! Are you kidding? You got tickets to the Sentras concert this weekend?"

Tory nods. "Yep. Al had a few he was giving away. His friend manages the Bear Creek Arena or he owns the venue or I don't know, his friend is important. Anyway, I snagged two."

"This was impossible to get tickets for. It sold out in like three minutes, months ago!"

"I know. I tried to buy some then too."

"Okay, you win. This perked me up."

"And that's the idea. They're yours."

"We're not going together?"

"Nope. Both tickets are yours. Go find a date. You know, a guy with a Qutor rank of one."

Quinn shakes her head. "I don't know anyone…"

Tory rolls her eyes. "Then how about a friend. Someone impossibly attractive, with wisps of amazing brown hair and who owns his own coffee shop."

"Oh…oh! That's what you meant by crutch."

"Yep. Crutch. Prop. A reason to go see Nick. Having tickets to a sold-out concert in the hottest area venue is a great prop to arm yourself with to go see him."

Quinn swings her legs off of the couch, moving the furry blanket to the side. "I could go up to Faze and see him. I could apologize for how my parents treated him and we could talk and then I could ask him to go to the concert with me."

"Exactly."

"And…" Quinn stands up, shaking her phone as she talks. "This is perfect. Bear Creek is outside of Austin so neither of us would know anyone there. It's like a neutral place we can go to get away from this stupid town."

"But there is one catch."

Quinn puts her hands to her face. "Is this going to ruin my

Cinderella moment? Because I'm totally enjoying my Cinderella moment. What's the catch?"

"Cinderella can take her prince to the concert, but you better not tell him where you got the tickets from."

Her eyes bulge. "You're right! If Nick knew these came from Al, oh…not good."

"Trust me. When Al overheard me saying that I might give these to you and Nick, he made this weird scowling face. So, to be safe, you need to tell Nick they came from me. End of story," Tory says. "And maybe this will earn me brownie points for the future when Nick might, maybe, ever talk to me again."

Quinn waves her hands and squeals. "Thank you, thank you, thank you." She jumps back on the sofa and grabs Tory for a hug. "I can't believe you would give up your chance to go to this concert so I could take Nick. You're the best friend I could ever imagine!" She lets go. "I should go tonight and see if he's in the office. He should be. I mean, he works so much this would be the perfect time to catch him. Oh, Tory. Thank you so much!" She flies toward Tory again with a quick hug.

Quinn's eyes fill with appreciation. "Time and time again, you always do the nicest things for me. One day, I'm going to pay you back for all of it."

"You let me stay here this summer. That's a pretty nice—"

"Thing to do? No, that's nothing. You do so much more. This…" she looks down at her phone, "this is beyond what a best friend does."

Tory shrugs. "Nah. This is just what I do."

Quinn smiles a dreamy, soft smile at Tory.

"Um," Tory says. "You're staring at me. Don't you have somewhere to go?"

Quinn snaps out of appreciation mode. "I gotta go shower!"

"Good idea," Tory says as Quinn jumps up. "Because I hate to break this to you, but girl, you stink."

* * *

Quinn's lucky. She found a parking space right beside the fountain at Town Centre. *That's a good sign.* After all, it's 7 p.m. and prime time for dinner at the busy restaurants all around here. And any time is busy time for a cup of coffee and a cinnamon roll at Faze. Landing a space this prime must mean luck is on her side.

She steps out of her car and eagerly looks toward Faze for what she hopes is another lucky sign. *Yes!* From here she can see the light in Nick's office is on.

She moves so quickly she forgets to look both ways for traffic as she crosses the road to get to the sidewalk leading to Faze. Her outfit feels breezy and fast: a flowing burgundy maxi-skirt with a lace camisole top and flat sandals so comfortable she could run a sprint in them if she had to.

And to think two hours ago she questioned whether she had the energy to get up and go pee.

She swings open the main door of Faze and quickly steps into the scent of cinnamon rolls. It's the scent of success. It's the scent of Nick.

It's crowded, again, though not as busy as when Wally B. was here the other night. She glances at the coffee bar. By now, knowing Nick, they already have a Sol de Flare on the menu.

She knows exactly where she's going and this time, she doesn't feel awkward walking through the back area. No one asks where she's going as she heads up the stairs.

Rounding the corner, she has a clear view of Nick's open office door. She hears his voice when a warning chill rushes through her body, begging her to stop. Her excitement has brought her this far. But she wisely remembers, he's not excited. He doesn't know she's here. He might not have even *thought* about her today.

Maybe this isn't a good idea. An apology ambush could backfire. But hearing his voice is too damn tempting…knowing he's *right there…*

Do it. She ignores her gut and pushes forward, now in the doorway of his office.

"Nick?" she calls, stepping inside.

Nick is leaning against the front of his desk, looking confident and in control, wearing a slender pair of dress pants and a dressy, white button-down shirt rolled up at the sleeves. He does a double take seeing her. "Quinn?"

She takes another step into his office and sees who he's talking to. It's a woman wearing a Faze nametag. She's gorgeous, the height of Charlize Theron with the wide eyes and thick black hair of Mila Kunis and the flashy smile of Julia Roberts.

Whoa.

"Um, hey, sorry. I didn't mean to interrupt," Quinn mumbles.

He stands up straight. "What a surprise." He looks to the woman. "Okay, are we good?"

"We're great. Thank you." She smiles like she just won an Oscar and walks past Quinn, leaving a sensuous scent of rose perfume dancing in the air.

Quinn knows that walk. She did it the other night. It's a walk fueled with pixie-dust magic knowing you were just alone with Nick in his power office.

Suddenly, Quinn feels dirty and ugly and, as Tory would put it, she feels like she's toast. She's not even wearing any intoxicating perfume!

"You okay?" Nick asks, looking at her face.

She pats down her face. *Is something on it? Lipstick smear? A wet mascara blink mark? Or is he noticing the look of panic and despair?*

"I was just, you know, moving fast to get here so maybe I'm a little flush." She fans herself.

He breathes in as if he just remembered he's mad at her. "What are you doing here?" He leaves his desk and walks to the door, closing it.

It doesn't matter what she looks like. Or smells like. And forget these nerves. *Just say what's in your heart.*

"I'm sorry for what happened Saturday. All of it. I didn't mean to put you in a position where anything in your life got worse."

The ice breaks with his slight smile. "That was a rough day I'd rather forget."

"Well, I'll never forget it. I'll never forgive myself."

She detects a slight look of forgiveness in his eyes.

"I still consider you a friend," he says, looking at her squarely. "And just a friend."

She gulps.

"That was awkward, at your parents' house," he says. "I felt like a boyfriend being punished by the parents and I'm not even dating you. I'm an adult running a successful business."

"I understand."

"Your parents have every right to ask me to leave, just like I have every right to ask them to leave if they ever came here."

"You would?"

"No, of course not. But my point is, I respected their space even though I disagreed."

"Nick, I'm so sorry this has gotten weird. I thought the party would be a great, safe place to hang out with you. Not dating, of course. Just hang out."

"Oh, I got hung out," he says with a boyish smile. He moves closer to her. "I'm glad you're here now. I wasn't happy with how it was left between us."

"Me neither."

His smile draws her closer. His arms open and she falls into him. He squeezes her with a warm hug. They separate but remain standing close. "You were moving fast to get here, huh?" he asks.

Perfect opening. Take it! "Well, yes. I was brooding over what to say and how to apologize and then something fell into my lap and you popped into my mind and I wanted to see you as fast as I could."

"Did you get hurt?"

"Hurt?"

"From what fell into your lap?" He smirks.

"Oh, ha. No, not fell, like that. I got an opportunity. An opportunity fell into my lap."

"So why did I come to mind?"

"Because you need an escape. I need an escape. Somewhere out of town where we can have some fun. As friends."

"I agree completely."

She smiles a smile that finally feels like herself again. At ease and happy, just being with Nick.

"I got two tickets to the Sentras concert this Saturday. Want to go with me?"

"Whoa! Sentras? I heard scalpers are selling tickets for over two thousand dollars. How'd you get the tickets?"

"Tory, actually."

He stands as straight as a board. "Tory. That's a whole other wound that's open."

"Nick, she's upset about hurting you more than you know. Try to understand, that's the world she's heading into. Sometimes, she may represent a client who goes against a company she likes, or against her personal beliefs. Or she may be on the opposing side from another lawyer she knows and likes. Practicing law can be brutal. But trust me, she can keep personal and business separate."

Nick's eyes drift away. "Why aren't you going with Tory?"

"She can't go," Quinn says. "And besides, Tory isn't the discussion on the table. The offer is you and me and a fun outing far away where no one knows us."

Nick smiles. "As friends."

"The best of friends."

"I accept your offer. I would love to go. Thanks for asking."

She feels her smile stretching. "Thanks for forgiving me."

A shadow of shame is gone from her heart. He's letting her back into his life. He clearly doesn't want to date, either her or the celebrity-looking bombshell who was up here earlier. And that's okay. Just being in his company is enough.

She's got to hide her true feelings. She needs to file them away in a folder marked "The Future." If she saw another woman gushing over Nick, she'd think they were being opportunistic. Like a gold digger, brainwashing him into a new relationship with the promise of support and love. That's not who she wants to be; that's not what she wants for him. She wants him to heal.

But she likes him so much it's beginning to hurt.

[NINE]

Quinn's voice already feels hoarse from singing and she's not at the concert yet. She's not even out of Nick's car.

They're stuck in traffic just outside Bear Creek arena. At least the scenery is beautiful, gentle rolling hills as far as they can see, with no businesses or homes within miles. The only thing out here is the state-of-the-art amphitheater complex, a venue so popular that bands go out of their way to schedule performances here.

Her hands are in the air; Nick beats the steering wheel, singing as loud and off-key as they can to *Glass House*, one of the hit songs from the Sentras' last album. They've sung all of the Sentras' other hit songs on the drive here.

Traffic inches forward and Quinn notices something else inching forward: dark clouds of a thunderstorm. Bear Creek is an outdoor arena and even if that storm misses them, the humidity might do a frizz-out number to her hair. If the storm hits them, she'll be rocking the drenched-rat look. Either way, she's starting not to care. Nick doesn't seem to be bothered by appearances, beautiful or ugly.

They enter the parking lot and notice the flashing lights from a Reed's Roadside tow truck.

"Ick, Reed's," Quinn says.

"I didn't know Reed's serviced this area," Nick says. "Their dealerships are only in San Antonio."

"Maybe they have to work out here because they need more money," Quinn says, adding a sarcastic wink.

Nick's eyes linger on the tow truck as they pass. Quinn turns the music down.

"Does seeing Reed's name make you think of Sienna?"

"It does. You know she told me once that she and Reed fought all the time. She shared some funny stories about him growing up. It was so odd how sweet she was and what an ass Reed is."

"Like, how can they be related?"

"Exactly."

"Does anyone besides Blaine actually like Reed?"

Nick shrugs. "Reed and I actually got along great years ago. Until he pulled a dick move and my fist met his face. He's had a beef with me ever since."

Oh my. Nick punched Reed once? *That* would have been something to see.

Traffic attendants direct them to a row and they pull into a space a fair distance from the arena. "Look how full the parking lot already is. And we're early!" Quinn looks again at the sky.

"I've got ponchos in the back," Nick says. They both get out of the car and Nick opens the trunk. "I thought we might be early so I packed this." He gestures to a picnic basket.

Any guy who owns a picnic basket is a keeper. "Amazing!"

He opens the wicker basket and holds up a bottle of wine. "I hope red is good."

She lays a hand over her heart. She'd probably drink lighter fluid with him at this point. "You're amazing. So thoughtful. It's perfect."

He opens the bottle and begins pouring. "You're treating me to a great show, it's the least I can do."

With thoughtful gestures like this, and forgiveness for her parents being jerks, plus being as hot as he is? He's doing more than he knows.

He hands her a glass and raises his.

She holds up her glass for a toast. "To friends."

"Friends," he toasts back.

"And a place where no one knows who we are!" she says.

"Let's hope!"

Other concertgoers have started their own tailgates and the parking lot fills with Sentras music. The looming thunderstorm hasn't moved, as if it's waiting to watch the concert too. They share their wine with some other couples and Nick enjoys a beer offered from a group of guys. Everyone begins to pack up their tailgates and Nick puts the trash into the trunk and grabs the ponchos.

Excitement pierces the air as they walk toward the arena. No rainstorm will dampen the mood on this night! They find their seats and strangers around them start up conversations as if they all have been lifelong friends.

Lights dim, the opening act takes the stage and the next hours are a blur of dancing and singing. Quinn keeps glancing at Nick, to be sure that the music isn't stirring up his emotions. But his constant smile tells her he's fine.

After the final song, the crowd screams for an encore when a clap of thunder sounds overhead.

"Want to beat the crowd and this storm and leave now?" Quinn yells.

Nick nods. He reaches for her hand and leads her out of the arena, through a capacity crowd growing rowdier by the minute, demanding an encore.

He doesn't let go of her hand even after they make it out of the gate, along with a few others who opted to leave early. Walking across the parking lot, he swings her arm. "That was amazing!"

Seeing his eyes on fire with excitement makes her soul jump for joy. *Perfect evening.* Drops of rain begin to fall and they look at each other with questioning glances. *Run? Walk?* He drops her arm and they both start to run.

Then the clouds open up and rain pours down.

"Next aisle!" Nick yells, nearing his car.

Quinn feels breathless from trying to run while laughing and attempting to unfold her poncho.

Nick races to her door, opens it and she jumps inside, throwing the wet poncho in the backseat. A split second later, he's behind the wheel.

They're wet and laughing when suddenly a vivid light turns the night as bright as day when a massive bolt of lightning strikes the parking lot and a booming crash of thunder follows. Quinn screams and Nick reaches over to wrap her with his arms.

"Oh my God, oh my God," she says. "We could have gotten hit!"

"Oh my God, that was close," Nick says, still holding her.

Her breathing hasn't recovered yet from the run and now her heart pounds from the terrifying thought of almost being electrocuted. Nick's trying to catch his breath too.

And he still hasn't let her go.

"Well," she says, looking into his eyes, inches away. A drop of water trails down her face and she resists her urge to wipe it away. She doesn't want to move from his arms. "If I had been hit with lightning, you should know, I would have been the happiest girl getting killed at that moment. What a night."

His face creases with a smile. "That's a little creepy, but I know what you mean. And I would have been the happiest guy, well, up until the moment I got fried to the pavement."

Another bolt of lightning strikes with an immediate crash of thunder. Quinn yelps and he squeezes her tighter. Rain unleashes on the car with a roar.

They're not going anywhere, anytime soon.

And he still hasn't let her go.

His eyes look vulnerable. His arms are protective. And he's so close Quinn can see the skin of his cheek under his beard.

Forget patience. Forget burying her feelings. She wants to kiss him. Just lay one on him and make it happen. Force the contact. Cross the line. Live in the moment. Rip off these clothes. Make love in this car right now!

Rain keeps up a steady roar and neither of them move. Then he turns his head, ever so slightly. She feels his breath on her lips.

He lowers his head, resting his cheek on hers. Tender. Sweet. But there's no kiss.

She has no words, not sure what to do. Their bodies are closer than they've ever been before, the romantic sound of falling rain surrounds them. But a layer of hurt seems to keep him from doing more.

Then, as suddenly as it started, the rain stops.

Nick leans away from her to look through the windshield at the sky. Thunder rumbles in the distance. Sounds of laughter and playful screams come from the parking lot as soaked, drunk people run to their cars.

Thanks, rain. Sixty more seconds might have changed everything.

"That was intense," he says, looking to her.

"I've never seen rain that heavy."

"No." He eases back into his seat, eyes on her. "I meant what just happened with you and me."

Don't say a word. Don't blow it. Don't agree or disagree or anything. Let him drive this moment!

She nods, adding a lip-biting smile.

Then the car alarm next to them goes off, lights flashing, siren blaring. A couple they met earlier runs up to the car, laughing and yelling and trying to turn it off.

The ruined moment crushes her heart. Nick seems content to smile.

"We should get going, to stay ahead of this traffic," he says.

She smiles in agreement, even though her heart feels a dull, disappointing ache. She buckles her seat belt.

A light rain still falls and Nick has a little trouble seeing out of his windshield. He backs up and pulls out of the row, following the lights of the car ahead of him leaving the parking lot.

"You buckled up?" he says, glancing over.

"I'm fine. I'll help you watch the side of the road over here."

A sea of puddles slows them down and Nick pumps his brakes to dry them out after driving through each one. Soon they are on the open road.

"On a wet night like this, I wish it was just a straight, well-lit road," Nick says, both hands on the wheel and squinting to see the car ahead.

"It hasn't rained in weeks. Does it feel slippery?"

"You know," he looks down at the wheel, "it does feel different. Very slippery."

"I'll watch for the turns and corners."

Thankfully, a large SUV is in front of them, giving them big, bright lights to follow. Then the SUV turns his flashers on.

"I hate that!" Quinn says. "Why do people do that! It's illegal to drive with flashers on. It makes it harder to see when it's flashing."

Nick doesn't respond. His eyes dart between the windshield and the dash.

"Everything ok?"

"There's no warning light but my car doesn't feel right. And these wipers flat out suck."

Quinn's having a hard time seeing straight ahead too. The idiot with his flashers is now farther down the road, making it harder to see him with his confusing, blinking lights.

"There's a crossroad up here," he says, nodding to his dashboard GPS map. "Let's pull off there and wait until this rain passes."

"Good idea." Safety first. Besides, the sound of rain is romantic. *What are the chances of them having another in-car snuggle?*

She gently places her hand on his forearm, giving him a soft squeeze.

He glances down at her hand and gives her a deep smile back.

Then he looks back up.

"Shit!" he screams.

The SUV ahead of them has stopped, their flashing lights in clear view as Nick's car comes closer. He hits the brakes and the back of the car spins, out of control, picking up speed and twirling wildly. Quinn screams, throwing one hand on the dash and the other on the window to brace herself.

"Hold on!" he yells, fighting with the steering wheel, turning the opposite direction of the spin.

Suddenly, weightlessness takes hold, as if a cloud has offered them a smooth and gentle ride. No screeching, no flashing lights. Only spinning darkness, the sound of rain and the stomach retching feel of dropping.

Bam! Glass explodes and an ear-splitting pop covers them with white powder as the air bags deploy. They're rolling. Rolling.

The car moans with bending metal as it slows, slows, slows…

Then quiet blankets the night.

The peace of a thousand white doves fills her soul.

And the car finally comes to a stop.

[TEN]

TORY

Adrenaline moves Tory's feet, panic sours her stomach and tears fill her eyes as she abandons her car in a reserved parking space and runs through the dark hospital parking lot.

Automatic opening doors will not be fast enough for her so she yanks the regular door open. The god-awful antiseptic smell of hospital hits her in the face and she's in no mood for anyone to be in her way.

She powers forward, grinding her teeth, until she sees the sign for the Intensive Care Unit, second floor.

No elevator's gonna box her in for no damn ride; she plows ahead to the stairs.

Motivated to move faster, she flies up each stair. *Fuck this; fuck life; this did not just happen.*

She bursts through the stairwell door to the second floor and into a quiet hallway, where pale blue paint is doing a hideous job of trying to make her forget she's in a hospital.

This. Did. Not. Just. Happen.

She looks right.

Then left.

There they are.

It's Daniel. And he's standing next to Nick.

Seeing them shreds her anger. She slowly becomes swallowed by a sad, weighty despair.

She would move, if she could.

Oh my God, Nick.

Daniel and Nick stare at her, not moving either.

Nick's face is puffy and bloody, his shoulders are hunched and he's got a sling on his arm.

Tory still can't move.

He's standing. Good. If he can walk away, Quinn will be fine.

She puts her hands on her face, closes her eyes and takes a calming breath in. *Nick is standing; Quinn will be fine.*

She finds the strength to move and slowly she begins walking toward them. The closer she gets the clearer she sees: Nick seems one breath away from a breakdown.

Step by step, she's closer to him. Daniel clears her path and moves away from Nick's side.

Trembling now shakes her body. Nick trembles too. His eyes are bloodshot and wet, cuts randomly dot his face, his hair is crazy out of place and she's beginning to imagine never seeing a smile on his face again.

She wraps her arms around him for strength. Support. He squeezes her, resting his head on her shoulder. In seconds, she can feel her shoulder getting wet.

Oh God, Nick. No. This did not just happen to you.

She stands still, and will stand like this for as long as he needs. For as long as *she* needs. She squeezes him tighter.

Gone are their arguments about friendly faces and loyalty. It doesn't matter why he was angry at her. It doesn't matter that breaking off their friendship had broken her heart. What he's going through is unimaginable.

She'll hold Nick for as long as it takes for him to be stronger. That's fine. But one of them needs to start talking and tell her where the hell Quinn is.

Daniel comes into her view. He's leaning backward to catch her eyes.

Thank God he's here. Daniel was the first person she called when she got the horrible text from Quinn's mom:

There's been a bad accident and Quinn's terribly hurt. We're at Methodist Hospital

Pam's text didn't need to say any more. Tory knew who Quinn had been with. And Tory rallied Daniel because he lives closer to this hospital and could get here faster than she could.

"Where's Quinn?" she whispers to Daniel, still holding Nick.

Nick loosens his hold and slides away, wiping his face.

"You need to stay calm, all right?" Daniel says in a low voice. He nods toward a set of double doors under the Intensive Care Unit sign. "She just got out of surgery."

Tory looks to Nick. "Is she going to be okay?"

Nick's eyes are paralyzed with fear. "Tory…I…don't know. It's bad. She lost a lot of blood."

Tory snaps her hands to her face.

"P.C. and C.C. are in there with her," Daniel says. "I talked with them. They said the surgery was to stop the bleeding. She was in surgery for a couple of hours."

Tory looks at her watch. It's 3 a.m. "I thought Quinn was late because she was having a good time with you." She looks to Nick.

He shakes his head. "I couldn't call you earlier. My phone is lost. I was in the emergency room getting admitted and x-rayed and scanned and they had to put my damn shoulder back into place. I didn't even know where Quinn was…"

"It's okay. I'm glad you're okay. If you could walk away, Quinn will be fine."

Nick goes pale and he shakes his head.

"Do you want me to drive you home?" Daniel asks him.

"No. No. I'm staying here. Right here. I want to know how Quinn is." He looks up at Tory. "Tory, it was an accident. I swear, it was raining and slippery and the car spun out of control—"

"Stop." She holds up her hand. "Nick, it's me. I believe you. All of the details will come out. I don't care about anything right now except that you and Quinn are okay."

They notice movement down the hall. Two police detectives are walking toward them. Nick tenses.

Oh shit. He needs representation!

The detective holds a paper. "Mr. Allen, here is the accident referral card." He hands it to Nick. "We'll be in touch when we finish the investigation but your statement tonight was very helpful. Thank you for being cooperative."

Nick looks down to the paper and nods. "I have absolutely nothing to hide."

Shit! Did they do a field sobriety test? Was he drinking? Should she say something now and advocate on his behalf before he says anything incriminating? Even though she's not a lawyer yet? Even though he's probably not guilty?

"Nick, do we need to speak privately?"

"I'm fine. I have nothing to hide."

The detectives nod, turn and walk away.

Her mind races with every lesson she learned in her Criminal Procedure class. "Let me call my dad. He can represent you. Even innocent people need representation."

Nick shakes his head. "No, not now. I don't care about the cops."

Her dad. She hasn't even texted or called her mom or dad! When they hear about Quinn, they'll probably rush up here, so she'll wait. It's the middle of the night and this hospital is on the edge of town. She'll call them in the morning. By then, maybe she will have seen Quinn and will know more.

She looks to the ICU double doors. "I want to go back there."

"Honey, they have strict visiting hours," Daniel says. "I don't think we can plow on back there."

Right now, she can't imagine anyone strong enough to stop her. "You said P.C. and C.C. are there?"

Daniel glances at his watch. "They went back about an hour ago."

The double doors open and an older couple, longtime neighbors of the Corbins, slowly shuffle out. They recognize her instantly.

"Oh, Tory," the woman says, giving Tory a hug. The man places his hand on Tory's back.

"Did you see Quinn?" Tory asks.

Tears fill the woman's eyes. She shakes her head, unable to speak. The man whispers, "She's very critical."

Oh shit no. No. No!

Tory turns to Daniel and Nick. "I'm going back there."

"If you go, I go," Daniel says, pushing up his sleeves and giving a stern, agreeing nod. Nick's chin rises and he follows.

"Tory," the neighbor says, squeezing her arm. "I'm so sorry."

Sorry? Sorry! Quit acting like this is the end of Quinn! For God's sake, accidents happen. Diseases get diagnosed. Fires burn. Floods flood. Shit is everywhere and a whole lot of shit has happened to Quinn tonight. But she's not a quitter. She's only twenty-four! People need to have faith!

Quinn will be looking for her; she'll want Tory to be strong. Quinn's always said she wanted to be as confident and strong as her. And Tory knows what she's about to see. Quinn will be battered and bruised and her hair is going to be frizzed out and look worse than after a run on a hot, humid day, but she's going to look up at Tory and want her to flash a confident smile and Tory's going to tell her what she always does.

You're lucky, Quinn.

You're fine, Quinn.

I wish I was you, Quinn.

It's the phrasing of their lives. She told Quinn she was lucky back in third grade when Quinn got Mrs. Quale as her teacher. Quale was the nice one, who brought fruit snacks and snuck in extra playground time for her class. Meanwhile Tory was stuck with Mr. Gregg, the grumpy man who always scratched himself. Years later she told Quinn she'd be fine after her first boyfriend Brian cheated on her with one of the sparkling pom-pom dancers in high school. Quinn spent weeks with cried-out eyes and a hollow heart, watching those two, walking arm-in-arm in the school hallway. But Tory ended up being right and Quinn was fine, really fine, after one of the big linebackers on the football team started dating sparkling pom-pom girl, leaving Brian crying beside his locker.

And now, in a minute when she sees Quinn, Tory will say *I wish I was you.* She'd trade places with Quinn in a hot second. Whatever is happening behind these ugly ass double doors, she'd switch places if it meant Quinn could be happy again.

Tory looks over her shoulder and into Nick's empty eyes.

She'd switch with Quinn if it meant Nick could be happy again too.

Tory leads the way, pushing open the doors into a long, brightly lit and stark hallway. She heads for a sink beside another set of double doors. She's watched enough television medical dramas to know, this is where you wash up before going into an ICU.

She and Daniel go elbow deep with soap and water then she helps Nick, unable to wash his hands because one arm is in a sling. She holds his free hand under the running water but even soapy bubbles cannot hide the burn marks on his skin, a constant, still-healing reminder of Sienna's accident. Now, those spots are dotted with small cuts, no doubt from breaking glass he was hit with tonight. As she gently washes his hand, her face is inches from his. His eyes look like a wild animal who knows he's about to be eaten. "Stick with me," she whispers. If anyone can handle Pam and Chet, it's Tory. And she will go nuclear if they don't allow Nick to see Quinn.

Daniel tosses his paper towel in a trash can and nods like a captain leading his troops into battle. Tory dries Nick's hands and faces him. Their eyes connect with a solid stare. They are both on point and connected in a way that feels familiar.

Daniel elbows open one of the doors and they cautiously walk inside. A nurse's station is the center of a large room. Curtains are drawn around patient beds; the lights are soft and low. The only sound comes from the faint beeping noises behind curtains. Tory shakes off a shiver.

A nurse spots them and opens her mouth but Tory speaks first. "We're looking for Quinn Corbin," she says in a hushed voice. "We know we're not supposed to be here. Please don't ask us to leave."

The nurse slowly nods.

That was too easy.

The nurse points to the corner and what looks like a private room within the unit. There's no door, only a drawn curtain, but there are walls on the sides where other patients only have curtains. *There's no way her condition is the worst up here. No way.*

Tory touches the curtain and pauses; Nick and Daniel are a paper-thin distance behind her.

Quinn's going to be okay. If Nick could walk away, Quinn will be fine.

Tory takes in a breath and gently slides the curtain open.

It's dim and cold. Machines beep, lots of big machines. Chet sits beside a big bed and Pam stands at the foot of it. *There's Quinn!* Bandages cover Quinn's hair and Tory can see her face. Quinn's sweet, sleeping face.

Pam spins around, looking past Tory to Nick. Her head shakes, her hands fist and her mouth clenches. She marches toward him when Tory blocks her path.

She locks eyes with the mother from hell. All of these years, Tory has acted nice to this woman, for Quinn's sake. But Tory knew Quinn had never felt loved. Quinn could never live up to Pam's expectations. And Pam's expectations were that Quinn be more like Tory.

"I've never asked anything from you," Tory says, eyes welling with tears. "Until now. Let him stay."

Pam's cheeks throb.

"It was Quinn's choice to be with him tonight. And she would want him here now," Tory whispers. She can only imagine what Nick is doing or feeling or thinking, standing inches behind her.

Pam doesn't move.

Tory does. Eyes on Pam, she walks around her and can feel Nick following. She steps closer to Quinn's bed, where Chet hasn't taken his eyes off of his daughter.

The pain of a hundred horrors hits Tory in her chest. Sudden coldness knocks at her core. She gasps, raggedly, and steps even closer to see dozens of small cuts covering Quinn's face. Her skin is ashen, paler than the white bedsheets her head rests on. The sheets are pulled tight, perfectly wrapping her body. Tory can't see anything below Quinn's neck. Wherever she was injured that caused so much bleeding must be hidden under these sheets, or under the bandages on her head. Quinn's eyes are closed and she's breathing on her own. Quietly. Steady. At peace.

Tory feels a hand pressing on her back. It's Nick, struggling to steady himself. She looks for Daniel, who cradles his arms around Pam as she looks to the floor.

An eerie peace covers this room…all of these people…and Quinn.

"Does she know where she is?" Tory whispers to Chet.

He shakes his head. "She hasn't regained consciousness since she was brought in."

Maybe she'll wake her up.

Tory leans closer to Quinn and the closer she gets, the more medical it smells, like a strong mix of antiseptic wipes and Lysol spray. "Hey," Tory whispers. "Time to wake up. I came to see you…to talk to you. I need to tell you something…"

No response; not even a twitch of an eyelid.

"Hey…I know you can hear me…right? And you need to wake up…we're all here. C.C., P.C., Daniel and even Nick. We're all right here."

No response.

Tory's desperation deepens and she can't hold her tears back any longer. Her words start to come out in a rhythm of sobs. "There's a lot we need to do, okay? We've…we've got to decorate your new classroom. Your camping theme classroom. Think about that. And…I've got to make my bed, right? I know it bothers you that I never make my bed but I promise… Quinn…I'll make my bed every fricken morning and you can watch me do it, but you have to wake up."

No response.

"I'll make you a cinnamon macchiato. Does that sound good? Or hot chocolate? I'll make as many hot chocolates as you want."

No response.

"Life…Quinn. We have so much life ahead of us. You promised me. You said I was…" Tory can't get more than a few words out in between her sobs. "You said…one day you were gonna pay me back…for being a good friend." She sniffles in, gasping.

"So…this is it…payback time. Wake up. That's what I want. We want to know you're okay." She sniffles. "That's all I want."

Nick squeezes Tory's arm and leans down toward Quinn too. "Quinn…that's what we all want."

Her eyelids flicker.

Tory gasps. "I saw that. See that?" She points to Quinn while looking at Nick.

He nods with his mouth open, trying to breathe and smile at the same time.

Chet inches forward in his chair. Pam moves to his side and Daniel breaks out a hallelujah smile, standing at the foot of the bed.

Quinn's eyelids flicker again.

Oh my God! She hears us!

"Buttercup?" Chet whispers.

Quinn's lips part open, ever so slightly, and her eyes lazily blink.

Ha! She's waking up!

No expression fills her face but her eyes keep blinking and slowly they widen, facing Chet.

She's awake!

"Oh thank God," Nick whispers.

"Hot damn, it's a miracle," Daniel says.

Her head remains still but her eyes begin to move, leaving Chet, then reaching Pam, then on to Daniel until they find Tory and Nick.

Quinn!

Her glassy eyes fill with messages Tory cannot understand. Quinn flicks a glance to Nick, then back to Tory, then back to Nick, then back to Tory.

"We're here!" Tory says, wiping her face. "We're all here!"

Quinn's loving gaze softens, as if this news makes her happy.

This means everything! She knows we're here, that Nick's alive, that Pam and Chet aren't yelling at Nick. She knows she's surrounded with love!

Then slowly, gently…Quinn's eyes drift closed.

"She saw us!" Tory looks back to Nick. "She knew us! She's gonna be okay!"

"She looked right at me, baby!" Daniel says proudly.

Tears fill Nick's eyes and relief covers his face.

An alarm rips through the room. Chet leaps to his feet. A nurse rushes in. Tory flies backward, hands in the air, afraid to touch anything and desperate to get out of the way. Another nurse rushes in. Nick wraps his arm around Tory and pulls her against a wall. Daniel flies to Tory's side, wrapping his arms around her. They cling to each other, watching the nurses feverishly hustle around Quinn's bed.

The nurses' actions remain fast…and real…but to Tory, everything seems to slow down. The voices blur. Even the alarm fades although these people don't seem to hear it. They're still in a flurry around Quinn.

Some strange, unnatural calm settles over Tory. She blinks, focusing, as the room gets brighter. The edge of her sight is fuzzy and white, like she's fallen into a white linen dream. *Is she about to faint?*

She looks to Nick and his eyes are fixed on the ceiling, his mouth agape and his face filled with amazement.

"Do you see something too?" she whispers.

He nods, with a look like he thinks he's lost his mind.

She turns to Daniel, still with his arms around her, but his eyes are fixed on the floor.

She and Nick must be about to pass out! She squeezes Nick harder, holding on like she's about to slip off of the spinning world as the commotion continues around Quinn's bed.

But Tory still hears no sounds.

A white haze seems to fill the room.

The ceiling flies away.

Then everything goes still.

The nurses stop moving.

Tory doesn't feel like she's falling off of the planet anymore.

The blur of white has disappeared and the room's dim color returns.

Tory hears sound again, coming from the machine next to the bed. It's the recognizable sound of one steady, drawn-out, low-pitched, dreadful tone.

Quinn Corbin has died.

[ELEVEN]

Two days later

A pot of noodles boils on the stove, the bubbles raging larger and larger. Suddenly, the pot overflows, the hot water meeting the stove's burner in a violent hissing fit. Tory stands next to the stove, looking down at the rising steam. *Guess she should turn that off.* She folds up the cuff of the pajamas she's wearing, the sleeves a little long since they belonged to Quinn, and she turns off the burner and slides the pot over.

Quinn used to cook noodles like this. It was her signature dish.

Tory wraps her arms around her chest, catching the sweet cherry blossom scent from Quinn's perfumed lotion woven into her pajamas. Tory looks into the pot. Overcooked elbow noodles float like confetti in the foaming, hot water. *Guess noodles ain't gonna be your signature dish.*

She throws her head back, looking to the ceiling. *Why. Why. Why.*

It's the question she's been asking herself for two days. It's the question she will ask for the rest of her life.

On the counter, her phone lights up with a text.

Did your dinner turn out okay? And did you eat it? You need
to eat something

Mom. Since Tory left her parents' house this morning, her mom has been keeping close tabs on her. She doesn't mind. She spent most of yesterday, the day after Quinn died, in bed at her parents' house. If it wasn't for her mom and dad's support, she's not sure how she would be handling this.

She's not sure how Nick is handling this. She hasn't spoken to him in a day.

And he has no family support.

She texts her mom back.

Managed to overcook and shred the noodles so no, haven't
eaten

She places her phone on her chest. Knowing her mom Jamie, she's already reaching for her car keys and thinking of the fastest place to get take-out food between their home in Shavano Park and her apartment. Well, Quinn's apartment.

Tory rubs her face, which still feels like she's been punched in the nose from shock. Her eye sockets are dry and they ache. She's trying to convince herself that she's back in classes at Texas Law and Quinn is back at grad school, happily learning how to be a teacher. That's how she's going to freeze this hurt. *Quinn's just away at school.*

She looks over to the white sofa, the furry white throw, the glass coffee table with a delicate rose-gold bowl, a historical romance paperback and three white vanilla candles. Across the room, a gold wire shelf holds Quinn's framed photographs and about a dozen dainty figurines, a collection of porcelain animals she had been collecting since she was a child. Front and center of the collection is Quinn's favorite: a small kitten, crouched in a playful pose with her tiny white porcelain tail in the air.

Tory can't pretend Quinn is at school when all of her stuff is still here, alone with her.

It won't be long and she'll need to leave this apartment. Pam and Chet will come in a few days and clean the place out. They'll want to cancel the lease and they aren't going to care that Tory lives here too. She burned a lifetime's worth of good-will on the night Quinn died by asking Pam to let Nick stay. Tory will need to live with her parents for a month while she finishes up at Indigo.

Indigo.

Tory glances to the counter, where a dozen fragrant, pink roses sit in a white vase. Al sent them and she's got to admit, he's been very generous, offering Tory as much time as she needs to process this loss. Still, with less than a month to go at Indigo, every day working will be a painful reminder of Quinn, and of Nick. The sound of a cappuccino machine will make her think of cinnamon macchiatos. The sound will also remind her of a buzz-saw, like how she cut Nick to the core by taking this job. She shakes her head to get rid of the thought.

With the pot of ruined noodles not helping her grumbling stomach, she has a sudden urge to get out of this place. She can't handle this hurt and this quiet. She needs fresh air.

She grabs her purse and puts one hand on the doorknob when she remembers she's still in pajamas.

Who the hell cares? Just go.

But Quinn would have never let her out in public looking like this.

Tory dresses in her favorite sweatshirt, jeans and flip flops and before leaving her bedroom, she gives another glance to her bed. It's immaculately made, the comforter's corners pulled tight and she even put the pillowcase on the pillows to honor Quinn. She heads out the door.

The days are longer now that it's late May and even at 8:30 p.m. she needs sunglasses to drive on the 410 highway. It's just as well. Sunglasses help hide her swollen eyes.

Her radio is off and her sunroof is open, creating a whip of wind that moves her hair. The oily strands blowing in her face remind her she hasn't washed her hair since Quinn died.

The farther she drives the more she starts to regret the trip. Everything she passes reminds her of Quinn. She speeds past a billboard with a photo of a full-busted woman in a yellow bikini top, an advertisement for a breast augmentation surgeon. Quinn used to say she wanted to get a boob job someday. Tory always thought that was nuts.

She passes Mama Margie's restaurant, one of Daniel's favorite taco haunts, and remembers the first time Quinn tried a beer-rita. She drank the frozen drink too fast and got a brain freeze, then got hyper from the sugar high and then started wildly giggling from the tequila and beer. Quinn used to always make fun of Tory's surprise slurs but that night, it was Quinn who was acting nuts.

This is nuts. Everywhere she looks she realizes: she's not going to be able to pretend Quinn is off at school.

Tory veers off of the highway, taking the exit to the Pearl, a revitalized area outside of downtown largely ignored by tourists. This is a place for locals, with a boutique hotel, craft brewery and unusual restaurants. It's also home to one of her favorite spots in town. And since she got back into town, she hasn't had time to come here yet.

Before she gets out of her car, she sends a text:

Changed my scene and just got to the Pearl. Going to sit on the steps by the river and relax. I'm fine and just wanted you to know I'll eat something here. I promise

Her mom responds:

Okay good. Text me when you get home

Tory smiles. *Super sweet.*

Tory steps out of her car, instantly unhappy with her decision to wear a sweatshirt on this hot night. But soon the sun will set, and whenever she sits by the river she always feels chilly.

She passes through the pedestrian streets at the Pearl, watching people in normal, happy conversations enjoy their evening. Young couples sit at outdoor tables and several dogs lie under or near tables next to their owners. Even the dogs are enjoying the night out.

Tory stops at a to-go counter at a restaurant and orders a chicken street taco. If she was in a better mood, she'd Snapchat a photo of this to Daniel, the expert of all things taco. But he'd ask where she was and then show up. Right now, she'd rather be alone.

She nibbles as she walks, moving like a normal person

through life. This doesn't seem real, to be walking and eating and listening and smelling. It's like she only has half of her body and no one can see it. *How long does it take to feel whole again?*

She reaches the river and her favorite spot: the Pearl steps. A set of about twenty, wide steps begins at the sidewalk and leads down to the Riverwalk. Across the river is another set of about twenty steps going up. Colorful pots with purple and pink bougainvillea line the steps and only one vendor selling souvenirs is here and they are way down by a limestone bridge that connects the two sides. This is the best part of San Antonio's Riverwalk because tourists rarely come here. It's not on the tourist maps. The only way they'd know it exists is if they paid attention when they sail past on the flat, barge-like Riverwalk boats cruising down the murky river.

A few people have come to the steps tonight and Tory slowly makes her way down a flight or two to find a spot to sit down. It doesn't matter that she's sitting on concrete. A nice evening breeze has kicked in and the occasional music and singing from a passing Riverwalk boat keeps her mind off of the prospect of a sore butt.

Also in her favor: this is a Quinn-free place. They never came here together. But she did come here before with Nick.

He showed her this spot—his secret spot—a long time ago when she was dealing with a tough issue. Maybe she should offer to bring Nick here this week. He'd probably appreciate the company, and the fresh air. When she feels stronger herself, she'll ask him.

Down by the river, two young women around Tory's age pose for a selfie just as a Riverwalk boat passes. So fun. So normal. So something she can never do with Quinn again.

Across the river on the opposite set of steps, a couple sits on a red-and-green Mexican serape blanket, enjoying a picnic. A warm shiver shoots up Tory's spine. Seeing normal things like this is beginning to irritate her. Maybe staying in bed another day, or five, would be the better way to go.

Then she notices something beside the couple. A young girl in a fun, flowery dress runs up the stairs near them. *Oh my God, no.* The little girl looks like she could be in second grade, old enough to have been in Quinn's upcoming class. Her wispy, blonde hair bounces with each step up she takes. And on the top of her head is a flower crown with long, colorful ribbons bouncing down her back.

That's it: peace out, Pearl steps.

Tory stands up to leave. What an epically bad idea to go out into the world of regular people and ghostly reminders. *Too much, too soon.* Right before she turns to walk up the steps, something else across the river catches her eye.

On the steps, a young man sits alone, staring at his feet. She can't see his face but she knows damn well who he is. His arm sling gives him away.

Nick.

He stretches out his legs and raises his head, his shoulders rising with a big breath. He notices the little girl running up the steps too, since she's only about an arms-length away from him. He shakes his head and looks across the river to Tory's side.

Tory smiles to herself, knowing in a few seconds his eyes will find her, especially since she's the only one standing up right now. Finally, he notices her and shakes his head in disbelief.

Smiling, she shakes her head too. What are the chances?

Well, actually, now that she thinks about it, the chances were pretty good. This is, after all, his getaway place.

She really doesn't feel strong enough to absorb his sadness. Two fatal accidents so close together? How can he even breathe?

His eyes haven't left her; he seems to be in shock.

She decides to go to him.

She begins walking down her side of the steps, reaching the sidewalk by the river. He's still watching her. She heads down the sidewalk, then up and over the limestone bridge. As soon as she's on his side of the river, one of the Riverwalk boats passes by, the captain singing loudly and off-key along with the twenty or so guests on his boat. Their hands are in the air, clapping along with their song. *Are they all…drunk?* Tory watches the boat chug past, then she looks up to Nick. He's standing up now too, looking bewildered at the boat of crazy people as it makes its way down the river. Then he looks back to her.

She shrugs. *Gotta love it. At least someone's having fun.*

His mouth curves with a smile.

She starts climbing the steps to reach him and he walks down to meet her.

He looks wrecked. He's still the best-looking man she's ever laid eyes on but he's covered in a grief-stricken, hasn't-slept-in-two-days, where-the-hell-am-I look. He looks exactly how she feels.

They meet together and immediately hug; she squeezes him warmly. He's squeezing her hard with the one arm he has to wrap her with.

"Tory, you seriously cannot be standing here right now," he says, pulling back from their hug. "I haven't stopping thinking about you and what you must be going through."

"I can't believe I just ran into you. Although, I just remembered it was you that showed me this spot in the first place."

He takes her hand, his hands shaking slightly. "Are you okay?"

"I suck. How about you?"

"I super suck."

"How are you feeling, physically?"

Nick lets go of her hand and gestures to the concrete steps. They both sit, close to each other.

"Everything hurts. My back, neck…top of my legs. The doctors warned me that a day or two after being in a car that fell and rolled like that would be my worst."

"The cuts on your face look better," she says, looking him over.

He doesn't say anything. Instead, he takes a deep breath. "I'd rather talk about you. I'm serious when I say you've been on my mind. You and Quinn were inseparable and I…I can't imagine how you're coping."

Tears warm behind her eyes. "I'm not admitting she's gone yet. I'm pretending, you know. I'm pretending she's off at school."

He nods with concern. "You're going to push this deep, aren't you? That's what I figured you might do."

Oh no you don't, champ. He's trying to draw a comparison to this and something bad, really bad, that happened to her before. And this is nowhere near the same. "I'll do whatever I damn well need to do and however I damn well want to."

He reaches for her. "Oh no, no Tory. I didn't mean for that to sound mean. I'm serious when I say I'm concerned. I totally didn't mean—"

She puts up her hand. *Girl, dial it down.* "It's cool. I'm sorry. I'm a little…I don't know…sleep-deprived and I'm kinda touchy with certain subjects. Quinn used to always say I bury my feelings too much so hearing it now from you…I don't know."

"Hey, I admit, I bury my feelings by working too much. It feels like Faze is the only safe place on the planet for me."

"You've already gone back to work?"

"Oh God, no. I wanted to wait until after Quinn's…you know…funeral."

Tory puts her elbows on her knees and buries her face in her hands. The funeral. In three days. Her parents will need to prop her up by both arms to give her strength to walk in. She looks up with a twang of panic. "Are you going?"

His eyebrows rise. "Um, no. I wish I could, for Quinn. But I know I'm not welcome."

She shakes her head. "It was an accident, right? I mean in a world with nice, understanding and forgiving people, they should understand it was an accident."

"I don't know what I could have done differently. I've been replaying every moment of that night. Maybe I could have sat in the parking lot and waited until it completely stopped raining, but it wasn't raining that hard when we left. And millions of people in the world drive in the rain every day!"

"You weren't drinking, right?"

"No. I mean, yes, earlier when we were tailgating, but I didn't have anything to drink for hours after. Nothing at the concert, nothing after the concert."

Tory's phone vibrates with a text. "It's probably my mom," she says, taking her phone out of her purse. "She's been amazing, checking up on me…" Tory glances down to read the text.

I finally found somewhere to go to without a coupon! Quinn's funeral! You'll be there, right? Because that would be a fitting place to see you again

Her phone slips out of her hands and she fumbles to catch it before it hits the concrete. Nick leans over to try to catch it too but it lands safely in her hand.

"What is it?" he asks.

She gulps down air to keep from screaming. *Jake's become a fucking freak.*

"Was that your mom?" Nick leans down to catch her eyes.

"No...no it wasn't." She looks at the blank screen of her phone, rubs her forehead and tosses her phone back into her purse. *Time for an action plan.* "I've got a little problem that hasn't gone away."

Nick's expression seems all-in. "Tell me," he says, kindly and sincere.

Look at him. Despite what he's been through...he's completely focused on her words at this moment. But this would be a horrible time to dump this problem on him. *Push your problem deep...*

She places her hand on his; his hand still covered with healing cuts and burn spots. "I will, but this isn't the time."

He shakes his head decisively. "Now I'll add this to the list of reasons I'm worried about you."

She warmly squeezes his hand, then lets it go. "So, we're keeping lists of reasons we're worried about each other, huh? Because my list for you is getting rather long."

"At least someone worries."

The pain behind those words cuts through her heart.

Laughter rises up from the sidewalk below as a group of young people walk by. Nick and Tory sit quietly, watching them pass.

"This is a great spot," Tory says, looking around. Many of the people who were sitting here earlier have left. The sun has all but set and even the vendor by the bridge has closed up shop for the night. The calm washing over the steps feels good.

"So, you're a south stepper?" he asks.

"South stepper?"

"Yeah." He points across to the steps on the other side. "The south side: people who sit on the south side."

"I…didn't realize the population was different."

"I'm a north stepper. This side is better. See? The view of downtown? Can't see that if you're a south stepper."

She stretches her neck to see the view. "Good to know. Because when I come to a place to have a quiet breakdown, view is important."

He smiles. "View can help take your mind off of your disasters."

"How long had you been sitting here tonight?"

"I just got here. It's the first time I left the house. I was hungry and couldn't take the quiet anymore."

Tory nods. *Preach.*

His eyes go blank. "I want to tell you something and I feel like you might be the only person I can tell this to."

His words sound almost as chilling as a Jake text.

"The night of the accident, something wasn't right. My car, it wasn't right."

She looks at him with uncertainty.

"My tires had zero traction and my wipers were almost non-existent. But my car had been driving fine on the way there. The hills and turns, it handled fine. A bird even crapped on the windshield and the wipers worked fine when I washed it off! My car should not have felt that way, even in the rain."

A warning voice whispers in her head. "Do you think someone fooled with your car?"

His eyes look desperate…desperate for her to believe him. "I can't think of how or can't imagine why, but all I'm saying is something wasn't right."

Why? He can't imagine why? She can! Nick has a long list of enemies. But screwing with his car seems like a wild revenge plot from a movie, not something that would happen here.

"I assume your car is totaled, but when will you get access to it?"

"After my insurance appraiser sees the car, and they won't let him near it until after they complete their investigation. Weeks, probably."

"Can you go see it now? And take pictures or something?"

"No. I can't even retrieve my personal things until after the appraiser sees the car. That's the rules for this police impound yard."

"Nick, I know you might think I'm overreacting, but you need a lawyer. I only have two years of law school and I can sense this might be getting complicated and over your head."

He looks away, uneasy. "It seems insensitive to Quinn for me to hire a lawyer. Getting one is like I've got something to hide."

"Oh no. Quinn would say it's smart. I say it's smart. It's not about looking like you have something to hide."

They're interrupted by the sounds from another Riverwalk boat passing down below. Thankfully this one isn't filled with obnoxiously singing tourists, but the amplified voice from the boat captain is enough to be annoying. They both go quiet for a minute, watching the boat pass and then their eyes turn back to each other.

"Nick, if you think someone might have messed with your car, you need someone to help you prove it. And there's another good reason why you should get a lawyer…"

He listens intently.

"…if the police investigation proves you were negligent with how you maintained your car," she swallows hard, "you could be arrested."

[TWELVE]

"Who are all these people?" Daniel tartly whispers to Tory as they sit in a pew at the Mission Park church.

Sad, depressing music plays: a perfect match to Tory's mood. She smooths out the lap of her dress and exhales her relief. She's seated now and can blend into the crowd. It felt like all eyes in the church were focused on her, her parents and Daniel as they walked down the aisle.

Tory and her parents have been friends with Quinn and her parents for so long, all of their old neighbors and extended friends feel like mutual friends. There's no doubt: they're all watching to see how she's handling this.

"You okay?" Tory's mom Jamie whispers, sitting next to her. Jamie's wide, inspiring smile can brighten Tory's worst moods. With her short, brown hair swept to the side, her signature single diamond stud earrings and classic but relevant style, Jamie defines Tory's goals of what she hopes to be when she gets to her mom's age.

"Made it this far, thanks to you," Tory whispers. Thank goodness Jamie offered her a sedative before they left.

The organist begins to play the opening hymn, cueing everyone to stand. Pam and Chet, followed by a pastor, make their way up the aisle. Tory turns to face them and is in a direct line of sight with Reed.

The taste of bile fills her mouth. He's in the same row as her, across the aisle. He's looking at her with earnest eyes behind his stupid hipster glasses, wearing a bow tie with a black jacket that probably cost over a thousand dollars. She's managed to avoid Reed since she got back into town. And today, or any day, isn't a day she wants to speak to him.

Tory's dad John turns back to look at her. John's a tall man with graying brown hair parted to the side. For the past five years he's worn a beard and mustache, which Tory thinks makes him look like a kick-ass legal eagle. He's a partner at Brink, Pearson and Taylor, a reputable law firm in Texas. John spends a hefty amount of his time on pro-bono work for people who can't defend themselves and rarely does he lose.

With John on the end of the aisle, he would have a clear view of Reed and probably noticed where Reed was looking. John's tender glance lands on her. He knows her contempt for Reed. He shares it. If this wasn't such a somber occasion, John might be crossing the aisle to remind Reed how much he dislikes him.

It feels robotic, standing and listening to people sing this dreadful song. Tory focuses instead on the multi-colored mosaics in the stained-glass windows over the alter, trying to decipher what each window means. She's not a stranger to church; she was raised a Christian. She's never really found a church she loves in Austin so she doesn't regularly go when she's in school. But she believes. And after what she thinks she saw and felt when Quinn died, she definitely believes in heaven and feels confident Quinn is there.

The hymn ends, a prayer begins and soon everyone takes their seat. Tory largely tunes out the parade of speakers who fill the next fifteen minutes or so. None of them knew Quinn like she did. Chet had asked her if she wanted to speak but she declined. No sedative could have calmed her down enough to publicly speak about Quinn right now.

But this is good, having people share stories of Quinn growing up. It's good for everyone to know what a beautiful person she was. Tory faintly hears her own name mentioned and looks up to the man speaking at the podium. Many people turn around and look at her. She was just mentioned, somehow. She wasn't paying attention though. Hopefully they weren't sharing an embarrassing story. Tory gives a slight smile and nods. People turn back around and the speaker continues. She leans over to her mom. "You'll have to tell me later what he said. I'm not listening."

Tory pulls her purse closer to her side. If this starts getting too sad, she's got plan B ready to roll. Her earphones are within reach and her phone is loaded with Quinn's preppy-ass playlist. She'd rather honor Quinn by listening to her otherwise unbearable mix of Kygo, Sia and Miley Cyrus songs than hear about how Quinn will never be able to see the eager eyes of her second-grade class, or how she'll never pick out a white dress and get married.

Tory shifts a bit in the pew, crossing her legs and leaning forward, looking down at her black pumps. Out of the corner of her eye she sees Reed lean forward too. She shifts her eyes ever so slightly to confirm: he is leaning forward and looking over at her. She sits straight back in the pew. *Get your weasel eyes off of me. And why is he here anyway?* He never really liked Quinn. He told her once she wouldn't ever understand his lifestyle because she never had money, even though Quinn and her family are upper-middle class. He's a spoiled brat, used to getting what he wants and if he doesn't get it, he flat-out takes it. Besides, it's barely been a few months since Sienna died. Why would he want to be reminded of death at a funeral for someone he never really liked?

All heads bow for prayer and Tory closes her eyes. She ignores the prayer being said and makes up her own.

Lord, please keep Quinn safe and loved. Please tell her I love her. Mention that I cooked spaghetti last night and she would have been proud.

Okay...you know I didn't cook it...but I really did pay attention to what my mom was teaching me and I'm going to cook it myself soon and make Quinn proud.

Please help all of us who are sad figure out how to be happy again. Ask Quinn for ideas, she was always good with perky stuff like that.

And please...keep Reed away from me. And if Jake's here, keep him away from me too.

But of all of my prayers, Lord, I ask for your help with Nick. He didn't cause this, I know he didn't, and for Quinn's sake, give me wisdom to find out if someone else did.

Quinn's the best friend I'll ever have. I owe it to her.

Music from the organ begins again and everyone rises for the exit hymn. Tory dabs her wet eyes and doesn't turn to face the aisle to watch the pastor leave, like everyone else is. She knows if she does, Reed will be anxiously looking at her again. Instead she turns the other way to face Daniel. "Let's go out your way."

Daniel nods, turns and leads their group out of their pew. Once in the side aisle, John wraps his arm around his daughter.

"I want to go straight to the car," Tory whispers. John squeezes tighter and the four of them move quickly, without stopping. It feels like everyone who sees them turns to let them pass. Those that know her would understand why. In minutes, they are in John's black 7-series BMW, pulling away.

"It was a beautiful ceremony," Jamie says, quietly.

"I didn't know Quinn took ballet and tap up until high school," Daniel says. "She's my spirit animal."

Tory stares out the window, sitting behind John's seat. Every so often, John glances back at her with worry.

They turn on the ramp up to highway 410, heading back home to Shavano Park. John merges and they join other cars, driving fast, all of them going to random places. The cars around them carry passengers who have no idea that this car carries people who are filled with such sadness.

Tory watches the cars. And something else. She watches their tires. Nick's words fill her mind. *Something wasn't right. My car, it wasn't right.* Who would try to hurt him, killing her best friend? It seems unlikely someone was trying to only hurt

Quinn. If it was Quinn they were after, they would have messed with her car, not Nick's.

Now on the open highway, their car picks up speed. Tory's anger starts to build too. Quinn believed, as she does, that what happened with Nick and Sienna was an accident. Quinn wanted to help Nick heal, and Tory did too. Now Quinn is gone from what could have been more than just an accident. Tory owes it to Quinn to find out the truth.

She also owes it to Quinn to fight what could be coming next.

"Dad?" Tory asks.

John glances in the rearview mirror. "Yes?"

"Do you think the Corbin's will sue Nick?"

John's eyes flick back between the road and the rearview mirror. "Knowing Pam, even if there are no criminal charges against Nick, I think the chances are good she'd file for civil damages."

"How good?"

"One hundred percent."

Tory nods. She thinks so too. And it wouldn't be Chet leading the charge. Chet's the type to put his foot down but not grind you to a pulp. But not Pam. She'd want revenge, even for something completely ruled an accident. She once got Quinn's dance teacher fired when Quinn didn't get a solo in the recital, which horrified Quinn. One time at the mall, Tory saw Pam yell at a sales clerk because she had sold her and Quinn matching shirts that Pam thought weren't age appropriate, leaving Quinn red-faced with embarrassment. Every time Tory has seen Pam take aggressive action, Quinn disagreed. And if Pam sues Nick, Tory knows Quinn would have been pissed.

"Another question…" she says.

John glances back, listening.

"There were no criminal charges against Nick for the accident with Sienna, but it was left wide open for Reed's family to sue Nick for civil damages. Why do you think they didn't?"

"Hard to say, especially since we all know how much Reed dislikes Nick," John says. "But remember, they still could sue."

Tory nods again.

They still could. But she's thinking they won't.

A civil suit opens up an investigation for more discovery. And more discovery might not be what Reed's family wants.

Tory's eyes drift back to the window and the world passing by. They speed past Dominion, the car dealership where her family now purchases their cars. Her dad bought this BMW from Dominion earlier this year, along with her birthday gift, her white BMW 350.

"I was curious about something else," she says.

John glances back at her. "Yeah?"

"You bought our cars from Dominion because you had some problems at Reed's, right?"

"Yeah, I had two lemons, both used cars. I haven't bought a car from Reed's since."

Jamie looks back to her. "What are you thinking about?"

Tory looks to Jamie and smiles, and tosses a glance to Daniel, who is looking at her with skeptical eyes.

"I'm thinking that my growing, formidable legal mind is analyzing all of the facts, like I'm supposed to do."

John looks back and gives her a sturdy smile.

All of the facts. Well, maybe after tossing around some wild speculation first.

What if Reed's Motors had been trying to sell a '66 Mustang known to have problems.

And Nick happened to be the customer who bought it.

Then the car did have problems, accidently killing one of their own family members.

Perhaps Reed's family isn't suing Nick because they're afraid of more discovery.

And maybe they're behind another accident intended to keep him quiet forever.

[THIRTEEN]

Gray clouds have formed a blanket of sadness across the sky, the overcast morning matching Tory's mood. It's the day after Quinn's funeral and even if the sun was shining brightly her mood wouldn't be better.

She slept restlessly last night, but not as bad as the night before. Still, her eyes are puffy from lack of sleep and from random bouts of crying. She stands in front of her bathroom mirror, swiping mascara on her lashes to hide the worst of her sleep deprivation. She took a little extra time to try and style her hair with long waves like Quinn naturally had. And she nailed it, for a few minutes. Then before she could cement her waves with hairspray, her hair rebelled and fell as flat as a pancake, proving once again that she'll never be like Quinn.

Taking a few minutes to fuss over makeup and hair is Tory's way of trying to be normal again. Lying in bed isn't going to make time go faster. And normal isn't going to happen anytime soon. But she knows she has to move forward, even if only an inch each day.

Tomorrow she'll go back to work at Indigo. She's been

texting with Al, who keeps checking in with her to see how she's doing.

Today though, she has another mission. Today is the day Nick said he'd go back to work. She's heading to Faze to surprise him with a shot-in-the-arm of emotional support.

He's rarely left her mind. She replays his haunted face at the hospital and his hurting eyes when they met on the Pearl steps. She knows it would have bothered him not being at the funeral. Besides, she hasn't been to Faze yet and Quinn had said the cinnamon rolls were delicious.

Tory slips on a pair of sandals with her dark jeans and a black off-the-shoulder shirt. She heads into the kitchen, where Jamie is chopping lettuce.

"Good morning," Jamie says, putting down her knife and pulling Tory in for a hug.

"I slept in a little…okay, a lot," Tory says, squeezing her mom.

They pull back. "Good," Jamie says. "You look fresh and on the way somewhere."

Tory sits on a barstool at the counter. Jamie pushes an empty mug toward her and then fills it with steaming coffee. "I'm going up to Faze to see Nick. I didn't talk to him yesterday and I know he will want to know how it went."

Jamie shakes her head. "I wish he would have gone with us."

"I know. I offered."

"And our offer still stands for him to stay here too. I hate the idea of him being alone."

"Nick's so independent. He's been on his own for so long, I'm not sure he'd know how to fit into and hang out with a real family." Tory sips her coffee. "Thank you though, Mom, for offering. I'm glad I came back here too instead of staying alone at that apartment."

"I'm glad you did too." Jamie wipes the counter. "Are you going to eat at Faze or do you want something now?"

"I'm holding out for a Faze cinnamon roll, thanks. So, Dad's already at work I guess?"

Jamie glances at the clock on the microwave. It's 10 a.m. "Yeah, the normal world has been running for a few hours now."

Tory shrugs. "Keeping track of time isn't something I'm doing very well right now. Maybe tonight I can talk to Dad some more about Nick getting a lawyer."

"Is Nick ready to hire one?"

"I'm trying to convince him he should. I have a feeling that things might be getting over his head."

Jamie leans an elbow on the counter. "Nick needs support. His brother still hasn't surfaced, even after all of this?"

"Stepbrother, remember. Same dad, different mother. I was going to ask Nick when I see him. At this point though, his stepbrother hasn't given him much support over the years so I'm not sure how much help he'd be now."

"Remember, Tory, that's Nick's side of the story. You don't know if his brother, um, stepbrother has reached out to him. Maybe he's tried and Nick's too angry to accept his help. Blended families can be complicated."

Tory takes a long, lingering sip. "There's a missing piece there too, with Nick's parents. I know his mom was much younger than his dad and I never really heard the full story of how his parents were killed, other than it was a car accident when he was eighteen."

"A car crash," Jamie says. "I remember it from the news because it happened not far from here. From what I remember, the other driver was at fault. So, if your formidable, growing legal mind was trying to make a connection with that accident and the recent two that Nick's been involved with, I'm not sure you can."

Tory gently places her cup down, rests her elbows on the counter and folds her hands.

Maybe not. Unless years ago, Nick's parents had bought their car from Reed's.

* * *

Tory stands inside the double doors at Faze, her nose overwhelmed with a sweet, cinnamon smell so amazing, it's making her mouth and her eyes water. *Why haven't I come here sooner?* She's in a delicious dream, surrounded with the deep, nutty aroma of freshly ground coffee. These colors! This furniture! Chill music! The vibe here! A man wanders past her holding a cup of coffee in one hand and a white plate with a fist-sized cinnamon roll in the other. And turquoise-blue frosting? Nick has nailed this concept. He needs to get a legal firm to represent him and franchise this to every corner in every city in every country.

Tory looks around at the happy, cheery faces. It's a little hard to take in happiness right now. Seems easier to hide under a table and ignore normal things. She can't imagine how Nick experienced this every day after Sienna. And now…

Tory walks farther inside, scanning the crowd and looking for a sign that says "offices" or something obvious that would lead her to where Nick might be.

She notices a woman with a Faze nametag that says "Gigi".

"Excuse me?" Tory asks the woman, who is looking the other way.

Gigi turns and Tory gets blown away with beautifulness. *Damn, she's like movie-star pretty.* This chick has a wild set of wide eyes like Mila Kunis and she's tall like Charlize Theron. Wonder if she knows her smile looks like Julia Roberts?

"Hello," Gigi says. "Can I help you?"

"Yeah," Tory says, curious to know if this woman has ever auditioned or modeled for anything because if she hasn't, she should. "I was looking for Nick Allen's office."

"It's upstairs," Gigi says, pointing to a hallway. "But he's not here today."

Tory's smile fades. "I thought he was planning to come back today."

Gigi's smile fades too. "You're his friend?"

Tory extends her hand and Gigi squeezes it. "Tory Taylor. Yes. Nick and I go back a few years."

"Oh, Tory! Oh, it's so nice to meet you. Nick talks about you all the time."

"He does?"

"All the time! Hey, I'm so sorry about what happened with Quinn."

Tory nods. "Thanks. I'm still in a haze. Nick too. He told me he was planning to come back today but I…guess he didn't make it."

Gigi shakes her head. "We visited him yesterday and took him a couple of meals."

Tory gives Gigi's shoulder a gentle squeeze. "Oh, thank you

for doing that. All day I was so worried about him and if he was alone."

Gigi's expression looks reserved. "We're trying to help. Nick's an amazing boss and all of us here would do anything for him. And from what he tells us about you, you seem to be his rock right now."

Whoa. "I think Nick and I are both leaning heavily on each other."

"Good," Gigi says with a warm smile.

Tory nods. "Okay, well, thank you for the information. I think I'll go over to his apartment and see how he's doing today. It was wonderful to meet you, Gigi."

"Same here." Gigi hugs her.

Tory smiles and turns away.

What a fun, warm place, filled with such happy people. It feels like Nick here; Faze has captured his spirit. This isn't what she feels at Indigo. Indigo has the same number of customers, but it's functional. Efficient. Operational. Where Faze feels like the proverbial place where you can go and everybody knows your name. It feels like family. Nick has created family to fill the family he's missing.

She sees an open table and sits down, pulling out her phone to text Nick, using the number she's had in her contacts for a few years now. If he's changed his number, she's about to find out.

Hey, I hear you're still at home today

Within a minute comes a reply.

Needed another day. How'd you hear that?

She takes a selfie, posing with a goofy grin and making sure the coffee bar is in the background. She sends it with no caption.

Wow you're at Faze

...looking for you

If I knew you were coming I might have tried to go in

Nah, it's all good. Don't rush your return to work until you're ready. Do you want some company now?

I would love some company now

I'll swing by then, maybe bring some lunch?

I haven't had bkfast so lunch is perfect

Tory smiles.

I haven't had bkfast either. Okay, c u in a bit

Perfect. She stands to leave but realizes she needs something very important. She texts him again:

I have no idea where you live

He replies by sending his entire contact information. Name, phone, address, personal email, business email, business web site, business address, business phone and fax. Guess she's got all but his blood type now.

Got it. Now I know everything about you. C u in a bit

He replies with two emojis: a smiley face and a heart.

[FOURTEEN]

It doesn't take long for Tory to get to Nick's. His apartment is in a small complex of urban lofts only three miles from Faze. She parks on the street and grabs the bag of sandwiches and cookies she picked up from a deli. She doesn't remember exactly what Nick likes or how he likes it, but she figures a hungry dude will eat just about anything.

She heads up the stairs to the second floor. Each apartment door has wide, vertical, dark-stained wooden slats with rectangular doorknobs. The look is clean and modern, and exactly the type of place where she'd want to live after law school.

Standing outside of Nick's door, she takes a big breath. Her heart is racing for some reason. *From one flight of stairs? Or nerves?* Nick's on the other side of that door, for heaven's sake. She could walk in with sweats and no makeup and he wouldn't care. *She* wouldn't care. *What's up with the jitters?*

She knocks and the door swings open.

"Tory." Nick hugs her with his one free arm. She hugs him back with her one free arm, since her other hand is holding the sandwich bag. His hug is about five seconds longer than a typical hug. She's noticed his hugs are always a few seconds more meaningful, but today it feels like he's hugging her like he's afraid to lose her.

Damn, he smells good. Like freshly washed man hair good.

They step away from each other, giving Tory her first real look at him. He's barefoot in a tight white t-shirt tucked into light gray sweatpants. The black straps of his shoulder brace cover most of his chest and his hair is tousled and damp. The cuts on his face have mostly healed and his slate-blue eyes look exhausted and hurt.

"How are you?" she asks. "You smell amazing." She leans closer and takes an obvious second sniff in. "Ah…the freshly showered smell of Nick."

A smile tilts his mouth. "You wouldn't have wanted to smell me fifteen minutes ago."

She tips her head. "Aw, you showered for me."

"Yep. Your visit inspired me to get off of my ass." He glances at the bag. "Need me to take that?"

She hands it to him and follows him to the kitchen, taking in his place. A one-bedroom apartment, high ceilings with spikey-cool stainless light fixtures. A light-blonde brick wall is on one side of the living room, covered with black-and-white photographs and art of different shapes and sizes. He has a brown leather couch in the center, with a reclaimed wood coffee table and modern, black-leather sling chairs to either side. It's man cave urban minimalist.

Nick places the bag on the counter, a polished slab of white quartz ringed by three silver metal bar stools.

"Your apartment is amazing," Tory says, stopping her visual architectural tour and looking back to him.

Nick glances around. "I love it here. But I'm starting to bounce off of these walls."

"Ready to get out more?"

He shakes his head. "Yes but no, not really."

"Well, Jamie wanted me to remind you that her offer still stands for you to stay at Casa Taylor."

His shoulders drop. "You mom's amazing to offer that. Thank you."

He opens his refrigerator and pulls out two bottles of water. "Is water okay?"

"Perfect." Tory takes two sandwiches out of the bag. "I wasn't sure what you like so I got two different things and you can have first pick."

His eyes smile at the corners. "No, you pick first."

She holds one up. "Turkey with girl-like veggies." She holds up the second. "Or roast beef with manly sauces."

"Would you pull my man-card if I take the turkey?"

"Not at all." She holds out the turkey.

Smiling, he grabs the roast beef from her other hand.

"Knew you would," she smirks.

He sits beside her on one of the stools, slowly unwrapping his sandwich with one hand. "This was very nice of you to bring these."

"I wanted to see you and check in with you, you know, after yesterday."

He takes a bite and says nothing.

She does the same.

"It's tomorrow that will be the worst," he quietly says. "One week."

"I know." She takes another bite.

He nods, looking at his sandwich, and then takes another bite. "How was the funeral yesterday?"

She swallows. "Lovely from what I saw, though I heard none of it."

"I hope they honored Quinn in a happy way instead of dwelling on the tragedy."

"They did, my mom said."

"You really didn't listen to anything?" He looks to her.

"Couldn't. Just couldn't."

He nods again. "How are you doing?"

She takes another bite and waits to speak until she finishes chewing. "I have these moments where I feel normal, like I think of something funny or pithy like I would normally do, then I hear music or see something and I get this feeling in my face, like I'm being slapped across my nose and eyes."

He nods. "I get that too. For me, I'll have energy and the next minute I feel exhausted."

She looks down at her almost-eaten sandwich. "Yeah, ditto. We have the same symptoms from the same disease."

"I wonder if there's a cure."

"There's not," she says, crunching up the wrapper from her finished sandwich. "I guess it's about finding the medicine so you feel better. But I don't think you ever get cured, not from losing someone as close as this."

He takes a deep breath in and nods, crunching up his wrapper too. Then he gives a slight eye to the bag, lying on its side. One of the cookies is sticking out and he looks like a kid who wants dessert but is afraid to ask his mom.

"You are adorably looking at that cookie." She grabs the bag and pulls it to her. "The one thing I did remember from years ago is that you have a sweet tooth." She bought four giant cookies, each individually wrapped and she holds them up like a hand of playing cards. "Chocolate chip, Chocolate with chocolate chips, peanut butter or vanilla coconut."

A boyish smile covers his face. "You pick first."

"Nope."

"You bought them!"

"For you."

"I don't want to take your favorite."

"Who said my favorite is here?"

"What flavor isn't there?"

She looks at her display of cookies. "Oatmeal raisin isn't here. That could be my favorite."

"Right. You like the nastiest cookie on the planet?"

"Why are you an oatmeal raisin hater?"

"Raisins is why."

Tory takes the vanilla coconut and gives him the other three.

"Knew it," he says. He looks at her slyly, then chooses the peanut butter cookie.

"Knew it," she says.

They unwrap their cookies and take bites.

"For the record, I really hate oatmeal raisin too," she says with her mouth full.

He looks over his remaining cookie while still chewing the hunk already in his mouth. "Cookies might be the next menu item I offer at Faze."

Oh...no. Tory chews slower. And slower. Her throat feels like it's thickening. "That's not a good idea. For you..." she mumbles.

Nick's chewing slows too.

He slowly looks to her.

She slowly looks to him.

And then he smirks. "Ahhh. Not a good idea for me? And why? Because cookies are a new, good idea for Indigo?"

She lowers her head and takes the last swallow of her cookie.

"So that's why they need a kitchen…" Nick says.

Not good. She just spilled her employer's secret! Indigo's plans for a kitchen are to create a new line of homemade cookies. Al wants to create a signature item with a to-die-for aroma, like Nick's cinnamon rolls. And she's the one working on the permits. This is worse than any one-drink surprise-slur she's ever blurted!

"I don't suppose you can get amnesia, like, right now," she says.

His tongue presses his cheek in a *"no way"* look. "Just tell me this…one little hint from the inside…" His eyes have brightened with mischief. "Are they going to have oatmeal raisin?"

She swats his good arm. "Hell yeah, as a matter of fact. Because their research found that sixty percent of people ranked oatmeal raisin as their favorite!"

"Wow, sixty percent?"

"You're having fun with this, aren't you?"

"Uh-huh. It's not every day I get competitor secrets handed to me on a silver—I mean—cookie platter."

She points a finger at his smiling face. "I had a one-time slip and you're never getting any insider information from me ever again. Ever!"

He smiles like he just discovered one of her ticklish spots.

She gets off of the barstool and gathers the trash, stomping into the kitchen. *Why did she spill that info? Ugh!* She looks at his sink and then to the left and the right. She has no clue where his fricken trash can is. In two seconds, she's about to throw this bag…

He's still on his barstool, watching her fumble around his kitchen. "To the right. Of the sink. If you're looking for the trash can. If you're looking for my secret cinnamon roll recipe, that's hidden in a different place."

She swings open the cabinet, pulls out the can, dunks the bag and closes it. "What am I supposed to do now?" She turns to face him. "Your kitchen at Faze is up and running. You could get an early jump and start your own cookie line now! Ethically, I have to tell Al I blurted this!"

Nick stands up, his expression not wearing as much mockery as he was a minute earlier. He moves into the kitchen, closer to her. "You and I just got to the place where I was afraid we might be."

"At least you're not mad and yelling at me, like the place we were before."

"No, no. And I shouldn't have reacted the way I did when you first told me you were going to work at Indigo. Friends work for competitors all of the time. And I'm sorry how I reacted that day."

Wow. Nice. "I couldn't blame you."

"We need to have a balance," he says. "I have to remember not to tell you my inside secrets."

"Agreed."

"And you are welcome to tell me all of theirs."

Her hands smack her hips. "If your other arm wasn't in a sling, I'd hit them both."

He smugly smiles. At least his eyes have softened from the

hurt she saw when she first walked in. Maybe the prospect of her professional demise is worth it just to see him be a little happy again.

"Just so you don't beat yourself up, I'll tell you a Faze secret," he says. "I had looked at cookies a long time ago. I really was thinking about pricing them again, even though there wasn't enough margin for me before."

Thank you, Lord. Then she scrunches her eyes. *Wonder what he saw in the margins?*

He leans closer, as if he can read her mind. "Raisins cost too much at the time."

His playful arrogance is making her temperature rise.

"Come on, let's sit down." He gestures to his living room. Tory follows him, sitting in one of the sling chairs while he sinks into the leather sofa. "Let's change the subject."

"Good," she says.

"What are your plans for the rest of the day?"

"I have an errand I need to run," she says. "Other than that, I was planning to sit and brood all day."

"Sit and brood: I know that show."

"Since we're changing subjects," she says, "have you heard anything from the detectives?"

"I have. They asked for my car maintenance records and I gave them everything I had."

"Good. And have you given any thought to hiring a lawyer?"

He shakes his head. "I still don't think I need one."

"You know I disagree. And I'm not saying this to push my dad as your lawyer either. I don't care if it's my dad or someone else. You need one."

"I don't like thinking about it."

She tilts her head. "Didn't we have a chat on the Pearl steps about not pushing feelings deep?"

He points a finger at her. "Oh yes we did. But not hiring a lawyer isn't about my feelings. It's about me being confident that they'll find out I did nothing wrong."

"Don't hide anything from them."

"I haven't. And I won't. How about you?" he asks.

"Me?"

"Yeah, you and hiding things."

"I'm not hiding anything. Well, except more classified Indigo secrets, of course."

"Of course," he smirks. "But that's not what I'm talking about."

She's not hiding anything. "What are you talking about?"

"The other night. On the steps. Your face went pale and you dropped your phone when you read a text."

Oh snap. Jake's creepy text.

"And you said you'd tell me what it was."

She shakes her head. "And this still isn't a good time."

He crosses his arms. "Is it your ex?"

How in the hell did he guess that!?

Nick leans forward. "You told me at the Fiesta party that you were having problems with him texting. And Quinn said she was getting scared for you. Is it escalating?"

Tory stares at him. He's been sitting around with too much time to think and he's evidently been thinking about this.

She looks to her lap. She hasn't talked to anyone about this. Not even Daniel. She was close to asking her dad for advice about restraining orders, but a quick internet search on stalking gave her the answer on what the criteria is to request that. And Jake isn't there, yet.

"It has escalated." She looks up to see Nick sitting forward, completely focused on her. "He hasn't threatened me, but the creepy factor has ramped up."

"How?"

"Yesterday when I got home from the funeral was the worst." Tory gets up and goes to her purse on the kitchen counter. She pulls out her phone and Jake's texts. "It seems innocent enough, but he said I looked beautiful at the funeral."

She offers her phone to Nick and he takes it. He scrolls, reading, and with each stroke of his scrolling finger his face stretches longer. "No coupon needed for Quinn's funeral? And then he tells you how beautiful you looked while you were there? What kind of a creep is this guy?"

"I could have handled our break up better." She sits down, leaning forward in her chair, almost knee to knee with Nick. "I was…I don't know…rude and I know it hurt him."

Nick clicks off her phone and hands it back to her. "What's the story with the coupons?"

"Is that a stupid reason to break up with a guy? I don't know…we never went anywhere unless a discount was attached and then we'd go out of our way to save a dime. He drove a nice Volvo and is getting his master's at Texas too so he has money but his couponing hobby was obsessive."

He arches an eyebrow questioningly.

"No, like, one time at the movies, after we got in with a coupon, he dug through a garbage can and pulled out one of those all-you-can-eat refillable popcorn bags and went up to the counter and…"

"No way."

"Way," she says, shrugging. "It's not like we had been dating a long time either. It was barely a month! He's not the kind of guy for me anyway. He's a comfortable settler and I'm more of an ambitious explorer."

"Where does he live?"

"Austin. I knew I'd need to deal with this when I got back to school but now, with him saying I looked beautiful, I don't know if he's here now and following me or what."

"He might have said that just to unnerve you, to make you think he was there."

"That's what I thought too. But it's starting to get into my every thought and I catch myself looking over my shoulder and jumping with every text."

"We need to deal with this."

We? She can feel the color changing on her face, blushing with a warm sense of security she hasn't felt for a while. "You're sweet to say 'we' but I know it's 'me'."

"Nope. Not anymore."

Oh, Nick. "You don't need to protect me anymore. This is why I didn't want to mention this to you. I knew you might do that."

"I can talk to him."

"No! I haven't talked to him myself since I broke it off. Sending a proxy—especially a guy—might make things worse."

"Why haven't you blocked his number?"

She looks at her phone. "I'd rather see what he's saying and not respond. If I block him then I won't know if things are escalating."

"I think you need to confront him. Tell him, nicely, to stop harassing you. And I can be with you when you do it."

Tory looks down to the coffee table, decorated with a black leather tray and some marble knickknacks. She looks back up into Nick's caring eyes. He's so protective of her. He always has been. But confronting Jake isn't the way she wants to go.

"I really do think he will get over me and move on. It's a matter of waiting it out. I have a plan now. I can protect myself."

Nick's eyes tell her he's not buying it.

She shakes her head. "Don't make me regret telling you."

He leans forward and takes one of her hands, holding it. "I want you to always trust me with no regrets, like I trust you. I've got your back in a nanosecond if you need."

She feels his sincerity coming through from the warmth of his hand, seeing the calmness of his eyes and hearing his reassuring words. Nick may be a train wreck with luck, but he's a much better person than Jake. What was she thinking when she told Jake she'd go out with him in the first place? And then again and again? In the future, she needs to hold any prospective boyfriend up to the Nick standard. He ranks a perfect one on the Qutor scale.

"I'd like to return to talking about your problems now," she says.

"I'd rather not."

She lets go of his hand and pats his knee. "I've been thinking about a couple of things."

"Oatmeal cookie recipes?"

She sneers. "You're good at trying to change the subject, aren't you?"

He sinks back into the sofa. "I do my best when the subject is me."

"Well focus for a minute and hear me out."

"Focused and listening."

"Did you buy your car from Reed's?"

"I did. I had my Lexus for about a year. Bought it used from Reed's."

"You had your Lexus and Mustang at the same time."

"Of course. The 'stang wasn't an everyday car."

"Have you gotten a new car this week? And more importantly, did you buy it from Reed's?"

"I did get a car. Another Lexus. Online and delivered to my door from Carvana. No way in hell would I buy a car from Reed's now."

"I'm suspicious. Very suspicious. After what you said about your car not handling well, I wonder if someone could have messed with your car. Intentionally."

"And that's what the detective seems to be honing in on: the maintenance of my car."

"You said your tires had been fine, until after the concert, right?"

"I thought they were perfect. One thing I was wondering is if Reed's had sold me a car with defective tires. But you'd think I would have noticed something earlier. It seems unlikely the tires would happen to fail exactly when they did."

"Unless bad tires were brand new to your car."

Nick quiets.

She leans forward. "Could someone have changed your tires while you and Quinn were in the concert?"

A shadow of concern touches his face. "Oh my God. I hadn't thought of that."

"There's got to be a reason why your car was fine before the concert, but not after."

Nick's eyes light up with horror. "Reed's Roadside! When we pulled into the parking lot, there was a Reed's Roadside tow truck off to the side, lights flashing, helping some car."

Her gut tightens. "Are you kidding?"

"After we saw the Reed's tow truck, Quinn and I started talking about Sienna and Reed."

"But Reed's doesn't have any dealerships around Bear Creek arena."

"There's nothing around Bear Creek arena."

"Where did you and Quinn park? Like, on an end aisle where people could see your car or in the middle?"

He shakes his head. "In the back! We were in the back! We both said we couldn't believe how crowded the parking lot was even that early."

"And people going to a concert wouldn't think twice about seeing a tow truck changing someone's tire."

"And if it was during the concert, no one would've been hanging around the parking lot long enough to notice them changing all four."

"This may be circumstantial...but how convenient for a Reed's Roadside truck to happen to be in the area...where you happened to be...parked in the back...and away from your car for hours."

"Son of a bitch," Nick says.

"We need to pull some more facts together. There's got to be a parking lot camera or some witnesses. Because if the detectives are focusing on car maintenance to blame this on you, and bad tires were put on your car, they're going to find a bad set of tires on your wrecked car."

Nick drags a hand through his hair. "If Reed had someone fuck with my car and that's what led to Quinn's death," he says, "I'm going after him."

[FIFTEEN]

Shadowy dark covers Tory's bedroom, except for the moon's glow filtering through the curtains and the dim light coming from the screen of her phone.

It's 3:10 a.m. on Sunday morning and she's lying in her bed, propped up with pillows, phone in hand and a half-empty bag of salty chips beside her.

She last saw Nick on Friday at his apartment.

But for the past two hours she's been texting with him nonstop.

They made a pact to do this, together. They wanted to be up and awake to remember Quinn, exactly one week to the minute when she died.

There's ten minutes to go. And Nick has been sending one message after another of thanks to Tory.

I never thanked you for standing up to Pam either. If she hadn't let me stay, I'm not sure what I would've done

Q would have wanted you there

Q knew we were there

Did you see her look back and forth between us, like she couldn't believe we were there?

I did. Maybe she thought I had died in the accident

Maybe she was trying to tell us something

Like what?

Not sure

Tory watches the three blinking dots pulse while he types.

I never asked you about something else

?

You looked around, like I was, you know, when the nurses came in

I thought I was fainting. Everything was white

I saw it too

I think it was peace. Pure peace. And it was a gift from Q

I do too. She said something to me, earlier that night

About what?

U might think this is weird, but we both almost died from a massive lightning bolt

Serious?

We just got in the car when it hit REAL close

OMG

Q said if it had hit her and she had died, she would have died the happiest person b'cause she had so much fun that night

Chills race down Tory's arms and she slides deeper under her comforter.

She was happy with you. Thank goodness she was with someone she was happy with

One minute to go

Oh God we were flat against the wall, freaking

Thank God I was with you

Right about now the roof disappeared

I thought that was my imagination

Tory wipes her eyes with the corner of her sheets.

Crying now

Me too

I miss her, Nick

3:20

Her tears are blinding her eyes. *One week ago. God, take care of Quinn.* She blinks to try to clear her eyes so she can see her phone, waiting for Nick's next message, but there are no blinking dots. He must be doing what she is: thinking of Quinn and crying. She reels from losing a best friend. He reels from losing a friend and from the guilt that he might have caused it. Plus, he experienced the accident with Quinn. He felt the pain, heard the screams, saw the blood. This moment has to be horribly profound.

There are still no blinking dots. *Why isn't he texting?*
Still nothing.
Another few minutes pass. She types next:

It wasn't your fault, Nick

No response.

We're going to figure it out, for Q sake

No response. He's got to be torn apart right now, she can't

even imagine. Maybe they should have done this together, in person, where she could hug him and push her face in front of his so he could see the eyes of someone who cares.

Nick?

She finally sees three blinking dots as he types the next message.

Don't leave me T

Tory clutches her chest and hot tears stream down her cheeks. *Oh God, Nick.* He lost his parents, Sienna, Quinn…he's terrified. She types back:

Not going anywhere

No response, so she types more:

I'm not afraid to ride in a car with you…

Still nothing.

…you oatmeal raisin cookie loving astronaut

That should draw a response! Suddenly, there're three blinking dots. *Good!*

Thank God you're in my life

She sniffles.

Thank God you're in mine

Nite, T

Wait! No! She's not ready to stop texting! She's not ready to let him go. Her phone feels hollow in her hands, knowing he might not be there anymore. Slowly she types one last message:

Nite, Nick

[SIXTEEN]

Two days later

The late afternoon sun beams through the skylight on the second floor at Indigo. Tory climbs the center staircase, heading back up to her office, holding a hot cup of coffee. When she sees the sliver of sunlight warming the center staircase, she knows it's time for her coffee break. And around here a coffee break is actually work.

Wooden floorboards creak with each step she takes. Since the special collection book room is upstairs too, there's a heavy, musty smell. Customers know Indigo as a vintage place, but the longer Tory's been here the more she's noticed: vintage is lacking upkeep.

She's felt slow on this first day back at work, heavy with thought and light with appetite.

She pulls out her leather desk chair in an office she shares with Robyn, Indigo's accounting manager, and gently blows across her coffee to cool it. Today's special is from Lake Kivu, one of the new brews Al is trying from Rwanda. Adding exotic coffee from regions in Africa is yet another idea he wanted to have in place before he retires at the end of the month.

Tory gives her coffee another gentle blow and takes a sip.

"Is it good?" asks Robyn.

"Mmm, a little bitter."

Robyn faces her computer, typing. "I liked the M one on Friday."

"M one? See, that's part of the problem. No one knows how to ask for it if you can't pronounce it." Tory looks through the papers on her desk and pulls out a memo. "Here's the list. Friday was Muhazi. Today is Lake Kivu."

"Tomorrow it's a Siberian Timbuktu blend or something. We're getting too weird," Robyn mumbles.

Tory smiles, turning to her computer to get back to work. She and Robyn share similar taste in coffee and logic. They also share similar tastes in people, particularly Reed. Robyn's been very helpful during Tory's internship by helping to keep Reed away. Every few days, he tries to pop into their office, hoping to see Tory. But each time he's been met with a closed door. Robyn has a tiny window that overlooks the center staircase and she can see when Reed is coming. She's so good, she can keep her eyes on her monitor and fingers on her keyboard while slightly rolling back in her chair so her foot can reach the doorstop and kick it out. By the time Reed arrives, the door has swung closed without her missing a keystroke.

She doesn't do the same for Blaine, since he is the boss's son. And in less than two weeks, Blaine will be running the place. Robyn figures she can't slam the door on him all of the time, even though she'd like to.

Also in less than two weeks, Tory will be back in Austin. She will have done what she can for Al in getting his kitchen expansion started. Now she knows why his law firm was dragging their feet. This isn't really work a firm would do and Indigo's city and state permitting is a mess. While trying to get their zoning and platting complete, Tory discovered Indigo didn't have a permit for the sign that's been outside for years. They've never had a license for the music they play inside. One reason they lost the Wally B. contract is because they didn't have a live entertainment license either and it was Wally B.'s team that caught the error. Tory also found out that the square footage of their new kitchen will make them too large for their current zoning classification. While Al dreams of handing over a perfectly ready project to Blaine, there's still much work that must be done. That is, if they want to keep it legal. From what Tory has gathered, city inspectors have turned a blind eye to what they've done so far.

She can only imagine the competitive smirk on Nick's face if he knew Indigo's behind-the-scenes problems.

This isn't the type of work Tory is interested in anyway. While it's been helpful to learn, she'd rather be understanding family law and how to defend victims. That's her passion. She hopes to do the type of pro-bono work her dad does now, only full-time and paid.

"Another gift basket heading up," Robyn says, glancing through her spy window while typing.

Since Al announced he's retiring, he's had a stream of gifts pour in and a parade of business leaders and politicians stopping by to say goodbye. Every evening he leaves with an armful of cellophane-wrapped baskets, bottles of wine and liquor and other gifts. Robyn calls Al the "don of coffeehouses".

A barista carrying the gift basket stops outside their door.

"Tory?" Tyler asks. "This is for you." He hands her a small basket, wrapped with clear cellophane and beautifully tied with a turquoise bow.

Me? Tory shrugs. "Thanks, Tyler."

Robyn stops typing and turns. "Nice."

Tory looks over the basket; she can't quite tell what's inside. Tucked under the bow is a small card and she pulls it out.

Caution slows her movement. *What if it's from Jake? Would he send stupid stuff to her office as his next move?* With Robyn watching her, she keeps her cool and carefully opens the card, holding it close to read.

Could sixty percent of people be wrong?
N

She puckers her mouth. *Oh no, Nick didn't.* She tugs the end of the bow. *Of course, duh, it's turquoise.* Inside the basket are a dozen individually wrapped oatmeal raisin cookies.

"Is that our afternoon snack?" Robyn asks.

Tory turns, smirking. She and Robyn always share their snacks and Tory is happy to part with this one. "Your snack now." She hands Robyn the basket, keeping the card but throwing away the cellophane and ribbon.

"Mmm…oatmeal raisin cookies!" Robyn says. "You don't like oatmeal raisin, do you?"

"I don't and I know you do, so enjoy!"

Robyn peels off the wrapper from one and takes a bite. "Now I need to go and get a cup of that Keevu Pond coffee to go with it."

Tory shakes her head. "Lake Kivu."

Robyn's mouth is full. "Yeah, too fancy, whatever. Hey, who sent these?"

Tory tucks the card into her purse and pulls out her phone. "A vendor who I don't think we'll ever use."

"They're really good," Robyn says, turning back to her computer.

Tory types a text:

Thank you for the thoughtful yet awful gift. Now it's on, cinnamon roll boy

Before Tory has a chance to put her phone back into her purse, Nick has replied with the cookie emoji and a message:

Bring it, T

Tory replies with the smiling poop emoji.

She puts her phone back into her purse, her mind racing with ideas of how to get him back. And she *will* get him back.

"Hey, watch the time," Robyn says, focused on her computer.

Tory glances at her watch. She has a meeting with Al in a few minutes. She was lucky he was able to fit her in his schedule. And she's not sure how to break the bad news to him on how messed up their licensing problem is. She also has to remind him she's not going to be around long enough to fix it.

She gathers her notes and stands up to leave when Robyn suddenly kicks out the doorstop and their office door gently swings closed.

"He's here, seriously?" Tory says.

"Right…there," Robyn says, looking through the narrow-slit window, watching Reed coming up the stairs.

Tory locks the door, then turns to gather more papers for her meeting.

A knock sounds. "Tory? Robyn? Are you in there?" Reed asks.

Tory rolls her eyes, continuing to gather her notes. Robyn keeps typing.

Reed knocks again. "Come on, I know you're in there and you have a meeting with Al in a few minutes."

Tory straightens. *What!?*

Robyn stops typing and turns. "How'd he know that?" she whispers.

"Shit, I'm trapped," Tory whispers. Her meeting is in three minutes!

Robyn looks through the slit window. "He hasn't gone downstairs yet."

"Keep watching!" Tory whispers.

"If he knew you had a meeting then he knows how long to wait!"

Tory presses her ear to the door. On the other side is a man she'd like to strangle, if she were prone to commit murder. She's tempted to throw open this door, pin him against a wall and fire off questions about Nick and Quinn's accident to see if he confesses. But she'd have to touch him to do that.

This is stupid. She should be mature and face him. Or maybe she could walk out of here and act childish by ignoring him. Either way…

Tory hears Robyn whispering in her phone. She hangs up and looks out of her secret spying window. "Help is on the way," she whispers. "Here she comes!"

"What?!"

"Listen," Robyn says, standing up and pressing her ear to the door. "Diane is coming up from the bookstore and will tell Reed that you and Al are downstairs…"

"Hey, Reed!" they hear Diane's muffled voice say. "What are you doing up here?"

"Waiting for Tory. I know she has a meeting with Al in a minute," Reed replies.

"I'm pretty sure I just saw her downstairs, at a table with Al."

Robyn peers out her spy window. "And…off he goes downstairs!" She turns to Tory. "Enjoy your meeting."

"You're amazing." Tory high-fives Robyn, opens the door, winks to Diane, then quickly moves down the hall, turning the corner heading to Al's office. His secretary sits outside. "Hey, Tory. Go on in."

Tory's about to bust out in a laugh. She has her reasons for avoiding Reed. But now giving him the slip has turned into quite an enjoyable game. For several people.

"Hey, Al," Tory says, stepping inside his office and closing the door behind her.

He gets up from his desk, his smile warm and his arms opening. "Welcome back." He wraps her in a hug.

"You've been the best boss ever. Thank you."

Al pulls out one of the guest chairs in front of his desk. His office is heavy with wood and musty smelling too, probably from the volumes of books stacked on his shelves. Dozens of framed awards and proclamations are on his wall. A few empty moving boxes are assembled and in the corner. His Louis Vuitton briefcase sits on his desk, where only one notepad, a cruise brochure, a pen and a folder lay.

Al sits beside her in the other guest chair. "I've been in meetings all day so I'm sorry I didn't say hello earlier. How are you, my dear?"

"I'm weird and sad. I'm glad I'm here though. Thank you for the flowers and all of the texts last week. My parents also appreciate the food you sent to the house."

"I know how close your parents are to the Corbins. Often the close friends carry grief as well."

Tory looks to her lap. "I'm sorry I missed a whole week. That was a huge amount of time to miss since I'm only here for a month."

"I intend to pay you for the entire month, even the time you missed."

"Al, you don't have to do that."

"I insist."

"Thank you." Tory looks around his office. "Getting ready to pack up?"

Al looks around too. "I am. So many memories here." He leans closer. "I should have told Blaine I was keeping this office and made myself, you know, CEO Emeritus."

The staff would celebrate if you did. "It's not too late, you know."

"Well, it is too late to cancel our trip." He nods to his desk and the cruise brochure. "I've promised my wife an exotic trip for years and boy, she's holding me to it."

"When do you leave?"

"A few days after I officially retire. We fly to New Zealand and board our cruise ship for a six-month sail to Europe."

"You deserve it."

"I've never taken a vacation this long. I've never left Indigo that long either."

"Blaine will have his hands full when you leave."

Al straightens. "That's why I've been working hard to get affairs in order before I go. I'm on a mission with a purpose."

"What purpose?"

He sits up, proudly. "I have spent my career working hard and watching all sorts of injustices happen around me. Politically and in business. I want to right the wrongs to be sure my legacy is cemented and that Blaine has the best chance to succeed."

"From what I've seen, your legacy is already cemented. You had the leader of the Texas State Senate stop by for coffee this morning! You're so connected."

"Yes, but politics can sometimes undo the good."

Interesting. From what she's seen, politicking has served him well. He's gotten away with multiple zoning infractions and licensing issues for a long time. Maybe he knows that when Blaine takes the helm, things will change. That might be why he's wanting Tory to clean this all up now.

"I have some updates if you would like to go over them," Tory says.

"I do, but I'm more interested in talking about you."

Tory tilts her head.

"The accident with Quinn was shocking," he says. "And I am terribly concerned that Quinn had gotten so close with Nick Allen. I know you and Quinn were close and you both considered Nick a friend."

Here it comes: a stay-away-from-Nick lecture.

"It's far too coincidental for Nick to have so many accidents and be so careless with his driving."

"But he wasn't careless. There were some unusual circumstances involved."

"There were unusual circumstances with Reed's sister's accident too."

Tory grips the armrests. "Which was ruled an accident."

Al shakes his head. "When we got those concert tickets and I heard you gave them to Quinn and Nick, oh Tory, I've been beside myself thinking what if you and Quinn had only gone. Quinn would still be here."

Tory narrows her eyes even as guilt tears through her. "Please don't put guilt on me like that."

"My dear, there are so many 'what if's' I've seen in my life. It's not guilt I'm trying to talk to you about. It's about making the right decisions so you have no regrets."

"Let me guess, a right decision involves no Nick."

Al nods. "He was so much trouble for us back when you all worked here together. I've never had the police come to Indigo to speak to one of our employees, except for Nick."

Tory squints. The dog hit-and-run? That's the only police-coming-to-Indigo incident with Nick that she knows of. And he didn't know he hit the dog!

"I appreciate your advice." She smiles to try to change the subject. "And with years of experience I know your advice is worth something."

"I want you to be safe, Tory." Al's eyes darken. "Sienna was killed in Nick's car. And now, Quinn. Keep yourself safe, Tory, and stay away from Nick Allen."

Tory nods. *Boy, this would be a horrible time to tell him Nick knows about his secret cookie plan.* She's got to steer him off the anti-Nick lecture and back to fixing his business problems.

There's a soft knock at the door. Al's secretary peeks her head inside. "The Mayor is on the phone."

"Finally!" Al says, his face lighting up. "I have been waiting all day to get through to him. Do you mind if I take this call?"

"Of course not. Just let me know when you want to go through these permits and licenses."

They stand and Al's gaze lingers on her. "I've known you for so many years. I want to be sure you stay safe."

"I will. Thank you, Al." She gives him a sweet smile and heads toward the door.

He's wrong about Nick, but she knows, Al's grieving too. He liked Quinn. From what Tory heard, he liked Sienna too. But his warning is focused on the wrong guy.

Al's secretary is sipping a cappuccino and doesn't look up as Tory passes her. A few steps later Tory turns the corner to her office when her knees buckle and she grinds to a halt.

Shit!

Reed leans against a wall, arms crossed, a smirk on his face and his heated eyes inches from hers. "Well hi there, Tory."

She's frozen. Can't move. Can't breathe. Not funny. *Not happening!*

"I've been trying to say hi to you for a while."

She's still frozen. Her jaw clenches and her hands fist at her sides.

"So sorry to see your meeting with Al was cut short."

She goes from frozen to boiling. "Did you just arrange a sabotage call to end my meeting?"

His eyes gleam with pride and he uncrosses his arms. "I want to talk to you."

Rage pounds her heart. "Did you seriously just intentionally end my meeting?"

"I have people who can play tricks too."

Her nostrils flare. "So you want to talk to me? It just so happens I want to talk to you."

"Good. Now that we're on the same page…"

Tory glances to her open office door. *Where's Robyn? Where's anyone?* There's no one in the hall who can witness this! Has Reed played another trick to lure them all away?

Screw this: she's on her own.

"Yeah," she says. "I want to tell you something."

Reed stands straight.

Tory leans closer to deliver the words she's waited over two years to blister him with. "There's no one on the planet more reprehensible than you and I will make it my life's work to destroy you if you even look at me, or talk to me, or think that you know me."

"Tory, stop!" he yells.

She clenches her teeth. "Stop? Stop? Oh really? I didn't think you were familiar with the word."

"You need to listen to me—"

"No. You are dead to me. And I don't make it a habit to listen to dead people."

She stomps past him, into her office and slams the door.

[SEVENTEEN]

Tory taps the steering wheel of her BMW, inching along in bumper-to-bumper traffic leaving downtown. For a Wednesday evening, rush hour traffic seems heavier than usual. Tonight, she won't be inching along with them for long. She's deviating from her usual home-to-work-then-home routine and heading to the Pearl. She's craving two things: chicken tacos from Socat, the restaurant she visited not long after Quinn died, and she wants to see Nick.

He's on the way to meet her, though his text said he's running late. Tory thought he might welcome a mid-week distraction. Heaven knows after her showdown with Reed on Monday, she could use a distraction too. And Nick's been doing the same thing she has: only going to work and then back home each day. Maybe together they can do small things like this to help them feel normal again.

She reaches the Pearl, parks her car and begins the walk down the pedestrian streets. Every step in her black pumps pinches her pinkie toes. Had she known this morning she'd be walking around the Pearl, she'd have chosen different shoes. The loose feel of her black and gray floral pencil skirt is also sending her a message: eat more. Maybe her regular appetite will return soon.

A delicious wood-burning smell of something spicy cooking fills the air. Young professionals sit at outdoor café tables, enjoying happy hour. Different music plays from the outdoor seating areas of each bar and restaurant she passes. Her walk feels hazy. Doing normal things like this still doesn't feel right.

The orange-and-red sign of Socat is ahead and Tory glances around to see if by chance Nick is already here. No luck. She stands in the middle of the walkway, waiting. She wonders what he'll be wearing and how he's feeling. All they've had are text exchanges and phone calls for almost a week and she misses him. But tonight, she better be prepared. He might be armed for revenge. Earlier today he should have received a delivery, a reciprocation gift from her for the oatmeal cookies he sent. She sent him a five-pound tin of plump raisins along with a note.

Found a great vendor with good prices.
Our margins will be just fine.

She can only imagine his reaction when he received it.

Tory looks around the crowd, wanting to see Nick before he sees her. Two guys her age pass her, wearing dress shirts and smiles, both giving her intriguing glances. *They're cute.* She grins. It reminds her of when she'd be at happy hour with Quinn. Guys would send them drinks and then come over to introduce themselves. She and Quinn knew it was unlikely they'd find the man of their dreams at happy hour. But it was fun to rate them with the Qutor scale and then collect their compliments. Sadly now, Tory doesn't have anyone to do that with. Except Daniel. And when she and Daniel go out, guys stay away, thinking they are a couple.

Another man hurriedly passes by, talking loudly into his phone and glancing at his watch. He's wearing a Nick-like outfit, a sport coat with a button-down shirt tucked into slim pants. But this guy's shirt is loose and his shoes match his pants—totally not the way Nick would wear an outfit like that.

Down the street she catches sight of another man wearing a Nick-like outfit and this guy is eye-catching and on point: fitted linen blazer tight across his wide shoulders with a tight white button-down shirt and slim navy pants with chestnut brown shoes. She does a double take: it is Nick! He's not wearing his arm sling! But he is wearing a big smile and heading her way.

It's got to be her imagination, but the crowd seems to part as women turn to look at him. It reminds her of how girls always seemed to get in line whenever Nick worked the Indigo cash register. It's no surprise to her: he's always looked incredible.

"Hey," Tory says as he pulls her against him for another one of those longer hugs. She breathes him in and then pulls away. "You've lost the sling!"

Nick looks delighted. "I was supposed to wear it for two weeks but I couldn't take it anymore."

"You're quite the rebel, huh?"

"I'm out of control with doctors' orders. But, I'll still wear it at home and in my office." He looks her over. "You look amazing. How are you doing?"

"What a week so far. And Reed…I just can't…"

"Unbelievable that he got Al's secretary to lie about the Mayor being on the phone."

"And she's the one who told him I had a meeting with Al so he knew where I'd be."

"I guess everyone has a price."

"Like paying for free cappuccinos for thirty minutes."

"Reed is disgusting to trick everyone to go downstairs for that."

"Thankfully I won't be there much longer to deal with any of them."

Nick looks down and then back up, the color draining from his cheeks. "I can't believe you're leaving in a few weeks."

"May has flown by."

"This was a great suggestion, to do this tonight. I need my T-time." He takes her hands and they twist together.

"I've missed you. I feel like even though we talk and are up to date, there's so much more to say in person."

He eases into a relaxed smile. "I've never felt like talking more to someone in my life as I do with you." His eyes drift up to the Socat sign as he lets her hands go. "So, this is the place?"

Tory turns to the restaurant. "I found this that night I ran into you on the steps. They have the best tacos I've ever had."

"Socat." He grins, looking at the sign. "I love it. Brilliant name. I appreciate savvy marketing."

"So…you figured it out, that fast?"

"Of course. Socat is tacos spelled backward."

He really does have something special in that brain of his. "And the menu items are described backward too. It's hilarious. Ready to eat?"

He rubs his stomach. "Well, I'm not super hungry. I had an amazing snack of raisins earlier."

She beams. "Five pounds of snackable, raisin goodness?"

"And thank you for all five pounds. Because four pounds wouldn't have been enough."

Their smiles light up the street.

"And, actually, I didn't eat any of them so yes, I'm starving," he says.

"Of course. Why would you eat raisins when you hate them?"

"But your raisins are why I'm late."

"How so?"

"I took them down to our kitchen and was talking with our culinary guy. He's going to work on a special cinnamon-raisin roll. Limited edition, of course. Because selling anything limited edition drives up sales."

She shakes her head.

He smirks. "I figure we should have a market for them, at least with those sixty-percent raisin lovers."

"Oh yes, you do."

"But you didn't hear that Faze secret from me."

"What secret?" She grins.

He nods to the restaurant. "Dinner's my treat tonight."

"You're sweet to offer, but there's no need."

He leans closer and the evening breeze sends her a whiff of his leather-smelling cologne. "I just thought of a coupon joke but figured I better not."

Her smile stretches. "There are times I really want to smack you."

"I'll take that compliment."

They move toward the restaurant door and he leans closer again. "Would it be okay if we ordered to-go instead and sat on the steps?"

Thank goodness he said that. "Actually, I'd prefer to. I'm not up for sitting inside a restaurant yet."

"Yeah, me either. The music and people…it's hard when you're stuck sitting someplace. I can handle this," he gestures around the open area, "but sitting inside is different."

They move to the to-go counter and Nick squints at the menu board. "This is hilarious." He turns to her. "Know what you want?"

"I'll try the chicken fajita tacos tonight."

He reads from the menu. "You mean, cream sour and gallo de pico, guacamole, tortillas corn homemade or flour of choice your with tacos fajita chicken?"

"I understood that perfectly. And I pick the flour tortillas."

Nick turns to the lady behind the counter. "I don't have to say my order backward, do I?"

She shakes her head.

"Okay, good. Two chicken fajita tacos, both with flour tortillas, and two bottles of water."

In minutes, they each have a paper bag and their water. Together they walk slowly toward the Riverwalk and the Pearl steps.

"I hate to break this to you," Tory says, "but you and I, we're about to have a big problem."

Nick jolts to a stop, eyes wide. "What?"

"Are we sitting on the north side steps or the south side?" She dips her chin. "Because as a south stepper, I'm loyal to my side."

They exchange smiles.

"You gave me a heart attack," he says. "If that's our biggest problem, I'll take it and come to the south side. But just this once."

Good. Because walking from this way, the south steps are right in front of them. If he wanted to sit on the north side, they'd have to cross the bridge. And at this point, her pinkie toes are screaming with every step in these pumps.

They reach the sidewalk where they can see down the steps. Step by step, they head down. Nick turns and offers her his hand for a couple of steps until they settle on a spot and sit down. Tory stretches out her legs and crosses them at the ankles and he does the same as they unwrap their tacos.

"I didn't ask you yet," Tory says, "how are you feeling?"

He grins. "We both keep asking each other that same question."

"I know. I like it when you ask me. And I ask you because I want to know."

He sighs. "Going back to work wasn't too bad, because I'm so comfortable at Faze I guess. I stay in my office mostly. I don't really want to go down and hang out with customers yet."

"What's the latest from your insurance appraiser?" Tory asks, taking a bite of her taco.

"He's getting irritated with the police not giving him access to my car. He thinks he'll see it by the end of the week."

"Good. Did you tell him to look at the tires?"

"I did. He'll take photos."

"And the wipers?"

"Same. He said it's a little uncommon that they aren't letting me see the car and get my personal items before he sees it, but it's not unheard of." He takes a bite of his taco.

"So many questions could be answered if you could only see your damn car." Tory takes another bite.

"At least the appraiser knows what I'm looking for. And…"

Tory looks at him, still chewing. "And what?"

"And I remembered something that I left in the trunk."

"Something valuable?"

He looks down. "Something alcoholic."

Her eyes widen. "Open bottles?"

"Empty bottles."

Her shoulders drop. "Oh no. What, like, how many?"

He's still looking down. "We had split a bottle of wine, so that was back there, and I had a beer with these guys we were hanging out with. And when we were all packing up, I put some of their cans and my stuff in my trunk." His worried eyes meet hers. "There wasn't a trash can around and I wasn't going to leave empty bottles and cans in the parking lot."

She rests her hand on his shoulder. "It's circumstantial. As long as you didn't decline the sobriety test and they have that result."

"I didn't decline. I passed. I wasn't drunk."

She squeezes him. "It's okay. It was garbage in the trunk. Every beer can be tested for DNA to prove you didn't drink them all. This can be defended. That is, if any defense is needed. There still might not be charges."

He inhales deeply and his posture straightens. Then he exhales through his mouth. "I didn't do anything wrong. There has to be no charges."

She pats his leg. "I agree with you."

Silence fills the next minute, both of them eating and thinking. A Riverwalk boat slowly chugs down the river, the boat captain not obnoxiously singing or talking loudly to his half-empty boat of passengers. A few people are sitting on the steps around them too.

The sun dips below the horizon, casting shadows on the steps but lighting up the potted bougainvillea plants lining the edge of the stairs.

"Look how the sun is now," she says.

His eyes wander toward the sunshine.

She points to the sunny side. "That was the beginning of May for me. Sunny, bright. And…look where I am now, sitting in the dark and the shadows."

His chin lowers. "Dark and in the shadows has been my year."

He finishes eating and crumples up his trash, taking her trash too and combining it in a bag. "Tell me about the new internship you have."

"I haven't even wrapped my head around it with all that has happened. My dad helped get me into a law firm in Austin. They always have tons of interns and even though all the summer spaces were filled, he found a partner with a spot. I'll be joining the other interns mid-summer, but it's better than staying at Indigo. I should have stayed in Austin all summer rather than come back to San Antonio."

"What else could you have done after your first internship fell through?"

"Anything but come back here."

"But if you hadn't come back, we wouldn't have reconnected."

Her chin trembles. "But if I hadn't come back, Quinn would still be alive."

Nick drops his arms and shakes his head. "No…no…how can you even think that?"

"I gave you guys the tickets…"

"I was the driver…"

"How do I not make a mistake like this again? How do I go through life and wonder if I take a different route home, will that be when I'll get in a terrible accident? If I take the first job that's offered, is there a better job I'll miss?" Her arms flail in the air. "Or if I go to one restaurant when I meant to go to another and then I get food poisoning? Or if the last time I see my best friend, I forget to hug her goodbye!"

Nick suddenly wraps his arms around her, squeezing her so tight and meaningfully, it quiets her. She throws her arms around him and buries her face in the nape of his neck. He presses his cheek on her head. They squeeze each other in silence; the power of his hold brings her close to tears.

He eases his arms. "You sounded like you needed that."

Don't let go. She squeezes him tighter. "I did. I still do. Don't let go." She closes her eyes and focuses on her breathing to calm down. *Breathe in. And out. Calm down. Nick's got you.*

After a few silent minutes, Nick gently eases back and captures her hand in his.

"I admit, I needed a hug too," he whispers.

She looks over his expression. "I hope that hug didn't hurt your shoulder."

He grimaces. "It kinda did but it was worth it."

She gives a hesitant smile.

"You asked a lot of questions there that I can't answer. This year, all I do is take wrong turns. But you, Tory, you have to live strong. Stay confident."

Fighting back tears, she sniffles. "I've got to learn from you."

"Me?"

"You've had these unbelievable tragedies and yet you come out strong because you believe in yourself."

His hands tighten around hers. "I wouldn't put it that way. Not sure I'm really strong."

"You're strong enough for me. And you always have been."

His blue eyes fill with warmth. He lifts his finger to stroke her cheek, wiping away a stray tear.

The way he's looking at her takes her breath away. Never before has a man given her this much unwavering support. She feels like he'd lead the way around the world to protect her and prove she's okay. The look in his eyes also just defined the moment when she realizes she never wants to let him go.

She shakes her head, her eyes wet. "Wherever I live, I've got to keep you in my life."

He sweetly smiles. "I can't imagine you not in mine."

"I'll have to drive from Austin every weekend for a Nick-hug like that."

"I'll drive to Austin if that means I can get me some Tory-time."

She sniffles. "See? That's the good that comes from this. You and I. We got this."

He warmly squeezes her hands again. "Thank God we've got each other."

* * *

Tory drives on air all the way home. Nick's hug felt like a giant Band-Aid covering her ugly and open wounds. Every minute she spends with him electrifies her soul and her brain races through her calendar, trying to think of how and when she can see him next.

This feeling is new. It's a feeling of completeness. She's felt funny things before, around guys she's wanted to date. Those were twangs of pleasure that spun her dizzy head off of her shoulders and made her body hot from the neck down. With Nick, this feeling of wanting to be around him…is different. And it's much more intense than the friendship she had with him back when they both worked at Indigo.

Her phone chimes with an incoming text. There's no way in hell she's going to glance at her phone while driving. If she did something stupid and got into an accident…she can't imagine what that would do to Nick. She knows it's Nick texting her something funny, maybe about raisins or astronauts. And he probably texted the words backward, like the menu at Socat. She's figuring out his moves. It's easy. His moves are just like hers.

Tory turns into the long driveway of her parents' Shavano Park home. Dramatic landscape lights shine up the stone front of their two-story house and she presses her garage door opener to raise her side of their four-car garage. She pulls in, turns off her car, closes the garage and starts imagining the conversation she's about to have with her mom. She'll want to know if Nick is okay. And Tory knows exactly how she's going to answer.

She opens her car door while grabbing her phone out of her purse to check Nick's text.

Her mouth goes bitter.

It's not from Nick.

Who's your new boyfriend?

EIGHTEEN

Robyn stands in the middle of a parking space outside of Indigo, twisting her hands. She makes eye contact with Tory as she approaches in her car and Robyn steps aside. Tory swoops her car into the space and has the car parked, locked and herself inside Indigo's double front doors in less than thirty seconds.

She and Robyn move quickly, up the center staircase and to their office, where they close the door.

"I can't live like this," Tory says, her heart racing, peeking through Robyn's secret spy window to see if anyone by the name of Jake has followed them up the stairs.

"I'll walk you to and from your car for as long as you need," Robyn says.

Tory presses her hands to her face and takes a calming breath. "Thank you so much, Robyn. I plan to have this problem with Jake resolved this weekend."

Robyn's already sitting down, opening a computer file. "How?"

Tory sits at her desk and opens her laptop. "First, I'm going to apologize for how I broke up with him and then second, tell him to stop harassing me. I'm going to ask to meet in a public place, where my dad and another friend will be nearby in case I need help."

Her friend is Nick and he's been beside himself with concern and anger since Tory called him on Wednesday after getting Jake's text. Her dad shares the same concerns and insisted he come along too.

"I hope that works. At least your problem with Reed got resolved," Robyn says, typing.

Hardly. Just because he's not panting outside their office door begging to be pet doesn't mean that the animal has gone away. If anything, Tory is more concerned that Reed will try to get back at her for lashing out at him.

Jake. Reed. Nick. There're a lot of guys with problems in her life and of those three, she's only interested in helping one. At least Daniel isn't barking up her tree with some issue. Who would have imagined a day when the only "normal" guy in her life was…Daniel?

A knock sounds on their office door and it swings open. Blaine walks in.

Super. Enter guy number four with problems, and his biggest problem is himself.

"Hey," Tory says, glancing up to him then back down to her computer.

He slides over to the side of her desk so she can see him. "I just heard our building contractor's contract hasn't been approved. What's the hold up here?"

She stops typing. "The contractor you selected has an expired license."

"So? I'm approving him."

"You're opening yourself to potential legal issues if you do."

"Then I'll have someone else here sign it. Robyn?"

Robyn stops typing. "You want me to sign off on something that I know isn't right?"

"I want you to sign off on something that is going to help our business."

"…that isn't right," Robyn says.

Tory exhales. It hurts her head trying to talk logic with Blaine, especially legal logic. He's miles away from understanding how businesses actually work. He should go back to what he knows, like how bristles wear out faster if you don't hang brooms up. Or he could stick to what he does best: admiring himself in anything that reflects his face. He's doing it now, she can tell. He just ran his hand over his hair while looking at her computer screen.

"Look, Blaine, having someone else sign doesn't resolve the issue legally. If you like this contractor so much, then call him and get him to renew his license."

Blaine sneers. "That's going to slow my project down. And everything with you makes me have to do something."

"It's called work."

"Blaine?" Al says, standing in the doorway.

"What?" Blaine says, straightening. "Tory needs to call our contractor to get this license problem fixed."

"Tory?" Al asks.

"There may be bigger issues to work on today. And you might want to sit down to hear them."

Blaine crosses his arms. "I'm a big boy and I think I'll stand."

What a putz. Tory stands up too and looks Al in the eyes. "You're not going to believe this."

"Oh no. What now?"

"You've been serving alcohol for special events but you've never had a liquor license for anything more than beer and wine."

Al turns to Blaine. "All of this was something you were supposed to take care of."

Blaine looks indignant.

"It gets worse," Tory says. "You may have a problem getting liquor sales approved for the new coffee bar because of St. Mark's."

"The new church across the street?" Al asks.

"It's within three-hundred feet of here." Tory lowers her head, knowing her truth-bomb just unexpectedly exploded in Al's gut.

"How did this happen?" Al says, focused on Blaine.

Robyn stops typing and turns to watch.

"I don't know," Blaine says, sassy. "I didn't open the dang church. What does being within three-hundred feet have to do with anything?"

Al shakes his head.

"It's the zoning ordinance," Tory says. "Um, what keeps you legal. Since the church is there, you may have problems getting approved to sell liquor now. If you had your license in place before the church opened, it wouldn't be an issue."

"You need to go talk to the church," Al says to Blaine. "Meet them first and ask if they have any issues with our plan. I can deal with the city."

"I'm not telling anyone about our plan!" Blaine says. "It's bad enough our legal student here knows what we're doing. I don't want to spread the word around town so Nick Allen finds out."

Tory rubs her eyes.

"You're not understanding the point," Al says, frustrated.

Tory's cell phone buzzes against her desk. She glances down. It's Nick! *Shit!* She picks up her phone, sends it to voicemail, then turns the phone upside down. Her eyes flash up to see if Al and Blaine saw who it was.

"If you have to get that, don't let us stop you," Blaine says.

Did he see it was Nick? Or is he just being pithy? "It can wait."

Blaine rests his hands on his hips, facing Al. "So, I go to church and get a blessing and then what?"

Al's eyes bulge. Blaine appears to be pulling the last straw of Al's patience and for a split-second Tory is imagining Al changing his mind about turning over Indigo to Blaine's control. How fast can she find and pop some popcorn to watch the fireworks that would ensue?

Her phone sounds a voicemail chime. Good, Nick left a message. And good, Al or Blaine didn't see it was him calling.

"You and I need to step into my office," Al says to Blaine, a vein in his neck throbbing.

Tory's phone vibrates with a text. And then another one. She flips it over and quickly sees they're from Nick and both messages are long. She flips her phone back over and puts it down on her desk. Can these guys hit the road with their family battle so she can read Nick's texts?

Robyn inches forward, on the edge of her chair, eyes wide like she's watching her favorite disaster movie.

Tory's phone rings again. She looks down at it, lying facedown on her desk. *What the heck is going on?*

Al looks down at her ringing phone too. "Someone sure is trying to reach you."

"I'm certain it can wait." Though secretly, she can't. She's dying to know why Nick is trying to reach her. It must have something to do with Jake and their plan for this weekend. Maybe Nick has another idea and is trying to catch her before she sets up her meeting?

Al glares at Blaine. "My office. Now."

Al disappears from the doorway. Blaine slumps his shoulders and follows.

Robyn's face stretches with a smile. "That was awesome!"

Tory shakes her head. She'd love to celebrate the awesomeness of witnessing a verbal Blaine beating but she needs to check her phone. She picks it up, reads the text and then grabs her face in panic.

Nick's been arrested.

[NINETEEN]

"I have to go," Tory says to Robyn, clutching her phone.

Robyn spins around. "Is it crazy Jake?"

Tory closes her laptop and grabs her purse. "Jake is the least of my problems right now."

"I can walk you out." Robyn stands up. "Wait. Al and Blaine are probably going to come back looking for you."

Crap. "They will. Can you just…just tell them I had a situation and had to leave but will be right back."

"What is it?"

Tory's hands shake as she replies to Nick.

On my way now and I'm calling my dad to represent you

Tory looks at Robyn. "No one is hurt, but I've got to take care of something. You should stay here in case they come back soon. I'll walk fast to my car and be okay." If this is the moment Jake wants to ambush her, he will have picked a very bad moment.

Robyn nods.

Tory rushes out of the office, reading Nick's texts while

she swoops down the center staircase. She's through the front door within seconds and has her dad's number already pulled up on her phone. As soon as she shuts her car door, she calls him.

"Hey, honey," John says, answering her call.

She backs out of her parking space. "Dad, I have a problem."

"What? Is it Jake?"

"No, not Jake. It's Nick. He's been arrested."

"No! How could they have finished their investigation this quickly?"

"I don't know. Can you help him?"

"I'm packing up right now. Where are you?"

"I just left Indigo. If you leave now, you'll beat me there."

"What are the charges?"

"His text said vehicular manslaughter."

"Okay. Second degree felony but it's his first offense so he should be able to get out on bail."

Tory stops at a traffic light downtown. So far, she's hit every damn one since leaving Indigo. "You know I wouldn't ask this unless it was important to me, but can we pay his bail?"

She hears her dad moving papers around and the phone sounds like he's got it squished between his ear and his cheek. "Absolutely."

"It's going to be $10,000."

"For what Nick did for you, we owe him," he says.

She lets out a huge breath of relief, now on the interstate.

"Thank you, Dad. You know I owe him my life."

* * *

The drive to the Bear County Sherriff's office feels like an eternity. Finally, she pulls into the parking lot and parks next to her dad's car.

Since she's been driving, she hasn't been able to text with him. Hopefully he's already got the paperwork rolling to get Nick released.

She barrels through the front door, only to wind up in line behind two other people at the reception counter. Her breath is hard to catch, from fear of what is happening behind an imposing set of double glass doors that obviously leads somewhere most people aren't allowed to go. She's also intimidated by this place. On the wall behind the counter is a massive painting of their seal with the motto: Protect and Defend. One of the visuals in their seal is a pair of handcuffs. God, she hopes Nick wasn't arrested at Faze and led through his own business in handcuffs.

The couple ahead of her are arguing about some traffic infraction and Tory begins to weigh what the charges would be if she jumps over the counter and runs through those double doors to the back area to find Nick herself.

The lights in this receptionist area are bright and harsh, the surrounding walls are too white and no one is smiling. Guess she needs to get used to this, being in law. Chances are stations like this are where she'll go to see and free her clients.

Isn't there anyone else to help here? Tory taps her foot as the couple starts to speak louder and grow more aggravated. Then Tory sees movement down the hall, through the closed glass doors. Dad! He's come out of a side room and is walking her way. Nick is behind him!

Her heart melts seeing the two of them, teamed up and

walking her way. *Be professional. Like a lawyer.* But what she really wants to do is run toward them like a teenager seeing their favorite boy band and scream for joy and hug them both.

Nick nods that he sees her. He looks relieved, happy even. *Oh, thank God.* She was imagining the worst and wondering if this might have thrown him into a dark depression.

Her heart beats harder as they walk through the doors. He's out! Her dad turns so Nick can approach her first.

Be professional. She hugs him, quickly, barely giving him a squeeze but he grabs her back with a hug so tight she's worried he'll hurt his healing shoulder. *Screw professional.* She closes her eyes and buries her face in his shoulder.

They say nothing, holding each other as if they are both afraid of letting go. Finally, Tory relaxes her hold and steps back to look him over. "Are you okay?"

He gives her a caring smile. "Now that you two are here." He glances back to John. "I thought today's big development would be that my insurance adjuster would finally get to see my car. The fact that they've completed their investigation and brought these charges is ridiculously shocking."

She turns to her dad and gives him a hug. "Thank you so much for coming so fast."

"Of course." He lets her go and nods to a corner for more privacy. They go over and huddle close. "We've got our work cut out for us," John says in a low voice.

Nick looks to Tory. "The main crux of their case against me is that I didn't maintain my car, which recklessly caused the death of another person."

"His tires were bald and the wiper blades had multiple cracks," John says.

"That's not how you kept your car, so your innocence should be easy to prove," she says.

John shakes his head. "Not when all of Nick's maintenance records have conveniently disappeared from Reed's."

"What!? Are you fucking kidding me?"

"All of them," Nick says, nodding with disbelief. "Even the oil changes where they ran a standard diagnostic report on my car. Those reports always had the tire tread and overall tire condition."

"What about your records that you gave them?"

"They've discredited them. There was no logo or anything official on the receipt so they are alleging that I forged them."

"Impossible. Then follow the money. The credit card company will have a record of the transaction."

John shakes his head.

Nick looks down.

"What?" Tory asks.

Nick looks back up. "I always pay in cash, except for major purchases. All of my car expenses I paid with cash."

Her head slowly rolls back.

"Listen," John says. "I'm going to go back in there and take a second look at some things. I don't want to waste any time."

Nick nods. "Thank you, John."

"We've got a long road ahead of us. My job is to prove your innocence so that this long road gets a whole lot shorter."

"Dad, thank you for dropping everything to do this." Tory hugs him again. "I don't know how Nick could have gotten out if you hadn't posted bail."

John raises an eyebrow. "I didn't post bail." He looks to Nick.

Tory turns. Nick's eyes light up with pride as if he's discovered a treasure buried beneath all of this legal rubble. "Did you bail yourself out?"

He shakes his head. "No."

Tory's eyes dart between them, both of them now looking like they've got a bombshell of wondrous news to drop on her. "If you didn't bail yourself out, and my dad didn't either, then who did?"

Nick excitedly smiles. "My stepbrother."

Tory feels like she's been swept off of the ground. "Your brother? Out of nowhere? He did this?"

Nick nods. "He's in town and wants to see me."

Whoa! Then why isn't he here?

John smiles. "This is the best news that has come out of this day. And I think you should go see him now. Honey," he turns to Tory, "can you drive Nick?"

She's floating with elation. Nick's brother has actually done something good and now this? Her dad is okay with her and Nick riding in the same car? After all of the bad luck surrounding Nick and cars, her dad trusts that his daughter will be okay?

She looks to John, then to Nick, then back to John. "Hell yeah I can drive him."

* * *

"Left on Broad Street," Nick reads from the GPS map on his phone, navigating while Tory drives.

It's late afternoon and Tory has already decided that her work day is a total loss. She texted Robyn and told her what happened with Nick and that she won't be back today but will be in tomorrow. She'd rather work on Saturday to make up for lost time than miss this opportunity to take Nick to see his brother.

"How long has it been since you've seen him?"

"Wow. Well, in the eight years since our dad died, I've seen him maybe three or four times?"

"Is he married?"

"Yes, with a daughter." He looks to his phone. "Right on Hubbard."

She takes the turn, not familiar with this side of town. Storefronts look like they were built in the seventies and several of them look vacant. They pass an old-fashioned gas station, one with only four pumps and a two-car garage for car repairs. She makes a quick lane change to avoid getting stuck behind a stopped city bus.

"Why have you and your brother been estranged?"

"We were never close to begin with. You know my dad remarried and my mom was a lot younger than my stepmom. My brother and I are twenty-four years apart with not much in common. Plus, he's busy with his career. I don't know too much about what he does because he never talks with me."

Tory drives in silence, remembering what her mom said. Blended families can be complicated and there're two sides to every story. She can't believe she's about to meet the other side.

"I wonder how he knew you had been arrested?"

"I have no idea." He looks down to his phone. "Turn right on Oak Street, and it's on the left." He points to a hotel, a four-story, typical chain hotel.

"This hotel?"

"Yeah. See, this is how vague he always is. All he said in this note he left at the station is to park and walk to the front and someone will tell me where he is. I guess he means we go inside to the front desk and ask for him."

"Okay." Tory puts the car in park. Why wouldn't he come out to meet them? Is this guy a criminal or something, like in organized crime? Is that why he didn't hang out at the police station, waiting? Maybe that's why he doesn't reach out to Nick. Is isolating him his way of protecting his little brother?

Tory and Nick get out of her BMW. Few cars are in the hotel parking lot and even fewer people are walking around. The only noise comes from traffic passing by on the road behind them.

The hair on her arms bristles. If Nick's brother is part of some organized crime ring, she wants no part of this. Her dad can pay this dude back the $10,000 and Nick can cut his ties. Nick has enough trouble. He doesn't need crap from a long-lost relative bringing him down.

Nick nods toward the main entrance and they move that way. At least it's still light outside. This would be totally creepy if they were doing this at night. Nick glances to her and she's pretty sure she's not doing a very good job of hiding her worry. He breathes in deep and takes her hand.

Okay. Fine. Holding hands with Nick is cool and sure makes her feel better, as long as some machine-gun toting hit man doesn't swing through this parking lot and wipe them out. *Ugh, be real.* Her imagination is working in overdrive. Tory squeezes her purse with her other arm. No need to watch for machine guns. *Just watch your purse.*

They walk past a heavily tattooed woman with a short, choppy haircut who is leaning against a side entrance door, smoking a cigarette. Tory squeezes Nick's hand as they pass her, now only a few feet away from the hotel entrance.

"Nick," the woman calls out from behind them. They both stop and turn.

"Yes?" he says.

She smiles, flips her cigarette on the sidewalk and grinds it out with her boot. She gestures with her head to the side door.

Tory's chest is beating so hard, it feels like it's moving her blouse. This is so super sketchy she's questioning why her own father would let her traipse off into the unknown with a guy who is known to be trouble, just to visit with some family member the known-to-be-trouble guy doesn't really know. Oh hell, she has no one to blame for putting her in this spot but her!

The woman opens the side door. Nick lets go of Tory's hand as he walks inside and she follows him. He turns back to read her expression and then takes her hand again. They follow the strange woman down a hall of guest rooms, turn to the right and continue walking down an even longer hallway.

Tory's squeezing Nick's hand hard and squeezing her purse even harder. No one says anything. All Tory knows is that the woman leading them down the hall reeks of cigarettes but she did have a nice smile that seemed oddly trustworthy.

The woman stops at a door, room 1564, and knocks three times. She inserts a key card, turns the knob and glances to her left and to her right before catching Nick's eyes. She smiles, nods and pushes the door open.

Tory's eyes feel like they are the size of dinner plates. Nick looks to her and then leads the way, walking into the room. She takes a deep breath and the brave steps to follow him.

Two lamps softly light the room, a standard-looking king room. Nick lets go of her hand just as the door closes behind her. The cigarette-smelling, tattooed lady has disappeared.

A man gets up from a desk in the room. He's short, a few inches shorter than Nick, but she sees the similarity in their eyes and expressions. He doesn't have a trendy five o'clock shadow like Nick but he is attractive and looks incredibly fit, like Nick. His eyes look relieved with a conflicted mix of happy and sad and he hasn't taken his eyes off of his brother.

"Nick," he says with a sincere smile that makes Tory's heart happy. He opens his arms and Nick opens his for a hug that seems to have three phases: initial, tight and even tighter. Their fingertips dig into each other's backs.

Nick pulls back. "I can't believe you're here and came to help me."

His brother smiles. "I have many years to make up to you."

Tory wants to squeal with happiness for Nick. The man with no family does have family, and this guy doesn't seem to be some monster. He looks like a super nice, fun and likely kick-ass kind of guy.

His eyes find Tory and Nick turns to her, seemingly remembering that he hasn't introduced her yet.

"Tory," Nick says, standing proud. "This is my brother, Frank Allen."

[TWENTY]

"Frank," Tory says, stepping to shake his hand.

His grip is warm, sending her nothing but comfortable, good vibes. His grip is also so strong she imagines he could probably crack a walnut in his bare hands if he wanted to.

"Tory, it's a pleasure to meet you," Frank says. "I guess if you're standing here then those directions made sense."

"Perfect sense, until the part where a mystery woman led us inside. Not gonna lie, I thought that was a little sketchy," she says.

Frank's smile puts her at ease. "I'm sorry about that. I'm on a case and unfortunately, my identity may have been compromised so I have to lie low for a few more hours."

"Is this the part where you finally tell me what you do?" Nick asks.

Frank looks to them both. "I work on fugitive recovery teams for the FBI."

Whoa. "Wow, I didn't expect that," Tory says.

"You always told me what you do is on a need-to-know basis," Nick says.

"I did. It's not that it's a secret to family and friends, but I don't openly tell people what I do."

"Or you never trusted me to keep a secret," Nick says.

Frank's expression sinks. "I've always seen you as someone much younger, and I know now that you aren't."

"Do you stay hidden, all of the time?" Tory asks.

"Oh no, just right now," Frank says. "We should be able to nab this suspect by the morning and then I go back to being a normal person."

Seems legit. Except for the part about the tattooed woman. "The woman who led us inside, is she your body-guard?"

He smiles. "She could be, but no. Daniella's my partner. Do either of you want anything to drink?"

Nick shakes his head and Tory does the same.

"Sit down," Frank says, sweeping his hand to offer a chair or the bed or the desktop. Nick sits on the low dresser. Tory puts her purse down on the bed and sits beside it. Frank sits in the desk chair.

As excited as Tory was for Nick's emotional reunion, she's downright giddy knowing Frank works for the FBI. *This is huge!* He must be here to help and she's anxious to get to work and start picking his mind about Nick's case.

"First," Nick says, "thank you for bailing me out."

"Of course. Sorry I couldn't stay until you were released."

Nick nods to Tory. "Tory's dad is a lawyer and was there to get the paperwork done."

Frank smiles at Tory. "Good. Very helpful." He turns back to Nick. "And I'm sorry to hear about the accident. Both of them. You look good though."

Nick holds out his hands, still a bit splotchy from his

accident with Sienna. "Some visible reminders still. Many invisible reminders though."

"I wish I could have helped you through the first accident. I was out of the country at the time."

Nick nods.

"I'm here now though. Once this case wraps up, I can stay here and help you through this."

Tory wants to clap her hands. "So, is the FBI taking on this case?"

"No, no...this isn't a case for the FBI. But I certainly can lend my expertise and the perspective I have to help prove your innocence."

"I haven't even explained what happened but you already think I'm innocent?" Nick asks.

"I do."

Nick's eyes glow with pride.

Frank looks to Tory. "Tell me a little about you. How long have you and Nick been dating?"

Tory's mouth flies open. "Um, well, we're not dating." Her face feels flush and she glances at Nick, whose eyes are lit with surprise. "I'm your brother's number one fan though."

"She's my rock right now," Nick says. "Tory was also Quinn's best friend."

"Is," Tory says. "I am Quinn's best friend. I will be her best friend forever."

Frank nods. "I'm sorry for your loss too."

"That's why I have a lot of skin in this game. I want to prove Nick is innocent and find out who killed my best friend."

"We're lucky to have your dad on our side then too. I'd like to meet him at some point. What do you do?"

"I'm a two-L at Texas Law."

Frank's expression softens. "Ah, a two-L. Only one year to go. How do you like it?"

"I love it."

Frank turns to Nick. "Seems like you are in good hands with Tory and her father."

"I don't know how I would be handling this without her." Nick dips his chin and looks to her with appreciative eyes.

Frank's eyes flash between them.

"So now," Nick says, "my world changed this morning with this arrest and I need to fight for my life."

"I've read the police report and the arrest warrant. But I'd like to know what really happened, with this case and also with the accident you had earlier, to know if they're related."

"They aren't related," Nick says.

"I think they are," Tory blurts. All eyes in the room go to her.

"You do?" Nick asks.

Frank's eyes narrow, his expression thirsting for details. "How?"

"I'll cut to the short version. Reed Brown of Reed's Motors is a nasty person who lives on revenge and is trying to get Nick back for two things."

Frank tilts his head. Tory continues.

"A while ago, I think Reed's Motors was trying to sell a vintage Mustang known to have problems. They don't have a good track record of selling the best cars, and my dad can tell you more about our own problems with Reed's. Anyway, I think Nick happened to be the one who bought the car. Then it did have problems, accidently killing one of their own family members. Sienna Brown is Reed's sister and she was driving Nick's car when it exploded."

Nick interrupts. "Sienna and I were only on our second date and I let her drive the Mustang because she loved it so much. She said it had been at her family's dealership for a while and she used to sit in it all the time but her parents wouldn't let her get it. So it didn't seem to be an odd request when she asked me to drive it."

Tory picks back up. "It was ruled an accident and Nick was never charged."

"And how do you connect it to the accident with Quinn?" Frank asks.

"I think Reed's was afraid of discovery if Nick had sued. I think they've built an auto empire on deceit, selling unsafe and bad cars for years."

"You think the second accident is revenge?" Frank asks.

"I think it was to keep Nick quiet forever."

"Tory, you never told me you thought this. We never talked about all of the dots connecting like this," Nick says.

"I didn't want you to think I was crazy."

"How could they have caused the second accident?" Frank asks.

"I think they switched out his tires and wiper blades at the concert."

Frank rubs his chin.

"Nick told me he and Quinn saw a Reed's Roadside truck up there and that's suspicious because they don't service that area. While Nick and Quinn were in the concert, I think they changed out his tires and wipers, knowing a storm was coming and knowing how remote the area was and how hilly the drive would be on the way home."

"That's plausible," Frank says. "But if they did this, then they wouldn't like the news today that Nick was arrested."

"Exactly. His criminal charges open it up for discovery. To be blunt, I think they probably panicked when Nick survived the accident."

"Of course," Nick says. "Instead of just recovering from an accident, now I'm fighting for the truth."

Frank stares intently at Tory. "You really don't like Reed, do you?"

"I don't. And I know how vindictive he can be. He just pulled a sneaky move on me at work to remind me."

"And," Nick adds, "he and I have a history."

"Okay," Frank says. "Let me reach out to my contacts and see if anyone knows someone at Reed's."

"Like, someone who already works there?" Tory asks.

"We may already have a source there, or one of our sources has access to someone there who can sniff around."

"But anything he finds wouldn't be admissible in court, right?" Tory asks.

"Depends on what he finds. Also, people on the ground like this can also smell the fire so the lawyer can prove the fire is there," Frank says.

"How many 'guys' you got?" Nick asks.

"As many as we need. I'd like to begin with a source at Reed's Motors and then also get someone to start trailing Reed himself. We need to watch him. If he wanted Nick quiet once, he may want him quiet again."

Tory's stomach tightens.

"I didn't think about how vulnerable I was," Nick says.

"In some ways, having these charges protects me. If anything happens to me now…"

"It could look like someone was trying to cover up your search for the truth," Frank says.

"These people we need to hire, I can cover these costs," Nick says.

Frank shakes his head. "No, I'd like to pay for any expenses."

"Just because you haven't been around doesn't mean you have to do something financially now."

Frank looks down to his lap and then back up to Nick. "I was your age now when you were born. I felt like Dad put all of his time into his new life with you and your mom. I froze you in my mind as the kid who was nothing but a handful of mischief growing up."

Tory grins at Nick, imagining how cute and fun he must have been as a young boy.

"I was the older one and I should have done more than I did keeping up with you over the years. Especially when Dad died."

Nick takes a hard swallow.

"I'm sorry, Nick, for not being in your life. Helping you now is the only way I know how to make it up to you."

Nick nods. "It takes two to be brothers. I could have done more to reach out to you too."

They share a caring smile.

"Um," Nick says. "What do you mean I was mischief growing up?"

Frank smirks and looks at Tory. "One year, at Thanksgiving, I was taking a nap on the couch and he put softened butter all over my hands."

"Epic." Tory grins.

Nick shrugs.

"Okay," Frank says, standing up. "I wish we could visit longer but I need to meet with Daniella about the fugitive situation we are working on."

"Let's regroup tomorrow?" Nick asks.

"I don't know when this will be wrapped up, so I'll be in touch to confirm. But, yes, that would be good."

Nick hops off of the dresser. Tory sinks her hands into the bed to stand up and the bed bounces, making her purse pop up. The purse tumbles to the floor, spilling everything.

Shit! She falls on her knees, rushing to push her stuff back in.

Nick throws his hands up with shock. "Tory!"

"Stop!" Frank barks in a tone that means business.

She freezes, kneeling on the floor, bent over the spilled contents of her purse and her big secret now lying in plain sight.

"You carry a gun?" Nick softly asks.

"Watch how you handle that," Frank says.

She never wanted anyone to know she has this. She only has it in case she has to defend herself! Carefully, she slips her gun back into her purse, along with her makeup and other crap. She gets off of her knees to face them.

"You got a Glock?" Frank says. "That's what we use."

"I do," she mutters.

Frank looks skeptical. "Do you know how to use it?"

"Yeah. I took the class I needed to get my permit."

"But," Frank says, lowering his eyes, "do you know how to use it?"

She takes a hard swallow. "If I have to use it, I know how."

"That's the Cadillac of guns. No safety either," Frank says, concerned.

Nick brushes her arm. "Have you always carried a gun?"

She looks to him. "It's a recent purchase. I thought…I wanted something to defend myself with…in case Jake showed up."

"Oh no." Nick rests his hand on her shoulder. "I knew you were worried but I didn't think he affected you this much."

Her fear pours into her eyes. "He affects me that much."

Frank crosses his arms. "And who is Jake?"

Dirty laundry time. "A guy I dated briefly and just broke up with. His texts went from salty to nasty to letting me know he's watching me. I…I have my reasons for wanting this. I'm legal in carrying it. I just preferred that no one knew I had it."

"I understand," Frank says, uncrossing his arms. "But I have two concerns."

She sucks in a breath, feeling like Frank's about to scold her like he's *her* big brother too.

"First, that you completely understand how to operate that gun. And if you aren't comfortable, I can take you to a range and get you comfortable. And second, if you have an ex who is following you, and we are meeting and gathering evidence to exonerate Nick, that means we all have an extra set of eyes watching us."

* * *

Highway lights speed by as Tory drives home. Nick stares straight ahead in the passenger seat beside her, his eyes distant.

"Thank you for sharing this with me," she says in a low voice, glancing his way. "This experience…meeting your brother. I know that was a huge moment for you and I'm glad you included me."

He drags a hand through his hair. "I can't believe he's here."

She passes under a highway sign indicating the exit to her parents' home. "Are you sure you want me to go straight home? It's no bother for me to drive you back to your apartment."

"No…no," he says. "I want to know you're home and safe. I'll Uber back to my place."

She veers off of the highway. Only a few cars are on the road in this evening hour.

Nick breaks out of his stare and looks around the car.

She knows: he's looking for her purse. "Does it bother you, that I have a gun?"

He glances to the backseat floor where her purse is, then he turns to look at her. "I'm more surprised. And like Frank, I want to be sure you know how to use it. But no, it doesn't bother me that you have it. What bothers me more is how I didn't pick up on how worried you were becoming. I was too wrapped up in myself to notice and that's not right."

Tory takes the final turn into her neighborhood and in minutes is pulling up the long brick driveway of her parents' home. She opens her side of the garage, pulls in and parks. Without saying a word, they both get out of her car.

Nick fiddles with his phone, ordering a ride. "They'll be here in four minutes."

Chirping crickets provide the musical background and a soft wind provides some temperature relief as they walk together toward the street to meet Nick's ride.

"What a day," she says.

"After I was arrested, I went from feeling hopeless to feeling like I'm on top of the world. Between your dad and now Frank, I feel like I can fight anything."

She leans in to him, brushing his arm. "You can."

He stops to face her. "I can do all of this because of you, Tory. You're the one who's lifting me highest, the one believing in me the most. Your dad has incredible legal knowledge and Frank has these secret spy skills but if I didn't have you by my side, I'd still feel lost."

She looks down to her feet. "I'm happy to help."

He covers her hands with his own and his touch brings her eyes to his. *Not unusual.* He's held her hand before. But he's not taking her hand to lead her somewhere, or holding it to comfort her. It's just him and her, standing under the cream-colored light of the moon, hand-in-hand and now eye-to-eye.

"You mean a lot to me, Tory," he whispers through a soft smile.

"You mean a lot to me too."

Headlights sweep over the road from a car turning down her street. In seconds, his ride will be here.

His eyes search her face and slowly he eases his hold of her hands. He lifts his finger and her eyes follow, watching as he gently brushes back a strand of her hair, moving with the evening breeze.

His ride pulls up to the curb.

Nick's expressive eyes are seeking something, some sign or signal, she's not sure what he's looking for. She's standing in a world filled with air but somehow on this driveway she can't find enough air to breathe.

He leans in and presses a soft kiss on her cheek.

Then he steps away, a relaxed smile tipping the corner of his mouth.

She smiles too, watching the profile of his body dark against the moonlight as he walks toward the street. He opens the car door and the inside light gives her a couple of seconds to watch him get in and close the door. Slowly the car pulls away and she waits until the faint glow of taillights has faded into the night before clutching her chest.

What the hell just happened?

[TWENTY-ONE]

Bright light from the rising sun blinds Tory just as she pulls into the parking lot at Indigo. She glances to the side to avoid the sun's glare and sees plenty of open parking spaces on this Saturday morning. Except for one space on the far left. That's Al's space and his black Cadillac SUV is here.

She parks next to his SUV, glances in her rearview mirror and rushes out of her car, squeezing her purse as she quickly walks toward Indigo's double glass doors. Squeezing her purse has a different meaning after last night. Now that Nick and Frank know she carries a gun, part of her is still embarrassed, but relieved. It exposed her weakness: that she's afraid. But it also showed her strength: that she's done something about it. Still, there's something about Frank and how he picked up on her lack of confidence with the gun. How can one man have such reassuring eyes that also seem to pierce her secrets?

Now inside Indigo's lobby, before she heads up the center staircase, she pauses. She *needs* a cup of coffee, not only to wake her up but to clarify her thinking after meeting Frank last night and especially after getting a friendly or maybe more-than-friendly kiss from Nick.

One of her favorite baristas, Tyler, is working today and he nods that he's seen her. He's already pouring her dark roast coffee, black.

"Morning, you guys," Tory says to everyone behind the counter, paying for her coffee.

"Working on a Saturday?" Tyler asks.

"Yeah, I got a little behind yesterday." She takes her steaming cup.

"Al's up there too," he says. "Hey, if you don't mind, can you take him this? I didn't have the Virunga brewed when he was down here earlier."

"Virunga?" Tory asks, carefully taking the hot cup that he's handing her. "Is this another regional Rwandan flavor?"

"Yep. Today's special," he says.

Tory nods. *Virunga. Virunga. Virunga.* At least she can try to memorize the name and sound impressive when handing this to Al, even though she agrees with Robyn that these coffee blends are becoming too exotic to remember.

With each step up the center stairs, she carefully balances the cups. Her coffee cup feels hot but Al's feels boiling hot. *Virunga. Vur. Rung. Gah. Virunga.* There's no way she'll remember this.

She passes the closed door of her office to go straight to Al and unload his Rwandan special. Down the hall she sees his office door is open. The lights inside are on and as she gets closer she hears his voice.

"You've disappointed me," she overhears him say. "What happened yesterday should have never happened and you need to fix it."

Tory pauses. Is Blaine in there? Or is Al on the phone?

She hears him slam down a phone. Poor Al. Yesterday must have been awful. Nothing that Blaine is working on is going well. So much for Al's dream of righting the wrongs and having the business ready for his son so Al can enjoy a smooth-sailing retirement cruise. Al probably spent most of the day pulling strings just to get the Indigo ship upright.

"Hey. Al?" Tory calls, several steps away from his door. She doesn't want him to think she was eavesdropping.

"Yes?" Al calls out.

Tory walks into his office, offering him a smile. "Coffee delivery." She walks in quickly, putting his coffee cup on his desk rather than hand it to him. "Dang that was hot," she says, shaking her hand and completely forgetting what the hell his coffee was called.

"What a Saturday surprise," Al says. "Were you standing there long?"

"Nope. That was burning my hand." She points to the cup. "Tyler said they just brewed it for you."

"And that's another thing not working. These daily blends need to be brewed and ready and this morning, this wasn't. Thank you though. What are you doing here and what happened yesterday?"

She lowers her head. "I'm sorry I had to leave in the middle of the day."

"More like morning."

"Yeah, morning. I came in today to make up the time."

He sips his coffee and leans back in his chair, rocking. "You went off to save Nick Allen, didn't you? I heard he was arrested."

Shoot! "Yes. It took many of us by surprise."

"Not me," he says, rocking forward and planting his elbows

on the top of his desk. "I've been warning you that he's trouble. And now, arrested in front of his customers? The shock and awe is never going to end when it comes to Nick."

Arrested in front of his customers? She didn't know that.

"Al, I can assure you that I am keeping Indigo work completely separate."

His eyes squeeze with doubt. "The lines do seem to be getting blurry."

She stands, silent.

"You left me in the middle of a big situation," he says. "I sent Blaine back to work with you and you were gone."

"I'll make it all up today."

"City offices are closed on Saturday. You can't make calls on our behalf to zoning offices that aren't open."

"I realize. But I can have my lists organized for those calls on Monday."

"Tory." He swivels in his chair and stands, edging to the side of the desk, closer to her. "You've been a good, loyal employee to us, years ago when you were a barista and for the few weeks you have been up here. And for the few weeks you have left, I need you to remain loyal."

"I understand."

"And here."

She nods.

"You've not heeded my advice to stay away from Nick. Now, he's been arrested for manslaughter for killing your best friend. You shouldn't be running off to save him. You should be running away from him."

She sucks in a breath. Her growing temper is starting to feel as hot as the cup of coffee in her hand. "Thank you, Al. I have my reasons for wanting to help Nick. And I promise you, I am keeping business out of it." *Except the cookies. Damn it, Nick knows all about the cookies.*

He squints. "Thanks again for bringing up my coffee." He turns and goes back to his chair, taking a seat and opening a folder on his desk.

Okay, then. Tory turns and walks out of his office, heading for hers. She deserved that. Part of that. She unlocks her door, flips on the light, steps inside, places her coffee on the corner of her desk, slips her purse under it and then closes the door behind her.

Splashed all over her desk are handwritten notes from Blaine, filled with exclamation points and scribbled either in anger or with the penmanship of a ten-year-old, or maybe both. She sits down and begins to sort through the notes.

This isn't good. She really did leave them at a bad time, putting Nick ahead of her job and for no reason. Her dad handled everything at the jail, so there was no need for her to drop work and go. She had already lost a week of work when Quinn died. And now judging from the look on Al's face, a glowing recommendation letter from him might be on the line.

Elbows on her desk, she buries her face in her hands.

Work is a mess and she's not doing a good job at it.

The fear of Reed keeps her locked behind her damn door.

Not knowing where Jake is has led her to buy a weapon she's still not confident she knows how to use. And now that Nick and her dad have more important things to work on, their "Jake sting" this weekend is obviously not going to happen, leaving her with more uncertain days.

She's fueled with vengeance, chasing a wild hunch that revenge has motivated Reed to kill.

And she aches with emptiness, missing the caring ear, glowing smile and fresh boho vibe from her best friend.

She's back at school. Quinn's just back at school.

Tory takes a slow, drawn out sip of her coffee.

Her best friend. What would Quinn think of Nick's lips on her cheek last night? This closeness Tory feels with Nick could go bad in a thousand ways and first on the list is how they're both betraying Quinn.

Her phone rings. She hunches over and drops her head, certain it must be Nick. What should she say? *"Good morning, hot lips. When ya gonna plant one on my cheek again?"* She pulls her phone out of her purse.

Thank God! It's Daniel.

"Boy oh boy, do we need to talk," she says, answering the phone.

"Oh, honey yes we do because you're never going to believe what happened," Daniel says.

Tory pinches her lips. "Can you top being arrested yesterday, re-discovering your long-estranged brother and then pressing your lips on the side of a friend's face with a kiss that could have a hundred different meanings?"

"No…why would I do all of that?"

She rolls her eyes. "Then tell me, sweetie, what happened."

"Listen to this. Last night, at Hamburger Mary's, I met a guy named Taco."

Having Daniel in her life *gives* her life.

"Taco?" she asks. "A guy with the same name as the food that makes your groin tingle?"

"It's a holy sign."

"Wait, you were at Hamburger Mary's? Did you meet Taco during the drag show and if so, are you sure Taco is a man?"

There's a long pause. "Well, it was Dining with the Divas but he looked and acted like a man to me."

"Let me guess," Tory says. "You want to go back tonight and you want me to go with you."

"Would you, please?"

"Daniel, I haven't really gone anywhere but home and work, and one time to a taco place at the Pearl, and I guess if you count the jail yesterday, then that's it."

"You went to a taco place at the Pearl without me?"

Tory rubs her eyelids, close to laughing. Mentioning "jail" and "arrested" can't get Daniel's attention but if she said "hard shell or soft shell" he'd be all ears.

"I had to research it to know if it was good enough for you."

There's a long pause. "I didn't know you weren't going out yet."

"Yeah, listen, I have a long, long list of stories to tell you."

"Meet for lunch?" he asks.

"I'm at Indigo, making up for a lost day yesterday."

"How did you lose yesterday?"

"Nick was arrested."

He gasps.

Finally! Got his attention!

"Nick? Mother of God, are you kidding? Stop!"

"Not kidding. Can't stop. Jesus has a mother but God does not. Why don't you bring lunch up here and we can catch up?"

"I would in a hot second except for the part where I hate Indigo."

"No one is here except Al and he's cool. It's Saturday! Trust me, Blaine would never come in on a Saturday."

Daniel stays quiet for a few seconds. "Nick really was arrested? You've got to be reeling."

"I am."

She hears him breathe in deep. "I'll be there in a few hours with something fabulous for lunch."

"Thank you, Daniel."

A couple of hours fly by when Tory hears a soft knock on her door.

"Yoo-hoo? Is this you?" Daniel's muffled voice calls through the door.

"Yoo-hoo, it's true!" She opens the door. He's stylishly dressed in slim white jeans, an untucked, checkered blue button-down shirt and flip-flops.

"Girl, I've been knocking on every closed door up here." He walks into her office, balancing a Raising Cane's food bag and two drinks. "Down the hall I think I knocked on a closet door but you know I came out of that a long time ago."

You nut. "When you worked here, you never spent any time on the second floor, did you?" she asks, closing the door.

"Hell no. With Blaine and his anti-gay rants, I avoided upstairs at all costs." Daniel lays the food bag on Robyn's desk. "Best thing I ever did was tell him off and impulsively quit that day."

"Blaine is a terminal jerk." She squeezes Daniel in a hug. "Thank you for the delivery."

He squeezes her hard and lets go. "I have missed you, sugar lips."

Sugar lips. Lips? Nick's lips? Now she's thinking about lips. "You don't know how timely that is."

He reaches into the bag, stained with greasy deliciousness. "I was in the mood for something fried, so good news, you get fried food too!" He hands her a wrapper with chicken tenders inside, neatly spreads out a napkin on his lap and starts eating his food.

"How long has it been since we've done something like this?" she asks, taking a bite of chicken tender.

"Um," he mumbles, chewing. "We've never picnicked in your office like this."

"I meant you and me, eating or hanging out or whatever."

"Quinn's funeral was the last time I saw you."

"I'm sorry I've been AWOL. I dove into this mission to find out who caused Quinn's accident and I've lost track of time, and friends."

"Who caused Quinn's accident? Is this a question where Nick isn't the answer?"

"A lot has happened. Turns out the detectives discovered bald tires and disintegrating windshield wipers on Nick's car. But that's not how Nick kept his car. We think someone switched out his tires and wiper blades while he and Quinn were in the concert."

"No…"

"Things are getting complicated. Then, after Nick was arrested yesterday, his brother emerged out of nowhere to bail him out."

"No…"

"And to make this long story short, I'm feeling closer and closer to Nick and he kissed me last night."

Daniel throws his napkin down. "No way! Like, a shift?"

"A shift?"

"Tongue on tongue."

"Oh God Daniel, no."

"A snog?"

"What the hell's a snog?"

"Open mouth kiss."

"No! He pecked the side of my cheek in what could be a friendly kiss, or it could be something more, so what do you call a kiss like that?"

"Oh, that's just a Yankee dime."

"Okay then, that's what it was."

"Wow, he Yankee dimed you? This is huge."

"I know. It's amazing and awful at the same time. I can't do this. Quinn really, really liked Nick. I can't even think about liking him too."

"Do you like him?"

"Yes, I do. I always have. But Quinn liked him more so I did everything I could to open the door for her. It was supposed to be her and Nick."

"What is it about this troublemaker that has all you girls going crazy?"

"Nick isn't trouble!"

"Look, you know my thoughts on the subject. Even though I've gotten to know Nick a little more, especially seeing him the night of the accident and all, I still think you're playing with fire."

"The only fire that will happen is if I start something with him. It's only been two weeks since the accident! It's so wrong to Quinn."

"So, you think his Yankee dime was meant to start something?"

"I think Nick had one of the biggest emotional days of his life yesterday. I'm probably reading more into his kiss than he intended. But I have to bring it up to him and clear the air right from the start. If he did mean to start something, I have to tell him."

"What?"

Her throat feels tight. "I have to tell him I can't."

Five o'clock. Quitting time.

On a normal day, it would be. For Tory, she has days of work still ahead of her. Daniel left a few hours ago but the mouth-watering smell of chicken tenders still lingers in her office. Her eyes wander over to her phone, lying next to her keyboard. She hasn't heard from Nick all day. This morning, she was afraid he might call and wouldn't know what to say if he had. This afternoon, she's wondering why he hasn't even texted.

Maybe he's regretting the Yankee dime. Or is the ball in her court? What's the protocol, post Yankee dime? This kind of crap is complicated for normal hot-blooded, relationship-seeking people. She's not relationship seeking and she didn't think he was either, making this five-layer bean-dip complicated. *Five-layer bean-dip. Dang, she's hungry.* Her vision is blurry. She's losing it.

Time to go.

She stands up to leave, glaring again at her phone. What she needs is a crutch. A reason to text Nick. Like how she gave Quinn concert tickets as a crutch to open the door for her to apologize to Nick. *Ah! Frank!*

She grabs her phone to text Nick.

Hi. Hope you've been okay today. Any word from Frank? Has his case wrapped up?

Seconds later Nick responds.

He's finished and with me now! At my apartment getting ready to order dinner in. Join us?

Her heart pounds like a middle-school girl who was just noticed by a cute boy. *Get a freaking grip.* Her imagination already has her in Nick's apartment, sipping wine and timidly staring at his tight, white t-shirt while she picks Frank's mind on legal and investigative matters. *What a nerd.*

Thanks for the invite but you should enjoy this time with your brother

Yeah, no, he wants you here and I do too. What kind of pizza do you like?

She shakes her head.

The same kind of pizza only two brothers should share. Thanks for thinking of me though

T! Please come

No. No way. They need to catch up and bond. Not the time for her to barge in. She sees three blinking dots…he's typing.

I have cookies

Her nose wrinkles with her smile.

What flavor?

Whatever flavor they deliver from this pizza place ;)

Compromise. You enjoy pizza time with Frank and I'll come for cookies and coffee later

Deal

I'm at Indigo now. Do you need me to bring coffee?

For real?

We sell delicious home brews...

Faze does too! And I have some! Or did I just spill a secret...

Her smile grows.

I'll drive slow so you can enjoy your bro time

Hurry. I like my T-time too

Her breath leaves her. *Line! Draw it! Now!*
If she doesn't, this is only going to grow.
Because the truth is, she likes her Nick time too.

[TWENTY-TWO]

After her barista friend Tyler walked her to her car, and after driving the long way and going around the block twice, Tory pulls into a guest parking space at Nick's apartment building. She twists the rearview mirror to look behind her and to the sides. No one followed her.

Jake must be back in Austin. Maybe time was on her side and now his creepy texting will stop. It would be nice to not feel an ache in the pit of her stomach every time she goes somewhere.

She grabs her host gift and heads up the stairs. Tyler hooked her up with a Rwanda blend experience package featuring five, two-ounce packages of ground coffee from Akagera, Lake Kivu, Kizi rift, Muhazi and Virunga. *Take that, cinnamon roll boy.*

Before she knocks on the door she catches her breath. What is it about standing here that makes her feel like she just ran a mile? *Get your nerves and feelings in check.*

Two knocks are all it takes before his door flies open.

"Hey," Nick says with wide eyes and a smile like he's won the lottery. His tousled hair isn't wet like when she came here before. Tonight, it's perfectly styled. He's wearing a faded blue, short-sleeve shirt with buttons pressing tight against his muscular chest. His jeans are dark blue and crisp, paired with casual topsiders. For a moment, she's back on her parents' driveway and his lips are on her cheek and instead of feeling guilty she's awash with the same happy feeling she sees in his smile.

He leans toward her for a hug.

"Hey," she says, giving him a quick hug, several seconds shorter than they normally would hug but long enough for her to breathe in the leathery smell of his cologne. She notices Frank in jeans and a polo shirt, standing up from the sofa. "Hey, Frank," she says, pulling away from Nick and stepping toward Frank for a hug.

She faces them. "I smell pizza, am I too early?"

"We're finished," Nick says. "Sure you don't want any?"

"Oh no. I'm holding out for cookies and coffee." She dangles the five little bags she was clutching in her hand. "Just in case your coffee doesn't come from the trendiest coffee-bean producing nation on the planet, I brought these."

Nick's eyes sear. "I'll never turn down a gift. Even one from Indigo."

"Actually, from Rwanda, but I get what you mean."

His grin devours her humor and surprisingly, he lets it go. Coffee bags in hand, he heads to the kitchen. She looks to Frank, who sits back down on the couch.

"Did your case come to a satisfying conclusion?" she asks, sitting down beside him.

"A satisfying apprehension is a satisfying conclusion." His eyes look brilliantly intelligent, a lot like Nick's. He seems like a guy she could talk to all day.

"Where do you live?" she asks.

"Tampa."

"I've never been. Do you travel a lot?"

"I do, for assignments like the one we just finished. That will come to an end soon though." He smiles.

Nick slides into a chair beside the sofa. "He's about to retire in a few years."

"Retire? You look so young!"

"About, meaning in two years when I turn fifty."

"See? You are young," she says.

"I'll retire from the FBI but still keep working."

"A second career?"

"It's common, actually, for former FBI agents to have second careers after retirement."

"You could run security for a large company," Nick says. "Or be a private investigator."

"You could be a bodyguard for a famous actor…or a rock band!" she says.

"Anything is possible," Frank says.

Nick taps her leg. "Did you want coffee now, or something else? Wine?"

"Not gonna lie, I was dreaming of a glass of wine."

"Frank?" Nick asks, getting up.

"I'll have whatever you are pouring. Only a small glass though. I need to hit the road soon."

Tory's eyes linger on Nick as he moves into the kitchen and she begins twisting a loop of hair around her finger. She catches herself and lets her twirled hair go. She turns to see Frank staring at her with a knowing smile.

"So where are you staying?" she asks him.

"A hotel. A different one from where we met, something closer to here."

"Good. And how long will you be in town?"

"Nick and I were just talking about that. I'll stay through the week, at least. I've identified a source at Reeds, so we'll be getting some information from there soon. I'd like to meet your father and start the list of places we need to go to gather our evidence."

"Like…"

"First is Bear Creek Arena to see if their parking lot cameras captured anything around Nick's car. Then, we need to get any evidence of Nick's car maintenance, anything outside of Reed's."

Nick approaches them, handing them both a glass of red wine. "I don't even have any pictures of my car, other than one selfie I took on the day I bought it and it didn't show the tires." Their hands gently touch as she takes her glass of wine. He looks to her, softly blushing; she looks to him, her cheeks feeling warm.

She hides her face with a sip of wine, then turns to Frank. "What can I do?"

"Right now, there are pieces of a plausible theory, but no evidence. It would be good to know more about Reed, to hone in on a firm motive."

She breaks eye contact and can feel Nick looking at her as he sits back down in the leather chair beside them.

"There's a long history there," Nick says.

Out of the corner of her eye, she sees Frank slowly nod.

"Tory?" Frank asks. "Do you have any ideas we can pursue?"

"I did have an idea and, I'm sorry to bring this up, but it's about your dad's accident."

Nick squints.

"Were you here then?" she asks Frank.

"I was not. From my understanding, it was an explosion…"

"From a pickup truck hitting my parents' car," Nick finishes.

"The police investigated?" she asks.

"They did and ruled the pickup driver at fault. He died at the scene too," Nick says.

Frank rubs his chin. "I see where you are threading this. Could Reed have caused that accident?"

"I was eighteen. That was before I met Reed," Nick says.

Tory nods. "Me too. Before we both worked at Indigo."

"Did Dad know Reed's family? Is there a connection there?" Frank asks.

"I don't think so," Nick says.

"Is there a way to look at that investigation, and be sure there's not something there that ties into Nick's recent accidents?" she asks Frank.

"Absolutely," he says. He takes a final sip of his wine and places his empty glass on the coffee table. "Listen, I'm operating on about two hours of sleep and it has caught up to me." He stands and Nick and Tory stand too. "And I owe Emma a long conversation."

"Emma?" Tory asks.

"My daughter. She's four."

Love it.

Frank turns to Nick. "I know tomorrow is Sunday, but are you planning to go to work?"

"I was, especially since I had to abruptly leave things on Friday."

"We should get together at some point tomorrow and work on this."

Nick nods. "I'll work around your schedule." They embrace in a hug that Tory will never tire of seeing.

"Pizza was a good call. Thanks too for the earlier conversation," Frank says.

Tory pulls out her phone. "Can I get your contact information to pass along to my dad?"

Frank pulls out his phone. She tells him her number and he sends her a text. "You got it now."

She watches her phone light up with the text. "Um, other than meeting with Nick tomorrow, did you have any other plans?"

Frank looks curious. "No other plans."

"Can you spare a little bit of time for me?" she asks, shrugging.

His eyes zoom in. *Damn him.* She can tell he already knows what she's about to ask.

"Of course," Frank says with a grin. "I offered, right?"

Her palms raise in the air. "How did you know what I was going to ask?"

He gives another sly squint. "We train for that."

"I...I'm not sure where to go."

"I'll find a range," he says. "Bring your Glock and magazines. We'll buy the ammo there."

"Thank you, Frank." She throws her arms around his shoulders and squeezes.

Frank squeezes her too and lets go, looking to Nick. "I guess I get some Tory time too."

Nick's cheeks begin to blush.

"I'll be in touch with both of you tomorrow," Frank says, opening the door.

Nick follows him to the door and closes it. He turns to her with pride in his eyes. "I'm really happy you asked him to do that."

"Frank's right. Frustratingly right. I'm really not confident with my gun."

"He always seems to be right."

"Does he do that to you? Like, look at you and know what you're thinking?"

He steps away from the door, smiling. "Always. It's irritating. And another reason why we weren't close. As a kid, he called me out before I had even done anything wrong!"

"Let's hope Frank's intuition helps us get your charges dropped."

Nick's expression fades, like he's finished with this subject because he just realized they are alone. "Let's sit down." He sweeps out one arm while his other hand gently presses into her back.

"I…I can't stay."

"Oh, okay. You're welcome to stay, though. Always welcome."

His hand falls from her back.

"The wine was good, thank you," she says.

"Yeah, you didn't have coffee though. And I really do have cookies!"

She feels her smile spreading. "Save them for me, for another time."

He nods.

"I would stay, but…"

Concern swims through his eyes. "Are you okay?"

"Oh…fine. It's just…last night. You know…when you were leaving. You gave me a kiss and…"

He straightens with a look like he's ready to kiss her again.

"But I'm not sure that's what we should do."

His shoulders deflate.

"I…I'm worried. My emotions…this is so soon since Quinn."

"I understand."

"She really liked you, Nick. And, I really do too, but it seems too soon…too insensitive."

"I know. I've thought about that too. I've thought about a lot of things sitting here, for hours and hours, days and days, staring at these walls. But Quinn and I, we were only friends. I was only friends with Sienna too."

"I know."

"I can't spend the rest of my life locking up my feelings."

"Oh Nick, no…no."

"What's happening with us seems so spontaneous but really, it's not. You…and me…we've never been this close before and we've shared some pretty intense shit together. For years my heart has been holding on to a space. My brain says I'm supposed to wait but my heart didn't last night. My heart has been waiting…for you."

"But my heart hurts too much for Quinn."

Any second now, he'll reach for her. She knows he will. He'll softly hold her hands or wrap her in a warm embrace. That's what he usually does at the exact moment when she needs him. Like when he wrapped his arm around her when she teetered on the bar stool at Indigo on the night of Al's party. Or when he held her in a lingering welcome hug at Quinn's parents' party. Or how they squeezed each other for loving support on the night Quinn died. And years ago, when he comforted her when she was in her darkest hour. But now, he's not reaching for her at all.

This is breaking her heart. "I should go."

He shakes off an emotion-filled expression. "I can ride with you and then Uber back."

God, this man is amazing. "I don't want you to go out of your way. How about you just walk down with me to my car."

"You sure?"

"I wasn't followed here. I'll be fine."

His body slumps with rejection.

Slowly they walk in silence, down the stairs, until they reach the parking lot, where the asphalt still holds heat from the day's sun. Nick gives a protective glance around the parking lot. She's only looking at him. By the time his eyes meet hers, she's about to cry in fear that turning him away is a massive mistake.

Push it deep.

"I'm very confused," she whispers, eyes wet.

He slowly nods and then finally he opens his arms, wrapping her in a hug that makes her flatten her body against his, pressing hard. She squeezes him as curls of confusion twist in her stomach. The guy she shouldn't have. But the guy she really wants.

"Raincheck on the cookies. Please save them for me," she whispers, pulling away.

"I will," he whispers.

She opens her car door, lays her purse on the passenger seat and slides in behind the wheel.

A bright light shines down from on top of a pole, casting a shadowy glow around Nick's head. His eyes look hauntingly sad but he manages a slight smile before he softly closes her door.

[TWENTY-THREE]

Muffled, sharp bangs echo through the indoor shooting range. Tory adjusts her protective eye wear, breathes in deep and looks over her shoulder to Frank.

His arms are crossed, a set of clear, protective eyeglasses across his face. "Again," he mouths, nodding.

She turns forward to face a paper target peppered with bullet holes hanging from a metal track from the ceiling.

Her Glock rests on the table ahead of her, pointed forward. *Deep breath. One, two...*

She grabs the gun, plants her feet, chin down, elbows in and with one hand supporting the other she fires four quick shots that pound her chest with concussive thuds. *Bam, Bam, Bam, Bam.* She lowers her gun, lays it on the table, nuzzle pointed to target and drops her arms.

Another deep breath slows her racing heart. Shooting shit has way better cardiovascular return than any exercise. She glances back to Frank, who holds up two fingers.

"Damn! I only hit two?" she says over the muffled sound of gunfire coming from the other lanes.

He moves beside her, hand on her shoulder. "Look where you hit." He points to the center of the target.

"I did?"

He lifts one side of her ear protection off so she can hear him clearly. "That's what we call a Bastard's Bullseye, because… poor bastard."

She pumps two fists in the air. She could play Frank's rapid-fire rounds all day. The way he's taught her is so much better than standing stagnate, pointing and shooting. He's training her the way a gun may actually be used.

The range master walks into their bay. "Good?" he asks.

"Can you approve her purse draws now?" Frank asks.

The range master nods.

Frank takes her purse, placing it on the table in front of her, unzipped. He checks her magazine and puts her Glock inside, then turns to her. "Slowly, show him how you will remove your weapon, point and shoot at the target."

She nods. Frank prepared her for this. He told her the range master has to approve any holster shoots or purse draws to be sure the shooter understands where their weapon points while they are in motion. The last thing the range owners want is an errant bullet hitting a shooter in the next lane. She's loosened her ear protection so she can hear.

"Keep your finger off the trigger," Frank says.

She steps up to the table with another deep breath and imagines a scene. Her paper target is Reed's face and he's coming at her. She reaches into her purse, grabs the gun, finger to the side, raises it, nozzle to target and yells "BAM!" She returns the gun to her purse and looks behind her, where the range master holds his thumbs up. He nods to Frank, and then leaves their lane.

"Let me see four shots," Frank says. "Remember to keep your finger off of the trigger until your sight is on the target and you are willing to shoot."

Another deep breath and she does it again, this time slipping her finger under the trigger and pulling four times, while brass casings fall everywhere.

Frank squints at her target and holds up two fingers.

"I'll take it," she yells. She places her gun back into her purse and walks to the back of their lane, removing her ear protection. Frank follows and removes his.

"I could mentally do this all day but my heart can't take it anymore," she says, shaking the reverberating fired-gun feel from her arms.

"Let's check out." Frank goes back to her purse and inspects her magazine. "Two shots left."

"Go ahead, cowboy." She winks. "Show me again whatchu got."

She puts her ear protection back on.

He doesn't.

He faces the target, wraps his left hand behind his back, raises her gun with his right hand and fires two shots right through the Bastard's Bullseye.

Damn him. He did the same thing earlier with a fresh target. The center bullseye was practically on fire from the heat of the repetitive bullets going through the same small area.

She takes off her ear protection. "Hey, those holes in the middle were on my target before your shot."

"Of course they were." He secures her weapon and zips up her purse. "And we're only in a twenty-five-yard lane. One day, we'll shoot in the fifty-yard one."

That's a deal.

They check out with the range master, wash their hands and then grab coffee at the small snack counter before settling down at a table in a corner. The closest person to them is the kid working behind the snack counter, who nods his head to the beat of something coming from his earphones.

"You were incredibly focused," Frank says, sipping his coffee.

"You said not to point the muzzle at anything I wasn't willing to kill."

"And whose face did you imagine?"

"I had someone in mind."

"I could tell. You fired with incredible anger too."

"Firing did feel good," she admits.

"I'm wondering if releasing that anger will inspire you to finally tell me something."

"What?"

"Number two," he says.

"Number two?"

"On the night we met, you said Reed is a nasty person who lives on revenge and is trying to get Nick back for two things. But you only told me one."

"Oh."

"Nick hasn't told me either."

She rubs her coffee cup.

"Tory, if Reed is trying to get Nick back for something else, this is a good time for me to know."

Dread sinks into her stomach. "But what if no time is a good time for me to tell you?"

He leans closer. "Then that sounds like a good time for you to talk to a counselor."

What the shit! "How do you do that? Like zoom into my thoughts?"

"It's not difficult when it shows on your face."

"My face? What do you see?"

"One thing we're taught for interrogations: don't put words into the suspect's mouth. I'm not going to put the words out for you. You tell me."

Her chest pounds. *Really...sometimes...fuck you, Frank.*

He presses. "Number two is big, I see it on your face. It has something to do with you and Nick, and he's not talking. But the sooner I know why Reed would want revenge, the sooner I can help get Nick cleared."

Her constant rubbing is wearing down the logo imprint on the side of her Styrofoam coffee cup.

"Tory, I'm here to help. If you don't want to talk to me, I understand. But you're holding some anger that you might want to talk to a professional about."

No...no! "No...I don't want to talk to anyone else. Just you."

He looks around the snack bar area and she does too. A few gun customers mingle at counters in the shop, a good distance away from them. They're still alone.

She takes a long, drawn-out sip of her coffee. It goes down thick and heavy, as heavy as her heart feels right now. *It's time.* It's time to stop pushing deep and let it go. For Nick's sake...*let it go.*

"Years ago," she mumbles, "when I worked at Indigo, with Nick and everyone else, Reed...he was such a pain in the ass and was always trying to get me to go out with him. He was a jerk and I kept avoiding him and..."

She takes another long sip of coffee. Frank shifts to the edge of his chair.

"One night…it was late and…I had to get cups from the supply room and…Reed followed me."

Her eyes fill with tears. *Push it the fuck out. Push it out!*

"He closed the door and surprised me…and I tried to push him out of the way but he…he held my arms and forced me back…"

Frank leans closer and lays his arm gently across her shoulders.

"He was saying all of this shit like he wants me and will make me want him and he always gets what he wants and he kept pushing me until I was backed up against a wall. I told him to stop and I kept trying to lower my arms…but he had both of my wrists in one hand. I…I started screaming and he was… pulling down my jeans and…he bit my mouth to cover it and… pushed me…and I pushed back and…"

Her breathing stays oddly calm and steady…her eyes are wet but no tears are falling. She sounds robotic…telling a story where it's not really her in the story.

"I was losing it…trying to scream but he kept biting my mouth and then…Nick…"

Frank leans even closer, still wrapping her shoulders with his arm.

"Nick busted inside that closet and…it was so fast…and so violent…he yanked Reed off of me and threw him into a shelf and I was trying to pull up my jeans but boxes were falling everywhere and Nick…"

She stops and sniffles.

"Frank…Nick beat the shit out of Reed." She looks up to Frank's eyes, inches from hers. "He beat the fucking shit out of him."

Frank nods. "Good," he whispers.

"There was blood and boxes and napkins and cups every-where and I couldn't move, watching Nick. But he stopped. I swear if he hadn't, he would have killed Reed. He would have fucking killed that jerk."

She sniffles again and Frank slides a napkin closer. She takes it and dabs her eyes.

"You and Nick, you didn't tell anyone, did you?" Frank asks.

"No…no. Why did you think that?"

"It's a common thing for young people to do, to handle something like this themselves. They may do it from fear of authorities or from confidence that they have handled it just fine."

She nods. "That's what Nick and I did. Reed ran away and I didn't…I never pressed charges. I…I quit Indigo not long after. I never told anyone, not even Quinn. Only my parents knew, and they found out when Nick drove me home. That was intense, Frank. My dad…I swear I think Nick stopped my dad from murdering Reed that night. My dad was screaming while Nick was screaming while my mom was trying to ice Nick's hand and I sat frozen, watching the whole thing. My dad has never forgotten what Nick did for me. And Dad never forgot what Reed did to me either."

Frank nods. "I understand now why your father is moti-vated to defend Nick."

"He'd do anything for Nick."

"And now I understand why Reed might do something significant to get Nick back."

She nods. "Not only because of beating him up, but Nick ruined Reed's imaginary romance with me."

"You really never told Quinn?"

"No. Quinn…I wish you could have met her. Quinn was always so happy. She always saw the best in people. We were so close but I could never tell her about the bad side of people. She knew I hated Reed, but I never told her why."

"Did Reed just disappear?"

"For a few weeks, he didn't come in to work. But I had already left when he came back."

"So maybe his family knew what Nick did?"

"Could be. I don't know where Reed went to recover or what he told his friends and family."

"And Nick has certainly kept your secret. I tried to get him to tell me his background with Reed the other night and he wouldn't."

"I know I can trust Nick with my life. And any secret."

Loud voices coming from the door of the firing range catch their attention. A couple is leaving, their weapons in cases and their rolled-up, bullet-riddled targets in hand. They approach the snack bar and their presence feels a little too close. Tory straightens and dabs again at her eyes. Frank moves his arm from her shoulder and straightens too.

Tory looks back at the range door. She doesn't feel like going back in there and shooting the crap out of a target anymore. Her body floats with relief, ten pounds lighter from telling a story she's been pushing deep for far too long. But releasing the truth has also left her feeling exhausted. And exposed. She dumped her biggest secret on a man she met less than forty-eight hours ago.

"Tell me why you bought your gun," he says.

She grits her teeth. "I might as well tell you what freaking color underwear I'm wearing. Geez, your questions go right to the belly of my soul, huh?"

He nods, those eyes piercing through her. "It wasn't because of Jake."

"I thought you weren't supposed to put words into my mouth."

"I didn't. I just read your eyes. Out loud."

"Jake triggered my weakness," she says, "that with a man, I might not be in control."

"Might not be in control, especially now that you're back in town, with Reed."

"God damn, you should be a shrink."

He shrugs. "In a way, that's what we are. Thinking like someone else helps us catch the bad guys. But enough about all that. You just released a trove of pent-up information. How do you feel?"

She puts her elbows on the table and rests her chin in her hands. "I feel incredibly grateful that you have come into my life. I never wanted to talk about this, outside of my parents. I sure as hell wasn't going to see a doctor or anything."

"Being the victim of an attempted rape is a significant event. You could benefit by talking with someone."

"I know. But I feel okay. Relieved. I'm glad you know every-thing. Especially if it helps clear Nick's name."

"I get the feeling you would do anything for my brother."

She nods.

He smiles. "And I get the feeling Nick would do anything for you."

She tips her head to the side. "I'm curious. The night we met, you assumed Nick and I were dating. How…like why did you think that?"

Frank eases back in his chair and folds his arms across his chest. "There's a whole science into reading eyes and I can tell a lot from a person when I meet them. I know from which way a person looks, like bottom right or upper left, whether they are telling the truth or lying. Lack of eye contact tells something too. And when I see two people together, rarely do I see two sets of eyes give the same message."

"Were Nick and I giving the same message?"

A grin stretches his mouth. "Eyes in love are easy to spot."

Her body quickly tenses and for a split-second her breath disappears.

No! She can't be. Frank didn't see that in her eyes. Or Nick's. It's not fair to Quinn to fall...

Frank dips his head closer. "Would you like for me to unpack your reaction there?"

She glares. "I'm beginning to not like you."

He smiles warmly. "I can have that effect on people. Tory, grieving means different things to different people. I think for you, the moment at Indigo years ago is when you built up walls to protect yourself. You probably saw Nick as someone who saw you at your worst. You and he haven't ever talked about that night, have you?"

She shakes her head. "Not since the day after."

"And now grieving for your friend...your dear, close friend...is keeping you from taking those walls down to let someone in who really, all this time, only saw you at your best."

Her arms feel as limp as a wet dishrag.

"Only you know how long your grieving process should be. And only Nick knows how long his should be. I can tell you this, after my conversations yesterday and today with Nick, he realizes now more than ever how short life can be. He's grieving, yes. But he's also made a commitment to not waste any time while he lives."

Tears begin dripping from her eyes. And she just pushed him away.

"I…I don't even know how to thank you for this conversation," she mumbles, wiping her eyes. "You're like my psychological soulmate, someone who understands me more than my mom, or Quinn, or anyone I've known before."

Frank squeezes her arm. "Thank you for the compliment, but I think there is someone who understands you much better than me."

She looks into Frank's eyes and for the first time, *she* can read *him*.

It's Nick.

[TWENTY-FOUR]

If there's one thing Tory's sure of, it's that she needs to see Nick. Now.

She's halfway to his apartment, her sweaty hands gripping the steering wheel as she drives a bit faster than she legally should. The late-afternoon sun is making her squint and she doesn't want to waste a split-second to try to find her sunglasses so she just flips down the sun visor to shield her eyes. She hugged her goodbye to Frank and rushed out of the firing range so fast, she didn't even call or text Nick to let him know she was on the way. Nick had told her: come anytime.

Even if he isn't home she knows where to find him. He'll be at Faze. He said he wanted to make up some time at work after he was abruptly arrested on Friday. Between checking his apartment first and then going to Faze, she will see him tonight.

Her radio is off; she's listening to her own voice as she practices what she'll say.

I shouldn't have pushed you away…

Weak. Try again.

I feel our connection too and I'm sorry I...

Too sappy. Be yourself.

I don't know what the hell I'm doing but I sure as hell want to do it with you.

Perfect.

She turns into the parking lot of his apartment complex and spots his silver Lexus IS parked under a blanket of shade trees. He's home.

Her heart beats a little faster as she swings back around to the guest spaces, pulls her car in and ironically parks in the same space she parked in last night. The worst night. The night she made a huge mistake by pushing him away.

Before she gets out of the car she checks her face in the rearview mirror. Her makeup seems flat and bland, her straight brown hair unremarkable. She's still wearing a black tank top, jeans and closed-toe ankle boots from the firing range. There's a good chance she smells like gunpowder too.

Going home to primp first was an option. But if she had, she might have lost her nerve. That would have given her too much time to think. Logic is already fighting with her heart. This is way too soon after Quinn's death to fall for the guy Quinn liked. But Nick is right. How long do you hold on to an empty space? When is too soon to give your heart to the man that you like too?

She swivels the rearview mirror back into place and picks up her phone to call him. He did say to come by anytime, but that might not have meant drop by whenever. He could be working on something or watching a movie or lounging with no shirt and a tight-fitting pair of cozy sweatpants which, actually, wouldn't be a bad thing to catch him in.

She presses CALL as she gets out of the car and starts walking up the stairs. This is it. They've only talked about what happened years ago right after it happened. Now, she's ready to bring it up again. She wants to clear the air and be sure he doesn't see her only as a victim. She's strong. She wants him to know it. And she wants him to know that she's his, if he will still have her.

One ring. Two rings. He answers and her heart thuds.

"Tory! Hey."

She's standing outside his door, her heart racing like she just shot two-hundred Bastard Bullseyes in the fifty-yard-long firing range. "Did I catch you at a bad time?"

"No. How was your outing with Frank?"

"Amazing and I wanted to tell you all about it, and more. If you have a minute."

"Where are you?"

She smiles and knocks on his door. "At your door."

She hears him unlock the deadbolt and the door swings open. He's still holding his phone, a look of shock on his face. He's wearing a crisp, white button-down dress shirt with the sleeves rolled up and untucked over a pair of dark jeans. He still has his chestnut-brown casual shoes on, so he must have just gotten in from work, or somewhere.

She loses herself in his steel-blue eyes, staring wide at her and if her heart would stop racing she could catch her breath and say something. She licks her lips.

"I…I hope I didn't catch you at a bad time."

He doesn't move, eyes wide, like he can't believe she's standing there.

She breaks his stare and looks down to her feet and then back up at him. "I was hoping we could talk."

He's still standing in shock and his eyes are so wide with surprise, it's freaking adorable. She can't help but grin, knowing what this must mean to him. He's got to know that big brother Frank has scored an emotional breakthrough with her, which has delivered her all but gift-wrapped to his door.

She dips her head down, still waiting for him to speak and invite her in. After all, just yesterday he asked her how long was he supposed to save an empty space in his heart. And she's standing right here, ready to fill it.

"Tory?" she hears a woman's voice call.

What? Tory sticks her head inside as Nick remains frozen, holding open the door.

Shock punches her gut. "Gigi?" Tory asks, looking in.

Gigi smiles warmly, sitting relaxed with her legs resting on Nick's sofa. Her feet are bare, a pair of heels kicked to the side of the coffee table. She sets down an almost-finished glass of wine and begins to stand on her long, toned legs, which look even longer since her skirt is so short. And tight. She straightens her floral blouse, which is so generously unbuttoned that even from the door Tory can see she's wearing an olive-colored bra underneath. "Nick?" Gigi asks. "Why aren't you inviting her in?"

Tory couldn't step in now even if he rolled out a red carpet.

"How are you, Tory?" Gigi asks, approaching her. "I've been thinking about you so much." She grips Tory's hands. Tory's hands and arms feel like cooked strands of spaghetti, the mushy kind of spaghetti like she makes. Gigi gently tugs her inside Nick's apartment.

A numbness Tory's never felt before has rendered her speechless. She looks down again to the wood floor and Gigi's shoes. Tory's been to Nick's place a couple of times, but never taken off her shoes.

"What's wrong?" Gigi asks, squeezing Tory's hands.

Tory cocks her head. "Nothing." She turns to Nick. "I'm sorry to interrupt."

"No, really, you aren't," he says, closing the door and walking closer to her.

Oh yes...yes she apparently is. She eases her hands out of Gigi's grip. "I just came from a great afternoon with your brother and I...I'm sorry I shouldn't have come right over." She steps backward, toward the door.

"Stay!" Gigi says. "Would you like some wine? We have cookies too!"

We?

"Cookies?" Tory mumbles. She's about to cry. "Oh no, no." She turns to the door and decides one good running leap would get her the hell out of here.

Gigi watches her with interest, her amazingly proportioned body moving closer to Nick's side. If Gigi touches him, Tory's heart will be shredded.

"Tory," Nick says, his eyes still wide, "please stay. How did it go with Frank?"

She's already at the door, squeezing the doorknob. Her chest burns but she manages to look Nick square in the eyes. "Frank is very wise about many things. But he's really wrong about some others."

She turns the doorknob and clumsily hits her head with the door in her rush to open it.

"Tory?" Nick calls.

She doesn't look back, walking away and then sprinting down the steps. She throws herself in the car and pulls away, her vision blurry on the edges yet she can see Nick, standing outside of his door, gripping the apartment railing, watching her.

In seconds, she speeds out of his view and is alone on the street.

Alone in her car.

Alone in her life.

* * *

The sour, coconut smell of sunscreen fills the air around the Pearl. "But mummy!" a little girl cries. "I want another ice cream!" she screeches.

Tory glares at the girl and her parents, all beet red with sunburn and wearing bright orange matching t-shirts as they pass her on the path to and from the Riverwalk.

Fucking tourists.

Tory lowers her eyes back down to her shoes, her feet plodding along, forcing her body toward the go-to place that makes her happy: the Pearl steps.

It's nearly sunset but it's after Memorial Day weekend so the tourists are out, even on this quiet end of the Riverwalk.

Tory kicks up some of the shell gravel as she walks. That shit looks like how her heart feels: scratchy and crushed.

What a fool. What an idiot. What an epic mistake.

Fuck Frank and his magic eye reading. Why did she buy into that shit? She should text him now and tell him his advice sucks. And to forget what she confessed. Oh, and to forget that she even exists.

Tory rolls her eyes and when she briefly closes them, she sees Gigi's breasts, curved and magnificently bulging out from the top of her olive-colored bra. Who wears something like that to their boss's apartment? Who hangs out barefoot in their boss's apartment? Someone who wants to screw the boss in the boss's apartment, that's who.

She nears the end of the gravel path and the top of the Pearl steps. The south side Pearl steps. *Fuck your north side loyalty, cinnamon roll boy.* Slowly she takes one step and then another down, eyeing the other tourists and locals who have claimed spots on the concrete steps. She chooses a spot about halfway down and with an unladylike thump, she sits.

A sliver of logic screams inside her scrambled brain. What she just saw at Nick's has to be a mistake. Twenty-four hours ago, Nick pledged that he never felt as close to her as this before. How could he emotionally pivot so fast? If Gigi and Nick are only friends, and what she walked into was a friendly visit, then why? Why are they hanging out? Why would Gigi's polished toes need to be resting on Nick's couch? Why did Nick let Gigi nosh on her cookies?

Maybe Daniel has been right all along. Maybe Nick *is* trouble.

Tory moans. This day hurts. Firing a gun hurts. Confessing what Reed did to her years ago hurts. Seeing Nick's untucked white shirt and wondering if Gigi untucked it, hurts.

She looks around to watch the normal people of the world.

Seems like the usual Pearl step scene: a few couples snuggling, a young family picnicking, a group of young professionals drinking. Over by the bridge, the vendor booth selling touristy crap is open, with a rack of colorful flower crowns dangling to entice shoppers. On the north side, a dude with bright ginger hair sits alone, which makes her think of Jake. It's been a whole day since she's thought about Jake's menacing texts and felt the fear of wondering whether he's creeping on her. *Come at me, bro. Come at what's left of me.* She's too numb to be scared anymore.

Then across the way, a beautiful, brunette woman in a flowing maxi-dress sits next to the ginger dude who had been sitting alone. She plants a lingering kiss on his lips. *Super.* Tory facepalms rather than watch their PDA.

Now Tory is the only one, north or south side, who sits alone.

The sound of clapping grows louder from a Riverwalk boat of tourists making their way down the river. If that wasn't bad enough, the boat captain is using his microphone to amplify some awful version of a rap song. Tory watches in horror as they make their way past. *People pay for that?*

She feels Nick's presence everywhere in these steps. He first took her here the day after Reed attacked her. He'd wrapped his arm around her shoulders, his hand swollen to twice its size from throwing all of those punches, and he sat here with her, helping her to clear her mind. They were close then, strangely close. And that's when she started pushing him away. She didn't want his pity. He saw her being attacked; he saw her vulnerable. And she didn't want him to see her like that. After she left Indigo, she left town. Nick was always on her mind though. He laid a lot out there when he defended her. But her freaking pride wouldn't let him in. Then when Quinn started crushing on Nick, Tory moved out of the way. She wanted Quinn happy. And she'd do anything she could for her best friend.

Even though Nick feels everywhere in these steps, he won't be here tonight. That's why she came. He's busy, with Gigi. Even if he did want to find her, it would be hard for him to rush Gigi out of his apartment. Those birdcage, high-heeled sandals of hers would take at least five minutes alone to strap on. They're the kind of sandals that don't just easily slip off either.

Tory's stomach rumbles from the absence of dinner. She'd love a taco from Socat, but she feels too damn pissy to get off of her ass and go get one. *Damn, she needs to clean up her language.* One day, the guy of her dreams will come along and she'll turn him off with her filthy mouth. *The guy of her dreams. Heh.* An hour ago, she thought she might have known who he was.

This pity-party is going nowhere. She needs to say her goodbye to the Pearl steps, forever. Next week is her last week at Indigo, then she'll be back in Austin. Distance wouldn't have worked with her and Nick anyway. Even with his promises to drive to Austin for his so-called Tory-time. He wasn't hers; she wasn't his. He's a free man to do whatever he wants and she shouldn't worry about it.

Nick's case is in her dad's capable hands. Nick doesn't need her to fight his charges. Frank's around now too. But after getting Frank's whopping bad batch of advice, she's wondering if his skills could decipher the backward menu at Socat. *What was she thinking, listening to the advice of a stranger?*

An easy breeze picks up the cool temperature of the river, carrying a chill up the steps and across her shoulders. She shudders and then suddenly, she starts to cry. Her head lowers, giving her tears nowhere to fall except to the concrete. One by one, her tears splash the steps with droplets that begin small, then spread larger. Her bones are starting to ache, her stomach is empty and she's in desperate need of a tissue to wipe her nose. Her purse, with her gun, is still in her car. All she has is her phone, a credit card and keys. She sniffles and wipes her face with the back of her hand.

Her falling hair makes a curtain around her face as she looks down to the tear-stained concrete. She can look from side to side without anyone noticing, so she does, just to be sure her crying is not causing a scene.

No one's looking at her.

Just as well.

She wipes her eyes again and runs her hands through her hair, sniffling.

Another riverboat passes below, this one packed with tourists and apparently driven by the most boring boat captain ever since none of them are even moving. They look like blurry bitmap images because her eyes are so wet. And so do all of the people across on the north steps. Except…

She blinks her eyes to focus.

Standing halfway down the steps on the north side, staring at her, is Nick.

[TWENTY-FIVE]

Nick came? He pushed Gigi out that fast? Tory blinks a few more times to focus through her tears. His shirt is tucked in. *They did it that quick and he got dressed that fast?*

She lowers her head, wiping her eyes. *Damn it.* She didn't think he'd come here tonight! What's she supposed to say? *Fuck that!* She's not saying anything! He needs to do the talking!

He knows she's seen him. He's moving, slowly stepping lower and lower toward the sidewalk by the river.

She wipes her eyes and sniffles, weighing the options. Flight feels the best. Just bolt from here and start running. There's a river between them with a bridge far enough away so he'd never catch her.

Facing him feels the worst. Plus, that carries the greatest risk. Because as clumsy as she was leaving his place, she's likely to trip and eat the concrete trying to walk down these steps to face him.

Good grief: grow up. Face his ass. Get it over with.

She sniffles in a wad of snot.

Slowly she gets up, staring at him.

He stands on the sidewalk, at the edge of his side of the river, facing her.

With each slow step down, she's starting to hate how good he looks. If there were one-hundred men on the north side all looking at her and ready for the taking, she'd pick him from the crowd. His brown hair looks unruly yet perfectly styled, the shadow of his beard throws a confident, sexy aura and his eyes stare at her like soft blue ribbons of passion pulling her in.

A riverboat approaches again, with the boat captain's robotic voice narrating some story about the Alamo. The boat's movement doesn't draw Nick's eyes away from her. He's still watching each step she takes. She reaches the sidewalk right as the boat passes, leaving only twenty feet or so of muddy, churned-up river between them.

She swallows what feels like marbles, facing him.

His shoulders rise up from the massive breath he's taking and his eyes flash fear. "That wasn't what it looked like," he says over the distance of the river.

She bats her eyes. *Good to know he realizes it looked bad.*

"I asked her to come over..."

Tory swallows hard. *That's not quite the direction she was thinking this might go.*

He mischievously grins with a smile totally not fitting the moment. He's...happy? *What the fuck.* He looks down to his watch and them back to her. "Right now, Francisco is proposing."

She rolls her lips in. *Fran...cisco?*

He's still grinning. "Francisco is Gigi's boyfriend, hopefully by now, her fiancé."

A warm feel of embarrassment begins to creep through Tory's body.

And Nick's still smiling. "My part was keeping Gigi busy so Francisco could decorate their apartment…their apartment…because they live together."

Her warm feel of embarrassment has escalated to a hot flush of humiliation.

His grin softens. "Francisco had candles and flowers and was trying to cook her dinner…"

"Oh," Tory chirps. "That sounds…romantic. For Gigi."

Nick looks like he's about to laugh. "I kept Gigi busy by talking about you."

What? Tory winces from the hit of a shame pie being smacked across her face. "Me?"

He nods. "You. All I've been talking about for the last two hours, is you."

"Ohhh." Her chin lowers to hide her embarrassment. "And Gigi…listened?"

"For a solid two hours."

There's nowhere for her to look except the ground. This is unbelievable. Sure, Gigi shows a generous serving of her boobs, but she's a patient saint, listening to him for two hours, babble about her. No wonder Gigi kicked off her shoes and laid back. It's a wonder she didn't doze off. And the wine? Maybe she was on her third or fourth glass just to keep sane. Tory looks back up to Nick.

Nick nods. "She's our number one fan."

Our? Our? Tory's about to crumble.

"I don't want you to think there's something there," Nick says. "There's only something here." He lays both hands on his heart. "For you."

Her knees buckle.

"I can't imagine…" Nick says with a rising voice, trying to talk over the approaching sounds from another riverboat. The boat chugs closer and this boat captain and his load of tourists are a floating party out of control. The ones that aren't shaking maracas are clapping and all of them are singing loudly and off-key, along with the boat captain on his microphone. The captain motions to the people sitting on the steps to clap along and shyly, many of them do, their faces expressing shock and surprise. "Come on, people!" he screams, trying to whip up everyone to clap with him while his boatload of tourists sings along. Tory's never seen one of these boats actually bounce before, but this one does as it passes between her and Nick.

She can't help it and nods along to the beat, eyes on the tourists and then she looks across to Nick, who's nodding his head too, and clapping. Everyone on the north side of the Pearl steps is on their feet, clapping along.

As the boat drifts past, Tory's eyes keep following it. *Best. Boat. Ever.* She glances back to Nick.

His clapping fades but his grin does not as he watches the boat float away. He looks to her and then down to the churned-up water between them. He looks back up to her with a hardened face of determination. He glances to the right and the limestone bridge, the only thing connecting their two sides, and then back to her. And then he sprints, running straight toward the bridge.

Her hands fly to her face in surprise.

Nick rips down the sidewalk, dodging people who are leisurely walking, side-stepping a little boy eating an ice cream cone and then jumping over a small dog. He grabs the side rail of the bridge, cutting a hard turn, then running across it while people dash out of his way. Nick swings hard left, now on the south side sidewalk, his hair bouncing back with the speed of his running as he barrels straight for her.

Tory's hands are still on her face from disbelief and delight.

People seem to notice Nick now and are getting out of his way. Everyone on both sides of the steps are watching him.

Nick flies past the souvenir vendor when his legs suddenly grind to an abrupt halt.

Tory drops her hands. *What?*

He raises one finger in a gesture to hold on a second and he turns toward the vendor.

Tory leans to see what he's doing but she can't see him. T-shirts on a sidewalk rack blow in the breeze and some shoppers on the sidewalk block her view. A few seconds later she sees Nick, leaping away from the stand, his smile a million miles wide as he grips a colorful flower crown.

Oh my God! Tory doubles over with surprise, grabbing her chest, with a smile that feels bigger than his.

Nick walks toward her with a swagger in his step, swinging the flower crown from his hand. People clear the way for him to pass.

He's an arm's distance away when she realizes her breath left her the moment he started running and now she can't feel her legs. All she feels is her heart, beating with incredible joy.

His eyes ripple with amusement, his mouth curved with a contagious smile as he reaches her.

"I said," he whispers, trying to pick up his earlier words, "that I can't imagine my life…with anyone…but you."

"Oh, Nick." Her anger scatters faster than confetti thrown in Times Square on a windy New Year's Eve.

He raises the flower crown and with two hands, rests it on her head. He moves his hands down, his fingers lightly stroking her hair, gently bringing some of the long, colorful ribbons toward her face in a move that makes her entire body roar with tingles.

"I'm sorry I thought…" she whispers and he presses his finger to her lips.

"I'm sorry," he whispers with a loving gleam in his eyes. "I'm sorry if that whole thing looked like anything other than…"

His voice breaks and he snaps his eyes to the side. Tory follows his gaze. A young couple is standing up, phones in the air, pointed at them. Tory looks behind her, where a gum-chewing teenager also stands with his phone in the air, pointed at them.

"What's happening," she mumbles, now looking over the river to the north steps. Half of those people are standing and most of them have phones or cameras in the air, pointed at them. Tory's mouth drops open. "I think…they think…you're proposing."

"Oh…my…God," he whispers, his hands frozen in place, touching her hair. He lowers his hands and straightens. "It's… an apology," he loudly says to the crowd on their side. He looks across to the north side. "It's an apology!" he yells, on the brink of laughter.

Over Nick's shoulder, Tory can see another riverboat coming. *Good.* Maybe they'll distract all of these people. She hears the boat captain singing on his microphone and thankfully this group isn't acting as rowdy as the last one. The boat approaches where they're standing and the captain looks left and right, noticing all of the people standing with their phones in the air pointing to them. He flips his thrusters in reverse, bringing the boat to a drifting stop and now all of the boat passengers are looking at them too.

Tory's eyes cross.

Nick shakes his head. "It's an apology!" he hollers to the boat captain.

"Well…" the captain says on his microphone, his words echoing up both sides of the steps. "Do it!"

She tries to suppress a laugh. No one's going to move until Nick does something!

Ribbons from Tory's crown catch the cool evening breeze and blow forward. Nick's finger gently brushes the ribbons away from her face. Her laughing quiets; she's sinking into the drama of his eyes. Every ounce of his attention is focused back on her. "I'm sorry if anything gave you any doubt about how I feel," he whispers. "Because my heart only beats for you."

Joy rolls through her body with a wild swirl.

His fingertip skims her jawline and then he lifts her chin, leans closer and presses a velvet-soft kiss on her lips.

Cheers erupt from the crowd and applause roars from the bottom to the top of the Pearl steps. The boat captain blasts two loud honks from an air horn as all of his passengers jump up to cheer. Bright flashes from phones and cameras capture Nick and Tory as he kisses her and she kisses him.

Nick sweeps her in his arms and dips her backward, her ribbon-flowing hair dangling to the ground. He lifts her up so quickly, her head goes dizzy. She flings her arms around his shoulders for a jubilant hug and he buries his face in her shoulder.

"Wow, just wow," she whispers, leaning back to look at him.

He dips his chin and raises his eyebrow with a "you betcha" look.

"I can't imagine your apology if you were really in trouble." She playfully tousles his hair.

His eyes drink her in. "Is this really happening? Can I kiss you again?"

She bites her lip and nods. "I hope it's happening. And please…kiss me again."

He slips his hands to the sides of her face and gently pulls her lips toward him.

She hears the boat motor sputter as the captain begins driving his boat forward again.

"Well played, sir. Well played," the captain says on his microphone, and then his voice and the sound of their applause fade into the distance.

[TWENTY-SIX]

Peace and beautiful quiet covers the Pearl steps. Tory and Nick gaze up at the twinkling stars, the few stars that are able to pierce the bright lights from the downtown night sky. They sit on a Mexican serape blanket that Nick bought from the sidewalk vendor before they closed up shop. A crunched-up to-go bag from Socat lies next to them and the air is filled with the smoky char-grilled smell from another nearby restaurant.

The stillness of the night also seems to have stopped the green river from flowing, at least on the surface. Riverboats haven't passed through in a while. Every few minutes, the breeze delivers the sound of a live band playing at one of the restaurants up at the Pearl. The tourists have all left and only a few locals are mingling and sitting on the steps. None of the people who are here now were here when Nick and Tory caused a scene about three hours ago.

"I don't want to leave," she mumbles, lowering her eyes from the stars to him. She traces a finger down his cheek, exploring the bristly feel of his beard. She can't keep her fingers off of his face.

He can't keep his hands off of her waist. "I don't want to either."

"I still can't believe this is happening."

"I can't believe I can do this…" He gives her another smoldering kiss, leaving her stomach tingling just as strong as when he gave her their first.

Her finger trails down his other cheek. "I've…I've never kissed a guy with a beard before."

"Oh really?" His eyes lower. "How do you rate it?"

"Rate it? The beard or the guy?"

"Either."

"You and your beard are a Qutor rank of one."

"Qutor?"

"Yeah. That was the scale Quinn and I used to rank guys. The 'Qu' of Quinn and the 'Tor' of Tory. You were the benchmark to beat at one."

"One is…good?"

"One is the best." She looks down at her lap. "I wonder if Quinn would be happy for me, for us."

"I think she wanted us together."

"How so?"

"Did Frank tell you about how he reads people's eyes?"

"Yeah. At first I believed what he was saying, but then after walking in on you and Gigi, I cursed Frank's stupid magic eye reading crap."

"You probably cursed my name too."

"Both of your names rolled off my tongue during my ugly hour."

He grimaces. "Well, I think Frank's right about how you can communicate with your eyes. And Quinn…she gave us that look at the hospital, right before she died. Remember?"

"Yeah. She kept looking back and forth to you and me."

"I think she was telling us something."

"You think Quinn was telling us to be together?"

Nick tips his chin up, looking at the sky, then his eyes come back down to her. "Why do you think only you and me saw the room go white?"

"Because we both were about to faint. But I don't dismiss that people can feel and see unusual things when someone they love dies."

A couple holding hands walks down the sidewalk by the river and they smile and point to Tory and Nick as they pass.

"He must be jealous because he doesn't have a blanket like this for his girl." Tory tugs the bright pink-and-blue blanket.

"He's jealous because you're not his girl." Nick's eyes gleam with pride.

"And, whose girl am I?"

"Finally, I hope—I think—you're mine."

Her heart bursts with happiness, and still a bit of disbelief, at his words. "So, what do you remember of me back when we were at Indigo?"

"Damn, Tory. Your jeans…"

Her eyes fly open. "What!?"

"Aw man, you had that pair of jeans, with that sexy fade in just the right places and I swear when you came into work wearing them I couldn't concentrate."

"No way. Even while you had a girlfriend?"

"Well, I was trying to break it off and what I really wanted to do was be with you."

"I knew you were trying to end things, but I never picked

up that it was me you wanted."

"Your smile, your humor…God I loved when we all hung out and you were there too. Being around you was so easy; you never had drama. And your style, then and now, classic but stylish. Simple but incredibly sexy."

Happiness gleams from her proud smile.

"What about me?" he asks. "When did you really notice me?"

"The day I met you. I remember the first time you looked up at me. Your eyes—those blue eyes—my knees went weak. You were the smartest one and your smile…your vibe was so hot. I just wanted to know you more and we became fast friends but I never thought a guy like you would want a girl like me."

His eyes intensely lower. "Oh…I want you."

Her body warms with his invitation, but her eyes look down.

"Earlier, I had come over to your place to talk about what happened years ago," she quietly says. "I should have never pushed you away when you were trying to help me. I didn't want you to think of me as a helpless victim."

"You're a beautiful, confident, strong and independent woman. Then, and more so now."

"You saw me at my worst. And I always thought that's how you'd remember me."

"No. Not at all. I wanted to protect you. Like I want to protect you now."

"Not because you have pity?"

He squeezes her waist. "No. No way. What I feel for you is the complete opposite. In all of my dreams about being in your life, I've never thought that of you."

His phone vibrates.

"Go ahead, answer it," she says.

He pulls it out and a smile rushes to his face. "Look, Gigi's ring." He holds up his phone and a text message with a photo of a massive new diamond on her hand.

"I'm so happy for her," Tory says.

Nick looks back at the photo. "Francisco showed me the ring before. He was so nervous." Nick starts typing a reply, reading out loud as he types.

I am so happy for you both. Tory too...we are together now

His phone lights up with a reply and he shows it to Tory.

I see that! I'm happy for you too

"She sees that? How did she pick up that we're together from your text?"

"She's dizzy with happiness, I guess." Nick tucks his phone back into his jeans pocket.

"I can't believe I thought that you and Gigi..."

"When you looked at her shoes on my floor, I died. And then when she offered you the cookies..." He plants his head in his hand. "Those were your cookies!"

"I damn well knew whose cookies they were supposed to be." She pokes him in the chest.

"I was like...stay...but then I knew if you stayed, Gigi would politely leave and I needed her to stay."

"How did you get her to leave so fast? I was only here for a few minutes before you showed up."

"Francisco finally texted her and she left. I was dying to find you, to talk to you. My gut drove me right here."

"My gut took me here because I knew you wouldn't be here. I figured you'd be busy with her so this would be the one time I could come here without running into you."

"I didn't care where I needed to drive or where I needed to go, I was going to find you tonight."

"That's how I felt leaving the firing range. Whether it was your apartment or at Faze, I was going to find you tonight."

"Fate," he whispers, his eyes melting into hers. "We found each other."

"And, now what?" she asks. "I'm only in town for a couple of weeks."

His face sinks and then suddenly, his eyes brighten. "We'll figure out next week next week. For this week, why don't we start with a date. An official date. Will you go out with me tomorrow night?"

"Like, a real date?"

He nods, his expression shy. "A date, yeah. Anywhere you want. Or if you're still not ready to go out anywhere, we can have a date at my apartment."

"Your place?" Her imagination races. The two of them, alone—really alone—for the first time. She'll be the one with her shoes off, and hopefully him too, and she'd be free to touch and explore more than just his face.

Her finger traces down his chest and she watches where her finger goes, stopping at the first button of his shirt. She lifts her eyes, inches from his raw gaze. "Your place sounds perfect."

He swallows hard.

She offers a suggestive smile.

His smile twists hot and mischievous, making her wish date night was right now.

Suddenly a camera flash lights up the steps. Tory and Nick blink and turn to face the light.

A couple standing on the sidewalk just took their picture. "Oh! We're sorry!" the woman says. "We didn't mean to interrupt. It's just that you two are soooo cute we couldn't resist taking our own photo," she hollers up from below.

The man holds a thumbs-up. "Nice apology, by the way," he says. The couple links their arms and walks away.

Nick's upper lip stretches. "How'd he know I had apologized to you?"

"That was hours ago," Tory says, her eyebrows scrunched. "They weren't sitting here all that time. Unless…" She pulls out her phone from her back pocket. She's missed a few texts from Daniel and some other friends. "My phone has blown up." She reads Daniel's message first.

Baby I hope u know what u r doing. 'Cause everyone knows u r doing it

He's put a link to his Instagram, where photos of their Riverwalk kiss have gone viral with hundreds of likes and dozens of comments. "Oh wow."

Nick looks at her phone too.

Many of the comments are sweet. But as she scrolls through more, her pulse begins to surge.

Hooking up with her best friend's killer?

Isn't this the guy who was just arrested
for killing her best friend?

Pro-tip on how to hook up with a guy:
knock off your best friend first.

Was the kiss an apology for killing her bff?

He's killed two women already this year
and now working on a third.

"Oh no, Nick!" Her mouth gapes open.

He covers her phone with his hand. "Don't read this. Don't read anymore."

"Oh my God! Think of everyone who has seen this!"

"This is why I stay away from social media. It's vicious and cruel. These people don't know us."

"They do now! Oh my God, look!" She holds out her phone again. "The Riverwalk shared some of these people's videos on their official Instagram! Romance on the Riverwalk? They're using our kiss to promote this place!"

He lowers her phone. "Don't look at it. There'll be way more bad comments than positive ones, so don't look at it."

She feels desperate. "Reed's probably seen it! Blaine? Oh my God…what if Al sees it? How can something so happy and special turn out so awful?"

"It's me, Tory. It's because of me. People always think the worst and that's what's happening now."

"What do we do?"

"We do what I've been doing all year. I go forward. One day, one step at a time. I know my sadness. I know my happiness. I know my heart." He points to her phone. "I don't listen to them." He looks up to her. "I listen to me."

Her trembling arms cling to him in a hug. *Nick.* The man she's liked for years. The man she finally lowered her walls for and has let him emotionally in. The man convicted in the court of public opinion for the accidental killing of another woman. The same man she stepped aside for so her best friend could find happiness. *Nick.* The man in her arms.

The guy also charged with a second-degree felony for killing her best friend. And evidently there are plenty of people who want to remind her of that.

[TWENTY-SEVEN]

A stack of contracts and notes lay on the corner of Tory's desk and gently, she eases a paper clip onto the corner of the stack. She peels off an orange sticky note, writes "City Issues" on it and places the note on the top.

She glances over her desk, organized with stacks of paper and folders color-coded with labels so clearly marked that even Blaine could figure out where something is. Tory glances at her watch. It's 8 a.m.

She came in early to get ready to be fired.

Her eyes feel swollen from lack of sleep and from the emotional toll of the craziest Sunday she's ever had. She barely remembers being with Frank and firing a gun on what began as one of the most exciting days of her life. But she clearly remembers the taste of Nick's lips.

If Al's seen the video or pictures of her kissing Nick, she knows she'll be shown the door.

Al's been a patient and understanding boss but he doesn't take kindly to people who don't heed his advice. Nick is more than someone Al doesn't like. Nick is his competitor. Now that Tory's been here a few weeks, she clearly sees why Al's been motivated to clean up matters before he retires. Blaine is all but certain to grind Indigo into the ground. The idiot can't even remember what a P&L statement is. And now that Tory's lips have been publicly photographed all over the owner of Indigo's rival, it will be hard to blame Al for taking action.

Her office door rattles and Robyn steps in, keys in hand.

"You're here early!" she says, perky, with a steaming cup of coffee in hand. "Whoa, your desk is clean. You must have come in here on Saturday." She plops her keys on her desk.

"I did, and I came in early today to get my affairs in order." Tory straightens another stack of papers.

"Do you think Al's going to be mad because you left on Friday to help Nick? I mean, you didn't even tell me you left for Nick until late so there's a chance he doesn't know."

"Oh, he knows. Al was here on Saturday and already knew Nick had been arrested. But that's only one problem. The other—"

A knock on their door interrupts them and the door handle turns. Tyler from downstairs sticks his head in. "Hey, the guys downstairs say Al isn't coming in today."

"Really?" Good to know so she doesn't have to ask his secretary, whenever that backstabber rolls in for the day. She hasn't trusted her since the bogus "the Mayor's on the phone" ruse she ran with Reed.

Tyler shrugs. "You might be able to keep your job, at least another day."

"Whoa," Robyn says. "You think Al's going to fire you?"

Tory nods and looks to Tyler.

Tyler slowly nods. "Anyone with Instagram knows that Tory's probably going to be fired." He looks to Tory with sad eyes. "Let me know if you need anything."

"Tyler, you have been the best. Thank you."

He nods and hesitates before closing the door. "Just remember me. I might need a good word put in if I have to apply at Faze when this place goes down in flames." He closes the door.

"Wow," Robyn mumbles, sipping her coffee. "What have you done on Instagram?"

Tory pulls up some of the photos and shows them to Robyn. Robyn also scans some of the comments.

"I'm sorry, Tory. You're really in a bad spot, although, I gotta say, Nick looks really good in that photo right there, am I right?"

Tory cracks a smile. "He's amazing in a photo and even better in person. It's been hard though to get over the guilt that this is too soon after Quinn died."

Robyn turns and starts up her computer. "You could have waited a year and done what? Cracked your knuckles passing the time until the strangers on social media decide when it's appropriate for you to move on? Who cares what they think?" Robyn glances up through her spy window.

"Give me the heads up if you see Blaine coming," Tory says. She wants to be ready. Even if Al's not here, he may have told Blaine to fire her on his behalf, a task he'd surely relish.

Robyn nods. "Someone's coming but it's not Blaine. It's Tyler again."

There's a soft knock on their door and Tyler turns the handle again. "Hey. When I got downstairs, a couple walked in asking for you."

A couple? Like Gigi and Francisco maybe? "Did they give their names?"

Tyler nods. "The Corbins."

Shit! Tory folds her hands into the praying position, pressing her fingers to her lips. Robyn stops typing. "Who are they?"

"Oh, well, you know, the Corbins are the parents of my best friend who died in the car driven by the guy I kissed last night."

Robyn's eyes light up with panic, as do Tyler's.

"How strong of a cup of coffee do you need?" Tyler asks.

Tory plants her hands on her desk and pushes down to force her body up. "My life is getting to the point where strong coffee won't be enough unless I have a pill to swallow with it."

Robyn nods.

"Thank you again, Tyler," Tory says, hand on his shoulder, and the two begin walking down the center stairs. Before she reaches the bottom, she sees Chet and Pam, sitting at a table with one extra chair between them, both of them gripping cups of coffee.

The only reason they could possibly be here is to scold her. They're not the type to sweetly check in with her and see how she's doing. They haven't reached out to her since Quinn's funeral, except to confirm when Tory was handing over her apartment key. The only other option for them coming here is if they've brought special mementos of Quinn's that they lovingly want to gift to her. But they don't have any bags or boxes. Anyway, Tory's already kept some things that were meaningful to her. Before the Corbins came to move out Quinn's belongings, Tory had what she wanted, like the margarita glasses her and Quinn stole from a sketchy Mexican bar after crossing the border south of Laredo one Saturday.

Now nearing the end of the stairs, Tyler leans closer to Tory. "In a minute, I'll bring over some coffee. Say 'thank you' if you're okay. Or if you need to get away from these people, say 'that looks hot' and I can spill it all over the table or down the front of the mean-looking lady if you need."

"Wow, that's a super clever plan."

Tyler smiles. "I did that once, for my girlfriend who wasn't my girlfriend at the time. She was trying to break up with her boyfriend and I was selfishly trying to help her."

"Good to know you have on-cue coffee spilling experience. Okay, I might need that." Tory winks her goodbye to Tyler.

Pam notices her and straightens. Chet turns. "Tory." Chet stands to give her a hug. He always was the kinder of the two, to her and to Quinn.

"C.C.," Tory says, hugging him back. Pam remains seated with a tentative smile. "Hi, P.C." Tory leans down to hug her and feels like she's hugging plywood. "What a surprise."

"Please, join us if you have a minute," Chet says.

Tory takes a seat in what feels like an electric execution chair.

"How have you two been?" she says through a smile. "I've been hoping that you've been okay."

"It's been a difficult two weeks," Chet says, looking to Pam.

Pam points her chin in the air, her shoulders strong and square. She's throwing the same shade she gave Tory years ago when Tory spent the night with Quinn and didn't make her bed the next morning. Pam takes a long, drawn-out sip of her coffee.

"Tory," Chet continues, "we know that Nick has been arrested for Quinn's death but we were surprised to learn that you and your father worked to bail him out."

Tory rests her hands on the table. "My dad has worked for

years representing people wrongly accused and I'm proudly following in his footsteps."

Pam slams her coffee mug down, splashing some coffee up and down the sides. "There's no way you can believe Nick is innocent," she quips. "All of the facts are against him and he belongs in jail."

"The facts are not against him. And actually, the team we're putting together is already gathering evidence to clear his name."

"How can you do this to Quinn? She was your best friend!" Pam sneers.

"Is," Tory says. "She still is my best friend."

"She would want justice and you are working to free a guilty man."

"She would want justice for an innocent man wrongly accused," Tory says. "She liked Nick and believed in him, as I do."

Pam nods with short, choppy movements. "She did like that man and now everyone in town is seeing how much you like him too. We've seen the photos, Tory. It's disgusting that you and Nick are out in public kissing and making a scene."

"There's a long story behind the moment in those photos."

"I'm terribly disappointed in you and how you are behaving," she barks. "I always told Quinn to be more like you, more confident and strong, but now I'm sorry I ever did."

Tory rolls her fingertips with an impatient tap. Then over her shoulder, Tyler appears.

"Here's your coffee, Tory," he says, holding out a ceramic mug, his eyes waiting...waiting...waiting for her words.

In a split-second she imagines this steaming, hot cup of

coffee spilled on the table and flowing Pam's way, forcing the end of this terrible visit. *Say the words "that looks hot" and it will happen.* Tory smiles instead. "Thank you, Tyler."

His eyes flash with surprise and his grin is all but giving their exchange away as he hands her the ceramic mug and walks away.

Tory repositions the handle, turning the cup to give her something to do as she finds her words. As nasty as Pam is, she's had a big loss too. *Have patience.* "Pam," she says, looking up. "I'm not going to sit here and listen to you be mean to me. I am not your daughter. I am a smart woman who knows more facts than you are willing to accept."

"Tory…" Chet interrupts.

"No, Chet," she says, and then turns back to Pam, who is grinding her jaw. "I know what the pictures 'look' like but until you want to listen and hear about what I've been through, what Nick's been through and what we know, I will not let you bash me."

"Why would I want to hear what Nick's been through? What about me?"

Tory leans in. "And what about me? You haven't even asked *me* how I'm doing."

"Okay." Chet raises his hands to stop Pam. "It's clear this is going nowhere."

"No, actually," Tory says. "It is going somewhere. Nick will be cleared."

"We're suing him," Pam blurts.

Tory sneers. "I'm not surprised. And we're ready."

Pam slaps her hands on the table. "I never thought the little girl I loved so much would turn on us like this!"

Loved? This bitch loved her? "I'm not turning on you. I'm doing everything I can to defend an innocent man." Tory turns to Chet. "If a day comes and you want to listen to Nick's side of the story, you should. Especially before you file a civil suit." She stands up. "Because if you sue Nick, we will win."

Pam gasps. Chet's eyes go hard.

Tory turns and walks away, heading for the center staircase. She grips the railing for balance, certain C.C. and P.C. are staring at her and this would be a hell of a bad time to trip. Now a few steps up, she knows she's in view of Robyn's spy window too. It feels like all eyes are on her. But is Quinn watching too? Would she be proud that Tory is continuing the fight to prove Nick isn't a bad person?

Tory reaches the top of the stairs but before she opens her office door she leans against the wall, pinning her arms against her chest. Her heart surges with confidence and confusion.

Nick. She's just gotten a taste of what he's been through. He's been painted as an evil killer by so many people in this town. Now she's glued to his reputation as the repulsive defender.

And the thought of being with him, paired together in this fight, is making her count the seconds until she sees him tonight.

[TWENTY-EIGHT]

The soft chime of the doorbell rings at the Taylor residence.

"That's him," Jamie says, taking a final wipe of the kitchen counter and draping the towel over the dishwasher handle. "Let's go, John." She tugs his arm, but John's feet stay planted in the kitchen, a wide smile and proud eyes on his daughter.

"You two are so cute," Tory says, glancing into a powder compact mirror, touching up her red lipstick. "You really don't have to run and hide. It's your house."

John turns to Jamie. "I do want to say hello to Nick. And besides, we haven't harassed a date of Tory's since she lived here, which was…when?" He looks to Tory. "When you graduated high school?"

Tory grimaces. The last time a boy came to the door to pick her up, John kept him one-on-one in his study for thirty-minutes talking about the weather, football and cars. Oh, the joys of living at home, even if she's only living here for another week. Tory flashes a sassy smile and does a model-worthy spin before heading toward the door. Her above-the-knee black Michael

Kors dress swings with her turn, her legs bare and an easy to slip on, or off, pair of black heeled sandals on her feet. The halter crisscross front of her dress looks sexy without being slutty. At least, it didn't make her dad blush when he first saw her come down the stairs tonight.

She opens the door and the sight of Nick makes her heart thump like a kernel of popcorn just popped inside it. His blazing eyes are looking at her, with his pearly white teeth dazzling in a wide smile. He's wearing black dress pants, slim and tight, with a white button-down shirt that looks custom fit to the angles of his chest.

"Good evening." His voice smolders and he extends a dozen red roses gathered at the stems with a white linen wrapping.

"Hello, handsome," she says, raising an eyebrow. Slowly, she takes the roses and then buries her nose in the arrangement. "They smell romantic. Thank you."

He scans her from head to toe. "You look beautiful," he whispers, stepping closer and slipping one hand behind the nape of her neck. He gently pulls her closer for a welcome kiss so hot it's a wonder the roses in her hand don't wilt.

"Thank you for the compliment. Come in for a second." She nods inside and he follows her. It's not the first time he's been at the Taylors. They hung out here before, at least a group of them did, before they went to a Fourth of July concert the summer they all worked at Indigo. Nick was also here the night of Reed's attack, when he drove a distraught Tory home and explained the incident to her furious father.

They turn the corner into the kitchen, where Jamie and John stand with enthusiastic smiles and their arms around each other.

"Now there's a beautiful couple," Nick says, extending his arms to give Jamie a hug, followed with a kiss on her cheek. He turns and shakes John's hand. "It's nice to see you in a social situation, not a legal one."

John nods, shaking Nick's hand and then letting go. "I'm glad we got to spend some time together today. I'm very impressed with Frank."

Jamie has already gone to the pantry to get a vase for Tory's flowers. Tory opens the wrapping while Jamie fills the vase with water. "It sounds like Frank got a lot done in one day," Tory says.

Nick nods. "He sure did. It's a little disappointing that the Bear Creek arena claims they don't have any footage of the parking lot, when Frank says a camera is clearly there."

"Did Frank give you any updates on Reed after our meeting?" John asks.

"He did. He's got two guys now following Reed, rotating their shifts. Reed spent the day in his office at the Lexus dealership, and Frank also confirmed they have a source inside the Lexus dealership too."

"And so it begins," Jamie says.

"And we will be patient," John says. "If Reed has covered his tracks so well to be sure the parking lot footage was erased, he's not likely to make mistakes going forward."

"But if and when he does, we'll know." Nick turns to Tory and smiles. She's leaning over the counter, sniffing her roses. "Ready?"

"You bet." She hugs her mom goodbye. "Don't ask me when I'll be home because, you know, I'm twenty-fricken-four."

"Do us a favor and don't wake us up," John says. He gives

a sturdy smile to Nick and shakes his hand again. "I know that you'll keep her safe."

Nick nods. "She's my number one priority now." He slides his arm around Tory's waist, which makes Jamie clasp her hands to her chest, smiling. "You kids behave," Nick says to John and Jamie as he and Tory sweep through the door.

They walk with excited steps toward Nick's Lexus, where he opens her door and she slides into the passenger seat. In less than a minute, he's behind the wheel, backing up and onto the street.

His car seems to float down the street with the smooth sounds of the chill jazz station he's playing. She's hiked up her dress a bit to give him a teasing look at her legs and glances over to him. "I've never ridden in a car with you as the driver before."

He gives her a nervous glance. "I haven't had a passenger in a car with me since the accident."

Wow. She strokes his cheek. "I'm not afraid."

His eyes quickly flash to her. "Well, I'm terrified. If anything ever happened to you—"

"It won't." She gently holds his forearm while he grips the wheel with both hands. "Don't worry, it won't."

In minutes, they arrive at Nick's apartment building and he pulls into a space and parks. As he walks around the front of the car to open her door, she has a chance to study him. His body looks so taut and toned, his shirt and pants molded to his muscular physique. Her cheeks feel flush, knowing that if things heat up between them while they're alone in his apartment, the only thing between her and seeing him naked is the word "no". And as he reaches for her door, she's quickly forgetting that two-letter word.

Hand in hand they walk together in a route familiar to her. Only the last time she was here, she was running away. Now she gazes at his profile as he faces his apartment door, turning the key.

"Date night in Nick's apartment," she says as he cracks open the door. "I wouldn't want to be anywhere else."

He turns to face her, using his back to push open the door and leading her by the hands into his apartment, filled with the flavorful aroma of sweet Italian spices. "Whoa, that smells amazing!" she says. His apartment is softly lit with lamps she never even noticed before, making the space feel cozy and romantic. Red rose petals are scattered on the coffee table beside unlit white candles, and the same set up is on the counter where two place settings are pre-set. Also on the counter sits a slow cooker with a steam-covered glass lid and the obvious source of the delicious smell. "Nick! You cooked?"

"Would you like to know what's on the menu?" He beams, walking over to the slow cooker and leaning down to lift up the lid. She follows him and rests her head on his shoulder. "Do you like Bolognese?"

Her lips press to his ear. "I don't know what Bolognese is but it's now my favorite."

He scrunches up his nose from her lips tickling his ear and quickly stutter-steps away.

"Oh! What have we here!?" she teases. "I found a ticklish spot?"

His eyes light up. "You'll drive me crazy if you do that again." He raises his hands up and she grabs them, the two playfully pushing against each other.

"What's wrong with going crazy?"

"Okay, tough girl, let's see how long you can last." He twists her hands down and presses his lips on her ear. "Red or white wine," he whispers with a few extra tantalizing breaths.

Chills zing down her body and she wiggles away.

"Ah-ha!" He drops her hands. "Looks like you have the same ticklish spot too."

She's smiling so wide, it's starting to hurt her face. His smiling eyes are irresistible, making her want him as an appetizer right now. She takes one step toward him. He reads her intent and steps closer to her. Their lips meet with an aggressive kiss. His hands plunge into her hair and hers grab his face. Their kissing makes their bodies start a sensual dance and kiss by kiss and step by step they spin in a slow circle of passion in the center of the kitchen.

"I…" he whispers, kissing her. "I haven't…" another kiss, "…even lit the candles yet."

Her laughter makes it harder to kiss him. She stops and presses her body against his, pinning him against the cabinets. Her finger gently strokes his lips, followed by her thumb, to wipe off her red lipstick marks from his face. "Oh, yeah…the candles. We should stop…for candles."

He nuzzles her cheek. "We can…you know…forget the candles." His eyes lower seductively and Tory's beginning to think if they keep this up, they won't be eating dinner anytime soon.

She leans toward his ear. "How about I light the candles and you open the wine."

His eyes drink her in and gently, ever so gently, he strokes a finger down her face. "Deal." He moves away but keeps his eyes on her before choosing a bottle of wine from a cabinet.

She looks around the kitchen. "Where's your source of, you know, heat? I mean, fire? You know, the way to ignite your heart, or candles?"

He slides open a gadget drawer and she picks up a lighter but he's looking at her with searing eyes so hot, his eyes could ignite the dang wicks. His hands grip the neck of the wine bottle and there's something about watching a man open a bottle of wine that she finds kinky. He twists and eases the cork out of the bottle while she imagines his strong hands twisting and touching her body. She flicks on the lighter to clear her smutty mind, lighting the candles by their dinner plates and the candles on the coffee table. When she turns to face the kitchen, he's coming to her with two glasses of wine.

"A toast?" he asks.

Smiling, she puts down the lighter and accepts her glass. "To?"

"You being here with me. Finally." He raises his glass and she gently taps his for a toast. As she sips she sees the raw appreciation in his eyes. So happy. So sincere. All he seems to want is her, here.

She lowers her eyes. "I'm a little jealous."

"Of?"

She nods toward the kitchen. "That you can cook."

He sips again, smiling. "I totally hosted the manly cooking hour here earlier when Francisco came over to show me how to make this."

"He did?"

"That's not to say I can't cook, because I can, a little, sometimes. But I wanted something special."

"Well, I can't cook, so to me this is super special."

Nick opens his stereo cabinet to turn on some music and together they return to the kitchen, their arms brushing as they walk. Nick plates two servings of spaghetti, topped with Bolognese and freshly grated parmesan cheese. They each sit on a barstool, enjoying their meal, wine and each other for over an hour. Tory clears their plates and rinses them in the sink and when she turns around, Nick is standing behind her with a massive smile and his hands behind his back.

"Whatchu got?" she asks, smiling and drying her hands.

"Dessert." He smiles proudly.

"Either dessert is in your hands, or dessert is you and I'd be really, really happy with both."

Hands still behind his back, he leans forward to give her a kiss. "Are you ready for something sweet?" he whispers.

His damn whispering is making her weak. "Yeah, I'm ready."

He straightens and whips out two individually wrapped cookies, the same kind she brought him once before. "Peanut butter and vanilla coconut with no oatmeal raisin in sight."

She smiles wildly. "My cinnamon roll boy has cookies!"

"Vanilla coconut for you." He gives her cookie to her. "Peanut butter for me." He opens his cookie wrapper and takes a sensuous bite.

She nibbles on her cookie, watching his lips and not feeling hungry for sweets anymore. His lips are captivating her and so is this music floating around the room and now that Nat "King" Cole's L-O-V-E is playing, she feels like dancing. "You like romantic, big-band music, huh?"

"There's nothing like some Frank Sinatra or the sweet, soul sounds of Etta James."

Eyes on him, she sets her cookie on the counter and brushes his hand as she takes his cookie from him and wraps her arms around his shoulders for a dance. Instinctively his hands find her waist and his hips begin to move, easy and slow, to the soft, musical notes. He leads her, gently nudging each direction he wants to go, and step by step they've danced their way out of the kitchen and into the living room.

"You're a great dancer," she whispers, kicking off her shoes.

"You're the perfect dancing partner."

"Where'd you learn how to dance?"

His eyes flicker. "My mom, actually. She'd turn on music like this and she and my dad would dance and then she'd take me by the arms and show me how."

Tory softens.

"I miss her. Especially with what has happened this year."

Tory tightens her arms around him as the music plays on and they press close, dancing. "No one can replace the love of a mother."

He squeezes her. "Absolutely right."

She eases her hold and stops dancing, gently stroking his cheek. What an emotionally ravaged man, who has risen up stronger. The hits keep coming his way but he doesn't lash out, doesn't pity himself. He just wants to be loved and give love. The music plays but they stand still, losing themselves in each other's eyes. She leans toward his lips and softly kisses him and he softly kisses her. They kiss again, and each kiss draws them emotionally deeper and connected with each other, deeper than anything she's ever felt with a man before. Their kissing builds up speed and intensity; she's getting lost in this music and lost in this man. He guides her backward, toward the couch. He wraps his hand around the back of her head and lowers himself with her to lie down. The weight of his body presses her and she squeezes her fingers into his back, enjoying his weight, enjoying this ride. He eases off of her to the side, still kissing, while one of his hands holds her head and the other finds the outside of her leg. His hand slips under her dress, stroking higher on the outside of her thigh and now inches from finding her lace panties. His eyes burn with a passion she wants to consume but suddenly, she smells cardboard boxes from a storage room and feels pinned against a wall, arms bound in the air, the stinging pain of teeth biting her mouth. She raises her hand to stop Nick's lips.

His breathing is ragged. "Too fast?" he whispers, stopping his hand.

Her chest rises and falls with her heavy breathing. "It's just..."

He lowers his head to his bent arm, keeping his hand on her thigh as they lie side-by-side, eye-to-eye. His eyes scream with worry.

"I want you to know something," she whispers. "I've not... you know...done anything this intense since what happened to me..."

His eyes widen. "Oh Tory," he whispers, sliding his hand out from under her dress. "I understand. Completely."

Her head bobs with short nods. "I want to do all of this, with you."

He presses his nose to hers. "Baby, we won't do anything until you're ready. Really ready."

She bobs her head again with short nods, absorbing the caring look of love from his eyes.

He holds her head with both hands and presses her lips with a slow kiss. His lips hover above hers and his eyes send protection, easing her fears, her insecurities. "Together…" he whispers. "You and I…we decide how far we want to go."

"How far do you want to go?"

"It doesn't matter as long as we decide together." He strokes her hair. "Only if we both say yes is when we take it further. Only if we both say yes is when we'll make love."

His words push ripples of pleasure through her body. *Make love. With Nick.* Something she's imagined, he just said. He's the guy. He's the one she wants to share herself with to clear the memory of what happened before. Just not tonight.

He presses his lips to hers so intently and hard, she feels it in her soul. Her eyes are tearing up and his are too in a moment so intense, it draws them closer than any physical act could. She trusts him with her soul. Her body. With her life.

Lying side-by-side, they stare into each other. His fingers stroke her hair; her fingers touch his face as she softly sniffles. Warm candlelight flickers through the room, while the easy sound of big-band romance plays in the background and with each soft stroke of his fingers she realizes that she has fallen completely in love.

A tingly feeling numbs Tory's arm. Her blurry eyes blink, waking from sleep. The music, the candles, the man inches from her face still holding her in his arms: she's still with Nick. His eyes are closed, his breathing satisfied and peaceful. *She fell asleep with Nick!* And she didn't watch him doze off so she must have crashed first. A few more blinks and all of her senses return. *Nick. Their kissing. Him on her. Her stopping him.* Her eyes study his sleeping face, carved with confidence but bruised with tragedy and hurt. He's cute when he sleeps. Hell, he's just as hot when he's awake. Lying like this, watching him sleep, she wonders what it will be like if they become lovers. *If? No, when.* If they were already lovers, she'd know how she'd wake him up now. She'd gently press warm kisses on his neck, roll her bare body on top of him and get his eyes to open by straddling him for a middle-of-the-night ride.

She grins at the idea; it's been a long time since she's had these kinds of thoughts. She shut down after Reed forced his way on her two years ago. She's never wanted to show her body to any other man. Certainly not Jake, who was a half-decent kisser but who never passed the compassionate test of someone who could share her emotional first-time-since-the-Reed incident. But Nick? He passed the compassionate test and she wasn't even intending to test him. He put her first by stopping. She should have drawn a clear line earlier tonight but she pressed him and kissed him and starting sending signals that all of the merchandise in her store was open for the taking. Instead of ordering an Uber and showing her the door, he vowed nothing would happen until they both agree. And now this: he's held her for as long as it took for her to be comfortable; so comfortable she fell asleep. *God, she loves him.*

Her shoulder twitches and her wriggling causes his eyes to flutter. A few blinks later, his eyes focus on her. "You fell asleep," he whispers through a sleepy smile.

He looks so kissable and cuddly. "And apparently you did too."

His eyes scrunch with pain and he pulls his arm out from under her body.

"My arm fell asleep too," she says.

"My arm could fall off and I wouldn't care as long as it had been holding you."

Her heart smolders.

"What time is it?" he yawns, answering his own question by lifting his watch. "Whoa, 2 a.m."

"Past my curfew."

He strokes her hair, his eyes now wide awake and one-hundred percent on her. "You need to go home?"

"I'm happy here. I'm happy with you." She kisses his cheek, the tip of his nose and finally his soft mouth. "But…I do have to work tomorrow."

"I guess it's good to be rested before you get fired."

"Something like that." She struggles to sit up and he offers her a hand. Together they stand up, facing each other. His messed-up hair and sleepy eyes look so sexy, she better leave here now and cap this perfect evening because if she stays, she'll be tempted to lead him by the hand into his bedroom where they can make memories until morning. And after just having that horrible flashback and needing to stop him hours ago, that's not what she should do until she's sure that flashback will never come back again. "I want you to know that earlier, it had nothing to do with you. I—"

"Tory." He squeezes her hands. "No need to explain. I know what happened to cause your reaction. I should have talked to you first."

"I want you to know, I feel good. You make me feel good, about myself."

"You're safe here. I want you to know, I won't let anything happen to you."

She absorbs the caring look from his eyes. "This was an amazing date. I hope we can do this again, soon."

His face lights up. "Same place and time tomorrow?"

"Listen to you!" She gently pushes on his chest. "I'd love to but I promised to take Daniel to Socat tomorrow night."

"Going out to a restaurant? With another man?"

She grins. "I owe him some quality time. But after dinner…" She presses closer, trailing a finger down his chest until it stops at his top button. "I'm completely available. All night."

"All…night?"

"Yeah, actually. Tomorrow night, Jamie and John are going to the Cattle Ball in Austin and staying at a hotel. After all this drama with Jake, I don't want to be alone, so I was going to ask Daniel to have a sleepover with me."

"A sleepover with Daniel?"

She gently pushes him again. "Footie pajamas and pizza at midnight like all the crazy kids have. No, seriously, not like that."

"Ohhh," Nick says, grinning.

"But, instead, maybe I could come over here after dinner."

"You could?" He presses closer, his eyes scanning her dress.

She lifts his chin so he looks her in the eye. "As long as someone keeps me company, all night."

"A sleepover at my place? Are you sure?"

Her flashback surprised her once and the only way to know if it will come back again is to see where this thing with Nick goes. She's focused now, focused on him. *Hell yeah, she's sure.* And she knows the word to say to prove it.

With her hand still under his chin, she leans closer to his cheek, pressing her lips against his ear.

"Yes."

TWENTY-NINE

Another morning, another cautious walk into Indigo. Tory wraps her arms across her chest, pulling the front of her navy, three-quarter sleeve cardigan together while scanning the parking lot. A few days ago, she looked around like this for any sign of Jake. Today, she's trying to find Blaine's car. She already knows Al's not here yet because she parked next to his vacant space. Either one of them could still fire her today.

A delectable aroma of ground coffee beans greets her as she opens the door. That's one perk of working here, it always smells comforting. Behind the counter, one of her favorite baristas notices her.

"Hey, Tory," the young girl says, already ringing up Tory's coffee.

"I've been thinking about you! Did you ever find your cat?" Tory says, paying.

"Last night!" she squeals, eyes wide. "I think my boyfriend had let her out on purpose."

Tory tucks her wallet into her purse. "If he did, that's not good. Be careful." Another barista hands her a cup of coffee.

"So, Tyler's working nights for the rest of the week, right?"

"Yeah, he'll be in later," one of the guys behind the counter says. "And none of us down here know if Al or you-know-who is coming in today."

"Thanks for reading my mind," she says, sipping.

"We all think Al would be crazy to fire you," he says.

Tory smiles. "Thank you. But in the end, this is his business and I have to respect his decision if he does. In the meantime," she looks at both of the baristas, "I'll work as hard as I can during the time I have left."

They both nod and Tory turns just in time to see the front door swing open and Al confidently walk inside. He's wearing his trademark warm, schmoozing smile and his Louis Vuitton satchel over his shoulder.

Okay, today's the day. Her breathing goes shallow as he walks closer. She's prepared for the worst but for all she knows, Al may have never seen the photos. She stands, waiting for him to come closer, while her hot cup of coffee heats up her hand.

Smiling, Al stops to greet a customer and lingers with their conversation.

Standing here for no reason while a cup of coffee boils in her hand feels awkward, so she heads up the stairs to her office. If fate is going to bring her a pink slip today, fate knows where to find her.

Within minutes, Robyn has joined her upstairs and the two leave their office door open. Throughout the morning, Al passes by a few times going to and from his office. Each time Tory hears his voice coming closer, she stops what she's doing to face the door, trying to see if he wants to catch her eye. And each time, Al passes her by.

Her phone vibrates with a text. It's from Frank.

Are you available for a coffee break? I'm close by

How lovely! She types back.

Absolutely! Text when you get here and I'll come down

Three minutes later, her phone vibrates.

I have arrived and am already at a table. No rush, come down when you can

Damn. When he said he was close by, she didn't think he was that close. She grabs her phone and hurries downstairs, not interested in getting any coffee but more excited to visit with him. She spots him at a corner table, sipping coffee from a ceramic mug.

"What a great treat," she says, approaching him.

Frank stands and they share a hug. "Time is a ticking and I'm busy working," he says, pulling out a chair for her. They both have a seat. "No coffee?" he asks.

She glances over to the counter, where there's a small line forming "No, I'm good."

He nods. "From what Nick tells me, much has happened since I saw you at the firing range."

She bunches up her shoulders and smiles. "It's been a roller-coaster but finally, I think we're both on the right track."

"Happy to hear this," he says. "I enjoyed meeting your father yesterday. We plan to get together tomorrow when he gets back into town."

"Good. So, what's the latest?"

A woman's laughter draws their attention. Al has just come downstairs, not too far from where she and Frank are sitting. Al gives a robust hug to the woman while a barista sets two cups of coffee at their table. Al and the woman have a seat.

"That's Al, right?" Frank asks.

"Yes. I'm not sure who he's with but for a while now he's been hosting all sorts of people who are stopping by to wish him well."

"He seems very connected."

"He is. There's no way Blaine will be able to keep up with all of the community, political and business connections like Al has."

Frank's eyes linger on Al. "He's connected, huh? Was it Al that gave you the concert tickets that Nick and Quinn used?"

How does he do this shit? "Frank, please don't let Nick know, but yes, Al was the one I got the tickets from. How did you guess that?"

"That concert was in high demand, so someone had to have known someone pretty high up, either with the band or the arena to get last-minute tickets. So, why do you not want Nick to know?"

"Nick is sensitive with this Indigo versus Faze thing and I never wanted him to know where the tickets really came from. I told Quinn to tell him they came from me, period."

"And who gave Al the tickets?"

"His good friend owns the Bear Creek Arena…" Tory stops. "Oh…wow. I see where you're going here."

Frank nods. "Maybe Al would have better luck if he asked his friend about the parking lot tapes."

"You don't think they were really erased?"

"I don't. I think the VP of Operations we talked to was inept and too lazy to find them. There's no way an arena the size of Bear Creek wouldn't keep their security tapes for at least ninety days. Too much happens during events, in the parking lot and in the arena. It's too great of a liability on their part if those tapes go missing."

Fear sinks her gut. "You want me to ask Al to ask his friend for something to help Nick? Al pretty much hates Nick! He's lectured me about staying safe and away from him."

Frank folds his hands, resting them on the table. "We need that high-level connection that only he has."

Her shoulders drop. "I'm walking on eggshells thinking Al's going to fire me any second! I don't know if he's seen the pictures of me and Nick kissing but I'm guessing he has and it's only a matter of time until he asks me to leave. How on earth can I sit down with him and ask if his friend can help Nick?"

Frank's mouth stretches with a wide grin. "You won't be asking him for Nick. You'll be asking for Quinn. Remember, proving Nick's innocence may help lead us to the real criminal. Even though my primary interest is to clear Nick's name, I'd also like to know who did this, for Quinn's sake."

Tory nods. *For Quinn's sake.* For Quinn's sake, she'll put herself out there and do anything. Frank's right. This isn't just about Nick. She looks over to the table where Al and his guest sit, smiling and sipping coffee. Who would have thought Nick's main competitor might be the one who can get the evidence to clear his name? Asking Al is worth a shot. And if she only has one chance to ask him for one thing before she's fired, she'd rather ask Al to do this than get a recommendation letter for herself.

"I'll ask him. When I get a chance, I'll ask Al."

"Good. Keep me posted. And another question, if you don't mind."

"Fire away."

"What does Jake look like?"

Her shoulders straighten. "Whoa. Jake? Why?"

"I'd like to know what he looks like."

Good thing she has her phone with her. She scrolls through her photos and finds one of the two of them together. "Wow. This was, like, the second time we went out." She stares at the photo as memories slam her heart. Jake seemed like such a nice guy at the time, with a warm smile and hilarious jokes. Hanging out with him seemed like it would be fun. They took this selfie before they went to a free jazz concert at Cantina Square. That April night was cool, the sunset painted with warm colors and they sat together, sharing a sub sandwich he bought from a grocery store with his loyal shopper discount card. She wanted to buy some cheese and wine with her own money but he wouldn't let her, because he didn't have a coupon. And she should have known then that any relationship with Jake wasn't going to work.

She shakes her head to clear the memory and forwards the picture to Frank.

He opens the picture and his expression tightens.

"What?" she asks. "Have you seen him before?"

He slowly nods. "I noticed a guy like that today, sitting alone on a bench."

"Where?"

Frank puts down his phone. "Here. Outside Indigo."

A sliver of afternoon sunlight reflects off the center staircase, serving as the call for the afternoon coffee break.

Robyn stretches her arms and stands up. "I'm going to grab a cup of something not from Rwanda. Want to join me?"

Tory stops typing. "Go ahead, I'm good." She doesn't want to leave this office until she's ready to go for the day, and hopefully by then either Robyn or Tyler can walk her to her car. Robyn already did a quick walk outside and didn't notice anyone on the benches near the door. If the guy on the bench that Frank saw was Jake, he's not there anymore. Besides, Tory wants to stay put because Al is down in his office and she's waiting to catch him the next time he walks by.

Robyn disappears just as Tory hears Al's voice. It sounds like he's standing outside of his office, talking with his secretary, the backstabbing bitch. Tory stops typing. His voice is getting louder. He's coming this way! She stands up and smooths out her black skirt, makes sure her white button-down blouse is tucked in and gives a gentle tug to her blue cardigan. She's counting his steps in her mind, timing her burst into the hall-way right when he should be close to her office. *Right about... now.* She pops her head into the hall. *Perfect timing!* Al sees her and his eyes widen.

"Hi, Al," Tory says, stepping into the hall. "Do you have a minute?"

"Tory," he says, tiling his head slightly. "What is it?"

Fine. She'll take that. "I hope you're doing well. I wanted to ask you something, unrelated to work." *Good! Pretend no pictures of her lips on Nick's exist!*

He glances at his watch. "I have a meeting downstairs with the Chamber President now."

"Oh, okay, I can walk with you."

His eyes tighten, irritated, and he begins walking toward the stairs, Tory beside him.

"I was hoping I might use your name for a call I need to make."

"What type of call?"

They're at the top of the stairs and it only takes a minute to get to the bottom. She needs to hurry!

"You know the owner of the Bear Creek arena, right?" she asks.

"I do. What, do you need tickets for a show?"

"Um, no, I needed to ask him for something else."

Al stops in the middle of the stairs and looks to her impatiently. "What do you need from him?"

"I needed to ask him about security procedures."

"Why?"

Here she goes, ready to be fired on the spot. But for Quinn's sake, and Nick's, do it! "I think they may have evidence to help prove who killed Quinn."

Al steps backward and almost trips on the stair behind him. "Who killed Quinn? We all know who killed Quinn."

"No, sir, we don't know who did, yet."

His cheeks pulse. "Why am I paying you right now? I'm paying you to help with legal work and contracting issues for Indigo. This isn't a conversation you should be having during work time."

He turns but she tugs his elbow.

"Al, I need your help."

He stops and turns back.

"Please, Al. I know Bear Creek will have what we need. They have surveillance video of the parking lot that will show the condition of Nick's car when it arrived and will show how someone tampered with it during the show."

His eyebrows tighten. "Is this what you really think happened?"

She nods. "I know it is. And as soon as I get the proof, everyone else will know too."

His eyes drift to the side in an expression she can't read. *Please say something!*

He gives a slight nod. "I have meetings here through dinnertime. After that, I'll call him at home."

She teeters on the steps. "You will? Oh Al, that's more than I was expecting. Thank you so much!" She opens her arms to hug him and he opens his, a little. They squeeze and she steps back.

His eyes still look stern and uncertain. "I can see that nothing is going to stop you. My thoughts on what you are doing with Nick Allen still haven't changed. You are putting yourself in danger. And it might turn out that this video proves his guilt and if it does, it would be something you should see."

There's no way it will. "Thank you, Al. You really are the best boss ever."

A voice from the bottom of the stairs calls Al's name and Al disappears down the stairs.

She lived! She didn't get fired! She might get a recommendation letter after all! And the icing on the cake is Al himself making the Bear Creek arena call! Forget what he said that this video may prove Nick's guilt. Hopefully by this time tomorrow, Al's inquiry will result in Frank getting the surveillance tapes. Soon, they may be looking at the proof of who screwed with Nick's car!

Tory dances up the steps and back to her office, her fingers typing a text to Frank, her dad and Nick.

This seems unreal. They really could be one short day away from finding Quinn's killer.

Tory glances at her watch: it's 5:30 p.m.

Robyn left for the day about an hour ago. Tory's humming a song, straightening her desk and getting ready to meet Daniel downstairs so they can ride together to Socat. This will be nice, spending some time with Daniel. And she doesn't need to worry about Nick having something to do because he and Frank are going out for dinner too. They'll probably go to a super-casual open-air restaurant, like she and Daniel are. Nick still isn't ready for normal things either.

This evening she feels like she's the frolicking bubbles in a glass of champagne. She has finally secured the proper entertainment, liquor and sign licenses for Indigo. She hasn't lost her job. She asked a major favor of Al and he's agreed. She can already taste the chargrilled deliciousness of chicken fajita tacos and can't wait to watch Daniel's face as he takes his first bite. And tonight, after dinner, she'll be alone with Nick until the sun rises.

She looks down to her white blouse and runs her finger down the line of buttons. If she's spending the night at Nick's, at some point this shirt's coming off. The question is, will it be her or Nick unbuttoning it?

Her cheeks warm with the thought just as a text vibrates her phone. It's Daniel and he's waiting at Indigo's front door.

Tory locks up her office and heads downstairs, passing the coffee counter and waving at Tyler.

"Night shift tonight, huh?" she yells.

He smiles. "Here 'til closing! Have a nice night!"

She flings open the front door and feels the humid air from a rain shower that just passed through. And in her view is Daniel's smirking face. "Well hello, sugar lips," she says, giving him a hug.

"We're drinking tonight, just a heads up," he says, flicking his hand in the air.

"What happened to your car?" she asks as they walk toward hers.

"They say it's the battery. The damn thing wouldn't start. And you know me, I've never had a hard time getting anything, or anyone, started before."

"No, you haven't," she says, laughing. They near her car, stepping around puddles in the parking lot. Tory looks all around. "Keep your eyes open for Jake," she whispers. "There's a chance he may have been around here earlier."

Daniel shrugs. "If he's hanging around watching you, you need to sit that boy down and have a talk."

She nods, unlocking her car. "Remember I'll be back in Austin next week. That's what I'm really worried about."

They get into her car and head to the highway ramp leading to the Pearl and Socat. The first traffic light she approaches turns red.

"I always hit this light," she says. "So, when will you get your car back?"

"Tomorrow for sure. I think."

She shakes her head, smiling. Classic Daniel: certain, maybe. The traffic light turns green. But a light on her dashboard catches her attention. "Oh great, look at that." She points to her dash and the brake warning light.

Daniel glances over. "Ha, now it's your turn for car problems."

Ugh. The last thing she needs is to lose her car for a day. This isn't surprising, though. She hasn't even taken in her car for an oil change in a while. There's a long list of normal life-tasks she hasn't done, like her favorite skirts have been waiting at the dry cleaners for weeks.

She starts driving again. "Maybe I can take you to pick up your car tomorrow and drop off mine," she says, winking his way.

"God, you multitask so efficiently."

Another traffic light ahead turns red but when Tory brakes to stop, the brake pedal feels like she's pressing a sponge. She pushes down again, finally stopping at the busy intersection full with pedestrians crossing the street during this rush hour.

"That didn't feel right," she says, looking down at her foot on the brake pedal.

Daniel stretches his neck to look at her foot too. "Your shoes are on point, by the way. I love a good sling back."

The light turns green and Tory drives forward, now only about three blocks from the highway entrance ramp. The next traffic light ahead of them is green but the pedestrian count-down signal looks like it's on single digits.

"Please punch it because I'm craving some carne asada," Daniel moans.

Tory hits the gas but the light turns yellow and she knows she better stop. She presses the brakes when suddenly the pedal sinks all the way to the floor. "Shit!" she cries as her car plows ahead. The light turns red and she barrels through the intersection, narrowly missing pedestrians who had already stepped out into the crosswalk.

"What's happening?" Daniel yells.

"My brakes are out!"

Tory's car speeds forward through the busy streets. She pumps the brakes, trying to get pressure back up. "I can't stop!"

"Oh my God!" Daniel screams, slapping both hands on the dashboard. "Turn the car off!"

"I can't! Then I wouldn't be able to steer!" She swerves around a parcel delivery truck parked on the inside lane. *This isn't happening!*

"We're gonna die!"

"Stop it, Daniel! We're not going that fast! Focus! Grab my emergency brake! Get ready to pull it!" She swerves back into the inside lane just as the light ahead of them turns red. *Shit!*

People start walking across the street, right in their path.

"Jesus! Mother of Mary!" Daniel screams.

The people closest to them have passed, but not the ones in the crosswalk ahead. She'll hit them if she goes straight! "I'm turning right!" She leans into the steering wheel, beeping the horn to stop anyone else from stepping into the intersection. A bicyclist wearing all red whizzes by beside her, flipping her off, as she makes the turn.

Daniel flips him back. "Fuck you, mister tight pants!" he yells. "No one looks good in red spandex!"

"There's room to stop now! Get ready to pull the brake!" Tory yells, then looks in her rearview mirror. *Damn!* Another car is right behind her! "No! Don't pull! That car's gonna hit us from behind if you pull that brake!"

Two blocks ahead, the light changes to yellow. Her car has slowed way down but might not be totally stopped by the time they hit that intersection! She'll have to pull the emergency brake and risk getting hit from behind!

Suddenly the car behind her pulls around her and swerves in front of her, braking.

"You're gonna hit them!" Daniel screams.

"I think they want me to hit them!"

The car ahead brakes to slow themselves to match Tory's speed. "Hold on! I'm gonna bump them!"

"Holding! Holding!"

She taps their bumper and they hit their brakes, slowing both cars. They both steer their cars toward open parking spaces by the curb, her bumper still touching the back bumper of the car ahead. Both cars come to a stop. Tory pulls up the emergency brake with her wobbly-feeling hands. Her whole body feels wobbly.

Daniel's hands are flapping so fast it looks like he might shake the skin off of his hands. "Oh my God, oh my God, oh my God."

"I can't breathe," Tory says, her heart pounding.

The door opens on the car ahead of them just as Tory recognizes the car. It's a Volvo. And the driver's getting out.

Her shoulders collapse. "What. The. Jake."

Jake runs up to her door. "Tory!" he calls, pressing his hands on the window. "Are you okay?"

She's gripping the steering wheel so hard she feels like she's bending it. She looks at Jake's face, painted with worry. He's trying to open her door but it's still locked. Daniel keeps hitting the lock button on his door to keep it that way.

She can't move but is aware of other people now running up to her car.

"Tory!" Jake calls. "Open the door!"

"That's...Jake..." she mumbles in a calm voice, looking to Daniel. His mouth has fallen open. Someone is pounding on his window, trying to get in to help or something. Daniel gives them a thumbs-up to get them to stop knocking.

"Okay..." she sputters, eyes on Daniel. "Okay...Jake is here." She turns her head and looks at Jake. *Jake? For real?* "Okay..." She looks back to Daniel to see if he can give her some sense of logic. "I'm...I'm gonna need to chat with him," she says, pointing back to Jake. "Can you make a super-quick call for me?"

Daniel puckers his lips. "Oh sure. We almost died and your ex is trying to break your window, so whom do we call?"

She reaches for her purse on the floor next to Daniel's leg. Her gun is in there, but that's not what she needs right now. She pulls out her phone and hands it to him. "Let's give Nick a ring."

Daniel nods. "You bet, my love."

Tory turns back to her window, where Jake is still knocking. This is so unbelievable, she still doesn't believe it. This must be a dream. A fucked-up nightmare. Nick will never believe this just happened. Frank is going to get here so fast, he's probably already on the way.

She unlocks the door and Jake opens it immediately, reaching in and protectively grabbing her shoulder. "Are you okay?" he asks again.

"I'm not sure…really…what…how are you…here?"

"What happened? Did your brakes go out?" Jake asks.

"I think…yeah…I think they did." She unbuckles her seatbelt and looks cautiously around. Daniel is hunched over, whispering into her phone. The people knocking on Daniel's window have stopped and are now standing on the sidewalk, staring at them. Both her car and Jake's are out of the lane of traffic, still touching bumper to bumper in a row of parallel parking spaces. Cars are slowing as they pass by, with people looking over to see what's going on.

She swings her legs to get out and Jake grips her elbow to help her. Before she stands, Daniel taps her shoulder, finished with the call.

"That call didn't go so well," he says.

She glances back over her shoulder. "Yeah…no…I bet it didn't." There's a good chance that Nick is on fire.

Jake tugs her elbow and she stands up, facing him. He looks different. His cheekbones are shallow, his eyes look ragged and his ginger-blonde hair looks like it hasn't been cut in a while.

"Thank you," she says. "I don't know why you're here but I'm glad you were."

"I saw you go through the light and I didn't know what was wrong."

She nods, hesitant. "But, you live…not here. Why have you been following me?"

His shoulders rise.

Tory realizes they are standing a few inches too close to the passing traffic. She closes her car door and walks to the front of her car, looking at where she bumped into Jake's car. It's dented, a little. Good thing she wasn't going that fast when she bumped him. She looks back at Jake's haunted and hurt eyes. Daniel has gotten out of the car too and stands next to the passenger door. The people lingering on the sidewalk have started to leave.

Tory rakes her hand through her hair and then crosses her arms over her chest. A few minutes of awkward silence pass while her brain races to process what just happened.

"We should talk," she says, facing Jake. "I should talk."

Jake looks around and then drops his eyes.

"Jake, I know you've been following me. And I'd like to ask you to please stop."

His eyes are on his shoes.

"I…I'm sorry for how I ended things with you. I know…I know I was rude and I'm sorry. But you didn't need to scare me with texts and following me."

He looks her in the eye. "You were rude. And I didn't deserve it."

"Fair enough. But I don't deserve what you've been doing, either."

His eyes go back to his shoes.

"You can't do that to me, Jake. You just can't."

A black Ford truck pulls up next to them, blocking traffic. Tory doesn't recognize the driver, but he's looking at her and her car. He pulls ahead of Jake's Volvo and parks, getting out of his truck and walking back to look again at Tory's car.

"We should get away from traffic," she says to Jake and he nods. They walk behind her car to the sidewalk. The man she doesn't know has now worked his way closer to her.

"Tory?" he asks.

"Um, yeah, I'm Tory."

Daniel moves closer to her side.

"I'm here to look at your car."

This crazy incident keeps getting stranger. They've been off of the road for less than five minutes and a road ranger is already here? But how'd he know her name? *Wait.* "Did Frank send you?"

"Yes."

Alrighty then. Evidently this is all just Frank's inter-connected, super-spy world and she just lives in it. How in the hell did he get someone out here so fast?

The man lies on the pavement and looks under her car.

Daniel leans toward Tory. "Honey, when you get a chance, I'd like to know who Frank is."

She nods, knowing that Jake is standing beside her. Now isn't a good time to blurt that Frank is Nick's brother who works for the FBI. Or maybe it is…

She points to her car. "So, you had nothing to do with this?" she asks Jake.

"No. No, Tory."

"You were just following me today. Casual."

His eyes go back down to his shoes.

"Did you see anyone messing with my car?"

He looks back up. "No. No. I wasn't hanging out all day."

An awkward feeling sours her gut. If Jake messed with her car only to be her hero, this isn't cool to be standing here with him. She's not sure how to read him right now.

A blurry silver streak from a car races past them. *Nick.* He takes a sharp turn in front of the Ford truck. In a split-second, he's jumped out of his car. Frank flies out of the passenger side.

Nick's panicked eyes find her. He runs down the sidewalk and swallows her with a sweeping hug. "T," he whispers, pressing his cheek to her face. "Are you okay?"

She squeezes him for strength. "I'm so confused."

His hands move to her face, his eyes hurrying to look her over to be sure she's okay. "Thank God you're all right." He pulls her in for another hug.

"I'm good, too," Daniel says, hands on his hips.

Nick steps back from Tory and then sweeps Daniel into his arms for a hug too. "Thank God you're both okay." Daniel pats Nick's back and then they separate.

Jake has taken a few steps backward and Nick notices.

"This is Jake," Tory says, turning to him. "Jake, this is Nick." The words seem to echo in her brain like she really didn't just say that. Who would have thought she'd ever introduce these two?

Nick's jaw ticks. "Why have you been following Tory?"

Jake's hands fist at his sides. "It's none of your business."

"She is my business. And not yours."

"I'm leaving." Jake brushes Tory's shoulder and heads for his car. But Frank blocks his path on the sidewalk.

"A few questions first," Frank says sternly. "Did you do this?"

"I don't know who the hell you are but I already told Tory, I didn't do this."

"I saw you earlier today, outside Indigo. Why are you stalking Tory?"

Jake clenches his fists again. "She needs to know what she did was wrong."

"And it's your place to tell her?"

"She acted like a smart-ass and needed to know what hurt feels like."

"That's a twisted world you live in, buddy."

Tory takes a step closer so the passersby on the sidewalk can't overhear them. "I have apologized to you, Jake. Now it's over. Leave me alone and I'll leave you alone. Especially when I get back to Austin next week."

Jake glares at her and then back to Frank, who stares at Jake without even blinking.

Nick steps in between them. "I will pay for the damage to your car." He pulls out his business card and hands it to Jake. "Thank you for helping Tory tonight. But now is a good time for you to leave."

Jake doesn't look back at Tory as he walks to his car. In seconds, he's driven away.

Tory's hands are on her face. Either that's the end of Jake, or this just ignited something bigger.

"Let's get out of here," Nick says.

The man who was looking under Tory's car is now standing by his truck, talking with Frank.

"What about my car?" Tory asks.

Frank turns to them, nodding them closer. "We're taking your car someplace safe to get fixed. You should go back to Nick's and I'll meet you there."

Tory goes to her car and grabs her purse and overnight bag. What a time to have her first overnight planned with Nick. With all of the anger pulsing through her body, it's going to take until morning for her to calm down.

She gives her key to Frank. Nick wraps his arm around her

shoulders and leads her to his car, opening the passenger door.

Daniel opens the back door. "This is one whacked-out taco night."

* * *

The minutes go by in a blur on the drive to Nick's. Tory finally is breathing normally, though her shoulders feel like they are carrying giant balls of stress.

Nick takes Tory's overnight bag and reaches for her hand as they walk up the stairs to his apartment. Daniel follows them. Nick unlocks the door and the three step inside.

Daniel looks around Nick's apartment. "Totes my style."

Nick's eyes linger on Tory as he walks toward his bedroom. He disappears and then returns without her bag. Even with all of this stress swirling around her, she can't help but grin. Then Nick heads straight to the kitchen and opens his liquor cabinet. He takes out a bottle of Tito's.

"I'll take a shot," Daniel says.

Nick looks to Tory and she nods. *God knows she needs it.* With three shot glasses poured, they gather together and throw back.

"The perfect poison for this princess," Daniel says, setting his shot glass on the counter and walking into the living room, looking at the black-and-white framed photographs on Nick's wall.

Nick pours himself another shot and throws it back. He's gripping the bottle, ready to pour a third, when Tory takes the bottle from his hands. "I know what you're thinking," she whispers.

He looks helplessly at the bottle and then at her.

"You didn't lose me tonight." She gently tucks a stray piece of his choppy hair back into place. "You're not going to lose me."

"I can't. I can't lose you. I have to keep you safe."

She's about to plant a kiss on Nick's lips to show him she's fine. The kind of sensual kiss that tells him she's here; she cares; she's his. She knows he's terrified.

Three knocks sound from Nick's door. Nick leaves Tory to open it and Frank hurries in.

He looks at Nick and then to Tory and Daniel. "You are both okay, right?"

"We're fine," she says.

"Shaken, not stirred," Daniel says.

"We had your car towed to a shop right around the corner. That was the owner who came to look at your car. He's a good friend of my partner, Daniella."

Tory nods. "Thank you. But what happened?"

"Someone cut your brake line with a hacksaw. In two places."

She grabs her stomach.

"Fuck, no," Nick says.

Frank nods. "They weren't deep cuts, meaning they were intentionally cut for you to have brake failure while operating the car."

"Who would do that to me? It's not Jake. I really believe he didn't do it."

"It's got to be someone who's after me," Nick says.

Frank nods again. "That's the most plausible theory." He looks to Tory. "You are clearly on Nick's team now. And whoever messed with Nick's car before has likely just tried to mess with yours to either hurt you or send you a message or both."

Daniel raises his hand. "Excuse me. You seem like a nice man, though full of dark news, but I haven't met you yet."

"Oh my God," Tory says. "I totally forgot. Daniel, this is Frank. Nick's brother."

"Oh, well hello," Daniel says.

Frank leans toward him to shake his hand. "Frank Allen. My apologies."

"You sound like a cop."

"Frank works for the FBI," Tory says.

"Stop!" Daniel says.

"But, this isn't a case the FBI is working on," Tory says. "Frank's here for a week, trying to help."

"And after tonight, we need to move quickly," Frank says. "My surveillance person who is following Reed said that today he went to a garage and repair shop on Luna Street. He was there for fifteen minutes and left. This is hypothetical, but that garage and repair shop may be where he knows someone who does his mischief."

"Interesting," Tory says. "Instead of using people from his own company."

"Or he could have been there to simply meet someone for legitimate business reasons."

Nick begins pacing. "Can we get someone to watch Tory? I don't care what it costs."

"No, Nick. I don't need someone."

"Yes," he says, forcefully. "I have to know that you are okay."

"Let's get our evidence, lock Reed up, and I'll be fine."

Frank nods. "We've got to turn up something that proves your innocence first."

"Well," Tory says. "Al said he'd make that call to his contact at Bear Creek."

"Good. In the meantime, we've got to work on our other leads," Frank says.

"What are you looking for?" Daniel asks.

Tory faces him. "First, we're looking for anything that proves how Nick maintained his car, particularly his tires. That's the crux of the case against him. All of his records at Reed's have disappeared, he paid cash for all his repairs so there's no money trail and there are no photos of his car before the accident. Second, we're trying to get footage that may show who changed out his tires at the concert."

"Nick, what about the people you tailgated with?" Frank asks. "Do you have any of their names or did any of them take photos?"

Nick shakes his head. "None of us were taking photos and I don't have their names. What about the beer cans? Can we run DNA to see if there's a match to a known database that would lead us to one of those guys? Then we could ask them what they remember about my car and if they saw a tow truck around it."

Frank pulls out his phone to type a text.

Tory leans toward Daniel. "This is what Frank does. He has all kinds of people he knows who can do things like this on the side."

Daniel nods, his eyes and fingers focused on his phone.

"Tory," Nick says. "Are there any parking lot cameras at Indigo that may have caught who messed with your car tonight?"

"Not sure, but I can check in the morning."

"I wonder if we should go up there tonight," Nick says.

"I think Al's working late tonight. If anything, I should go up there alone. It wouldn't be a good idea for you to go with me."

Frank puts his phone back in his pocket. "Our guy who was already running DNA tests on all of the beer cans can speed up his tests. What other ideas?"

Tory looks at Daniel, still playing with his phone. *Gee.* She knows he's new to the world of crime solving but she thought he'd be more interested than this.

"Hey," Tory says. "What about any other business that you regularly go to that would have images of your car on videotape?"

"Gas station?" Frank asks.

"Even if we got an image, how can you see the detail of the tires?" Nick asks.

"There are experts that can take a grainy photo and find something as small as a bloody fingerprint on it. So, it should be easy for them to identify the brand of tire that you had compared to the brand found on your car. Any photo of a tire is helpful."

"Any photo?" Daniel asks, looking up from his phone.

Frank nods.

"Well, how about twenty?" Daniel asks.

"Twenty...photos?" Nick asks.

Daniel cocks his head. "Twenty." He holds up his phone.

"What?" Tory yells, looking at his phone. "Oh my God! I totally forgot about these!" Chills shoot down her legs and she grabs the phone out of his hand to scroll through the pictures.

Nick darts to her side.

"Where were these taken?" Frank asks.

"This was a week before the accident. At Quinn's house!" Tory says. "Her parents had a final Fiesta party and look." She holds up the phone so Frank can see. "Nick parked on the street and we all posed for pictures with this crazy cowboy boot balloon. In most all of these photos, Nick's car is in the background!"

Frank's eyes are devouring the pictures. Tory takes the phone and forwards them to herself, Frank and Nick.

The four of them scroll through photo after photo. The first few are the ones Tory took, with Daniel alone with the boot. The next ones are of her and Daniel that Quinn took. The next ones are of her, Daniel and Quinn that Nick took. And the last few are the one's Nick took, when he smooshed himself into the balloon for the final round of selfies.

The chill racing through Tory's legs now pulses through her from head to toe. *Quinn. Sweet Quinn.* She was smiling, with Nick. Her whole life was ahead of her and only a week later, she'd be gone. *God, she misses her.*

Frank steps into the kitchen, talking to someone on the phone. He hangs up and comes out. "I'm sending these to be analyzed by a photography expert. This one here…" he holds up his phone, "is remarkable because it shows all of Nick's car."

Nick nods. "I took it. And I take bad photos. I barely got the people in the picture."

A feeling of peace, happiness and sadness builds up tears in Tory's eyes. "Look at Quinn. You guys, look at where she's pointing."

They stare in silence at the photo of Tory, Quinn and

Daniel. All of them are smiling, but only Quinn has her hands in the air. And her right index finger is pointing straight to Nick's car.

Nick straightens, his face twisted in fury and pain. "Where the hell is Reed right now," he asks Frank.

Frank types a text and immediately gets an answer. "Our guy following him says he's at Indigo."

Nick turns to Tory. "I'm going up there."

"Hell no you're not," she barks.

He steps to the door. "I'm going to show him these pictures and—"

"And what?" Frank says, moving closer to the door too. "That is an incredibly premature move, Nick."

"I'm not waiting another minute," Nick says.

"You need to wait quite a few more minutes," Frank says.

"No. Not this time. I'm not a little kid, Frank. I've got to stop this. Now. Tonight." His voice rises. "Tory's in danger! Because of me! I'm going to tell that mother fucker that we've got the evidence that proves I'm innocent."

Frank grabs Nick's arm. "But we don't have the proof yet that Reed did it."

"I know he did! He knows he did!"

"Nick, calm down," Frank says.

"No! If he tried to hurt Tory today, he'll try to hurt her tomorrow. He's hurt her before. It's got to stop. Now."

Tory's never seen this side of him. He's becoming unglued! "Nick, no!" she pleads.

He shakes off Frank's arm, grabs his car keys and goes to her, shaking his head. "No, I'm going to keep you safe. I'm not going to lose you."

"Then stay here with me! Don't leave to do something stupid like this!"

"Daniel," Nick says. "Can you stay here with Tory? Both of you, stay here, until I come back?"

Daniel crosses his arms. "Even Captain Obvious would say this isn't a good idea."

Nick shrugs him off. "Frank, you can stay here too or you can come with me but I'm leaving right now." Nick heads for the door, giving a panicked, lingering look to Tory before racing outside.

"Nick!" Tory calls out.

Frank's wild eyes look back to her. "I'll stop him before he gets there. Stay here." He rushes out of the door.

Daniel slaps his legs, turning to Tory. "You're just going to stand there? You let those boys talk to you like you're some helpless kitten who can't get wet?"

Tory grinds her teeth. She knows where Nick's heart is. She knows where Nick's source of panic comes from. She's angry too, angry at herself. Every day she feels regret about giving Quinn those concert tickets.

Suddenly she's hit with a cold chill, an icy cold smack of reality. *The tickets...*

"I need you to stay here," she says.

"Oh my Lord, what's with everyone wanting someone to stay here!"

"I don't have a key to lock up Nick's place!"

"And where are you running off to, honey? Because I'm supposed to be babysitting you."

She grabs her phone and opens her rideshare app to order a ride.

"I'm going to Indigo." She looks up to Daniel.

"Why? Because you don't think Nick and his beefcake brother can handle Reed alone?"

She looks down to her phone. Three minutes until her ride arrives.

"They can handle Reed just fine. There's just one, tiny problem."

Daniel looks confused. "What?"

She swings her purse over her shoulder. Sure, Reed would be motivated for revenge against Nick. But there's a huge problem with their theory. Reed wouldn't have known Nick was going to the concert. The only way someone could have planned this—someone who brought old tires that would fit Nick's car all the way out to the remote Bear Creek arena and switch them out—would be if someone knew where Nick would be. Someone who knew Nick had her concert tickets. Someone who could cover their tracks by using their connections at Bear Creek Arena.

"Their problem?" she says. "They're going after the wrong guy."

[THIRTY]

"You can pull into the parking lot, right there," Tory says to her rideshare driver.

The young man pulls into the parking lot at Indigo. Tory gets out and immediately sees what she's looking for: Al's car is in his parking space.

She steps around puddles still dotting the parking lot from the earlier rain shower. The blue light from the Indigo sign bathes the wet sidewalk with a warm glow. It reminds her of the beginning of May, when she arrived back in town. When she walked arm-in-arm with Quinn into Al's retirement party.

Now, Tory walks alone, clenching her fists.

She didn't notice Nick's car here, so maybe Frank was able to stop him from confronting Reed. Tory tugs open the front door and walks into the sounds of coffee beans grinding and the murmur of laughter and voices from Indigo's usual evening coffeehouse crowd. She scans behind the counter, looking for Tyler. He spots her and smiles. "What are you doing up here?"

She moves closer. "Had some business upstairs. I see Al's car, so he's still here?"

"Yep," Tyler says, pumping cane sugar sweetener into a

mug. "He had some dinner up there with someone a while ago. I'm coming up in a minute with a coffee he wanted."

"Good," she says and Tyler looks surprised. "Hey, remember when you offered to, you know, help me that one time? You said you could spill a coffee if I said 'that looks hot'?"

Tyler nods, wiping the counter.

"I might need that in a little bit."

"Everything okay?"

"Not sure but I'll know soon."

Tyler nods again and Tory turns to go up the center staircase. So far, no sign of Reed, Nick or Frank. Maybe Reed had already left because all she hears is happy conversations and laughter. If he was still here with Nick and Frank, there wouldn't be any laughter.

Tory quickly dashes upstairs and down the hall leading to Al's office. She passes her office door and stops to open her purse. The only sound in the quiet hall is the sound of a zipper unzipping as she opens her gun case. Having a gun does make her feel bolder, though she has no intention of using it. Still, it's not a bad idea to have it ready. What she does intend to use is the recording app on her phone. She launches the app, presses record, puts her phone in the outside pocket of her purse and walks ahead. This whole visit is about catching Al off guard to get more evidence, especially before he leaves the country on his retirement cruise. And he sure won't talk if Nick is with her. This is a perfect chance and she needs to hurry. Because when Nick heads back to his apartment, Daniel will tell him where she went. It's a safe bet that he will race up here to find her.

Al's door is open and bright lights from his office light up the dark hallway. There's no one talking, so he must be alone.

Perfect. Let's get this conversation started.

She stands in the threshold with a clear view of Al. He's sitting behind his desk, looking at a stack of papers and holding an ink pen in his hand. He's well dressed, as he always is, with a blue sport coat dotted with brassy gold buttons. It's his signature look. A look she's always admired. But if her hunch is right and Al had anything to do with Quinn's murder, the only outfit of his she'll admire now is an orange jail jumpsuit.

"Hey there," she says, loudly.

He jumps slightly, looking up to her. "Tory?"

"You weren't expecting me tonight, were you?" she says, boldly stepping in.

Slowly he sets his pen down. Even though she's steps away from his desk she can see that he's just taken a hard swallow.

"I wanted to thank you," she says, now beside the guest chairs in front of his desk. She sets her purse down on one of the chairs, the side with the pocket holding her phone facing his desk. She sits down in the other chair so she can look him in the eye.

"For...what?"

"For offering to call your friend at Bear Creek. That was very generous of you. Have you heard from him yet?"

"I haven't had time to call, Tory. Is that why you came up here tonight?"

"Proving Nick is innocent is all I work on, you know, in my off hours."

He pushes down on his desk and rolls back in his chair. "Then I think you need some new hobbies."

"Good suggestion. I might take up something new, like a class on automotive repairs. So next time I'll notice the brake fluid under my car after my brake line has been cut."

His chin slowly rises. *Oh, you son of a bitch.* His slow, not-surprised movement tells her all she needs to know. Anyone coming into his office this late and babbling about a brake line being cut would certainly draw out more of an emotional reaction. Something organic like "what happened" comes to mind. But Al sits, quiet.

She snaps her fingers. "Oh, my bad. I forgot to mention: brake line cut in two places."

"I'm not sure why you are telling me this," he says robotically.

"Just so you know that I know."

"Know what?"

"That my brake line was cut, in two places."

His breathing deepens.

"I know you're leaving on your cruise next week so I also didn't want to miss the chance to thank you for this job. I've learned more than I ever expected."

His eyes narrow.

She stands up and walks over to a bookcase. He's packed up most of his proclamations and awards, but some books on leadership are still on the shelf. How ironic is that? Maybe he's planning to leave them behind for Blaine. "I know you're worried about Blaine. And after seeing the state of Indigo's business affairs, I'm worried for him too. Especially since he'll be in direct competition with Nick and Faze."

"Nick isn't competition. Nick is a criminal."

"Nick was charged for a crime he didn't commit. He's no criminal."

Al swivels in his chair to face her. "Your loyalty to Nick is a big problem."

She shrugs. "It's nothing that a hacksaw to my car's brake line can't solve, right?"

"What's this all about?" he asks, swirling his hand impatiently in the air.

"You'll do anything you can to level the playing field for your son. He doesn't have the natural skills like you do. And you don't want to return after a six-month cruise to see the business you started, be ruined."

"And what's wrong with that?"

"Nothing. Until you try to eliminate the competition."

He stands up, trailing his fingers on his desk. Her heart thumps. Maybe she's pressing too hard. She's chirping in the same tone she used the night she broke up with Jake. Her bitchiness set Jake off. And even though Al's using measured responses, it feels like she's on the brink of igniting him.

"That's a big accusation from a young law student."

She nods. "A young law student, armed with evidence." Her insides twist. *Damn, what a misleading statement.* She only has one piece of evidence. What a way to dangle bait to try to get him to tell her more.

"What evidence do you have?" he asks, stepping to the edge of his desk, still keeping the fingertips of one hand on his desk.

"You've had years to work with Blaine to get him ready to take over the family business. But you didn't. You cut corners and worked back-room deals. You skirted the rules and laws to give your business a competitive edge. You've always gotten your way. Then when you realized Blaine wasn't going to cut it, you tried to get legit. But you couldn't resist a golden opportunity to get rid of a competitor. A competitor who was beginning to crush your business. A competitor who had just suffered a tragedy and you saw a chance to pile on. No one would have thought twice if Nick had died in that accident. He's dangerous, right? And negligent with how he handles cars, right? But instead, you killed my best friend!"

Al rushes toward her. "You need to shut your mouth!" He grabs her arm. Tory punches his chest with her other arm while he frantically tries to grab it too. *Not the reaction she expected!* Squeezing her arm, he flings her into his desk. She hits the corner and a sharp pain stabs up her back.

"You didn't listen, huh?" he yells. "I told you to stay away but you kept poking around."

She pushes him again with her free arm and he staggers backward. She hears yelling and commotion coming from the hall.

"Tory?" she hears Nick calling. *Thank God!*

Al flings her again by her arm, throwing her into a bookcase. *Shit!* In a split second, he opens his top drawer and pulls out a gun right as Nick, Frank and Daniel run into the room. Al yanks her toward him, tight, thrusting the gun against her head.

"Don't move or she's dead!" Al screams.

Tory has one free arm and she quickly weighs whether she should punch him now or freeze.

"Don't hurt her!" Nick yells. He has both hands out, standing across from them, his face blanched and terrified.

Tory's panicked eyes dart between the three of them. Nick is closest to her, Daniel stands in the middle of the room and Frank is off to her left, by the guest chair. By her purse.

Al's an outnumbered old man. If she can get this gun off of her head, they'll easily have him.

"Tell them why you did it, Al," Tory chides.

"I should finish it here, now, Nick," Al taunts.

Nick's nostrils flare and he looks like he could rip Al apart with his teeth.

"One squeeze of the trigger and another girl of yours will be gone," Al says.

"You're sick!" Daniel yells.

"That would be, what, Nick? Three women you were responsible for killing this year, right?" Al says.

"No." Nick shakes his head. "You killed Quinn. It was you, not me. I just realized it was you that night. Downstairs, we just parked next to your car, by your reserved space. Your Cadillac SUV with the long, vertical brake lights. That was you in front of me that night. I know those lights. You had your damn flashers on and then you hit your brakes causing me to skid. And you kept going."

Al squeezes Tory. "Damn straight I wasn't stopping."

"You sick, twisted…" Nick steps closer but Al jerks his arm tighter around Tory, causing her to yelp. The cold metal from the gun's nozzle is zig-zagging against her temple from his shaking hand.

Tory desperately looks at Frank and then down to the chair where her purse is and then back up to Frank. He gives the slightest nod. *He got it! He knows what's in her purse!*

"Hey, Al?" a friendly voice comes from down the hallway and a second later, Tyler walks in, holding Al's coffee mug. "Shit!" he screams.

"Don't move!" Al yells.

"You're trapped, Al," Nick says. "Let her go."

Al's whole body starts shaking. "She goes if I go."

"Shoot me!" Nick yells. "It's me you want to get rid of! Take your shot!"

No, Nick! If she feels this gun move away from her head, she's knocking it free. No way she's going to let Al take a clear shot at Nick!

"Go ahead, Al!" Nick yells. "I'm standing right here!"

Al's shaking so much, Tory knows she can knock his gun up with her free hand. She just needs a split-second diversion. *Tyler!*

"*Tyler!*" she yells. "*That looks hot!*"

Tyler's face widens in shock, then he throws the ceramic mug, hot coffee and all, toward Al's desk.

Tory hits Al's arm and the gun launches up into the air. Nick rushes toward her. Frank flies toward the chair with her purse. Daniel screams, ducking down behind the desk with Tyler. Al is no match for Nick's anger and he easily tackles Al to the floor.

"Freeze!" Frank yells, pointing Tory's gun at Al.

Daniel screams again, huddled on the floor.

"Tyler," Tory yells. "Call 9-1-1!"

Tyler runs out of the room.

Frank steps closer, his rock-steady hands aiming at Al.

Nick has Al's arms bound tight behind his back. "Tory? Are you okay?"

"I'm fine! Hold him hard!" she says, her pulse racing. She carefully kicks Al's gun out of the way and under a chair.

"Is everyone okay?" Nick calls out.

"I don't know!" Daniel yells, crouched under the overhang of Al's desk.

"Tory," Frank says, "come take your gun."

"Your gun?" Daniel asks from under the desk.

Frank hands it over to her. "Secure it," he says, never taking his eyes off of Al.

The metal feel of her gun weighs heavy and it's not from the gun's weight. This weapon means something different after having one pointed at her forehead. She stares at the gun, then shakes off her thoughts, opens her purse and puts the gun back into the case. "I've got it all recorded," she says to Frank, and then stops the recording.

"Good," Frank says, eyes still on Al. "I'll take him, Nick." Frank puts his hands on the back of Al's neck like Al was a helpless tiger cub and Frank was the five-hundred-pound tiger mother. Nick gets off of Al's back and Frank pulls Al up and stuffs him in his desk chair. "Don't even think about moving," Frank growls.

Nick rushes to Tory, gathering her in his arms. "Thank God you're okay," he whispers into her hair. She sinks into the cushion of his arms, squeezing him tighter than she's ever squeezed a human before.

"Is it safe to come up?" Daniel asks.

Nick eases his hold on Tory, cracking a smile. Tory steps away from Nick and extends her hand to Daniel. "This has been one fucked-up taco night, my friend," she says. Daniel latches on and she pulls him up.

Nick turns back to see Al, slumped in his desk chair, with Frank hovering over him. Nick gives a satisfied nod.

"But this has been a great night to finally get justice for Quinn."

[THIRTY-ONE]

It's after midnight when Tory, Nick, Frank and Daniel get back to Nick's apartment.

Nick plops his keys down while Tory puts her purse on the counter. Daniel rubs his eyes and Frank stands straight, eyes wide, like he has the energy to do this whole thing all over again.

Daniel has made his way into the kitchen, where the bottle of Tito's is still on the counter. He opens a couple of cabinets before finding four iced-tea size glasses. "We're doing generous pours, y'all," he says, pouring double shots for all.

Tory rests her hand on Daniel's back. Her surge of adrenaline is gone, leaving her exhausted, yet alert. Nick stands across from her, glass in hand. Frank reaches around Nick's arm to take his glass.

Their eyes search each other, silently processing what has happened. Without saying a word, they all throw back.

Frank sets his glass down first. "Your dad will be back in the morning?" he asks Tory.

"Early, I'm sure. It was hard to convince him not to drive back tonight he was so excited."

Frank nods then looks to Nick. "Your charges should be cleared by tomorrow."

Tory clasps her hands, drawing her arms to her body. "I've never felt so sad for something so exciting."

Nick nods somberly and then pulls her into the circle of his arms. "It's closure. A very difficult closure."

Daniel sets his glass down and steps into the living room. "I never would have pictured Al as being so aggressive."

"I can," Nick says, pulling back from Tory's arms. "If things weren't going his way."

"Frank," Tory asks, "do you think Al felt bolder than usual because of all of these politicians and business leaders stopping by for weeks, giving him attention? Does a sudden ego play into uncharacteristic action?"

"Absolutely," Frank says. "Someone who feels invincible is more likely to make bolder moves. Especially when pressed to the wall with a deadline or when presented with an irresistible opportunity. I've seen cases like this dozens of times."

"Do you think the video footage at Bear Creek did exist but Al had his friend erase it?" Tory asks.

"Highly likely."

"When he grabbed me, it felt like an out-of-body experience."

"Sure," Frank says. "This was a man you only knew as kind and supportive. But after listening to your recording, I heard how you clearly pushed his buttons."

She rests her elbows on the counter and buries her head in her hands. "He sent me flowers. Sent my family food. He even paid me for all the time I missed from work. All when he knew he was behind the accident."

"From guilt, probably," Nick says. "He liked Quinn. He was always trying to set her up with Blaine."

"Then why did he do this, knowing she was in the car?" Tory asks.

"Because he's stupid," Daniel says, yawning.

Tory straightens and smiles at Daniel. "But you're not. What a hero, finding the photos and then telling Nick where I was." She turns to Nick. "If you hadn't gotten there right when you did, I'm not sure what I would have done."

"I don't know, Tory. You're pretty damn resourceful. That prompt you had with Tyler sure came in handy," Nick says.

"Tyler wants to work at Faze, you know," Tory says.

"I'll hire him in a second. I have a feeling that with Al's arrest and Blaine now in charge, things aren't going to be running smoothly at Indigo."

Tory shrugs to herself. Things weren't running smoothly before all of this happened. "Speaking of not running smoothly, what about Nick's records disappearing from Reed's? How could Al have done that?"

"I'm not sure now that anyone intentionally erased any records," Frank says. "Our source there did an oil change today on a lady's car. A few hours later, all of the information he had input into their system was gone. From what he's told me, Reed's has some major problems with record keeping on their service side of the house."

"They need to be held accountable for that. And after what happened with Sienna you would think they would fix it. They shouldn't be selling cars that aren't right or not keeping records on the cars they service," Nick says.

"That is a different battle for another day. We have a long

day ahead of us tomorrow," Frank says. "Daniel, I can drive you home."

Daniel's mouth stretches with another yawn and he walks like a zombie toward the door. Poor guy. His body shuts down without food. Sugar lips never did get his taco night.

Tory hugs Frank, and then Daniel. "Love you both, very much. Thanks for, you know, saving my life and all tonight."

Nick gives Frank a hug. "Now you can fly back home sooner," Nick says and Frank smiles. Nick reaches for Daniel and hugs him too. Daniel yawns again.

"Goodnight," Nick says to the two of them as they leave. He closes the door, locks it and turns to face Tory.

His eyes have no shadow of worry. They are lit with a blissful happiness. Together they share a moment with their eyes on each other, elated and alone.

"You're free," she whispers with disbelief.

"You believed in me all along," he whispers.

Her shoulders are weakening, tired from the late hour and the emotions of this day. But her mind is energized and alive. "I could use a hug."

In one forward motion, Nick has her in his arms, the contours of his body pressing into the curves of hers, sinking into an embrace so magical, so intense, she can't imagine ever letting him go.

"It's over," he whispers, stroking her hair. "Now it's time for us."

She's melting into his chest and can hear the beating of his heart. *Time for us.* Words she never thought she'd hear from Nick. And now he's hers until sunrise.

His lips slowly lower to meet hers. Warm. Sweet. Intimate.

He stops kissing her, gently sweeping her hair back from her face. "Let's get comfortable."

Her breath catches in her throat. "What do you have in mind?"

His glance floats over to the kitchen. "Let's split that bottle of wine over there, turn on some music and because I know how important candles are, let's light some of those too." His smile stretches into a smirk.

"I'll get the music and candles," she whispers, letting him go. He's right behind her, heading into the kitchen. "And now I know where you keep your source of igniting things," she teases.

He reaches for the wine and glances at the sleeve of his shirt, dotted with coffee stains from when Tyler threw the mug in Al's office. "So that's why I keep smelling coffee." He grabs her waist and pulls her close. "Give me a minute to take a quick shower and I'll be right back." He brushes a gentle kiss across her forehead. His eyes are still on her as he steps away. "Feel free to get comfortable," he says and disappears into his bedroom.

She suddenly has no interest in lighting candles or drinking wine. She takes a few curious steps, following his path into the bedroom. When he said a quick shower, boy he meant quick. He's already in the bathroom and the door is partially closed. This is the first time she's seen his bedroom. A pecan wood platform bed with a gray comforter and black pillows is centered against a white-washed brick wall. Two matching saddle-brown leather chairs are beside a window, her overnight bag lying on one of them. A rust-colored shag rug looks so soft she can't help but imagine the feel of her bare skin lying on it.

The sound of water rushes from the bathroom as Nick

starts his shower. And a smile stretches her face. *He said to get comfortable...*

She slips off her cardigan and kicks off her sling back pumps. Her fingers pause on the buttons on her shirt. Earlier today she was wondering if she, or he, would be undoing these. Now she knows the answer: she'll save him a step. She races to unbutton her shirt and drops it, and her skirt, to the floor, leaving her standing only in her blush-colored panties and matching racer-back bra. Her pulse races with naughty excitement as she gently presses on the bathroom door.

Warm mist greets her as she cautiously steps in. Nick is surrounded by a steam-covered shower glass enclosure and has no idea she's here. Her heart pounds and her hormones race, knowing he's naked and she's only one steamy glass door away from seeing him. A couple of white towels are rolled up on a shelf and she takes one. *Ready or not, here she comes.* She unfurls the towel and snaps it over the top of the shower wall.

Nick swipes a finger to clear the steam from the glass and his eyes bulge. He swipes again to give himself a larger view and his eyes beam with a devilish look as he makes no attempt to hide that he's watching her.

His reaction is one-hundred percent instant-on, good-to-go, horny man. A sensual smile covers her face and she slowly bites her lip as she unclasps the front of her bra. His wide eyes eagerly watch as she releases herself, letting her bra fall to the floor.

He breathes in so deeply, she can hear the rush of his breath over the sound of the running water.

She slowly bends forward, easing herself out of her panties, facing him with nothing but a bare skin invitation.

He pops opens the shower door.

Now the only thing between their naked bodies is a wispy cloud of hot steam. Slowly she steps closer, eyes on him.

He seems to be trying hard, real hard, to keep his eyes on hers but he can't and lowers his gaze to scan her body. She steals a glance of him too, watching the water ripple over his chest muscles and admiring how generously he's aroused.

His eyes go back up to hers and he extends his hand. She clasps on to him and he pulls her closer, under the running water. She tips her head back, letting the hot water drench her hair, her face, her body.

His mouth brushes over her neck with feather-soft kisses and she rolls her head to give him more neck to kiss. His lips hover over her ear. "Oh my God, you are beautiful," he whispers, lightly kissing her ear.

She shakes her head to get his mouth off of her ear before he drives her bat-shit wild.

"You said to get comfortable," she whispers.

His grin devours her. A manly leather fragrance from the soap he was using smells intoxicating and with his eyes on her, he lathers up his hands. Slowly he caresses her arms and then up to her shoulders. His soapy hands begin gliding down her chest and her eyes flutter closed, knowing where his hands are going next. She's on the brink of losing it as he takes his time discovering her there.

His soapy hands continue skimming down her body to her hips. Then he presses against her, clutching her waist, giving her passionate, tongue-thrusting kisses. Her bare backside pushes against the cold tile while the warmness of Nick's body presses her from the front and his relentless tongue pushes her toward ecstasy.

She squeezes his face and gently pushes his mouth off of hers.

Water drips down in between them, both of their chests rising and falling with their heavy breaths. His eyes burn with hunger for her.

But she's hungrier.

"Take me to bed," she whispers under the stream of water.

His eyes flash urgency and in a hot second he's turned the water off and tugged her towel down. He opens the towel and she turns backward as he wraps the towel around her, drying off her back, shoulders, chest and then hair. She does the same to him, pulling down his towel and opening it. With a grin, he backs into his towel and she wraps him, squeezing his shoulders, his chest. She spins him around and with her eyes on him, she drops her hands, using the towel to dry the part of him she's super interested in playing with now. His eyes close and a small gasp escapes from his mouth with each of her soft, drying squeezes.

His eyes open and he takes her by the hand, leading her out of the shower and into the bedroom. They stand beside the bed, wearing nothing but smoldering stares and damp towels.

She's never felt braver. Bolder. And more on the cusp of frenzied pleasure.

He gently cups her face. "Are you sure?" he whispers.

Oh, she's sure. She raises an eyebrow and yanks his towel off of his shoulders.

He gives her a sinful grin and gently pushes her towel off of her shoulders.

He slips his hands behind her head and lowers with her, down to the soft comforter. Skin-to-skin they kiss and roll: him on top of her and her on top of him. He pulls a corner of the comforter back and they both slide underneath, kissing. He presses his body on hers and looks down to her with eager eyes.

"Tory," he whispers between quick breaths. "Do you want me to do this?"

There's no smell of cardboard boxes. No painful flashbacks. Nick Allen is on top of her and he's patiently asked her so many times if she's okay and ready. But she can't wait another second. "Make love to me."

He lowers his lips to hers. Her vision blurs, her world spins. Electricity arcs through her body as the man she loves shares himself with her and she shares herself with him.

[THIRTY-TWO]

Two months later

The only thing hotter than a Texas afternoon in June is a Texas afternoon in July.

Tory veers her car off of the exit toward downtown San Antonio and glances down at the temperature gauge on her dashboard; it reads one-hundred and three degrees. Even with her air conditioner blowing she feels the heat through the windows, especially since she's been sitting in her car for over an hour fighting the Friday evening traffic out of Austin. Now she's about two minutes away from Faze and she knows one-hundred degrees is nothing compared to the heat she plans to generate with Nick this weekend.

She slips into a parking space and rushes out of her car, leaving her weekend bag waiting in the trunk. Five days away from Nick is five days too long. She hears the echo of her black pumps clicking the sidewalk with her quick steps, her slim, black ankle pants and embellished white linen shirt a perfect work-to-dinner and easy-for-Nick-to-take-off, outfit.

Opening the door at Faze, the blast of cool air conditioning is as big of a treat as the smell of freshly baked cinnamon rolls. The delicious scent makes her mouth water but eating one now would ruin her appetite for their sushi date tonight. Then again, eating sushi might not be the best idea. Lately, she's had a hard time keeping food down.

"Hey, Tory!" Tyler calls out from behind the coffee bar, busy with a line of customers about five people deep.

She holds up her hands in the shape of a heart, so thrilled that Tyler works here now. Tyler gives her a happy smile back. She'd love to stop and talk, but she didn't just claw her way through rush hour traffic in a ninety-minute drive for him.

She flies up the stairs, heading for Nick's office. Even after dating for two months, the thought of him makes her nervous in an excited kind of way. It's what she used to feel when she stood outside his apartment door, only at the time she couldn't admit to herself that it was okay to like him. Now, all day, every day, he's on her mind. She'll catch herself doodling his name on notepads during her internship at the Austin law firm where she works or smiling whenever she smells coffee in the breakroom or from any restaurant. And now she's steps away from seeing him to begin another magical, memory-making weekend.

"Hello," she calls, stepping into his office.

"Tory!" Gigi squeals from the conference table where she and Nick are sitting. Gigi abandons their meeting and rushes toward Tory for a hug. "Thank you for the picture you sent of the sunflower centerpieces!" Gigi pulls back. "Francisco loves the idea and that's what we're going to use for the reception next summer."

"Perfect!" Tory says, glancing over Gigi's shoulder to the conference table.

Nick has gotten up and is leaning against the table with his hands in his pockets. He's absolutely delectable. His summer gray button-down shirt is fitted tight, sleeves rolled up, tucked into a pair of navy pants that she guesses will be no trouble at all for her to take off. His eyes seem to twinkle, waiting for her to pay attention to him, and all she can imagine is the fun she's going to have riding him all night.

Gigi graciously steps aside and Nick comes for Tory. They collapse together in a hug like they haven't felt each other in a month.

"You two are so adorable," Gigi says, going back to the table to gather up some papers from the meeting.

"I love the weekends," Nick murmurs into Tory's hair.

"Mmm, Friday has a whole new meaning," Tory says, squeezing him hard.

He eases back so he can face her, touching his lips to hers with a kiss that makes her lips want to sing. He pulls back and tenderly runs a finger down the edges of her face. "Was traffic okay?"

"Totally sucked," she says, stepping back. "But you are worth every second of the drive."

"Okay you two, I'm out of here. Anything else you need, Nick?" Gigi asks.

Nick turns back to her. "We have a meeting in a few minutes. Can you watch for him and bring him up? I think you know Reed Brown."

Gigi nods. "Sure do and sure will. If I don't get a chance to say goodbye later, have a great weekend."

"Thanks, Gigi. You and Francisco too," Tory says.

Gigi leaves Nick's office, pulling the door closed behind her.

Nick turns to Tory. "Are you ready for this meeting with Reed?"

Thinking of that creep still makes her shudder. But facing him to finally get him off of her back is overdue. "No, not ready, but I want to get this done."

"Me too," he says, gently stroking her shoulders. His eyes shift to worry and he looks her over. "Were you okay on the drive? Have you gotten sick since this morning?"

"I felt a little nauseous, but no, so far I only throw up in the mornings."

He lowers his hands to touch her stomach. "Did you bring a pregnancy test with you?"

She nods.

"Okay. We'll do this together, tonight. If we're pregnant, we're in this together."

Tory melts every time he says "we". She already has a hunch that her life has changed. Every symptom points to her being pregnant. Loss of appetite, nausea in the morning, plus her swollen boobs that Nick sure has enjoyed playing with for the past few weekends. "I can't believe this may be a reality."

"It's my mistake. I should have made sure one of us was on birth control."

"No, it's just as much my mistake too."

He strokes the edge of her face again. "Doesn't matter if it's a mistake. If we're going to have a baby, I'm going to love him or her just as passionately as I love you."

"I can't believe how calm and supportive you've been while I've been terrified. How will I get through my last semester of law school if that's when I'm due?"

He squeezes her arms. "How? Because I'd move to Austin."

"What?"

"Come here." He takes her hand and leads her behind his desk. He pulls up some images from his computer. "Look what I've found. Several beautiful homes available to rent. We can have a temporary nest together, you can decorate a nursery however you want and we can bring our baby into the world the way we want while you finish school."

"Are you kidding?" she says, her voice higher. "Nick! These homes are beautiful! But this can't work. You can't walk away from Faze!"

"I wouldn't. I can work remotely and come back here maybe two days a week. I was thinking of promoting Gigi to run things while I'm gone, plus I know she can use the extra money for her wedding. And I'm so impressed with Tyler, I was thinking of promoting him to manager."

Whoa. "This…that could work."

"Look at this house here." He leans down to click on a listing. "It's modern with an outdoor fireplace and it's four bedrooms so we could have a guest room and maybe Jamie can stay with you when I'm back here."

Gramma Jamie. She can't even imagine what her mom and dad are going to say but she has a hunch her mom would have a smile on her face packing her suitcase every week to come play with her grandbaby.

Tears build in Tory's eyes. "You did all of this research, for us?" She faces him. "You would go to this expense, for me? And our baby?"

"I love you, Tory. It's just the beginning of how I want to share my life with you."

She falls into him with a hug. "I love you, Nick." His arms

wrap her with confidence and love. Then she hears him sniffle. She draws back to see his eyes are brimming with tears too.

"You believed in me, Tory. I'll never forget that for the rest of my life. You went to war for me at a time when I could have gone to jail for who knows how long."

She sniffles. "Two to twenty years."

"Is that what it was?"

"Yeah…vehicular manslaughter, second degree felony, Texas penal code nineteen point zero four."

He grins. "I like having a lawyer as my lover."

Soft knocks sound at the door.

"That's probably Gigi with Reed," Nick says, letting go of her arms. "Do you need a minute?"

She sniffles again and dabs at her eyes. Her tummy is gurgling and she's not sure if it's from a first trimester of pregnancy or from her body's instinctive revolt when in the presence of Reed. "No, I'm fine. Let's do this."

Nick nods. "Yes?" he calls out.

Gigi opens the door. "Reed Brown is here," she says, swinging the door wide.

Reed slowly walks in, his hipster glasses looking as stupid as ever. He's wearing a caramel-colored blazer with slim black pants and he's only making eye contact with the floor.

"Thank you, Gigi," Nick says. Gigi nods and closes the door behind her. "Reed. Thank you for coming." Nick gestures to a chair at the conference table without attempting to shake Reed's hand. Reed takes a seat, finally looking Nick and Tory in the eyes.

Nick sits next to him.

Tory sits next to Nick, making sure he is between her and

Reed. It's also the chair closest to Nick's bathroom. With her queasiness, it's good to be close to the bathroom in case she needs to run and vomit.

"Thank you for finally agreeing to meet me," Reed says, folding his hands and resting them on the table. A shine from his Rolex watch catches Tory's eye. "I owe you an apology. Both of you."

Nick takes a sturdy breath in.

"I believed in my heart that you were responsible for Sienna's death and I'm sorry for the trouble that I caused."

"You know I would have traded places with her," Nick says. "I live with that guilt every day knowing that it should have been me driving my car."

Reed nods. "I didn't believe you at the time, but I do now."

Silence.

Tory stares at the grain patterns of the reclaimed wood table. She's not ready to say squat, yet.

Reed continues. "The investigation into Quinn's accident showed that we, as a business, have some problems we need to address. I was shocked that we had no records of your car's maintenance. It led us to also look at the records from your Mustang and we didn't have those records either. This isn't the way my family intended to run our business. Not knowing how we service our vehicles may have cost us more than customers. If that Mustang had problems and then we sold it to you…" his voice trails off. "We can't get Sienna back and it's something I may never get over."

He pauses to take a deep breath.

Tory closes her eyes thinking about Sienna, a young girl she never knew. A young girl who would still be here today if her family had only done things right.

"We've hired a consultant to revamp the systems in our service division and I thought you would like to know," Reed says.

Nick nods. "Good. If you don't mind, there's been something else on my mind. The night of my accident with Quinn, we saw one of your tow trucks at the arena, but you don't usually service that far from San Antonio."

"We don't. But I called them that night. I was there, with Blaine. His car engine light had come on."

"You and Blaine had been at the concert?"

Reed nods. "We had VIP tickets and backstage passes."

Tory rolls her eyes, still looking down. *Of course, they did. Makes sense that Al would give the best free tickets to his son.*

"Um, Tory…" Reed says.

She stiffens and looks the other way.

"Since you came back to town I've been trying to talk with you. I'm a different person now." He pauses, searching for words. "Years ago, I was dealing with many issues. I should have never forced myself on you and done what I did."

She manages a slight nod. *Okay, done. He said it. He can leave now.*

"This isn't easy for me to—"

Shock spins her head to face him. "Easy? For you?"

He straightens. "I realize it wasn't easy for you either."

"You're so full of yourself. Do you even have any idea what I've been through? Living with that feeling of losing control and not being able to defend yourself? Looking over my shoulder all of the time and wondering if every guy will hurt me too? All of the issues I've had to overcome to be strong and get the memory of you *forcing yourself* on me, out of my mind?"

"I know there's no excuse. All I can do is apologize and tell you what I was going through."

She slaps her hands on the table. "Then I come back into town and you're hovering around me everywhere. I was being stalked by one ex and then you're lurking around Indigo, trying to catch me at every turn."

"I was trying to talk to you."

"By paying for everyone's cappuccino to trick them to go downstairs? Tell me, how much did you give Al's secretary to lie that the Mayor was on the phone?"

"By that point, I didn't know what else to do to get you to have a simple conversation."

"I mean, even at Quinn's funeral, you kept staring at me and—"

"No, I wasn't staring at you."

She glares at him. "Yes, Reed, you were. During the speeches you were looking over at us."

"That's right," he says. "I was looking your way, but I wasn't looking at you!"

"If you weren't looking at me, then who were you..." She stops cold. *Oh no. No...no...no.*

An awkward silence covers the table.

Nick slowly turns his head to her and then back to Reed. "You must have been—"

"I was looking at Daniel," Reed blurts.

The floor falls out from under Tory's world.

"Oh," Nick says with wide eyes.

Tory buries her head in her hands, struggling to think of the best curse word to adequately release her shock.

"Daniel?" Nick asks.

Reed's shoulders have shrunk.

Nick folds his hands now too and rests them on the table. "So, these issues you have been dealing with, have to do maybe with your—"

Reed's head rises. "I wanted to talk to Tory to ask her about Daniel."

"I see," Nick says. "And back when we worked at Indigo, you forced yourself on her—"

"Because you were struggling," Tory finishes. "I wouldn't go out with you, no girl wanted to go out with you and the whole time you were figuring out if going out with a girl was what you even wanted."

"I know I should have handled things differently," Reed says.

"But you're best friends with Blaine, who made Daniel's life at Indigo miserable because he was gay," Nick says.

"Blaine doesn't know everything about me yet."

Tory holds her unsettled stomach, pressing back a surge of strange emotions. This feels like having empathy for a poor person who robs you at gunpoint. Her compassion for Reed's sexual struggle is there but forgiveness for nearly raping her is still hard to find.

"Reed, thank you for sharing this. I realize you didn't need to tell us this much information, but I'm glad that you did," Nick says.

"I'm proud of who I am now, personally and in business," Reed says with his typical smugness. "I know that who I was before was not me in my finest hours."

"Okay," Nick says, looking at Tory and then back to Reed.

"I'm glad we met face to face to clear some of this up. I know it's unlikely that we'll be friends going forward, but I certainly don't consider you my enemy anymore."

Reed nods.

Nick stands, and Tory and Reed stand too.

"Good luck, Reed," Nick says, extending his hand.

Reed shakes it. "Thank you, Nick. Good luck to both of you." Reed's eyes hunt for some response from Tory.

Say something! "I'm sorry I'm not saying much," she says. "This is…this is a lot for me to process and I hope you understand."

Nick slides his arm across her shoulders for support.

Reed nods and turns for the door.

She believes him. She really believes Reed has turned a page and is moving forward with a better life. She still doesn't like him. Hearing his voice makes her want to sprint away in a different direction. But his hipster glasses, trendy style and expensive lifestyle would be attractive to someone she loves.

"Tacos," Tory blurts.

Reed stops and turns, looking at her with a questioning glance.

"Daniel has a soft spot for tacos."

Reed gives a hesitant smile, then walks to the door, opens it and disappears.

Tory and Nick stand motionless, staring at the door. Then he turns to her.

"Are you okay?"

She leans into him and rests her head on his shoulder. "I'm not sure. It's like Reed is a book where you like the ending but you sure hated the first part." Her arms slip around his waist.

"I was surprised you gave him the taco hint."

"I'm already regretting that I said that. I'm not sure how I feel about Daniel and Reed together but if it's something that may make Daniel happy, it's really up to him to decide. Thank you, though, for arranging that visit. It really was good for me to hear what he had to say, and tell him what I needed to say."

"We're moving forward. You and I. We can put this behind us now."

She slips out of his hold to face him, her eyes studying his expression, absorbing his love. The faint smell of cinnamon rolls fills his office, making her feel warm and comfortable. After losing Quinn and everything they've been through, now she basks in his attention. His love. His support. He got her through those tough times. And now here he is, ready to support her through what might be her biggest challenge yet.

She skims her finger gently down his cheek. "I'm ready to start my weekend."

He generously grins. "I'm ready for anything with you."

[THIRTY-THREE]

Two years later

The delicious aroma of cinnamon rolls lingers downstairs, and upstairs, in Nick Allen's newest coffeehouse, Faze Two. Caterers rush around under Gigi's crisp direction, setting out dishes and table settings for tonight's grand opening party. Tyler arranges turquoise and silver balloon bunches throughout the main room. Nick seems oblivious to everyone bustling around him as he stands at the bottom of the center staircase, looking up. To her.

Tory stands at the top of the stairs, looking down to him. After wearing jeans and a t-shirt helping to set up for tonight, she's changed into her off-white, A-line party dress. She can tell Nick's already noticed her dress's deep, plunging neckline. She can see his raised eyebrow from here.

"Mr. Allen," she flirtatiously says, beginning her walk down the staircase so familiar to her. After all, she worked in this building twice before, back when it was known as Indigo Exchange.

Nick's smile seems to sparkle and he holds out his hand. "Mrs. Allen."

She reaches him and slips her hand into his, and then he spins her around in a romantic twirl just like he had done on the ballroom floor during their wedding reception a year ago. Dizzy, she stops in his arms.

He gives her another once-over. "Every day when I think you look beautiful, the next day you look even better," he says, pressing a warm, lingering kiss to her lips. "I believe the last time you wore a white dress as stunning as this was our wedding."

"You're right," she says, straightening the turquoise tie on his light gray suit. "And tonight is right up there on our list of life celebrations that are important for us. I mean, how many times do you get to re-open a place with as many memories as this?"

"Memories that are good ones and not so good ones."

"It's all part of history," she says, flicking some lint from his shoulder. "Everyone knew it was only a matter of time before Blaine drove this place into the ground. And thankfully," she kisses him again, "you're here to save it."

"And you are downstairs just in time," Gigi says with a smile on her face and a clipboard in hand. "Are you ready to greet our guests?"

Nick glances at his watch. "We have fifteen minutes until the party starts, right?"

"It's always good to be ready early," she says.

The front door swings open and someone carrying a massive bouquet of white roses walks in. The flowers are blocking his face but he can't hide from Tory. She recognizes his sassy walk and his slim white jeans. "Yoo-hoo! Is that you?" she calls out to Daniel.

He peeks out from behind the bouquet. "Yoo-hoo! It's true!"

She rushes over to greet him and he holds out the bouquet for her. "Some classy grand opening flowers for my classy, coffee shop girl," he says.

Tory kisses his cheek. "Thank you, sugar lips. Hey, Gigi?" Tory calls and Gigi comes over. "Where's the most visible spot for these lovelies?"

Gigi reaches to take the vase. "Let's put them front and center on the coffee bar," she says, taking the roses across the room.

Tory reaches for Daniel's hands. "Thank you, my friend, for the flowers, the love, the support. You are my treasure."

He lets go of her hands to fan his face, fighting back his misty eyes. "Oh, please don't make me cry."

"Oh honey, that's nothing," she says, smirking. "I'm about to make you ugly cry." She looks over her shoulder. "Hey, Nick? Gigi? Tyler? Let's tell Daniel our big announcement!"

Daniel's eyes spill over with the same excitement as when Mama Margie's has two-for-one taco night. "What is it? Are you renaming this place after me?"

"No! You nut!" Tory, Nick, Gigi and Tyler line up in front of Daniel. "Are you ready?"

Daniel clutches his chest.

"Tonight…" Tory says, "we're having…"

And then they all yell, *"A taco bar!"*

"Stop!" Daniel excitedly flaps his hands.

Gigi points to the catering station. "Hard shell or soft shell, corn or flour, beef or chicken all with sour cream, pico, tomatoes, Cholula…everything is there! All you can eat!"

"You guys!" Daniel says with joy. "You turned a place I

hated into paradise!" He pulls Tory in for a hug. "Thank you!"

Nick puts his hands on his hips. "What about me?"

Daniel drops his arms from Tory and sweeps Nick into a quick hug. "Thank you, too."

Tory holds her face watching their embrace. At one time Daniel swore he'd never touch Nick, except if Nick ever sat in his chair begging for a haircut. And now, Daniel is practically part of their family. Especially how he refers to himself as Uncle Daniel.

He releases Nick from their hug. "Hey," Daniel says. "We're missing someone. Where's my princess?"

"Any minute she'll…" Tory says and then the front door opens.

John and Jamie walk in, bringing Nick and Tory's eighteen-month-old daughter.

"There's my princess!" Daniel yells. "Welcome to the party, Lilly Quinn!"

Lilly Quinn Allen squirms out of Jamie's arms. Her white-lace party dress bounces with her running, the ribbons from a colorful flower crown flowing behind her brunette hair. "Taniel!" she squeaks, running toward him.

Daniel picks her up and spins her in a circle.

John and Jamie reach Tory and Nick's side, exchanging hugs.

"She couldn't wait to get up here," Jamie says, watching Daniel spin Lilly Quinn around again. "But have you noticed? She's really mastering her use of the word 'no'."

Nick grimaces. "I know."

John leans toward Nick. "She reminds me of Tory. You know, Tory was a handful during her terrible-two's."

Nick smiles lovingly at Tory. "Like mommy, like daughter."

Tory tips her shoulder up. "Only if you're lucky." She opens her arms and calls out to Lilly Quinn. "Hey, baby girl!"

Daniel sets Lilly Quinn down and she toddles over. "Mommy!" Tory rushes to scoop her into her arms, kissing the baby-smooth skin of her cheeks. Since the day Tory and Nick found out they were pregnant, Tory uncovered the deepest love she could ever know. Lilly Quinn's entrance into the world was stressful; after a ten-hour labor she finally arrived right in the middle of Tory's last semester of law school. Tory only took a week off before dragging her exhausted and healing body back to class. Thanks to support from her parents and Nick, she graduated on time and later passed the Texas bar. Now, she enjoys working part-time in her father's office and has taken over a majority of his firm's pro-bono cases. She also helps Nick with Faze's legal issues, though thankfully, Faze runs a much more legit operation than Indigo did. But this, having Lilly Quinn in her arms, burying her nose in the baby-powder smell of Lilly's hair and being able to watch their loving miracle grow up and discover this world, is the best career she could ever have.

Lilly Quinn extends her tiny hands toward her daddy. "Up!"

Nick expertly snatches her from Tory's arms and gives her an easy, two-handed toss-up into the air. Lilly's party dress billows out as she floats down, adorably giggling as the colored ribbons of her flower crown tickle her face. "Again!" she squeals and her daddy obliges.

Watching him play with her brings tears to Tory's eyes, every time. Heck, watching his blue eyes open every morning and look at her brings tears to her eyes too. After everything they've been through to become who they are now, it's all been a magical journey she feels damn lucky to be on.

Nick notices Tory's stare and stops tossing Lilly Quinn in the air. He holds her on his hip and steps closer. "T, are you okay?"

She cups his face with one hand and Lilly Quinn's face with the other. "I love you so much."

He falls into the love of her eyes, his gaze deepening into hers. But their loving moment isn't exciting enough for their daughter. She squirms out of his arms and toddles off to Daniel, who picks her up to show her the balloons and how to punch them. Tory and Nick stand together, ignoring the arriving guests and the music now playing from a jazz band. Soon, they'll need to greet everyone and in a few minutes, Nick will need to say a few welcoming remarks. But right now, they only have eyes for each other.

"I love you, Nick," she whispers. "My cinnamon roll boy."

A smile creases his face. "Thank you for this moment," he whispers. "Tonight, celebrating our success. You are my rock and my love. I owe it all to you."

"And to think you used to be the bad boy in this town."

Nick tosses his hands in the air. "Now look: I'm on my way to owning most of it!"

And he's not kidding. Opening Faze Two is just the beginning of Nick's plan. The renovations he's done to bring the once-boarded-up Indigo up to trendy Faze standards are remarkable. Upstairs, the musty-smelling rare collections book room has been renovated into Gigi's office, since she will run Faze Two full time. Al's old office has been split into two offices: one for Tyler and one for Robyn, who was thrilled to join the Faze team once Nick promised they'd never offer exotic coffees that no one could pronounce. Nick's downstairs renovations were substantial too, stripping down the old wood floor and refinishing it with a glazed gray stain and adding the decorative stainless steel and white leather touches Faze is known for. He also gutted the space Tory always avoided: the storage closet. Nick had the walls torn down and added some bright paint and soft couches as a break area for the partners. And his national franchising plan for Faze is well underway. Within five years, they'll be opening Faze Three, Faze Four and Faze Five in San Antonio and then expanding throughout Texas and other states within ten years.

But for now, tonight, Nick's priority is here at Faze Two.

Downstairs is filling up with guests already enjoying complimentary coffee and cinnamon rolls. Then a man approaches Nick and Tory, pressing a hand on Nick's shoulder. *Frank!*

Nick turns to give Frank a hug and Tory does the same.

"You're here!" Tory excitedly says. "How are you!?"

"I cannot believe you came tonight!" Nick says.

Frank's eyes are wide with energy and delight. Now retired from the FBI, he's beginning a new career that they once joked about. He now runs security for the Oscar-winning alternative rock band Plebeian.

"I'm so glad I could come by, even just to say hello. I'm on my way to Dallas to review the security protocols for Plebeian's live televised concert next week. This worked out perfectly to stop by."

"We'll be watching next week! I love Plebeian's music. We always play their songs," Nick says. "How do you like it?"

"Everyone is wonderful, the work is challenging and I couldn't be happier."

"Tell me about Lauren Logan," Tory says. "I can't imagine how she's dealt with sudden fame and everything else she's gone through."

"She's amazing. Smart. Funny. Super talented and loves her kids like crazy."

"Two teenagers, right?" Nick asks.

Frank nods. "Yes. Two boys. And actually, Tory, Lauren reminds me of you."

"You're kidding me," she says.

"Lauren's pretty feisty and can handle herself, but in the end, she's a big romantic."

"A romantic…who can sing. Really well," Tory adds. "Which I can't."

Frank smiles and searches Tory and Nick's eyes. She knows he's trying to read them.

"What do you see there, Frank?" she asks.

His smile stretches. "Two people in love."

Nick wraps an arm around Tory's waist.

"I know you need to start your party and I do need to leave. The plane is waiting on me."

"Plane? You're on a private plane?" Nick asks.

"Yes. Lauren's personal plane. It makes everything efficient. I will get this venue check finished by early morning and be back in Tampa by lunchtime tomorrow."

"Well, I know under your watch, nothing bad will happen," Tory says.

Frank crosses his fingers. "We have our share of crazy fans giving us problems, that's for sure. Some lady followed our keyboardist Michael around the grocery store the other day. The guys in the band nicknamed her 'Banana Girl'. With any luck, she will be the worst of our problems."

Tory nods. *Surely, she will be.*

"I do miss you, Frank," she says, pulling him into another hug. "I know your new job will keep you very busy and I'm not sure when we'll see you next."

"I miss you both as well. I'll give Lilly Quinn a hug on the way out." He looks Nick in the eye. "I'm proud of you, Nick. I'm proud to call you my brother."

They lock their arms around each other in a robust man-hug and then let each other go.

"You've taught me everything I needed to know about how to be a good brother," Nick says. "I hope I never let you down."

Frank shakes his head. "Never. You never will." Then Frank looks to Tory, flicking his thumb in Nick's direction. "I know he can get into trouble. Take care of him for me."

Tory proudly nods. "Don't you worry, Frank," she says, standing tall and looking into Nick's eyes.

"I can handle him."

The End

Acknowledgements

It's easy to write a book alone. But you can't get it finished without the input and help from friends. Thank you to:

Alex Lum and Ben Judkins, for your guidance on legal and medical matters.

Daniel Lee, for inspiring a character so full of fun and life I simply had to name him after you.

Walter "Wally B." Jennings, the real Wally B.

Karen Cowan, for your special area of expertise.

Sarah Wilson Thacker, for another spectacular book trailer.

My amazing editor, Mandy Schoen.

And my incredible squad of beta readers: Jill Reagan Healey, Keri Riegler, Amber Marcellino, Kathryn Barry and Marta Vittini.

Books by Debbie K. Lum

Want to know what happens next to Frank Allen? Find out in the Plebeian Series.

PLEBEIAN REVEALED (Book One)

When Lauren Logan, an introverted wife and mother, records a secret movie soundtrack with her ex-boyfriend, she gets more than sudden fame when their band Plebeian is revealed.

PLEBEIAN IN DANGER (Book Two)

Lauren thought her stage fear would be her largest challenge during Plebeian's world tour. But a series of bad luck has given her bigger problems.

The world tour is unraveling and it's all according to plan. By the time Lauren discovers the enemy within, she's already fallen into a trap. Now she must face a killer to stop this, and resist his love.

PLEBEIAN REBORN (Book Three)

Lauren has survived remarkable challenges as the lead singer of Plebeian. Now she faces her biggest challenge yet—her mistakes from the past. When tragedy strikes and secrets are revealed, she unravels in a downward spiral. Only one man can save her, and Plebeian, now. And it's not her husband.

THE DOCTOR, THE CHEF OR THE FIREMAN

Find out why THE DOCTOR, THE CHEF OR THE FIREMAN was called "A quick, satisfying romantic mystery." by *Kirkus Reviews*

Kendra King ran away from her boyfriend so fast, she almost left her favorite Louis purse behind. Newly minted doctor Christopher Randall had been the man of her dreams, until she uncovered his dangerous secret.

Moving from Richmond, Virginia to nearby Cory City was easier for the 26-year-old than confronting her ex, and she busied herself with her new career. Soon, handsome fireman Matt Livingston softens her broken heart and life in Cory City looks as rosy as the flowers Matt sends her every week. Even daily breakfast at the local diner seems magical, and she quickly bonds with a misfit group of regulars including young chef Nolan Ford, who warms her soul with his blueberry pancakes and adorable southern smile.

But when one of her new friends becomes suspiciously ill and scandal engulfs the fire department, Kendra sets out with Matt to prove his boss is crooked. She learns nothing in Cory City is as it seems and when her ex arrives in town, Kendra's not sure who to trust. She begins to uncover the good, the bad and the ugly among the three men closest to her: the doctor, the chef and the fireman. And if she's not careful, she might unleash the evil in one.

About the Author

Debbie Lum has enjoyed a 28-year professional career in marketing, where she loved turning big, complicated problems into smooth, organized programs. She's travelled from the beaches of Turkey, to the volcanoes in Italy to the bricks of Red Square, Moscow. And no one can drink more unsweetened iced tea than her.

After seeing a self-esteem campaign encouraging little girls to dream big, she wondered why not grown women too? She challenged herself to do something she knew little about: reading and writing novels.

I CAN HANDLE HIM is her fifth novel.

Debbie's website: www.debbielum.com/

Follow Debbie on Twitter: twitter.com/Debbie_K_Lum

Like Debbie's Facebook page: facebook.com/authordebbielum/

Follow Debbie on Goodreads: www.goodreads.com/author/show/14613663.Debbie_K_Lum

www.ingramcontent.com/pod-product-compliance
Lightning Source LLC
Chambersburg PA
CBHW070824190726
48292CB00006B/2096